US/THEM

Edited by
Carol Hightshoe

WolfSinger Publications ⌇ Security, Colorado

Acknowledgements

Re-Humanized © 2021 by Natasha Gordon-Polomski
A Grey Area © 2021 by Birgit Gaiser
Pin-Hole on a Nice Neighborhood © 2021 by Madeline McEwen
Boxed © 2021 by Maria Simbra
Boys Play © 2021 by Ginny Venton
The Colors of Community Organizing © 2021 by B. Craig Grafton
E Pluribus Rot © 2021 by J.J. Smith
The Flower War © 2021 by Laramie Wyoming
For Remembrance © 2021 by Liam Hogan
Killing Stephen Miller © 2021 by Brad Shurmantine
In Other Words © 2016 by Lisa Timpf
Previously published in *One Thousand Words for War* – CBAY Books 2016
Ten Pfennings Worth of Chocolate © 2021 by Charles Robertson
The Enemies © 2021 by Thomas Cannon
Initiation © 2021 by Charles Kyffhausen
Time for Murder © 2021 by John Taloni
Labels © 2021 by Bob Rich
Previously published in *Lifting the Gloom: Antidepressant Writings* – Loving Healing Press 2021
Second Wind © 2021 by Tammy Higgins
Standing for the Flag © 2021 by B. Craig Grafton
Suspicious Words © 2021 by Duane L. Herrmann
The Green Line © 2021 by Sarah Edmonds
The History Songs © 2021 by Russell Hemmell
The Killers © 2021 by Carlton Herzog
Us Versus Them: An Aged Fable © 2021 by Christopher Welch
Are we a Thing? © 2021 by Bennie Rosa
The Limit of the Sky © 2016 by Holly Schofield
Previously published in Perihelion - 2016
Photo Sympathy © 2021 by Ray Daley
The Long and the Short of It © 2021 by DJ Tyrer
The Other Side of the Cage © 2021 by Radar DeBoard
Humanity © 2016 by Joanna Michal Hoyt
Previously Published in *Mythic Magazine* – 2016
Acceptance © 2021 by Steven T Lente

For permission requests, please contact WolfSinger Publications at:
editor@wolfsingerpubs.com

ISBN 978-1-944637-07-1

Printed and bound in the United States of America

TABLE OF CONTENTS

Re-Humanized

Natasha Gordon-Polomski

I guess I saw myself in you
that day you shed your tears,
I hadn't known that we had felt
the same way all these years

With all those silly taunts and jeers
and battles going on,
It seemed that we were made too blind
to see what we had become.

In my eyes you were all but lost
and I in yours, a waste.
But when the lines had all been crossed
we both could see our own disgrace.

I guess I saw myself in you
that day you told your fears,
when the barricades had fallen down
and we had put down all our spears

And I guess that I had always known
that someday it would end,
but I hadn't known that when it did
I could ever call you friend.

~ * ~ * ~

Natasha Gordon-Polomski is a young writer living in London, currently studying for a Bachelor of Arts and Sciences alongside volunteering and activist work. She is interested in politics, social theory, anthropology and psychology; and is particularly interested in the intersections between social justice issues and mental health. You can find her on Instagram at @onbecomingnatasha.

A Grey Area

Birgit Gaiser

"Things are rarely just black and white. Most decisions happen in grey areas."

I considered the woman across the table from me. She was tall but sat with a careless posture, as if she was trying to blend into the crowd. She wore no make-up, her salt and pepper hair was trimmed but not styled, her clothes clean but unassuming. She was, if you will, extraordinary in her carelessness.

Nonetheless, people like her stand out. They spend their lives cultivating an air of being special, respected, even revered. It simply isn't possible for them to switch it off at will. Luckily, that charisma makes them easier to spot for us and those in the community who help us by keeping their eyes open. We always find them in the end, whether by tip-offs, mugshots or the way they carry themselves. Always.

This one had stayed hidden for five years.

"What do you mean?" I asked.

"The grey area. The place where things aren't clear-cut, where there's no one hundred percent good or bad decision. If you're lucky, it's maybe ninety to ten, but it's always gonna be a *little* bit split. Otherwise, you wouldn't have to make a choice.

"People like you and me, we make difficult calls based on incomplete information, on imperfect outcomes, on the lesser of two evils. Some people don't make a call, but you and me, we always do. That's why we're sitting here now."

She smiled at this, a bit sadly, I thought.

"Are you saying nothing is ever clearly right or wrong?"

"Oh, sometimes, sure. But anyone can make the right decision when it's obvious and doesn't come at a cost. The difficult decisions are the ones that make the hero and the traitor."

"And which one are you?"

She chuckled and took a sip of champagne. "I've got a feeling we're not going to agree on that one. What do you think?"

"Indeed we won't," I said.

She wasn't defending herself, denying her identity or justifying her actions. Maybe she was tired of running and hiding, thankful for it all to be over.

She gestured to the waiter for a second glass, filled it from her bottle and offered it to me. "Cause for celebration, surely? You've got me. Congratulations."

I smiled thinly. "Never on the job. That one's not in your grey area."

She shrugged, clinked the two glasses against each other and took a sip from each.

"Mind if I finish the bottle? I assume it'll be my last drink for a few decades."

"I should think so, yes. If you're lucky."

I enjoy these situations, maybe a little too much. Arrests are one of the redeeming features of life in the federal service. I half wished I had accepted that glass of champagne, but I might celebrate with something a little stronger later in the evening.

Demagogues, terrorists, religious fanatics, murderers, nearly all of them feel the need to tell their story before their arrest. Some scream it in your face, some tell it slowly and timidly like a confession, some preach it, some threaten you and say the truth will come out and you will pay the price, but they all feel the need to get it out and share.

I wondered how she would tell her story, whether she would try to explain her choices. I had a feeling she just wanted to sit there and talk, to savor her last evening of freedom, her last night in a busy bar, the feeling of being surrounded by people not wearing prison uniforms.

But I am not a betting man. I would find out how she would tell her story when she told it, so there was no point in second-guessing and presuming. Presumption leads to mistakes, and I don't like making mistakes.

"Are you just going to sit there and watch me drink?"

She was taunting me. Understandable, given the circumstances. We could link over a hundred deaths directly to her and her cell. She was unlikely to go down without chalking up a few points on her personal score sheet first.

"You wanted to finish the bottle. I'm waiting. That's all."

I was not interested in a sparring match, at least not yet.

"No other terrorists to catch tonight then?"

Her jibes began to irritate me. I wondered whether I might have to cut her champagne session short after all. This was disappointing.

"What do you think?" I asked.

"No, probably not. I'm a big fish, aren't I." It wasn't even a question.

"You got it."

I could see she was starting to get impatient with me, too. Par for the course. I'm not a golfing man, either. In fact, I find it deadly boring, devoid of strategy and generally played by people with more money than brains, but I like that phrase. Par for the course. Very fitting.

"Anything you want to ask me?" She spoke so softly I had to strain to hear her over the background chatter from the surrounding tables.

The confession type, then. I liked that. These did not tend to require much work once they got going, and they rarely put up a fight at the point of arrest.

"Yes. The bus bombing. How did you pull that one off?"

"Ah, the bus bombing."

She seemed vaguely amused about this. I did not share the sentiment.

"The bus left the barracks at six forty-five every morning. That was no secret. The problem was getting someone on the bus to plant the bomb.

"We'd been trying to infiltrate the place for months. A few of our members had made it to cadet status, but they were all exposed before they had a chance to sign up for prison camp duty. As you know, the army had badly decimated our agents by then."

I nodded. "I'm aware."

"You would be." I would have liked to think that her smile was forced, but it did appear genuine. Maybe the deluded type after all?

"Well, as I said, in the end we didn't get anyone into the barracks. So all the nineteen-year-old boys and girls you shot afterwards were innocent. Not that a little additional collateral damage would matter much to you, I suppose."

She was into her fourth glass of champagne by now, downing the drink at a speed that clashed with her calm composure. I did not mind too much. The more inebriated she was, the more likely I would get an unfiltered version of events. Of course, I was miked up. A technician and a second agent heard and recorded everything she said from the comfort of the van at the back of the building.

"We didn't execute anyone unless there was evidence against them." I could feel myself getting defensive. Not the persona I wanted to display. I made a mental note to rein in my indignation.

"If you say so," she shrugged. "Back to where I was, then. We managed to bribe the driver. He was a civilian and didn't like you any more than most of them do."

"The population has expressed…"

"…'*overwhelming support for the president and her policies,*' I know. Spare me the fucking propaganda."

She filled yet another glass, upending the bottle to get every last drop out. I let her. The staff at the place she was going to had seen worse than drunks and cleaned up worse than vomit. I would not be the one who had to deal with it.

"So, the driver."

"Yes, the driver."

She giggled, then caught herself and cleared her throat.

"He was, as I said, well, he didn't like you. If you insist, he liked you less than the rest of the population did, or whatever doesn't clash with the seven o'clock news.

"His son was killed when your lot took over, and he lost his job as a teacher due to his so-called 'misalignment'. Someone must have found it amusing to make him drive your guards to the internment camp."

I raised an eyebrow. It did indeed sound like something our pettier middle managers would have found amusing. I kept the thought to myself. Anything I said would, after all, also be recorded.

"Unsurprisingly, he appreciated the opportunity to get back at you. So much so he was happy to die for it. In his words, he didn't have much left to live for anyway. He hardly needed encouragement.

"Of course, we checked him out. He was sound.

"We delivered the parcel with the explosives to his house, and he smuggled them onto the bus, one by one, over weeks, and installed them when he could.

"On the last day, he set the timer. The charges exploded just as the bus passed the gates to the camp. Thirteen people died, twelve of them yours. Sixty-eight innocent people escaped."

"A grey area?" Even I could hear the sarcasm dripping from

my voice.

"A grey area. It was one of my toughest calls. Some of the guards were hardly more than boys themselves, and no doubt indoctrinated from childhood. But the number of people in the camp! With most of them having done nothing—*nothing*—to justify their internment.

"If only we'd had a way to warn the prisoners of the explosion, maybe more of them could have escaped."

She finished her final glass. I had heard as much as I wanted to. It was all getting predictable now and following patterns I had seen plenty of times before.

"I think it's time to go," I prompted gently. No point in being uncivil so close to the finish line.

"Ah, but you see, I don't intend to go."

"We can take you if you don't come willingly."

"I know."

"Then what's keeping you?"

She smiled again, that thin, genuine-looking smile that seemed so entirely inappropriate for her situation.

"Nothing. I just don't want to go."

"I understand. Will you, though? Even if you don't want to?"

"No."

"You want us to carry you out?"

"If you must. I doubt it will swing anyone's political allegiance."

I sighed, then gestured.

Four plainclothes officers rose from surrounding tables and unceremoniously grabbed her arms and legs. As they pulled her away from the table, I saw a blinking light reflected in a window. Her body must have been hiding it from view before.

"Bomb!" I screamed.

~ * ~ * ~

Birgit Gaiser lives in Edinburgh, Scotland. They write short speculative fiction and have a soft spot for the slightly bizarre and characters who view the world with a healthy dose of sarcasm.

Working as a scrum master by day, they also have a PhD in toxicology, which they consult for the occasional (literary) poisoning.

Visit them on Facebook www.facebook.com/BirgitKGaiser

and Amazon www.amazon.com/author/birgitkgaiser.

Birgit's work has been shortlisted for the Edinburgh Flash Fiction Award and published or accepted by WolfSinger Publications, Black Hare Press, *Daikaijuzine, Black Ink Fiction,* Ghost Orchid Press and *50-Word Stories.*

Pin-Hole on a Nice Neighborhood

Madeline McEwen

I'd escaped from my houseful of building contractors for an afternoon, and by the time I returned home at nine, it was dark. The car's lights spanned the street, highlighting our corner lot. The house was exposed to the public without the privacy provided by our flattened, thrown to one side, fences.

A dogwalker, on my side of the street, paused as I pulled into the curb. The woman's face was gaunt, blanched by the headlights. Wiry hair haloed from her head, and she held an extendable dog leash in each hand. The dogs' red eyes turned toward me. The witchy woman, Mrs. Witchy—no, she wouldn't be married, no man would have her. So, Missy Witchy raised one arm, shielding her sparse, overplucked eyebrows. Otherwise, she stood frozen to the spot, flip-flops planted two feet apart, a sentry holding her ground, challenging my right to return home. Who did she think she was?

Remaining in the driving seat, I observed with disgust as one of her huge hairy hounds, the white one, squatted and defecated on the edge of our driveway. Seconds later, Missy strode purposefully to the other side of the street. The dogs bounded ahead of her, out of my line of sight, disappearing into the gloom.

The nerve of some people. Californians are renowned for their wacky ways, but for that woman to pollute this beautiful, leafy suburb of San Jose is beyond the pale and beggars belief.

Switching off the lights and engine, I grabbed my shopping bags. I struggled out of the Silverado and down onto the ground, shoving the door closed with my shoulder. I peered along the dimly lit street to catch a glimpse of that treacherous lawbreaker. I wanted to shout at her but, decided against it because people can be weird. What if she ran back and set her dogs on me? They'd smell the steak in my grocery bags and make mincemeat of me, tear me apart, gorge on my intestines and devour my entrails.

Instead, I hurried inside. Dumping the bags on the kitchen island next to an open bottle of scotch, I called for Frank, a big bear of a man, but the only babe in my life. Where was my husband when I needed him?

"I'm in the den, Karen," he replied.

"Frank!"

"What's up?" he called.

Leaving his recliner, he hurried to my side, now tuned into the tone of terror and indignation in my voice.

I gave him a brief and fulsome account of what had transpired. I steadied myself against the counter; the surface gritty with a fine layer of stucco dust. Lightheaded, I feared I might faint, overwhelmed by a confusion of mixed emotions.

"Frank!" I said, more forcefully than I intended. "What are you going to do about her?"

Frank stood still, his thoughts rippling across the furrows of his broad, heavy-set brow. For all of his bulk, six-foot-two and two-hundred and seventy pounds, he was never quick to make decisions.

"Well?" I said, expectant, hoping to prod him into action.

Frank opened a drawer, removed a Ziplocked bag and a flashlight, grabbed the Ram 1500's keys, and stomped heavily out through the front door, slamming it closed behind him.

Dashing after him, I caught up with him as he reversed from the driveway into the street. I had no idea what he was going to do, but I was damned sure I wasn't going to miss this spectacle. Frank was a timid man at the best of times, and I don't think I'd ever seen him this riled since his best man spilled a glass of Dom Pérignon champagne on my wedding dress more than twenty years ago.

Frank turned his face toward me, and I read his look of determination. We were in this together.

Jumping into the back seat, I slipped into the footwell out of sight of our antagonist, should we find her. The pickup lurched forward and rumbled down the street. The air conditioning roared, keeping us fresh despite the hot night air of August. To think that some woman, a neighbor no less, could befoul our home and believe she wouldn't pay the price. Well, she could think again when there are men like my Frank to be reckoned with.

After what seemed like only a few seconds, Frank slammed on the brake and rolled down the window. His forearm rested the length of the open window, knuckles raised, thumb tight and tucked into his fist. He stuck his head out.

"Hey, you!" he shouted.

My face rose inch by inch until I could see through the window.

That was her. He'd found the right woman, our prey. Close up, she looked older than I first thought. Scrawny too, like when skin thins and withers with age hanging loose from her upper arms—bat-woman from hell. She held the dogs in, shortening their leashes, close to her body, in front of her for protection.

"Yes?" she said.

She had an accent. Australian? Was she faking? Good actor, though. She did a great job of pretending she didn't know what Frank was about.

"Why don't you pick up after your dogs?" Frank said.

"I do," she said, raising one of the leashes with three, obviously full, black doggy bags attached. "See?"

Frank wasn't expecting that—a flat denial. Neither was I. And yet, does anyone take responsibility these days? What would he do now? Back down? Let her get off scot-free?

"My wife told me your dog fouled our driveway just now."

Typical Frank. Always putting the onus on me. However, that made the match two against one. We were right, and she was so very wrong. She was the kind of woman who had tattoos hidden under her clothes and a ring through her navel. And cheap too. Every which way you looked at it, she was no better than a thief, stealing our peace of mind.

"I think you're mistaken," Witchy said, shaking the leash and the bags again. "My dogs have already toileted."

Toileted? Who talked about their dogs like that? What was that accent of hers?

"My wife was in her car and saw you and those dogs right in front of her."

Good job, Frank. Told her right, no wriggle room.

"Maybe it was some other dog," Witchy said, "at some other time? Earlier, perhaps?"

That woman was a phony, a sneaky cheater. And bold, so brazen and entitled.

"Are you saying my wife is a liar? She saw your dog do it with her own eyes." Frank thumped the side of the car with his fist. "Now, are you going to go and clean it up?"

Frank! The man was my hero. Decisive, determined, and authoritative.

"You want me," the woman said, "to pick up after some other

dog?"

"No, your dog."

"Okay," she said. "In the spirit of neighborliness, I'll do as you ask."

I watched her turn around and walk back up the street toward our home. Frank reversed, made a three-point turn, not an easy maneuver in that narrow street with such a huge truck, and followed her at a slow and steady pace, like a pirate forced to walk to plank back to our desecrated home.

While the engine idled, Frank watched. I watched too as the shiny-eyed woman tore off a baggie, removed the offensive material, and secured the baggie next to the others attached to the leash.

Frank turned off the ignition, and the night fell into silence and darkness. He said, "Have a great night" because he is a great man, a giant of good manners and civilized behavior.

The woman said nothing, brushed her cheek with the back of her hand, and switched on a tiny flashlight as she retreated; her humiliation complete. I could almost see the tail between her legs, the stupid bitch.

Satisfied, Frank and I giggled. I gave him a smack of a kiss, my chivalrous knight defending his household's honor. A wrong had been righted, and I felt a shiver of gratification.

After that, cozy in our soon-to-be-perfect partly remodeled home, we did have a great night, the two of us rekindling our spirits in the privacy of our bedroom.

The following morning, I was much calmer until the contractors arrived at seven o'clock sharp to begin another earthshattering day of mess and misery.

~ * ~

Summer dwindled into fall, and soon our remodel was complete, the bills paid, and the contractors moved on to their next project. By that time, I'd forgotten all about Missy Witchy, although I still kept a wary eye out for her in the evening because they're like that, aren't they? Dog walkers are creatures of habit. They take the same route and repeat their well-worn paths. Besides, women like that lacked the imagination to try anything new, unlike my designer planned, state-of-the-art, technologically advanced kitchen.

So I was caught unawares that weekend, when I visited my

neighbor, Melanie's, at-home craft fair as I did every year. Melanie hosted the fair in her sunny open front yard. The neighbors brought their home-made gifts to sell, everything from jewelry, hand-made soaps, and festive floral arrangements.

Melanie circulated with a tray of hot chocolate and warm rum punch to encourage extravagance in the dazzlingly bright sunshine. I swirled the syrupy drink with a cinnamon stick when I spotted a huge, white hairy dog prancing past Melanie's bare-branched hydrangea. I recognized it immediately. That was not a creature I would easily forget, not with that distinctive tail arched like a scimitar over its back. The dog's dark eyes clouded by cataracts turned towards the guests. Its nostrils flared, taking in the tantalizing assortment of odors. A few moments later, the second dog, the curly black one appeared too, followed, shortly afterward, by Missy Witchy herself shrouded in a yellow and black striped pompom hat, a matching wooly scarf, and a pair of chunky, round-lens sunglasses. She looked like a bee or maybe a hornet.

I glanced around for Melanie, to identify Missy Witchy as the culprit in my tale of woe. Melanie loved nothing better than a bit of gossip and was horrified when I told her what had happened in August. She, too, was impressed with Frank's masterful control of the nightmare.

"Oh look," Melanie said, "there's Cara."

"Cara?" I said.

"Yes, Cara means friend in Gaelic. She's Irish originally, but grew up in New Zealand."

I knew she'd had an accent, but it wasn't like any kind of Irish accent I'd ever heard before.

Witchy, or rather, Cara, paused and turned toward the yard. She slapped her thigh, and both dogs ran to her and sat at her feet, awaiting a treat. Digging into her pocket, Cara gave them both something to chew on.

"Hello there," she said to Melanie.

"Why don't you come on in," Melanie said, "buy some early holiday gifts."

Cara raised both her hands, each attached to a retractable leash. "Sorry, but I don't think I can trust these guys around all that delicious smelling food."

Cara had a loud voice, almost shrill, and the sound of it drifted over the yard, carried far further than I would have imagined.

"Good decision," I said, taking a step back toward the crowd of shoppers milling around the different tables. An autumnal breeze fluttered through the branches of the almost leafless trees. An air of agitation irritated my jangled nerves. I couldn't face a showdown on my own. Pulling out my phone, I shot off a quick text to Frank. "Witchy is here. Come rescue me."

Melanie and Cara continued their conversation as if I were invisible, which, in a way, was some relief. I noticed the two women, Cara and Melanie, were similar in height and build, that is to say, petite, rather than robust. I caught snatches of their chattering while I scoured the street for Frank's arrival. Would he come? Why hadn't he replied?

Then, I saw him jogging down the driveway, his red plaid shirt-tails flapping over his black t-shirt. For some unknown reason, instead of crossing the street, he climbed into the truck and drove the twenty-five yards from our house to Melanie's.

As he clambered out, I noticed, to my horror, he was still wearing his favorite, suede, threadbare, moccasins. They robbed him of the stature he so richly deserved, but maybe nobody else would notice.

Frank hurried to my side. He flung his arm around my shoulders and rested his chin on the top of my head, a protective gesture for which I was eternally grateful. I grew taller and braver with him by my side, united against a common foe.

Sensing a change in the atmosphere, I glanced toward Witchy who's stony stare grazed my face.

That prompted Melanie to introduce us.

"I'm so sorry," Melanie said. "Where are my manners? This is Karen and Frank Wright. We've been neighbors for years since my kids were in grade school. And this is Cara O'Leary. Her family owns the Cape Cod house on Blossom Avenue, the one with the gorgeous garden."

Garden! Garden? Who cared about some dumb outside yard when I had a unique pristine kitchen inside?

"Ah," Witchy said. "Actually, we are acquainted, but were never formally introduced."

"How so?" Melanie said, her brow crinkling with curiosity.

"I'm sure I told you about this last time we met."

Witchy's voice was noticeably louder. The shoppers paused, some glanced over, their attention anticipatory, their interest piqued.

"Yes," Witchy said, "remember the guy who harassed me, back in August?"

"Of course," Melanie said, "that hideous, power-crazed tormentor."

"Tormenter?" Frank said, in a voice bathed in disbelief.

"That's a bald-faced lie," I said, backing up Frank.

"Karen?" Melanie said. "You've heard about this too?"

I stayed schtum and lowered my gaze to a bare patch in the lawn.

The shoppers moved as one block away from the tables and toward the street, forming a crescent-shaped wall of bodies, an audience awaiting satisfaction. I gripped Frank's arm for support.

"It was all a misunderstanding," Witchy said. "You see, I was out walking Curly Sue and Noggin around the neighborhood late one evening when this truck came barreling toward me at high speed, headlights on full beam and practically blinded me. No signals, no indication of where they were going, and stopped right in front of me, pulling into the curb on the corner without warning. I was utterly terrified. That was why I didn't notice Noggin take a dump on the side of the road, on their driveway, I suppose, although I didn't realize it at the time. My fault entirely, of course.

No one came out of the truck, it just sat there, headlights burning. Eventually, I drew the courage to move away. I assumed the truck had stopped there and wasn't about to move. Perhaps the driver had pulled in for a phone call or to text. Who knew? So I crossed over to the other side of the street and carried on my way.

"Anyway, I continued down the street toward home, when another huge truck tore down the street after me and braked inches from my ankles. Noggin started barking, and Curly Sue wrapped her leash around my legs in terror, trying to escape. I mean, some trucks are bloody monster-sized, like that one!"

She pointed at the Silverado's shiny chrome fender, and the crowd nodded their agreement.

"It was eerily scary," Witchy continued, "especially in the dark. It was so hot, the sweat was pouring off me as if some crazed stalker was after me. This time, I could see the driver because he stuck his head out of the window. Such an angry, blotchy face, and he shouted at me. I couldn't understand what he was saying. The engine burbled and rumbled, and he kept hitting the accelerator, revving up. All the while, I was trapped in a pool of light by those hot headlights in a sea of inky darkness. The whole experience was surreal. I half expected him to pull a gun on me.

"Eventually, I understood he believed Noggin had fouled the pavement, which, as it turned out, was true, but I didn't know that at the time. I gave up in defeat and returned to the corner lot. Noggin was tired. At his age, arthritis makes him slow. The truck driver hovered behind us for each painful, plodding step as we retraced our route in the fetid night air.

"I cleaned up the driveway while he, the driver and his truck, stood guard over me, glowering and bristling with hatred. Then, when I turned to leave, he roared at me again."

"What did he say?" Melanie asked, glancing toward Frank, her eyes traveling from his moccasins up his hefty body to his pink-flushed face.

"He shouted, 'Have a *greeeeaaat* night!' It was as if he spat the words on me. The utter contempt in his voice was indescribable."

"How horrific," Melanie said. "What did you do then?"

"What could I do?" Witchy said. "I walked home as swiftly as Noggin's legs permitted."

"Is that why you've changed your routine," Melanie asked, "walk during the day not at night?"

"I never want to feel like that again," Witchy said. "Daylight's safer."

"I'll say it again," Melanie said, "you should have filed a police report. Not just for your own peace of mind, but to protect others. We can't tolerate that kind of behavior in this neighborhood."

"What?" I said, before I could think.

"Karen," Melanie said, "do you disagree? Isn't it better to get these things out in the open? Thugs can't go around bullying innocent people and not expect to get called out."

"Thugs!" Frank repeated, squaring his shoulders. "Can't a guy put people straight?"

Curly Sue, Noggin, and Cara took a collective step backward. The crescent of shoppers took one step forward.

"You may not realize, Frank," Melanie said, "but big guys like you can be intimidating."

"Especially at night," one shopper said.

"Or if they're high up, like in that truck," another said.

"But he was one guy," Frank said, "against two ferocious dogs."

The onlookers examined the dogs who were large, but otherwise benign, dopey, dewy-eyed, house-pets.

"A lonely law-abiding guy," Frank said, "against one evil-minded, lawbreaking, ball-busting bitch."

The shoppers, all women, took in a collective gasp.

"You've got to see both sides," Frank said. "We live in a democracy, plus innocent until proven guilty, right?"

"Good point," Melanie said. "In fact, why don't you, Cara, go back to the house. See what he's got to say for himself? What's the address? You said it was a corner lot, right? Which street?"

I dug my fingernails into Frank's forearm. He winced and shook me off, his body as tense as a bull before the matador's final sword.

Witchy turned away from the yard to glance right and then left, leisurely, as if weighing her options. I saw the tension in her sinewy turkey neck. She swung around, removed her sunglasses, and stared at us with cold, dead eyes, crow's feet crinkling the corners as she smiled.

She replaced her sunglasses, took a step off the curb, and the dogs followed her lead.

"Well," Witchy said, "these suburban streets are so alike, I'm not sure I can remember accurately enough to condemn."

~ * ~ * ~

Madeline McEwen [she/her] has enjoyed publication in a variety of different outlets both online and in traditional print.

Her fiction and non-fiction focuses primarily on disabilities [ableism] and humor.

She has numerous short stories and a few stand-alone novelettes. Her latest short story, "Stepping On Snakes", appears in the *Me Too Anthology* edited by Elizabeth Zelvin published by Level Best Books, and "Benevolent Dictatorship" published in *Low Down Dirty Vote Volume II* edited by Mysti Berry.

BOXED

Maria Simbra

"Mom, what am I?"

My daughter looks up at me quizzically from her school forms. The dreaded race box question. I dread it, because I am philosophically opposed to marking such a box.

To me, in a color-blind society, the box shouldn't matter. We are *people*, not boxes. We have no choice into which box we are born. I resent being judged and grouped based on characteristics beyond our power to control.

I am so against this; I never mark it on any of my applications or information forms. As a result, I have been every race under the sun, it seems.

For instance, on my birth certificate (not that I had any choice at the time), I am "White." Because in 1967 in Nashville, Tennessee, the only options available on birth certificates were "Black" and "White."

When I did my year of residency at Georgetown University, I left my race blank on my personal information form. I discovered the residency office later marked me down as Hispanic, presumably because my name is Maria.

For my year of television classes at Robert Morris University, again, I left it blank on my registration materials. Later, as I looked at my student ID, I saw some mysterious force classified me as "Black."

Whatever. It didn't matter to me. But clearly it mattered to someone.

Perhaps being a statistic in some underrepresented group helped the educational institution in some way—federal funding quotas, alluring admission rates. I wish it weren't so. I wish that kind of information wasn't important to how society operates.

My staunch stance about resounding blankness came to a head during the 2010 census.

I was amenable to filling out how many people lived at our address. I conceded the government should know how many people lived in the United States and where. But that was all.

In my opinion, it was not appropriate for the census to ask what our relationships to each other were, what our commute times were, how much I made. The government has marriage licenses and birth certificates, highway cameras, tax returns, and plenty of other ways of figuring out the nosy stuff they were asking about.

My face turned crimson with anger at the government asking what color we all were.

Of course, the government didn't see it that way. In bold italics on the survey form, you were ordered to fill out the information truthfully and completely. If you didn't, you could face fines and/or imprisonment.

The government also warned if responses weren't furnished, it would send census workers to determine the information in other ways. They might call your home and use accents, dialects, and speech patterns to make the designation. Or they might visit in person to visually inspect and give their best guess that way.

How horribly racist.

True to my form, I didn't mark the race box. And I understood I could go to jail.

Part of me wished the census police would arrest me, make an example of me, and I could get on my soapbox. Not that I expected anyone to adopt my point of view, but I wanted people to at least hesitate before committing and consider for a moment what it means to subscribe to a particular race.

My husband thought I was crazy, but knew better than to argue with me.

True to the government's form, the next level of probing began. For weeks, the phone rang off the hook. Luckily, the answering machine picked up; the pre-recorded bureaucrat left its message—please provide the missing information. I didn't return any of the calls.

Then an unfamiliar car appeared near our house. At first, I didn't think anything of it. Maybe it was a contractor or visitor for one of our neighbors.

But it was consistently parked out front. My stomach dropped as I realized—to collect the missing information, a census worker was now SURVEILLING ME.

I did not want to give the watching and waiting census worker any clues about "what I was." So, each evening, when I came home from work, I clicked the garage door open, scurried into the house, and did not reemerge. I stayed away from the windows, aside from a quick peek to see if the strange automobile was still there.

Eventually, the doorbell chimed. Like the phone calls, I didn't answer. I knew who it would be.

This cat and mouse game went on for weeks.

I told my blond-haired, blue-eyed work bestie, one of the news photographers, what was going on. He was incredulous at my bold defiance of the census.

"Just mark it. What's the big deal?"

"NO! I will not! You know how I feel about this. It shouldn't matter what color any of us are. I will go to jail before I mark that damn box!"

He got quiet, leaned back, and looked at me hard.

"You're gonna go to jail." He gasped, haltingly, with the tone of a child admonishing, awww, you're gonna get in trouble. Then his expression softened into worry as he realized I was truly going to fall on my sword over this issue.

To steer the conversation in a lighter direction, he patted his chest and grinned matter-of-factly. "Well, I'm White."

I smirked at his smugness.

On another day, I relayed my census woes to an African-American photographer I was working with.

He couldn't relate. "I like to know where all the other Black folk are." He blithely chuckled about that, and at my dilemma, and thought I should just mark the box and make the problem go away.

That night, after work, I pulled onto our street with trepidation, anticipating the car, the doorbell, the evasion.

To my surprise, the car wasn't there. Nor was it there the next night. Or the night after. In fact, it never came back.

Huh, I thought, *I guess they finally figured out they weren't going to get what they wanted from me.* I felt victorious! And life went back to normal.

Then, a few weeks later, the doorbell rang. In an unguarded moment when I was expecting a neighbor, I answered. I found myself face to face with a mousy, petite woman with glasses and an official-looking notepad in the crook of her arm.

The census worker!

Our eyes met. Mine grew wide. She opened her mouth to speak. But before she uttered even a syllable, I swiftly shut the door.

How could I have been so careless? She must have parked out of eyeshot. *Dammit!*

I felt defeated. She had seen me. She had all the information she needed to make her pronouncement.

I never saw or heard from her again. And I was relieved, yet disappointed, I didn't go to jail.

I wonder which box she marked.

Another reason I hate picking a race, or having it picked for me: inevitably, someone will mentally conclude, "Oh, you're one of *those*." As if any behaviors or decision-making leanings could be predicted by a "box," which is what I believe the government aims to forecast with its big data.

Would my box predict I'm an only child? That I became a mom at age 41? That I have a proclivity for country line dancing? That I consider myself a disgruntled Catholic, who, in my rebellion, goes to a non-Catholic church? That I lust equally for Ricky Martin and Rick Schroeder?

If we're going to be technically correct about the "appropriate" box for me, based on my genetic origins, traditionally, it has been Asian/Pacific Islander, though more contemporary choices actually include Filipino.

Sure, my relatives might indulge in lumpia and pancit at extended family get togethers, and my mom makes a kick-ass flan, but I'm no more Filipino than a bottle of vinegar. (That's a joke. In case you're not familiar, Filipinos do everything with vinegar. Cook with it. Clean with it. Baptize their kids with it.)

There is a selection I would prefer. I identify as AMERICAN. In all its technicolor glory.

I was raised on the Star-Spangled Banner, the First Amendment, McDonalds®, Coca-Cola ®, and Michael Jackson. I've been imbued with Happy Days and MTV. I hold sacred baseball and Kevin Costner movies, and I, too, like in Bull Durham, believe in the small of a woman's back, the hanging curveball, and slow, wet, deep kisses that last three days.

But American isn't a choice.

The world is made up of lumpers and splitters. I would gladly be lumped together with my fellow Americans, but demographic forms, by their nature, are splitters. And my heart breaks as my daughter calls to me. "Mom, what am I? What do I pick?"

My heart breaks because my daughter is a most splendid lump of Eurasian DNA. She descends from Hansies and McNallys, Farabaughs and McIlnays, as evinced by her natural red highlights, with which she can celebrate St. Patrick's Day with conviction. Her Enriquez-bestowed, almond-shaped eyes aren't as dark brown as mine, and they have glints of her father's hazel.

When she was in preschool, she'd say with a satisfied smile, "Mommy is coffee with milk, and Daddy is light peach. And I am dark peach." And I loved that, glad at her recognition and embrace of all of her genes. She had not simply favored one side based on appearance, which, with her blended features, isn't really that simple at all.

I look over her shoulder at the choices before her. Dark peach isn't one of them. None Of Your Effing Business isn't, either. I don't want the box Nazis to come after her if she leaves it blank.

"Other." I nod and point to the empty, surely underrepresented, square. "Mark 'other,' honey, and be proud to represent that."

~ * ~ * ~

Maria Simbra is a memoirist, on page and on stage. She chronicles her careers in neurology and TV news, as well as her unconventional path to motherhood. Words in lit mags of quirk, verve, grief, menopause, and baseball, and at performances of the Avant Garde. She takes cream in her coffee, adores peaches, and opposes boxing.

Boys Play

Ginny Venton

Theodore Gunderson says:

Lou Tanner knocked my brother off his tricycle, right in front of me, which was like asking to have the crap beat out of him. On my way up the block to do just that I thought about it. I hung out with guys—Bobby, the two Mikes, Carl—who got our kicks playing sports or biking to the parks and climbing trees or messing with Carl's chemistry set. The Tanners were part of a crowd that did things like knocking little kids off their trikes and getting into fights. I mean, my guys would fight if we were attacked, or if some idea of justice was violated right in front of us—but we didn't feel *obligated* to fight. By which I mean, if I went after Lou, his boys would fight for their guy, and *my* friends—not necessarily.

So, such an obvious affront to my sensibilities had to be a trap: even Lou Tanner wasn't that stupid. He had to expect I would cream him.

Then his friends would cream me.

And my friends would…agree that was a horrible thing to have happened.

It was a trap.

I was going to get killed if I killed Lou Tanner.

But I did. I chased him, caught him by the shoulders, threw him to the ground and kneed him in the stomach. He'd messed with my *brother*. No way he was walking away.

My brother was crying. I walked him home. The Tanner gang wouldn't do it then, wouldn't be looking for me yet; they'd wait for some time when I didn't expect it, when I'd see them gather and march up the block, when I'd have no escape except to run further and further from home.

So, there was time and I used it well. A past issue of Captain Candew comics, I remembered, had illustrated lessons on mastering some of Captain Candew's deadly martial arts moves. That became my life. I practically lived in the basement, the comic book laid out on the washing machine so I could swing and kick and hop around.

I say I was "practically" living in the basement because I was also spending time in the backyard practicing with my pea shooter. My parents hated the pea shooter so I had to act like I only used it for target practice; but I was practicing hitting that target not just straight on, but while turning, while running, rapid fire—phwitt pip, phwitt pip, phwitt pip, beans and little stones (hardly ever peas) from my mouth through the tube, bouncing noisily off the tree. I got to be not too bad. I practiced climbing the tree too, in a hurry, figuring the Tanners weren't too smart, and if I had to get up high to pick them off, they'd realize only that I was picking them off, not that I was trapped in a tree.

A few times I saw Tanners—Jimmy Julie or Harold or Gags —walking by innocently, as if they were doing just about anything but checking out where I was since I wasn't at the park or the Little League field or anywhere else they expected to find me. They couldn't just invade my backyard: parents were like the Olympics, in that, around them, everyone was so friendly and happy to just be hanging out with each other. No, they had to kill me elsewhere.

I was a hermit for over a week, and was starting to get the itch to play some ball when, what do you know, Bobby showed up out front with his mitt, calling, "Hey The Gun, Hey The Gun."

They call me The Gun.

Bobby says:

There's this guy, Jimmy Julie, who comes around a lot and says sometimes he's my friend but mostly is mad about something so he's grumpy and just yells or pushes and then leaves, and he came over and said something like, "I haven't seen The Goon for a while," and I said, "Me too" and Jimmy Julie said, "He's your friend, ain't he, you ought to go get him play some ball."

He was talking about the Gun, Theodore Gunderson, who imagines he's called The Gun, and he is, mostly, by me and Carl and the Mikes and some others, but actually it's The Goon 'cause they say their name like "Goon-derson" and he's got that "The" in Theodore so it looks like The Gun, but it sounds like The Goon.

You don't say The Goon by his parents, though because, you know, that would be insulting to them and parents are like, this other world and there's no point raising any trouble for no one.

I don't look for trouble generally, and I do good in school. Well, for *behaving* I do good, but the *grades* aren't always *that* good. That Jimmy Julie sat next to me last year, and I don't know how he gets through it, slamming his desktop and always drawing instead of listening and making weird noises when the teacher turns around and lots of other stuff. He hangs out with those Tanners a lot, and those guys are mean and bad. But Jimmy, like I say, he comes by sometimes and asks, "What are you guys up to these days?" I tell him maybe we might ride our bikes out to the airport, or going to build a clubhouse in the vacant lot or whatever we got on our minds at the time— though a lot of times we ended up *not* doing what I said, because Tanners happened to show up and we didn't want trouble.

So when he said I ought to go get The Goon and head out to play ball, I thought that I had been wanting to do that too, but hadn't seen old Theodore for a while, maybe a week or more, so I grabbed my mitt one morning and headed over there.

"Hey The Gun," I called, and he looked out and saw right away it was me and what I wanted and he was anxious, it seemed, and he came right out and off we went to the Little League Field.

"Hey," I said as we were scanning the street as we walked, for things to pick up and toss at trees and lampposts, "that Jimmy Julie might be there with some guys."

"Jimmy Julie?" The Gun said, and he stopped walking. He tossed a pinecone. "Why him?" Jimmy Julie wasn't very good, it's true, so come to think of it he didn't always come out wanting to play baseball. "Other Tanner boys too?"

"I don't know, Gun. He just come and said we should play," is what I explained, and The Gun thinks a second and gets this weird smile and look on his face, like maybe he just saw the future or something like that. He says to me "Okay, you done your job." And off he goes just like before, like I hadn't said anything about Jimmy Julie. I was thinking, what's that mean, I done my job? I done my job telling him Jimmy Julie was coming, or I done my job calling on him, The Gun, to come play? Seemed like stuff was happening I was a part of but didn't know about. Like if there were a big old rock rolling down a hill about to crush the house while I was just sleeping there, not hearing nothing. Maybe people other than me was planning *my* future.

The Gun says:

So this was it. Jimmy Julie tricked poor Bobby, got him to lead me into a trap. That's what he thought. The truth was it was me who had set the trap, and Jimmy Julie and the Tanners and everyone associated with them was about to get hurt. I had that pea shooter in one of the fingers of my glove, and some beans in one of those little sandwich bags which I stuffed into my pocket, and now I had the glove looped looking all innocent with the bat over my shoulder and my hat pulled down to the middle of my forehead.

So we went walking in the street, early in the morning, past the bungalows with their worn out lawns and under the bright dewy leaves on the elms along the way, me happy and Bobby holding back a little now, until we came around the corner and saw the field and some guys gathered and their bikes tossed around the parking lot like they had fallen from the sky. Then Bobby said, "There's Carl and Tall Mike!" And, he took off running past me, so I ran, and we raced to the fence and jumped over. I was looking for Tanners, for their friends, because I knew they were coming. This was their game. Carl threw the ball to Bobby on the run, and Bobby threw it at me but I wasn't paying attention and it hit behind me with a thud on the grass and rolled away. Tall Mike called something that sounded like "lagoon" and I was already picking it up. It was wet with dew, like it had fallen into a lagoon all right, but it would dry, the grass would dry. Soon we'd be sweating and wishing this really *was* a lagoon out here.

If we made it that long, that is. I looked up and there, riding into the parking lot on his stripped Schwinn was Mel Tanner, the big one, the oldest of the Tanner boys, leader of the Tanner gang. I tossed the ball carelessly back toward the infield, toward Carl, and I watched Mel drop his bike and grab his mitt off the handlebars just as Lil Mike came speeding in like he always does, turning as he braked and hopping away as his bike bounced and the front wheel jumped crazily like a broken neck.

Mel saw Lil Mike, and waited for him, leaning on the fence separating the field from the bleachers down the right field line, and I thought this was it, Lil Mike was going into a headlock, I was supposed to run to help him, and a mess of Tanners would pop out somewhere and the fight would be on. I was looking around for where they might be, but there was no one gathering, just the guys on the infield playing catch and someone who may have been Lou Tanner crossing the street way beyond the parking lot, in no hurry to get anywhere if it were in fact Lou Tanner. They'd be saving me for him, since I had beaten him so badly, but this guy was just taking his time, and it turned out it wasn't Lou but Tommy, the middle Tanner, and he was just strolling along, flipping his mitt in the air and dropping it more often than he caught it. He was a horrible baseball player.

But I didn't think there was going to be a game, and I turned back around expecting to see Lil Mike on the ground and Mel kicking him and looking my way.

But there they were, and I didn't know what was going on now: they were just walking and talking and once Mike looked over at me, but just for a second, and not like he needed help. Then I noticed others looking at me, too. I guess I was just standing there, alone in center field, and everyone was wondering why. So, I took my time walking on in to the third base dugout, looking at my mitt, looking up at the sky—like I didn't have a care in the world. This Little League had dugouts on both sides, not really "dug" but built out of wood with cement floors and a water fountain, and these cubby holes and shelves where I could stash the pea shooter until it was time, so that's what I did, keeping the beans in my pocket.

Jimmy Julie showed up, and some others, and pretty soon there were lots of guys so we picked sides, and anyone not picked would go home or go into the parking lot and play Home Run Derby the other way, with their home runs landing on the field, because their "over the fence" would be our "inside the park." This usually happened when there were too many guys. So, they chose up, two of the bigger guys, and I ended up with Bobby and Lil Mike and, wouldn't you know it, Tommy Tanner. One guy *not* picked was Carl, who really should have been taken over Tommy Tanner, so he headed out to the parking lot with some little kid I didn't know, just smiling and chatting like nothing was wrong. That made me realize Lou Tanner wasn't there. He was probably around somewhere, behind a tree or creeping through the parking lot. I didn't see him, but I made sure I was sitting next to where I had stashed the pea shooter.

We batted first, and I saw Mel Tanner was playing shortstop

for the other side, and they had Jimmy Julie over at third. My first time up they gave me a low inside pitch that I know what to do with, a line drive right down the third base line about an inch off the ground—easy double, which is what I wanted, thinking I could slide hard into Mel Tanner and get a jump on him before his gang could charge from whatever shadows and rocks they were slithering around. But he didn't cover and there was no play, but I slid just to show him what I could have done, and he just took the throw from left field and looked at me lying there, and casually tossed the ball to the pitcher. Maybe I'd bump him on the way to third base.

But he inched over while there was some kind of talking going on at home plate, and he said, "Hey, man, thanks for taking care of Lou like that."

This is it! Man, my pea shooter's in the dugout, but I have my hands and feet and martial arts. Mel says: "I don't know what's wrong with that guy. How old's your brother, like three? Pushing a little kid like that. I hope he learned something."

I glared at him, tense, ready. "What you mean, Mel?"

"The way you clobbered him. He deserved it." He kicked some dirt and looked down. "I'm really sorry. Hope your brother's okay."

Oh, man, what are they up to? Tanners are just violent people, they're all a bunch of jerks, and they don't apologize for hurting someone. Everybody knows that. So, this is part of the trap, and it's getting really deep, really tricky.

There was a fly ball and I moved to third, and Jimmy Julie's standing there right on the bag. We really don't like each other. "Glad you made it. Where you been?"

"You'd like to know," I said slyly.

"We're gonna beat you bad."

"I'm waiting." But then there was a hit and I scored. Bobby pounded the bench next to where he was sitting, so I sat there, and I told him what was going on.

"You get a chance," I said, "you slide hard into that Mel Tanner, take him down, hurt him."

"I do that he'll start pounding me," Bobby said, not seriously —I mean like he didn't think *I* was serious.

"They're up to something, acting real nice," I insisted. "So I'm thinking. Get them to move before they want to. Take him down. Then I'll come out there and let them all have it."

"'Them' who?" Lil Mike was sitting on the other side of Bobby.

"Tanners. That's why Jimmy Julie wanted you to get me out here. They're gonna get me for getting Lou."

"You're nuts," Mike said. "Mel told me he was glad to see you, he's sorry for what Lou did to your brother."

"That's his plan, man, that's his plan. Then when we're not looking, they come out of nowhere and gang up on us all."

"I ain't doing it," Bobby said suddenly.

"Just take him out. He'll be mad, but I'll be on him and then he'll be sorry. Then Jimmy Julie then Tommy and by the time the others show up I'll get them all."

"Look, The Gun, there's that old guy there, he'll tell, they'll be breaking it up before you get *anyone* and then the Tanners will be after us forever." Lil Mike grabbed his mitt as he said that—inning was over. He was right, there was a guy sitting in the bleachers in left field.

But I had to do something.

That Old Guy says:

The boys gathering, as the morning came into focus, and I like to grab a Coke and go sit in the bleachers and watch the rowdy games, the games of spontaneity, the ones with no supervision. We used to do that all the time, before this was a manicured field, and fences. We played on empty lots. Not many empty lots around anymore, but this used to be one, played into a ball field, base paths made by the insistent running of me and my friends and the boys who did the same thing before us, the ground lumpy and weedy so it was dangerous to get in front of a ground ball, and sliding was just a crazy thing to do. Now the field is designed for ground balls and sliding, but the boys are the same, not even vaguely aware anything they do might hurt them, might be dangerous. Maybe because boys that age are still with their parents and not aware of all the things they're being *protected* from, not aware something as simple as catching a ball carries peril, that riding a bike is a very difficult thing to do.

Soon enough they'll stick their heads out of that cocoon and see the world is crazy and murderous. I remember getting old enough to be aware, and becoming aware of assassination, suppression, war, trickery in the highest circles. And how running can hurt, muscles get pulled and sprained and worse.

But they don't know that yet, here now, in the morning games. The boys just play.

This one's just a regular game for the most part, slow, and with some yelling. Everyone getting dirty as the morning evaporates, and the dust kicks up. There's a dispute or two, decided by figuring who's more determined to not let the game go on until he gets his way—just the way we used to solve things.

So, it was kind of a shock when an actual fight started, especially when there was no reason, nothing leading up to it. This kid just came running out of the dugout with his hand up at his face, charging at the bigger kid playing shortstop. The bigger kid ducking, swatting the air around him. Then, in a flash, he was charging the first kid and I don't know, don't remember the exact sequence. There was pushing, and then a pile of kids. It seemed like, legs and arms just kind of, well, *bouncing* in this pile. Appendages moving violently and only once in a while colliding with something else. But, mostly just bouncing off other arms and legs.

But, I thought someone might get hurt eventually, so I yelled at them and when that didn't do anything—in my day, an old guy yelling from the sidelines, we wouldn't have done anything either— I got up and went down there.

I have to admit to a bit of apprehension tingling up my spine the closer I got to the scrum. I'm 71, in fair shape and kind of a big man; but, still 71—*and* alone and about to confront maybe fifteen or twenty young boys.

Would my age, or rather my adulthood, be authority enough? I started speaking with authority as I crossed the base path. "Stop it now!" I commanded. No one looked up from the fight. I could see now what was happening. The boy who had started it was squaring off with the kid he had attacked and appeared to be trying, ridiculously, to karate chop him from five feet away. Other boys were pushing each other, and there may have been a headlock somewhere. What was curious was that there was no lateral movement, all the movement was in the arms and they were barely kicking up dust. It was like each one had picked a specific spot to fight, and nothing could move them from it, not even if the opponent was out of reach.

Some of them saw me coming and stopped their little dances and a few retired to the dugout—or rather, they ran away. Authority! That was me, and it was good to see some fear there, some respect. They were all sweating, I was too, because the sun was high now; it was like high noon. There were the two of them in front of me now, the smaller kid who started it with (I could see now) a pea shooter at his feet, the bigger kid staring him down in angry disbelief, ready to pounce at the touch of a breeze.

Neither saw me, though I was talking, or muttering, something like "Hey, Hey." I touched them both, on the shoulder, meaning to say It's okay, nothing we can't work out, just play the game and it'll be all right.

But I guess they were too wound up. I thought the smaller kid flinched, made some angry movement, poison in his eyes. The other's head jerked. So I don't remember which one—or maybe it was both at once—but someone gave me a punch to the gut. I felt something bad and fell to my knees first, then to the ground, fetal position, arms wrapped around myself, gasping and, somewhere inside, gurgling. Maybe someone touched me, maybe someone said something, but whatever they were doing it was no help. When, in a minute of two, I got some breath back and looked around from the infield dirt there was no one there, just some running footsteps in the distance and the clatter of bikes being put to use.

Bobby says:

I was holding off Tommy Tanner, or he was holding off me, when someone said that old guy was coming. No one stopped, especially The Gun. I might start just calling him The Goon now, though, to his *face*. I mean, why did he do that? Grabbing that pea shooter, I didn't even know he had it, and for no reason charging at Mel Tanner, and then trying to kick and chop him. No one could believe it for a second or two—it was so crazy. He'd been talking about something all day, but I figured that was just The Gun flapping away. But no, it turns out it was working himself up into The Goon.

So, I might call him that now. Especially after how it all turned out.

We'd seen that guy in the bleachers. He's there a lot. I never saw him up close though, and when we turned around and there he was; all wrinkly with little wisps of silver hair like threads unraveling and his big used up eyes, man, we thought the dead were walking around that Little League field. I went to a wake once, for some old uncle, and just seeing the guy from the back of the room was enough for me; it was like they just slapped something together out of old parts and said, "Here, look at this and pretend it's a person." That's what I felt then—that something put together for the purpose of scaring us was coming, pointing, croaking out, "Stop, boys!"

So, me and a bunch of guys took off. I was climbing the center field fence when I saw it, saw the man on his knees and grabbing his stomach, and then falling all the way with Mel Tanner taking his first steps towards his bike and the Goon looking really freaked, like a cat was puking on his shoes or something. Really surprised, really freaked. He said something, and kind of nudged the guy with his foot, and the guy lifted a hand and said something back, and then The Goon took a few steps backwards, slowly, and then he turned and ran into the dugout and I don't know why but I though he was getting a bandage or something, but instead he came out running with his mitt, looking back once at the guy lying there looking like he was just a bag blowing across the infield, and The Goon hopped the fence and caught up to me.

"Call nine-one-one!" he yelled. "He'll be okay then, won't he? Right?"

So, I called 911 when I got home, in case The Goon forgot, and I guess that man *is* going to be all right. Something inside him just got whacked out of place. I don't know. He was in the hospital a while and then out again, and I saw him watering his lawn a few days later.

But before that, running home with the Gun—man, it just seems so odd to be calling him The Goon—I said "So, what, man? What are you doing?"

"That guy had no right!" he said suddenly and quickly and angrily. "He had no right. He just watches, you know? He's not even supposed to be there, Bobby, it's supposed to be just us, just boys playing. Why didn't he just let us boys play? He had no right."

His voice cracked then and I noticed he was almost crying or about to cry.

So, I let him go and haven't seen him now for a while. Someone told me he had to go visit the guy in the hospital. That his parents made him go and apologize. So I guess he's grounded for the summer. I suppose that's good. Tanners are looking for him now. That Jimmy Julie jumped on Lil Mike at the Runza a few days ago but I came by in time, so he just spit at us.

I might go see The Goon tomorrow or maybe sometime soon. I can't get over it. Did he think he was going to get rid of all the Tanners? Even I know that's dumb. All he did, with all his planning and plotting and jumping Mel for no reason—all he did was make sure we can't get up a game of baseball anymore. City chases us off the Little League field now when we try.

Man, I can't get used to calling him The Goon. Maybe we ought to go with Theodore.

~ * ~ * ~

Ginny Venton is a trans woman, living in San Juan Capistrano, California, close to her family (former spouse and three of their five children).

Her writing has been largely for radio, as she was a successful morning show host in Omaha, Nebraska, for many years. She has written for the Omaha Magic Theater, the Sweetness and Light Satirical Theater, and *Omaha Magazine*. A few of her short stories have been published online. She keeps herself busy performing music (she writes songs too), writing stories, and transitioning.

The Colors of Community Organizing

B. Craig Grafton

Tytus Pittman decided to attend the meeting after all. He didn't live in this neighborhood anymore, but he owned three fourplexes there and he wanted to hear what these community organizers had to say and how it might affect his income properties. So, he sat in the middle of the crowd at the Martin Luther King Center and watched as a cast of characters, black and white, milled around and talked to each other on the stage. Finally, a young man, a white tow-headed youth, went up, grabbed the microphone, tapped it to confirm it was working, cleared his throat, and spoke up.

"Ladies and gentlemen let's begin now. My name is Sven Lief and I'm from the…" Mr. Pittman did not catch the name of the organization Mr. Lief said he was from only that it was a nonprofit tax exempt corporation which he proudly made a point of and therefore a tax deduction when one gave them a donation, which he encouraged them all to do of course. Mr. Lief then introduced each of the local people sitting in a row behind him who acknowledged themselves by nodding their heads and the audience acknowledging them in return by clapping after each one was introduced.

Tytus Pittman elbowed the old man next to him, a man he didn't know, and said to him, "What the hell is this organization doing here by sending a Swede to talk to us."

The old man whispered back jokingly, "Well you know what they say, us negroes we's just Swedes turned inside out." The man chuckled slightly to himself. Mr. Pittman did not appreciate this lame attempt at humor. He had never heard that one before in all his sixty-six years of existence and didn't appreciate hearing it now even if it was from a fellow black man.

He responded with his usual. "They? Who's they? Tell me who they is. I don't know who the 'they' are that you're talking about." It annoyed him to no end whenever someone said, 'they say.' He always countered with his 'Who's they speech?' "Give me some names, phone numbers and addresses of these 'they' people so I can contact them," he always said knowing that inquiry usually killed the conversation on the spot and put the speaker in his place which was the intended result of course.

And it worked here as the man in the chair next to him shut up, turned away from him, and pretended to be paying attention to the speaker.

Mr. Lief droned on and on, promising how his organization can unite this underprivileged neighborhood, bring them all together for a better life, and give them a meaningful voice in community affairs. But he spoke in the same old general generic dull boring terms, nothing new, nothing specific as far as Mr. Pittman was concerned. Mr. Pittman had heard all this before for years and now hearing it from some young white man he'd never seen before was to him just plain too much to bear. As far as Mr. Pittman was concerned this young man was just one more community organizer come to town to preach to them and tell them what to do. Like he would know—never having lived here. And even though Mr. Pittman wasn't buying any of this, he knew the local folk here were. They always did.

"And another thing we can do," Mr. Lief rattled on, "is get some of these rental properties owned by the slumlords fixed up and become livable for families, so they aren't a haven for drug addicts and drug dealers."

Mr. Pittman immediately came to attention with that accusation. *Good thing I showed up after all*, he said to himself as he rocketed up from his seat.

"Hold on there a minute young fellow," he hollered. "Who you calling a slumlord?" His anger was palpable. Tytus Pittman had retired from the federal government as a civil engineer. He had worked hard all his life and had saved up and invested in properties here in the neighborhood. They represented a substantial part of his retirement income and his retirement time as well. In fact, it seemed now all of his time was spent keeping up his units and dealing with tenant problems. And he wasn't going to sit here and take any of this bull lying down. He wasn't going to be called a slumlord when he worked hard to keep his places up and presentable.

The youth was taken back by Mr. Pitman's outburst, not expecting anything like that. Actually, the naive youth had not been expecting any resistance, of any kind, from anyone. He thought everyone would be glad to see them and welcome them with open arms and go along with whatever he said.

Behind him sat the Reverend Malcolm Wright from the local Baptist Church. He sensed the youth's awkwardness in dealing with the situation and rose from his chair, went up to him, took the microphone from him and came to his rescue.

"We don't mean you Ty. We know you keep up your properties."

Tytus Pittman hated Reverend Wright with a vengeance. He called him a thug behind his back, and 'Reverend Alright' to his face. Reverend, hell no, he was some former gang banger from Chicago who suddenly got religion and came here downstate to preach to them. He was just another outsider who had no business here at all as far as Mr. Pittman was concerned. In fact, he and the reverend had tangled a few times already about church policy. Mr. Pittman had grown up here in the neighborhood and though he had moved away he remained a lifelong member of the church in which Reverend Wright now preached. That they were not friends went without saying.

"But you could be a little more diplomatic with your tenants, Ty," Reverend Wright added. "And be more considerate of immigrants and their ways. Mr. Lief's organization can help you with things like that."

It had become personal again. The Reverend had hinted at the problems Mr. Pittman had with the Nigerians he recently evicted.

"Look here, *Reverend*," Mr. Pittman shouted. "I did that all legal through my attorney. I followed the law." He kicked out the Nigerian family because of their cooking. He didn't know what they cooked, some food they ate in Nigeria, but it reeked something awful and had a terrible obnoxious nauseating aroma that filled the entire building. The other tenants constantly complained about the smell and asked him to do something about it. Furthermore, the fifty-pound open sacks of rice they left on their patio drew mice. Some of his good tenants even threatened to move if he didn't correct these things. So, he gave the Nigerians proper notice when the lease was up; but they didn't get out. He got a lawyer. Eventually they were gone after it cost him a few hundred dollars in attorney fees and court costs which he knew he would never recover from them even though the judge had awarded him fees and costs in the judgement per the lease.

"Well," Reverend Wright countered, "that doesn't change the fact they were immigrants and we as Americans should try to help them, make them feel at home here. Make them welcome here."

"Our organization encourages helping immigrants," Mr. Lief added. "After all that's what America is all about. Welcoming newcomers. Helping the downtrodden."

Mr. Pittman was smart enough to keep his mouth shut. He knew he couldn't win this kind of a b.s. hokum argument. He originally tried to help this family but it just didn't work out. *Try to help people*, he thought, *and they hate you for it.*

Then as if on cue one from Reverend Wright, one of the church's deacons, one of Reverend Wright's flunkies as far as Mr. Pittman was concerned, stood up and asked him. "And why did you kick out that young white gal and her baby awhile back, a single mom on food stamps and all. Tell me why'd you do that Ty?"

Mr. Pittman had tried to help that person too but when she didn't pay rent for three months, she had to go. She had cost him more money in lost rent and attorney fees and court costs too.

Mr. Pittman kept silent. This was none of their business anyway. But these community organizers had done their homework. They knew how to counter punch him when he spoke up. They were ready for him. After all, Ty Pittman had a reputation for speaking his mind.

"These are the things we can help you with Mr. Pittman," Mr. Lief continued. "One of our goals is to organize a diverse community here. That's what America's all about too, diversity you know."

That did it. That diversity nonsense that is. That pushed Mr. Pittman over the edge. The dam burst. He had had enough. "Bull! It's obvious your goals here are to tell us what to do. Take over our community, run our lives. You already got your people taking folks to the store, handing them pamphlets with calorie counts, nutrition value etc. etc. on them. Telling them what to buy, what not to buy. What to eat. Like they're too dumb to feed themselves and their families. Telling them to come to you if they have landlord problems and you'll take care of everything for them. Telling them you'll put those blankety blank slumlords in their place." Mr. Pittman stopped to catch his breath. Then continued.

"You're always thinking you're doing good by trying to help people. Hell, nobody helped my folks when they lived in this neighborhood and raised us four kids in the two-bedroom tar-papered run-down shack of a house we all lived in. But now there's grants to bring foreigners here. Grants for housing, food stamps, free medical care etc. etc. Grants for everybody for everything. Hell, we never had any assistance of any kind when I was growing up. Didn't need any. We took care of ourselves. We pulled our own weight. No one helped us and we don't need any community organizers to help us now either. We already got township, county, city, state, and federal laws regulating and organizing us enough. Telling us what we can and can't do. We don't need any more organizing. We've been organized to death."

Mr. Lief interrupted him. "If I could explain please."

"I don't need any explanation young man," Mr. Pittman said. "The explanation is simple. Your organization gets a government grant to operate doesn't it? But it's just us taxpayers funding you anyway through our stupid politicians. Enough is enough for God's sake. It's time all this nonsense stopped. It's got to the point of ridiculousness. You can take your traveling circus show, pack it up your you know what, and leave as far as I'm concerned."

And with that said and with a stiff upper lip Mr. Pittman sat proudly and defiantly back down in his chair. His back ramrod straight. His head erect, arms folded. His chin stuck out. His shoulders squared away. A few in the audience started to clap their approval but went quiet when Reverend Wright stood up and glared down at them.

"Mr. Pittman," Lief youth said. "A lot of good can come out of our organization. Give us a chance. Don't forget the President was a community organizer for us in Chicago and got a lot done there." The youth said all this hoping the popularity of the President would resonate with the audience.

"Oh yeah," Mr. Pittman said. "Those neighborhoods he 'organized' I bet they are gardens of Eden now. I bet you'd want to raise your family there. And oh yeah, don't forget about that other great Chicago community organizer, Al Capone."

A few chortles burst forth and then quickly fizzled out as Reverend Wright took the microphone back from Mr. Lief. His former gangsta demeanor came through loud and clear and intimidated the audience into silence. But not Mr. Pittman as he was on a roll and not to be stopped.

"We didn't ask you here did we? Yous just decided to show up on your own and force yourself upon us." Here he paused, thought about what he was going to say next, smiled, and then continued. "Cause we's all jess poor underprivileged black folks ain'ts we?" He said all this in his best 'darkie' accented voice letting Mr. Lief know he didn't appreciate his condescending attitude.

"Tell me," he continued, "how many white communities have you organized? I'll bet the farm it's none. You're always trying to help us poor underprivileged black folks. Why aren't you trying to help poor white folks? Aren't they underprivileged enough for you? Answer me that."

Reverend Wright shouted out, "Ty that's quite enough. if you're not going to behave and be respectful, we're going to have to ask you to leave."

"Oh, now you're trying to 'organize' my right to free speech. Trying to bully me into keeping quiet huh."

"Ty if you don't behave, I'm going to have to ask you to leave."

"What you gonna do? Call the police on me?"

Reverend Wright nodded to a man in the back of the room, a big man, a big muscular linebacker type of man. The man took his cue and started his robotic zombie-like lumbering walk toward Mr. Pittman.

Mr. Tytus Pittman saw the handwriting on the wall, or rather the machine coming at him, and started for the door. The muscular man ground to a halt. Mr. Pittman had left the building.

He knew he couldn't fight these community organizers. Knew they would keep on pushing their agenda to ensure their jobs. To ensure their weekly paycheck from the federal government subsidy. Knew they wouldn't stop until they got what they wanted. They always did. And the ironic part as far as he was concerned was a lot of people here would actually believe them and be convinced their organization was necessary, was doing some good, and welcome them with open arms. After all this had been going on for years now. Nothing changed.

"Too bad I wasn't born white," Tytus Pittman mumbled to himself as he slammed his car door shut and started the engine. "Then I wouldn't be needing any community organizing."

~ * ~ * ~

B. Craig Grafton's latest book *Willard Wigleaf: West Texas Attorney* is a legal fiction humorous western thriller about the diversity of and social issues of the American West in the 1880s. His next book, released in September 2021, is *Jill Driver: Trail Boss.* It is the story of a female trail drive boss and her crew of many ethnicities on a trail drive from Texas to Missouri. Both are available on Amazon.

E PLURIBUS ROT

J.J. Smith

"Must kill Charlie," the large man said. He appeared to be homeless and spoke as if demented, which frightened Woodrow Lyttle, who had been trying to pass the man with no success. The man's husky frame prevented Woodrow from rushing down the Van Ness station subway escalator in order to catch the next Red Line train to downtown Washington, D.C.

Woodrow was determined to catch that train because he was running late for a meeting at the health-insurance think tank where he worked as head of the federal policy group. As head of that group he developed strategies to get Americans to believe government health-insurance programs were socialism, price controls on health insurance were socialism, and access to health care is not a right. His efforts were so successful, he occasionally provided input to the legislative and regulatory committees established to prevent any intrusion of the health insurance industry. For Woodrow to achieve that goal, it was necessary to live within Washington's beltway. At the same time, having to live within Washington's beltway seemed like a huge drawback to life in general to Woodrow for, while he loved the federal community and the drama that went with it, he hated the local community and the drama that went with that. So, except for the many fine restaurants, theaters, and shopping available, he did everything he could to keep from getting involved with his neighbors, and the other local residents, including all classes of the homeless, especially homeless veterans ranting about "killing Charlie."

However, before Woodrow could completely ignore him, the ranting veteran said, "Don't make me kill villagers. I don't like it."

To which a totally surprised Woodrow said, "What?!"

"Don't make me kill villagers. I don't want to hurt anyone," he said.

Woodrow leaned back to get some distance from the man, but he was still close enough to see the man was crying. *He really is unstable,* Woodrow thought, and then quickly wondered if the man was dangerous and if his work fighting insurance payments for mental health care was the right thing to have done. But Woodrow didn't have a lot of time to ponder those questions. The escalator's descending stairs had reached the bottom, and the unmistakable sound of a train pulling into the station filled the gateway area. The man stepped off the stairs enabling Woodrow to pass and make his way to the gates where he fumbled with his fare card, and trotted down another escalator onto the single platform, where he ran to the nearest train car just in time for the doors to shut in his face. "Motherfucker!" he said, as the train pulled away. There was an electronic sign on the platform that said, "Next Train, 15 min," so Woodrow took a seat on one of the granite benches that was a feature of the entire the Metro system. As he sat there, the man from the escalator took a seat on the same bench, but facing the opposite direction on the single platform that sat like an island between the two, river-like tracks on which trains sailed through the station. The man continued to mumble whatever he was saying on the stairs because Woodrow again heard "Kill villagers…won't do it."

Not knowing exactly what he was going to say, Woodrow then turned around and saw the man was bent forward, his hands up over his ears as if he were shielding himself from a loud noise, but there wasn't any such noise and there wouldn't be until the next train roared into the station. While the man really did look pathetic, that didn't stop Woodrow's temper from getting the better of him. "Hey shit-for-brains, I don't know what your problem is, but you caused me to miss that train and now I'm going to be late for an important meeting. I know you don't give a shit about that, but I want you know there are some of us who are actually doing something important with our lives." He paused and there was no reaction, which infuriated Woodrow further. "Hey loser, if I was as pathetic as you, I'd kill myself. Did you hear that, loser?" Again, no reaction, causing Woodrow to shake his head and turn away so he sat facing the tracks on the opposite side of the platform. He produced a magazine and focused his attention on reading, remaining that way until the lights at the edge of the platform began to blink signaling a train was approaching. Woodrow rolled up his magazine, picked up his briefcase, stood, and took a few steps from the bench positioning himself so he could glance into the train cars as they sped past to watch for an empty seat. Looking down the tunnel he saw the headlights on the train switch from high beams to low as it entered the station. The train slowed, but remained at a good pace, so within seconds it had traveled half the distance of the platform and was an eyeblink from where Woodrow stood. That's when the man from the escalator went flying pass Woodrow and dove into the path of the train, the lethal impact occurring during the time it took Woodrow's heart rate to soar from witnessing the suicide.

In what can only be described as a blur in slow motion, Woodrow saw the part of the lead car that reached the operator's waist smash into the man, breaking his body as if it were a sack of glass. Blood shot out of the man and splattered onto the tracks, the platform and the wall, and the man's sneakers went flying ahead of him, while his head sort of flattened on the front of the train. All of that occurred in an instant, and just as fast as the death happened, the train passed, ending the horrible tableau, at least for Woodrow, who then saw the train's cars flash by carrying passengers who had no idea of what had just occurred. However, the same couldn't be said of those on the platform who reacted to the horror they just witnessed with screams and panic. But, the noise of the train drowned out most of those shrieks. At the same time, the train came to a halt, and the initial shock experienced by those on the platform grew as the enormity of what just happened started to manifest beyond the platform causing some riders to turn away and vomit, while others collapsed into sitting positions—like they were at a campfire—and took deep breaths, while some, more hardy souls, ran to the front of the train apparently to inform the operator of what happened (what they didn't know was an incredible amount of blood had splattered over the windshield, so the operator was very aware). Many others stood in shock and stared as they tried to process what they'd witnessed. Woodrow was among those who stood and stared, but he was processing more than the suicide. He was also thinking about something he saw at the instant the body hit the train, something that made him question his own mental health.

What he saw was so strange he believed it was likely his mind had concocted it to soften the blow of seeing someone kill themselves by jumping in front of a train. What Woodrow saw was—at the very instant the life was knocked out of the man—some type of rubbery vapor emerge from a crack in the subway station wall and hit the top of the man's head, but it didn't stop there. It then shot out of the man's head, like the colors of a rainbow exiting a prism, and it struck everyone on the platform who witnessed the death. It happened so fast that if Woodrow had blinked, he would have missed it. But he didn't miss it, which left him with two possibilities. The first was: he had hallucinated the whole thing, which wasn't out of the realm of possibility. But, if it was a hallucination, it was as close to reality as he'd ever experienced it. The second possibility was: it really happened. No matter which scenario was correct, seeing the man die left him both in shock and speechless, and he remained that way until a subway official directed everyone to move to the upper section of the station where they would be questioned by police. When an officer finally talked to Woodrow, he was tempted to tell the full story of all he'd seen, but at the same time he was sure he'd be labeled a crazy person, so he held that part back, along with calling the man a "loser" and that he should kill himself. The officer took Woodrow's statement and moved on to the next witness. The subway official then returned and informed Woodrow counseling was available, and offered a paper containing details of who to contact if he felt the need to talk to a professional. That was it. Woodrow left and, despite living a short walk from the subway, he resolved not to return to that station for as long as possible.

~ * ~

"Paige, it was surreal," Woodrow said to his wife in the comfort of their parlor. "He was a crazy homeless person...he killed himself in front of everyone, and then I saw colors jump off the man and splatter onto peoples' faces. I can't explain it."

"Woody, tell me again about the part where you saw...whatever that was." Paige Tovah had been married to Woodrow for 15 years and was the only one who ever called him "Woody". The reason she kept the name "Tovah" had more to do with not losing the family identity than with feminist politics. The family identity was forged by her great-grandfather after the war when he immigrated to the U.S. She told Woody that prior to changing it to Tovah, his name had been Dachauer and he, along with his family, had been sent to the camp of the same name. After surviving such, he refused to carry the name of the place that murdered his family.

Paige had graduated from Brandeis with honors, and, after gaining some experience at a university press, she now worked at the Holocaust Museum as director of academic publications. In addition, she was gorgeous. Immaculately coiffed auburn hair, green eyes, and a hint of freckles all on top of a five-foot-eight frame that she enhanced on a pedestal of pumps. She was also gifted with an intuition that served her both professionally and personally. It enabled her to sense when a paper should be published, and when she was getting hit on at a cocktail party, or a Smithsonian reception. With her looks and charm, it wasn't unusual for her to be hit on by some government official, administrator, or even horny historians, but, while she flirted—it was the nature of the Washington political scene—the federal Casanovas didn't stand a chance. She truly loved her husband.

Woodrow continued, "I don't know if what I saw really happened. I think I was in shock, so it's possible I hallucinated the whole thing. Wouldn't that be just as bad?"

"Tell me again what you saw," she responded. So Woodrow again described how the vaporous tendrils emerged from the crack in the wall, and how it appeared to touch all those who witnessed the death. When he was finished, she asked, "So, no one else saw that?"

"I don't know. If they did, no one said anything, which means it was probably a hallucination caused by the trauma of witnessing such a horrible thing, but I don't know. All I'm sure of is, I had a splitting headache afterwards."

"There's another possibility," Paige said, then paused to ensure she had his attention.

"What's that?"

"The station is haunted."

"Oh, for Christ's sake!"

"Don't dismiss it like that. The Washington area is one of the most haunted places in the country," she said.

While Woodrow didn't fully concede Paige's supposition, he did consider the possibility the station was haunted, and decided that for the foreseeable future when he needed to ride the subway, he would access the system through a different station. However, "the foreseeable future" for Woodrow turned out to be only a fortnight.

~ * ~

Two weeks had passed since the incident at the station, and Woodrow suddenly found himself running late for a meeting scheduled for that morning. He was giving a briefing on an upcoming senate bill, and that created a quandary.

He had been avoiding the Van Ness Metro station since the incident with "Charlie", and had been walking to the much further away Cleveland Park Metro station. But Woodrow did not have the luxury of a leisurely commute, so he kissed Paige, said "Goodbye", and made his way out the door headed to the nearest station. As Woodrow hit the sidewalk, he quietly said, "Haunted or not, here I come."

However, despite his determination to fearlessly access the station, apprehension crept up Woodrow's back as he rode the escalator down, and a nervous heat rose through him that stoked his fear. That caused a type of hyper awareness to assert itself through him, making him cognitive of the sounds echoing through the station, especially the sound of the escalator as it creaked along. He was even aware of the tangy smell of the stainless steel on which he stood. It was a bit overwhelming, and he was happy to reach the bottom. When he stepped off the moving stairs, his increased level of awareness diminished slightly, and he made his way through the gates as he had hundreds of times before. It was when he was standing on the platform that he noticed the changes to the surroundings.

The first thing he noticed was the curved walls of the giant tubular station had taken on a darker tinge. Because he was in an underground section of the subway, the cavernous dark was to be expected, so was dirt, but in this case the walls seemed dirtier than most subway stations. Grime and water stains had gate crashed their way into the station through cracks in the concrete, and while a certain amount of unhealthy filth was expected, what was on the walls seemed to have surpassed "unhealthy" into toxic. Because the platform was nestled between the tracks, Woodrow was easily able to walk up to the edge of each side and closely examine the filthy walls. As he did so, his imagination played tricks on him because he started to see images embedded within the stains. At first the crud looked like vague, unidentifiable figures, but as he focused his attention on each patch of grime, they started to become recognizable. Woodrow was convinced he'd seen these before. *But where?*

he asked himself as he studied the stains, the images becoming more and more discernible, until it hit him. *How is it possible?* he silently asked himself. But there it was, the pictures were there, all anyone had to do was look hard enough and they could be seen, but again *How?!* Woodrow suddenly become obsessed with the images, obsessed to the degree he forgot about the project briefing he had to give, and he would have remained at the station entranced by the images had it not been for the arrival of a train. The thunderous roar snapped him back into the present, and he recalled he had a meeting. He boarded the train and made it to the meeting on time. However, the images dominated his thoughts, causing Woodrow to make a half-hearted, nonsensical presentation. However, this was Washington, and everyone said it was "brilliant," or "a triumph," or "awesome". Despite the praise, as soon as the meeting was over, he made his escape, telling his team he had to leave early for personal reasons, which no one questioned, and he was gone.

Soon, he was back on the station platform, again marveling at the images made out of dirt and slime. That was when he got the idea to confirm what he was seeing. He ran up the stairs and back to his home. Once there, Woodrow went straight to the computer and quickly found what he needed and sent it to the printer. Now he only had to wait for Paige.

~ * ~

As soon as she walked in the door, he said, "You need to come with me."

"What is it? Is something wrong?"

"No," he said. "But you have to come and see."

"See…see what? I was about to make dinner."

"Forget that for now. We'll eat out tonight. I hear there's a new restaurant called 'Epicurean' that's gotten high marks."

"Okay, but what's so important?"

"Paige, this is…I don't know what this is, it's too hard to try and explain, you have to see it yourself." Woodrow held up an "Interoffice Mail" envelope and covered his face with it like a mask, holding it so she wasn't able to see it touched his forehead. After a few seconds, he said "Come on," and turned for the door.

Grabbing her purse, Paige followed.

Once outside, Woodrow took her arm and didn't let go until they arrived at the subway station.

Paige was aware her husband had been avoiding the station near their home, so she was mildly surprised when he led her there. They rode the long escalator in silence and she followed him through the gates onto the tiled platform where he ran to an edge, pointed to the wall across the tracks, and said, "See it?"

She looked at the dirty wall and said, "See…what?"

"The images, the pictures. They're more like a cave painting, you know, by cave men, than murals, but they have as much to do with cave paintings as they do with the Sistine Chapel's frescos."

Paige again looked at the stain and after a minute of intense concentration she said, "What are you talking about?"

"You don't see it? There're dozens of images, all of the same subject, but different events…the images…they're of war crimes."

She looked again, this time concentrating on the stains that covered the walls, and after a minute she turned to him and shrugged her inability to see them. This despite her being the most intuitive person Woodrow knew, and who worked in a museum dedicated to documenting the murderous actions of one of the most morally bankrupt regimes in history, yet she couldn't see what was right before her.

A little exasperated, he said, "My Lai…the stains on the wall …they're images of the photos of the massacre at My Lai."

"What!? Woodrow just what are you talking about?"

He unrolled the pages he'd printed and examined them before picking one. He held it up towards the wall and said, "There, that one there is the picture of the old crying mother, she's standing in front of a group of young women and some children, you can see the terror on their faces, and, according to the information I found, that girl in the background, the one buttoning her shirt, she's doing that because she'd just been raped by a G.I." He paused for a few seconds, then said, "The old woman is trying to protect the girls from the troops…our troops…U.S. troops. Also, according to what I could find, the soldier who took the picture reported all of the women were shot seconds later." Woodrow looked at his wife for another few seconds, then moved onto the next large stain.

"Over here, this is the picture of the body of a young boy, the kid looks to be about seven or eight, and he's with a man, probably his father. There's a basket with goods just sitting in the middle of the road. It was full to the top, and the contents aren't spilled out all over the road. That was evidence the basket had been gently set down by whomever had been carrying it in the expectation of lifting it up again. The way the two are lying, it doesn't seem like they were running, and the boy's clothes are torn to shreds, probably from the bullets." When Woodrow was done describing the image, he moved onto the next, as if he were leading a gallery tour.

"This image is of two boys, probably brothers. One is older, about ten, and he's still alive, but they are both on the ground, the older boy is trying to shield the younger boy, who looks to be about five, but the younger boy looks dead." That explanation completed, he proceeded to the next.

"This picture is one of the most famous of the massacre. About twenty bodies strewn across a road, with some of the youngest victims naked, or with most of their clothing missing." Pointing to the center of the stain he said, "Right in the center is the body of a baby...the baby is naked and lying face down, and the infant's head is covered by the bare legs of another child who's about nine or ten years old and of indeterminate sex. That child is only wearing a shirt, no pants and his or her legs are spread in death, but the youngster used his, or her, hands to cover their private parts. It indicates the kid died trying to keep their dignity."

There were plenty of other images described by Woodrow, including those of G.I.s rounding up and holding villagers at gun point; of U.S. troops burning huts, of plenty of corpses, some missing limbs and soaked in blood. During the tour, Paige hadn't said anything. She just stared at her husband and the stains on the wall until he was finished. "So what's your point?"

"What...? Paige, what do you mean?"

"What you're ranting about occurred decades ago. Most people have forgotten about it, and at the time, a huge number of people didn't think it was a big deal, and, by the way, all I see are dirty stains. But you obviously want me to go the full Rorschach, so I'll say they look like a cross between sea anemones, and brain tumors. With that said, I'll ask again, what's your point?"

"You think it wasn't a big deal...you're wrong, when the pictures hit the newspapers it helped turn America against the war, that's how big a deal it was."

"That might be true, but people don't care about that anymore. At best it's ancient history to most people, at worst it's something no one wants to admit happened, much less admitting they see it on the subway station walls the way other people see Jesus in toast."

Playing Devil's advocate, that's my Paige, he thought before sheepishly saying, "Unfortunately, I think you're right." Suddenly, he felt dizzy, which caused him to stumble back, and he was soon tottering on the edge of the platform. But as he saw the headlights of a train entering the station, the flash of the lights blinded him, and when his eye readjusted, he found himself standing at the edge of the train system, but on the other side of the tracks looking out at the platform and Paige, who was about eight or nine feet from Woodrow and looking right at him. However, he could tell there was something wrong with his wife. Her eyes were glassy, and she didn't seem to be aware of where she was. That's when he heard her say, "Must kill Charlie." Woodrow then held out his hand and screamed "NO!" And everything stopped.

~ * ~

Woodrow saw not only was Paige frozen in mid-step, but the roughly score of passengers surrounding her were also frozen. Despite that, he kept reaching out to her in an attempt to catch her or push her away from the edge. That's when he heard the voice. "You're aware of the images that adorn the subway walls, you've seen them…the details, yet they don't draw you to them in despair, why?"

Woodrow was sure that for his, and Paige's sakes, he needed to respond. "I think because my job is to shape public perception, I can identify when such images are being used to do that." He paused, then added, "But aren't you out to cultivate despair to the point of suicide. I mean I saw the effect they can have on people when that homeless guy jumped in front of the train, isn't that what you want?"

"No, not suicide…suicide is the problem. Our leadership isn't out to foster a few dozen deaths each year, not when government policy has the potential to annually kill hundreds of thousands… millions. Artwork of such quality is meant to influence…to inspire fear of the other, to incite hate and violence against them, but the overriding emotion so far has been sadness."

"Who are you?"

"The Malebranche. We live behind the walls. We've always lived behind the walls. World governments are aware of us and have been long before there was a United States. Some have tried to destroy us by destroying those who follow us. When that has happened, we take some of our followers into hiding underground. When they emerge, they are not the same.

"Currently there is a silent partnership that stretches back to the end of the last great-war, that was the hostilities your kind called 'the Cold War'. Under the agreement, the cult that worships us and provides appropriate sacrifices, is allowed to quietly operate. In exchange, we help in manufacturing consent when needed."

"Consent? What do you mean?"

"Past policies of chattel slavery, genocide of the indigenous, general violence against 'the other'. To pursue such polices requires the consent of the governed. Therefore, those in power need to channel that propensity for hate and violence in order to achieve their ends. To achieve such requires both free speech, and exploitation of all the mediums in existence at the time. That has not changed. However, now it seems a sense of 'regret' has gotten a foothold in the populace. The Malebranche won't let regret replace us, which is why I kept you from the front of that train. You've been observed, and it is believed you are competent enough in your occupation to produce a concept, or message that will stem any regret, or self-reflection that might be creeping into the American psyche and poisoning that propensity for hate and violence. In exchange, you and your woman will remain safe. Do you have any suggestions?"

"Actually, I believe I do."

~ * ~

Paige was falling forward when an arm appeared across her waist and pulled her back keeping her from stepping off the platform. A second later a train raced past her causing a scream to escape from her mouth. She then heard a familiar voice, it was Woodrow. "You're okay, everything is going to be okay, we're going to be okay."

~ * ~

After the incident at the subway station, Woodrow took Paige home and contacted their employers telling them what occurred and that they needed to take some time off. Paige needed to recover, and he needed to tend to her. They would use accrued vacation time if necessary. However, in both cases the H.R. departments were sympathetic and immediately approved three-weeks off, with an option for more time at the direction of a doctor or therapist. That was Woodrow's next call, finding a therapist who was in their insurance network, and he was provided several options. When he did find one who specialized in trauma and could quickly take Paige, he made the appointment. The therapist was of great help calming Paige, and then helping her get past how close to death she came. It took a few weeks, and during that time he saw to her needs, but when he wasn't caring for his wife, he was working on his other project.

Woodrow had some art talent, mostly as a sketch artist, or illustrator, and probably could have pursued it professionally, but had found the wages to be insufficient. But, while he'd put his ability to draw in the closet, it never left him. When he arrived home with a sketch pad and a set of 50 colored pencils, Paige asked, "What's going on?"

"A project. It's not going to keep me from seeing to you, that will never happen, but I'm going to slip this in while we're home... okay?"

"Okay," she said, before returning to the couch next to the end table where the pills prescribed to calm her and help her sleep sat. The first day, as Paige watched a movie she fell asleep during, Woodrow sat in the kitchen and drew. It continued like that until the next day, when, as Paige napped, he went into the basement and again drew, and that became the routine. He would make Paige her meals, take her to the therapy sessions, see to it she was comfortable at home, and then draw whenever the chance presented itself. At the end of two weeks, he put the colored pencils away, and left the house with the sketch pad, returning about an hour later without it.

"Honey, I think it's time we went out," Woodrow said after a week passed.

"Where to?"

"The subway."

~ * ~

Paige was hesitant, but after Woodrow assured her he would hold her arm and keep her next to him at all times, she agreed. Soon, they were standing at the machines that dispense Metro cards. "Stay here, I'll be right back," Woodrow said. He then walked up to the "station box" where Metro employees monitor the station's operations. He knocked on the window and exchanged words with the employee on duty. He gestured to Paige to join him and they passed through the entrance gates. Woodrow then went to a door located on the platform side of the station box and the missing sketch pad was passed out to him. He again thanked the worker, and rejoined Paige. Holding up the pad, he said, "I left it here, and it turned up in the lost and found."

Woodrow then led her further into the system. Once on the platform, he repeated what he had done the last time they were there, and led her on a tour. "Look around and tell me what you think," he said looking up at the walls. Paige was a little hesitant, causing Woodrow to say, "Take your time, there's no rush."

That increased her confidence and she did as instructed, taking in her surroundings, seriously scrutinizing the entire subway platform. After a few minutes she said, "I'm thinking of the TV, and the washer and dryer, and the refrigerator, and stove, and our house, our car, and…money," she replied. "Why am I thinking of those things," she asked looking confused

Woodrow opened the folder he carried and showed her the drawings he had been working on some weeks before. They were drawings of their television, and washer and dryer, refrigerator, and stove, their car and house, and money—of a ten, twenty and one-hundred-dollar bill. What she didn't know was those items were now embedded into the images of the My Lai Massacre that adorned the station's walls. They were also embedded in other dirt and slime images that decorated other stations of the Washington Metro system. Those stations included the Capitol South Station, which is adjacent to the Congress, and had washers and dryers in the images of the 300 Lakota Sioux massacred at Wounded Knee, South Dakota; and at Metro Center, the largest station in the system, and was its hub, and which now had televisions, cars, a swimming pool, and money peppered among images of whippings and lynching of hundreds of blacks. There were also the upper and lower decks of the Pentagon Station that had images of the aftermath of the nuclear attacks on Hiroshima and Nagasaki. Those images showed the flattened landscapes, of a human shadow burnt into stone steps, of hundreds of charred bodies, and of a Japanese baby with a brick sticking out of his or her skull. Next to the baby were images of diamonds and gold jewelry.

The station closest to the White House was McPherson Square Station. It is a single tube structure with the platforms on each side, separated in the middle by the train tracks. On each side of the station, staring from the platforms and working up were images of the mushroom clouds over both Hiroshima and Nagasaki, with all types of consumer goods plastered on the walls almost as if the blast had thrown those items sky high. Madison Avenue would be proud.

There were more such images at all the underground stations, with the images of torture and murder designed to remind those who would question such actions that this is what we've done to those who stood in our way, and if you don't watch yourself it could happen to you. It also reminded those who were prospering from those actions that possessing homes, cars, TVs, and all the rest, is the American dream. That the tree of prosperity must be refreshed from time to time with the blood of losers.

However, at that moment, Woodrow saw Paige's face still expressed confusion. "I'll tell you why you're thinking of those things? Because that's what people want…that's what's really important to Americans…and we don't care what we do to get that stuff." She still looked confused, so he said, "I'll show you."

He then turned and hurried to the escalator just as a train arrived. He wanted to get to the ascending escalator before the train's doors opened and the passengers exited like lemmings, and he made it just as the first passenger, a man wearing a jacket and tie, stepped onto the escalator. Woodrow looked at the man and said, "Sir, would you share your opinion of what happened at My Lai?"

The man stopped, considered the question and said, "As far as atrocities go that wasn't so bad. Others have done worse." He then turned his attention upward as he ascended.

Woodrow waited, allowing a few passengers to pass, and then said to a woman "My Lai, would share your opinion please?"

The woman, who was in her mid-20s, certainly born long after the war in Vietnam ended, said, "I support the troops, they're so hot."

She was followed by another man who said, "Too little, too late. Should have taken the gloves off earlier."

And another who said, "Calley for president."

Woodrow waited for a few more passengers to pass and picked a man who was dressed a bit more relaxed. "What do you think of U.S. actions at My Lai?"

"If the gooks didn't want to get shot, they shouldn't have lived there."

"But that was their home?"

"What, are you, a commie? Go back to Russia commie!"

Behind the man an elderly woman said, "Got what they deserved...we should have wiped out the whole goddamned country."

A young man right behind the elderly woman said, "I've produced a game."

"A game...what game?" Woodrow asked.

The male, who looked to be in his 20s, held up a cell phone, and in bold letters the text on the screen read, "Getting Some Payback: Massacre at My Lai"

"How do you play?" Woodrow asked.

"What do you mean?" His tone of voice changed. He paused for a few seconds then, as if he were explaining something to a toddler, said, "You round up Viet Cong into groups and shoot them."

Woodrow had heard enough. He turned and hurried back to other end of the platform, but as he walked away he heard someone say, "How dare you bring that up, you commie! Those guys had an impossible job, but they did their duty. I bet you didn't even serve."

"You're wrong." Woodrow hurried back to Paige. On finding her, he kissed her forehead, then took her hand and led her to the point on the platform furthest from the escalators. At that end of the platform there was only the train tunnels. Once there, Woodrow looked at her and said, "I'm in their service now. They'll never let me go, but you can leave."

"But why you? Why do they want you?'

"They've always had me. I just didn't know it."

Paige started to speak, but Woodrow placed a finger on her lips. But that didn't stop her from asking, "Will I ever see you again?" Her eyes filled with tears.

"No," Woodrow replied, quickly adding, "They're going to…" He paused as if someone were speaking to him. After a few seconds he said, "it's better you don't." He then turned and disappeared into the tunnel.

As Paige emerged onto the hustle and bustle of upper Connecticut Avenue, she thought she heard someone say, "Must kill Charlie."

~ * ~ * ~

J.J. Smith is a writer living in the Washington, D.C. area. He's been a hard-news reporter for international news services, and newspapers for nearly 28 years, and after 16 years of reporting on the U.S. government he now spends his daylight hours writing summaries of House and Senate hearings. However, when the sun goes down he writes short stories that have a gooey center.

His work has appeared in the anthologies *Good Southern Witches; Blood & Blasphemy; The Big Book of Bootleg Horror Volumes I and IV; Depraved Desires Volume I; Dark Magic: Witches, Hackers & Robots; Halloween Shrieks;* and *Tales from the Witch's Cauldron*, and in Horror Bites Magazine.

J.J. is a proud Ojibwa

.

THE FLOWER WAR

Laramie Wyoming

There were two round islands bound in the lake, each about equal in size, and both were swarming with activity. People on the West island ran up and down the streets; people on the East island paced up and down the avenues.

In the calm center of the West island, Sergeant Ted sat in his office with a soldier standing before his desk. Sergeant Ted was a solid, unflappable-looking man with a thick brown moustache. He was wearing the standard green uniform of his party. He was a sergeant because he would do anything for his side. The soldier's hands were clasped behind her back and she stood at attention. She was wearing the green uniform, too.

"Project Ten-AX-Five is almost complete," Sergeant Ted said in a commanding voice. "We only need twenty more pounds worth of iron. Soldier, I have found one of the last places with some left. There's a power plant in disuse off Pine street. All the piping is pure iron. I am tasking you to go and collect this and bring it back to the construction site behind here as quickly as you can."

"Sir, yes, sir."

"You will be walking."

"Sir, yes, sir."

~ * ~

Sergeant Fred was in his office, the safest, calmest room on the East island. A soldier was standing before his desk. Sergeant Fred was a mountain of a man. He did not have a moustache. He was wearing the standard orange uniform of his party. He was a sergeant because he would do anything for his side. The soldier's hands were straight at his sides as he stood at attention. He was wearing the orange uniform, too.

"Soldier, I need you to go and collect more steel. There is a cluster of houses on Mango Avenue which still have corrugated steel roofs. We are almost complete with Project Five-XA-Zero-One, and I only need one of these roofs, if you can take the entire thing. Just take from the first one of the houses when you round the corner."

"Sir, yes, sir."

"When you have the steel, please bring it straightaway to the construction site behind the offices."

"Sir, yes, sir."

"You will be walking."

"Sir, yes, sir."

~ * ~

The green soldier set out in her green sneakers. They had no cars left on the island; they had all been taken apart, to be used for Project 10AX5. Everyone walked everywhere. The green Soldier, at least, knew she had been losing weight because of it, which was something she was relatively happy about. The military had not taken her because she was in tip-top fighting shape. They just needed people, and her previous job, sewing custom lace, had grown useless when people lost interest in frivolities. They all had less and less money, and besides standard military types, the green army was primarily made up of the standard custom-lace-sewing types.

As she walked down the street, she watched the people around her. Storefronts were empty. The poor dry cleaner had been the first one to go. Their space had been filled with pipes and machines, all precious iron.

"Renovating!"

"Reopening soon!" signs in the windows of places said. Most of them had closed temporarily, for the good of Green. As soon as Project 10AX5 was carried out, they would defeat Orange, and that problem would be gone. Then everything would reopen, hopefully. They had faith in Sergeant Ted and the people in his cabinet. That exclusive group held the only Green people who *knew* quite what Project 10AX5 was. Not even The Green Soldier knew exactly what it was. Like the rest of the public, she figured it must be a giant weapon that could be unleashed on the Oranges and somehow bring them to their knees in one fatal burst. At least, this is what they all hoped. It's even what some of them prayed for. Except, of course, for The Town Lunatic, a flaming redhead who always wore white rags, and would pray in the streets for the Orange as well as the Green.

The Green Soldier turned a corner, and entered the residential area. There were two types of people on a street like this: people in plainclothes put-puttering about, and soldiers in green uniforms, walking places or carrying things with straight backs.

~ * ~

The Orange Soldier rounded the corner onto Mango Avenue. Like Sergeant Fred had instructed, The Orange Soldier went to the door of the first house he saw with one of the corrugated steel roofs. He knocked on the door.

A Lady in plainclothes answered the door. He could see the home behind her, a well-maintained, cozy space. There was the sound of children playing in a room further off. There was a faint smell of oatmeal.

"How can I help you?" The Lady asked, as was proper when a soldier knocked on her door.

"Sergeant Fred, highest rank of the Orange Office, has instructed me to come to Mango Avenue and collect a steel roof for use in Project Five-XA-Zero-One, Ma'am."

"You mean you're collecting *my* roof?" The Lady asked.

"Yes, Ma'am, unfortunately."

"Well, why don't you come in for a moment, we can talk," she said.

"That's very kind of you, but it's not in my schedule," he said.

The Lady frowned, and a small note of suppressed hysteria entered her voice. "Why can't you take the neighbors roof?"

"These were my orders, Ma'am. But it may make you feel better to know the steel you are providing us with will be used for one of the completing touches on Project Five-AX-Zero-One. Your generosity is helping to lead the war effort."

She sniffled. "Okay."

"Thank you, Ma'am. Deconstruction should take only about an hour. Is there somewhere you and your family can be for an hour? It won't be safe here."

She nodded. "We can go to the neighbors. Ms. Dawn lives next door, and she doesn't have any children." She wiped her eyes. "I have three."

"I'm sorry, Ma'am, this is just the way I was instructed to operate."

"No, I understand. I guess…well, to get those damn Greens, I guess it will be worth it."

"Well, thank you for your understanding." Without breaking his perfect posture, The Orange Soldier shuffled his feet.

~ * ~

The Green Soldier was walking down the sidewalk amongst mainly plainclothes people, carrying the iron piping. She had a green wheelbarrow to carry it all, which another soldier had left there, probably in anticipation. It was hurting her back, but she didn't let her expression, let alone her posture, show she was in pain. A grunt or groan was completely unimaginable. Complaining was not something they did in The Green Army, and complaining was not something The Green People did when it came to the effort. How many times had The Green Soldier said this to her daughter at the dinner table? Her little girl would pick at food and say "I wish you had your old job. I liked the real butter better."

"No," The Green Soldier would say. "We don't speak like that. You should be grateful your Mommy is helping to fight against The Orange. When you complain, it sounds as though you don't really support The Green, and aren't appreciative of all The Green Army is doing for you and your people."

"Why can't I like The Orange?" her daughter would ask. "I mean, I *don't*, of course, but why can't I, if I want to?"

"Because you *are* a Green. And you're entitled to your opinion, you're allowed to do what you want, but I don't think many people around you would accept you if they knew you like The Oranges."

"You mean I wouldn't have many friends?"

"Probably not."

"Would you still like me?"

"Of course I would."

The Green Soldier was now passing her own childhood home. The island was small enough she never passed a place she didn't know. All of her best memories were contained on this one piece of land. But here was the home, someplace truly special to her.

Her house was small, not very different from those around it. It was made of bricks and it had a Green flag flying in its front yard. Next to the flag was something newer: a plastic sign with little wire legs in the ground. The Green Soldier paused in her duties to inspect it.

The sign only had words on it, which were written in white

block font on a black background. "RECLAIM!" it said, and then, beneath that, in slightly smaller text "'ORANGE GREED IS DETRIMENTAL TO GREEN HAPPINESS AND FINANCIAL PROSPERITY!!!!'—*The Green Island Gazette*". The Green Soldier wasn't sure if her parents had put up the sign themselves. They were ardent Green supporters. At the same time, it was not uncommon for soldiers to put these signs up on behalf of the army, to inspire people further. Nobody who received these signs would ever protest by taking them out of their lawn.

~ * ~

The Orange Soldier dropped off the metal he had collected from the roof. A few other soldiers who happened to be on the street had helped him out. Now, the group of soldiers checked out with a watchman on the construction site, and walked out together, laughing and talking. "What do you call a Green Soldier who runs everywhere?" one of the soldiers asked. Before he could get to the punchline, The Orange Soldier's phone rang.

"It's my boyfriend, I have to take this," he said, and rolled his eyes. He and his boyfriend had been fighting before they both left for work that morning.

"Hey, what's up?" The Orange Soldier answered his phone.

"Nothing, I'm just walking home, I knew your break was coming up, I wanted to talk to you."

"You're still mad?"

"No. The opposite, actually. I realized you were right."

"What? Really?"

"Yes. I was in the teacher's lounge earlier today, and they had the TV tuned to Gold News, and they were saying exactly what you were trying to tell me this morning. That apparently there are a lot of people on the Orange Island who speculate our army might be going too far with weapons, considering all the resources we have used to make Project Five-XA-Zero-One. And like I was telling you, that's just what I had been thinking, that with all we've taken out of the island, it must be for some really destructive weapons. Apparently, a lot of people don't think that much force is necessary when the Green haven't attacked us yet...but then they showed footage, and—" his voice broke. "They showed footage of The Green Island, where they're burning replicas of Sergeant Fred and

Orange Soldiers, they're burning these wooden dolls in Orange clothes in their town center. I just can't believe it, how people could have so much hate in them. Doing a thing like that! I mean, if they're doing that, think how violently their government must be planning to attack us? Just think about that!"

"I know," the Orange Soldier said.

"I'm sorry…I was wrong, I think the government is making the right decisions."

"I know," the Orange Soldier said.

~ * ~

Sergeant Ted straightened his green tie before standing up at the roundtable. "We have maintained this project as top secret," he said to his cabinet, "And I would like to thank all of you for that. I have deployed a few more of our Loyal Green Soldiers out to collect iron from some power plants with excess piping. They are expected to return later this afternoon, and it is my opinion we should deploy Ten-AX-Five as soon as possible. Our counterintelligence has shown The Orange are also planning an offensive move, and it is imperative we strike first. If we can achieve this, then I don't think The Orange will ever have the opportunity to strike back.

"Now, I know we have talked about this before, but it is time to finalize it: where will we put Ten-AX-Five? I know we have referenced before a civilian exposure. Our people will most certainly come out; out of patriotism and out of curiosity—truly nobody outside of this room knows what we're going to be wheeling out. I think this is a good idea. The people seeing the project, and the people seeing the people seeing the project. I mean the people at home watching TV news will all be proud of the sacrifices they have made. In seeing our might in what we have achieved, as Mr. Dill has noted before, it will further inspire people, and they will believe wholeheartedly an attack on The Orange, by The Green, is completely justified."

Across the table, Mr. Dill, who, like everyone in the room, wore a green uniform, nodded as he frowned with approval. "Even the few who had their concerns will see The Green army is truly fighting for them, and has done good by them. Any sympathies they may have had for The Orange will turn irrelevant in this light."

"Exactly!" Sergeant Ted said. "Now we'll get the news out to the people. Just work with some of The Soldiers, make sure the path is cleared. We have determined the optimal tactical location is directly on the waterfront, off Leaf Street?"

"Yes, sir," the coordination planner and aerodynamics physicist, Mrs. Pickle said.

"Alright then. As soon as the soldiers bring the final iron, we'll begin to roll out. Mrs. Pickle, talk to the on-staff soldiers about clearing the path to the waterfront. Mr. Brush, please alert the press."

~ * ~

Sergeant Fred led a group of ten soldiers as they wheeled Project 5XA01 out from the construction site. Before they saw the people, they heard the people: cheering and clapping and shouting and whistling and whooping bled into every avenue and alley. When they did round the corner, and the sea of people on the sidewalks saw 5XA01 at last, the noise was deafening. People jumped at the barriers, their mouths wide open as they screamed. "Orange!"

"Get those Greens!"

"Kill The Green!"

It was an undeniably impressive machine: a cannon, taller than a house, with a muzzle big enough to fit a whale-sized ball of steel. Each spoke of its wheels was as thick as a human, and taller. The whole thing was painted, of course, Orange.

Every street on its path was walled in by audiences. Sergeant Fred smiled at everybody, waved his hand like royalty. He couldn't stop grinning. He felt a happiness, a giddiness beyond his control. The last time he could remember feeling that way was when he was a teenager, playing soccer and about to win the biggest game of the season. Everyone in the stands had been chanting his name, and he knew he had to run, whether he wanted to or not, whether he thought he could do it or not. And when he scored the winning goal and won the game, his teammates had carried him on their backs, and he hadn't been able to stop laughing.

"Yes!" he shouted now, and the crowd quieted to hear what he had to say. "Those Greens are gonna pay!" The cheering intensified, and then the cannon was at the waterfront. Sergeant Fred stood in front of the cannon, where nobody was permitted access except military personnel. He faced The Green across the water, so his crowds couldn't see him. It was just like the soccer game. Sergeant

Fred could not stop laughing.

~ * ~

The Green cannon stood on the waterfront, facing The Orange Island. Sergeant Ted disappeared from the scene and picked up his phone. He pounded his wife's number onto the screen. "Hello? Hello?" he breathed heavily.

"Ted?" his wife asked.

"Yes! Yes, honey, where are you?"

"Fern Street, Ted. I saw you go by. I'm so proud! Nobody believed me, I kept saying 'That's my husband! That's my husband!' —but what's up? Why are you calling me? Why aren't you letting off the cannon?"

"Go home."

"What?"

"Get off the street so we can talk better. Nothing is going to go wrong, but I need you to go home."

"Is something going to happen?" she whispered.

"No, no, nothing's going to *happen*." To his own surprise, his hands were shaking. "I'm just worried. What if The Orange counterattack quickly? What if something goes wrong here? I don't know. But go home. Really."

"What's going to happen, Ted?"

"*Please*. Nothing. Just go, please."

"I am, I am, I'm on my way downtown now."

"Okay. Text me when you get home, okay."

"What am I, Ted—fine. I'll text you when I get home. *You're* safe?"

"Yes. Yes, I'm okay. God, I…I'm okay. I don't even want to hurt them, that's all. I just don't even want to do this anymore. I can't really hate them. But it'll be over, right? I'll come home tonight to you, and it's going to be alright. It'll all be over, won't it?"

"Yes, Ted, it will."

"Goodbye. I love you."

"I love you, too."

He hung up, his hands still shaking. He pressed them together to keep them steady, and then turned back to the cannon. He walked around to the front of the crowd, where he would be when they fired. The people were silent in anticipation, breathing behind him in one, solid mass. "You ready boys?" he asked.

~ * ~

Sergeant Fred's mouth suddenly twisted, and his laughing turned to sobbing. One of the soldiers on guard at the cannon saw this, and walked over to him calmly.

"Sergeant, what's wrong?" The soldier really didn't know what was happening, and he was speaking more out of concern for himself and the cannon than out of empathy for Fred.

"I just remembered," Fred said, as his body wracked with sobs again. "I just remembered a boy, I used to play soccer with him, we were on the same team, he was from the Green Island, and he was so good, such a good person. We're going to kill him now, Soldier, we're going to kill him now." He buried his face in his hands. "I loved him, I loved him! We can't do it." He felt himself starting to hyperventilate. "We can't do it. We can't do it! *I* can't do it," he gasped. "I can't really hate them."

"Okay, okay," the soldier said, patting Fred's back awkwardly. "Sergeant, you just need to give the order and it's all over. Let's go and get it done with, hey?"

"I can't do it. I can't do it."

The soldier turned and gave the signal to all the men by the cannon. The crowd began to cheer again.

~ * ~

The two round islands bound in the lake, each about equal in size, were bouncing with excitement and turning their heads in shame. Their cannons, made from their towns, were pointed at one another, loaded and ready to fire. There were fantastic twin bangs that sent the water and the crowds rippling. And then everything was quiet. The West Island was sprinkled with orange crumbs, and the East Island with green.

~ * ~

The Orange Soldier was in the crowd, close to the shore. He caught one of the falling flowers in the palm of his hand. "What?" he gasped. Green flowers were raining down as far as he could see. He turned around, he looked everywhere, up, down, left and right. Apparently, nobody knew what was going on.

"Flowers!" Sergeant Fred said, and the soldier with him looked to where he pointed across the water. Orange flowers were falling gently all over the Green Island. "Flowers, my God!" He laughed before he passed out.

~ * ~

Mrs. Pickle was the first person on the Green Island to speak. "The orange flowers, they came from our cannon," she said. "I'm not sure how that could've happened. Maybe the winds from both cannons pushed the flowers backwards as soon as they came out. I do not know!" she laughed. Sergeant Ted picked up his phone and dialed his wife again, while Mrs. Pickle exclaimed: "From the cannons! Flowers!" The lady laughed again and shook her head in disbelief.

~ * ~ * ~

Laramie Wyoming is a writer from New York City. She is currently attending Oberlin College, where she studies archaeology. She enjoys fall weather, poetry, and taking her cat, George, on walks (though George is less a fan of this pastime). This is her first published story.

For Remembrance

Liam Hogan

"'Ere, what's all this, then?" The woman scowled as Private Anders pushed past her and into the rooms beyond. "You got a bleedin' warrant?"

"We don't need a warrant, Mrs. Hartley," Captain Lowcroft said, following once Anders had signaled the all clear (though I'd already told him I couldn't hear any threat). "Not under the Psi Protection Act. Not if there's a suspected psychic on the premises."

"A psycho? Hah! Don't make me laugh." Mrs. Hartley, a stained and faded apron over her matronly girth, crowded the corridor as I traipsed after the Captain. She reeked of onions, sweat, and bleach. A pair of pale eyes peered from a child's cot in the corner of the room, not *rooms*. "An' why's it always the wimmin you brutes pick on?"

Private Goldmark slammed the door behind him and stood guard at the end of the drably painted corridor. He had more space down there than we had. It was the usual six-man squad; Corporal Tanners, our medic and only woman, and Private Dawson, our monosyllabic driver, had stayed with our transport. Even minus Goldmark, the combined sleeping and living area was strictly standing room only.

The Captain glanced at the signs of some cottage industry, mending clothes or the like. A little extra income on top of what Mrs. Hartley's cleaning job brought in. Strictly illegal, but hardly worth the mention. "*Please,*" he drawled. "Everyone knows the Psi mutation only appears on the X chromosome."

Mrs. Hartley looked at him blankly. "Chromo-what? And what about *him*?" A blunt thumb stuck out in my direction.

"Your genes, Mrs. Hartley. Your DNA," I explained. "And you make a valid point. While women are statistically twice as likely to display psychic abilities as men, a man still carries one X chromosome." I sensed the Captain's growing impatience and shook my head. "But this is hardly the time for a lecture on genetics. In any case, it's not your gender that brought us here."

"Don't *he* talk proper!" Mrs. Hartley exclaimed.

Of more interest was the fact she'd pegged me as the squad's tame psychic. 'Takes one to catch one,' they always said, correctly in this case. But I was wearing the same uniforms as the rest of the men, even if I was over a decade older. A lucky guess, or…?

Only one way to find out.

The Captain was a fraction ahead of me. Jumping the gun, yet again. "The Doc will examine you, Mrs. Hartley. Do try and cooperate. Everyone else, helmets on!"

"Ooh, a Doctor, is he? And what are the 'elmets for?" Mrs. Hartley scoffed. "'Fraid I might get inside your tiny male minds?" I wished she'd shut up, or at least calm down. By the way the Captain pursed his lips she was pushing him too hard. And that might backfire, badly, with a squad not accustomed to civilian duties.

The helmets contained an embedded skull cap. A fine mesh of exotic metals that tripled their manufacturing cost. Standard issue for soldiers. Always worth spending a little more to avoid being shot at close quarters by one of your own.

And I *was* a Doctor. Not of medicine, nor of anything relevant to these times. I'd got my PhD the year the War broke out, the year everything changed.

I didn't know I was a psychic when I was drafted. I found out in training. Tested, the way I test now. I'd always been told the voices I heard were inside my own head, taught to suppress them, to ignore them.

I wish I still had that ability.

"No, Mrs. Hartley," I said, taking my helmet off. "They're worried *I* will. This may get uncomfortable."

The thing with reading minds is it's never just one way. A psychic broadcasts as well as listens; they can't help it. And they sound very different from the mundane, the normal people. Like the difference between eavesdropping through a wall and being in the same room, being part of the same conversation. The test was designed to get Mrs. Hartley to talk whether she wanted to or not.

Assuming she was telepathically able, which I strongly doubted.

"'Ere!" she remarked, eyes going wide. "I can smell rosemary!"

"For remembrance, Mrs. Hartley," I said through gritted teeth as I concentrated.

"For rem'brance of strong wimmin, more like."

That old wives tale. And yet…. They'd once used the existence of rosemary in a spinster's garden as proof positive she was a witch. And psychics in the bad old days were frequently accused of witchcraft. Assuming they *were* psychics and not just old maids, lonely widows, and those with absent or weak husbands. Scapegoats for when harvests failed, disease struck, or war came calling.

Of course, Mrs. Hartley didn't have a garden. No-one did around here.

Anders and the Captain were looking bored. They shouldn't be. This was the most dangerous part. If a psychic realized they were about to be forced into the open, they might lash out. But then, the Captain and his men were new to all of this. Recently transferred from border control, the dust still ingrained in their uniforms.

I let the rosemary fade. There had been no echo. I almost wished there was, as then I wouldn't need to proceed to the arduous next step. I took a deep breath and let the pain come flooding out.

Mrs. Hartley rocked on her stout heels, recoiling as though slapped. Her face contorted into an ugly mask, her eyes screwed up, jaw clenched.

Nothing…. Still nothing.

I called the memory of the War back into me. The War, and the aftermath. Tucked it away once again, to fester and remind me to follow orders.

Mrs. Hartley looked at me in disgust. "You…*filthy* bugger! What's next, you monster? Going to rape my poppet?"

I'd almost forgotten the young girl in the cot. I wasn't the only one. Helmeted heads swung towards the corner where she silently sat. A slip of a girl, in a slip. Thin, flat-chested. Too big for the cot, but not by much. Couldn't have been much older than nine, maybe ten, maybe an undernourished eleven.

"How about the girl?" the Captain asked.

I shook my head. "Psychic abilities don't tend to manifest until puberty."

"You hear that, pretty one?" Private Anders leered, and the child cringed away from the unwelcome attention. "We'll be back to test *you* in a couple of years."

"Can it, Anders," the Captain ordered without much enthusiasm. "Leave the little girl alone."

There was an ugly bark of a laugh from Goldmark that had

me chalking Anders down as someone to avoid. Especially if I ever had a daughter. Which, given the current climate against my kind would be an incredibly stupid thing to do.

"Who's the father?" the Captain asked.

Mrs. Hartley spat. "He ain't around no more. He wasn't even around that much when he was busy giving me Lottie."

"But who was he?"

"A soldier," Mrs. Hartley said, staring me down. "Like you lot."

The Captain laughed, following her gaze. "Doc here is no soldier. Not a real one, leastways."

I absently rubbed the scar on my left hand. A nothing; a bottle-top sized piece of shrapnel that tore all the way through and left an ugly mark and two fingers palsied. The only visible sign of my three-year glorious War service.

The *real* damage was inside and would never, could never, heal.

I guessed the Captain wouldn't score too highly on an IQ test, let alone a Psi one. But then, none of the squad were old enough to have seen action. What age was the Captain when the War ended? The War we won, whatever that meant.

When the scientists introduced the skull caps—the first ones rather bulkier than today's versions—it changed the War. After that the only people the Psi-corps could target were other psychics.

And non-combatants, like Mrs. Hartley and her kid.

The things they made me do...

The things the army did, to protect themselves, when every civilian, on either side, could potentially be turned into a deadly weapon.

After the War, it was the psychics who took the blame. We were traitors, spies, and agents of propaganda. Any and all atrocities could be defended by saying the troops were under the mind control of enemy, or rogue, psychics.

The witch hunt was brutal. If I hadn't been compliant. If I hadn't been useful. If I hadn't been *male*.

I kept wondering if the Government might belatedly realize the disadvantages of disappearing their psychics. If they might allow selective breeding within the camps, arrange early testing and train-ing, all within a tightly controlled environment, of course. Armed and helmeted soldiers at the ready for any signs of disobedience. I wasn't sure which would be worse. Neither slow extermination nor forced propagation and slavery treated us as humans. But to them we weren't. *Human.* We were mutants, psychos, puppeteers. Something to be hated, to be feared. The other. The unknown.

I could still hear Mrs. Hartley as we traipsed back down the external stairwell.

"Hush now, there-there," she said, voice trembling but with a softer edge than it had had before. "The nasty men are gone."

"Not yet, mummy. *That* one…he's still listening."

The hissed reply was in Mrs. Hartley's internal voice. An unconscious echo of her daughter's wordless warning.

I didn't hear the girl at all.

A useful skill that, especially in one so young. Hiding in the shadow of her formidable mother. I'd not seen such accomplished psi stealth since—

The Captain tapped me impatiently on the arm. "So, no follow up?"

I shrugged. "No, Captain. Mrs. Hartley is no more psychic than you are."

He grunted. A childhood wish, thwarted? Lucky bastard whether he knew it or not.

"And the tip-off?"

"You know how it goes. Someone thinks they're being read, when in reality a nosy neighbor simply put two and two together. Or a drinking buddy spilt a secret they were sworn to keep. Let me guess; it wasn't exactly the most specific of reports, was it?"

He laughed at that, though I hadn't intended it as a joke.

"Good. Let's get the hell out. The locals are getting restless."

I blinked. I hadn't realized we had an audience, still too focused on the cramped room three floors up. Now that I broadened my mind's gaze, I picked up the dull throb of resentment, spiced by sharp spikes of anger.

Not many. A couple of young men lurking in pock-marked concrete doorways. A cadaver of a lady draped over her windowsill above us, watching with beady eyes, an ember of a cigarette in the corner of her downturned mouth.

Overall, though, there were fewer windows lit than when we'd rocked up, fifteen minutes earlier.

There wouldn't be any trouble. Not tonight. We were leaving empty handed and before word could spread. The adults were still cowed, still remembered the price of peace, even if the young only knew that times were better, once.

It was an ugly atmosphere. And these were not the enemy, the occupied; these were our own people.

It wasn't that they supported mutants. But the residents of this densely packed part of town weren't exactly fans of the army that patrolled their streets. That enforced the will of the stentorian government, who kept the food and fuel and jobs rationed, who kept the bomb-damaged slums bottled up.

A government that wore their own version of the Psi-blocking skull caps, sans helmet. Elegant lace filigrees proudly on display to show how *they* at least weren't being manipulated, weren't being controlled.

A jingoistic government that had begun to turn covetous eyes on our vanquished foes. Hadn't they gotten off too lightly for their transgressions? Were the people of this righteous nation not still suffering, five years on? Wasn't our victory more like a prolonged, suffocating stalemate?

Those oppressed on the other side of the barbwire and mine-fields had it far worse. So I heard. So I believed.

There would be war, again. Unless the hawkish leaders were tumbled from power. Unless the people on both sides of the border rose up and said: "No more."

"Helmet, Doc," Captain Lowcroft reminded. As if he and the rest of the squad wouldn't want to be in the confined space of the truck with an unshielded psychic, even one supposedly on their side.

I wondered what they would do if I tried to get on without it. Or if I began to fiddle with the stiff straps mid journey. Would they scramble to put their own helmets on? Or would they take more lethal action, using their side arms in the confined space?

It wasn't an experiment I was in any hurry to try. Though I thought of it too often for my own good.

Before I donned my helmet and clambered aboard the troop transport, I beamed out a swift: "Stay hid."

From a child's cot three floors up, from a dozen darkened rooms and from alleyways all around, silent nods echoed back.

~ * ~ * ~

Liam Hogan is an award-winning short story writer, with stories in *Best of British Science Fiction*, and *Best of British Fantasy* (NewCon Press). He's been published by *Analog, Daily Science Fiction*, and Flame Tree Press, among others.

He helps host Liars' League London, volunteers at the creative writing charity Ministry of Stories, and lives and avoids work in London.

More at http://happyendingnotguaranteed.blogspot.co.uk.

KILLING STEPHEN MILLER

Brad Shurmantine

Rebecca listened to the loud and funny conversation ricochet all over the place. It was Friday happy hour, but instead of being in a bar they had gathered in Dawn's apartment and were sitting in her tiny living room knocking down a pitcher of margaritas and passing around a joint. Joanna Newsome was playing in the background.

Six of them were getting loopy and waiting for the pizzas to be delivered. Queen Dawn sat in the big easy chair that dominated the room. She told a funny story about that chair. She bought it for fifteen dollars at Goodwill, and called an Uber to get it home. The driver was an old guy who had a crucifix hanging from the rear-view mirror. He didn't want to mess with the chair, almost drove off, but she coaxed and flirted with him, made him think he might get some action when they got it back to her place. They carried the chair upstairs and she gave him a beer and thanked him. He got no action. That was never in the cards. It was a funny story, the way Dawn told it.

Dawn was in the chair, Robbie and Ben were on the couch, she and Dominic and Nathan were sitting on the floor. This was Rebecca's new crowd. She had met Dawn at the Napa Women's March. Rebecca was new in town and trying to get connected. Dawn was wearing a pussy hat and carrying a funny sign: "Does this ass make my country look small?" under an unflattering picture of Trump. She complimented Dawn on her sign, and Dawn complimented her on hers. Rebecca was proud of her sign. It was a "Bible" quote: "Let He who Hasn't Raw Dogged a Porn Star after the Birth of His 5th Child with His 3rd Wife Cast the First Stone." And she attributed it to "donald JOHN trump 1:21," because that was the date of the rally. They hung out together for the rest of the day.

She had come to Napa to work in its Planned Parenthood office. Just when Oakland had become too intense for her, this job opened up. It didn't pay much and it certainly wasn't a promotion; Napa was a little outpost, a place you went to escape pressure and responsibility, not impress the bosses and move up the ranks. But she was tired of all the outrage in Oakland, everywhere you turned.

She thought Napa would be a quieter, calmer office, where she could counsel women without the angry circus of distractions. So, she was surprised to find protesters camped outside that office too. They didn't do abortions there; it was basically a health clinic. But a few elderly men and women from a local church brought their signs and their folding chairs every day and sat on the sidewalk and tried to discourage poor Latina women from getting pap smears.

"Hasn't someone told them we don't do abortions here?" Rebecca asked a co-worker.

"Oh god yes, we've told them dozens of times."

They were not violent and ugly people, like some in Oakland. Rebecca used the back entrance anyway, and tried not to notice them.

It was crazy expensive in Napa, but she kept asking around and finally found Nathan, who had a two-bedroom apartment and needed a roommate. Through Nathan she met Robbie, and through Dawn she met Dominic and Ben, and eventually they all got together. Of course Nathan and Robbie knew Dominic and Ben because they went to high school together. So here they were, one more Friday night, getting drunk and high and entertaining each other.

The guys were funny, smart Bernie bros who had strong opinions. They spent a little too much time laughing about high school days, but they were liberals and egged each other on when they talked about Trump.

They were telling funny stories about a teacher at Napa High who was Hispanic, and that got them talking about all their friends in Napa who were Latino, many of them Dreamers. And that got Rebecca talking about the horrible things that were going on at the border, the forced separations, the kids who were dying in custody, the hundreds of children the government had lost track of, who just got swallowed up in the system. And that got them talking about Stephen Miller.

It was Robbie who took the conversation to a dark place. Robbie. A 4th grade teacher.

"I've been thinking. I got a buddy, Dane, in Minnesota, who creates board games. Well, there ought to be a board game, a fucking Milton Bradley board game, called *Killing Stephen Miller*. You start with all the pieces in the center and you follow winding paths out to the four corners, where you kill Stephen Miller. It's a race to see who gets to kill him first. Only two to four people can play. You roll dice and move your piece along the paths. The paths are all twisty and have spaces on them where you get to draw a card. The spaces contain Trump tweets. *I am disinviting Stephen Curry to the White House. Pick a card.* And then the cards are all stuff that actually happened. *Brett Kavanaugh is confirmed! Move back two spaces.* Or, *A Federal judge rules the Muslim ban is unconstitutional. Move ahead three spaces.* It's a killer game!"

"But you kill Stephen Miller at the end?" Dominic asked. "What the fuck, man?"

"Yeah, it's like *Candyland.* At the end of each path it's all lolli-pops and unicorns because Stephen Miller dies. There's even a death scenario."

"Somehow I don't think Milton Bradley will carry this game," Dawn observed drily.

"No, it will be my bud in Minnesota who gets it going. But we can help him. We should think of ways to kill Stephen Miller that are funny and inventive, or at least ironic and inventive."

Dawn and Rebecca looked at each other, their smiles draining from their faces. Rebecca felt a little guilty, listening to this. She didn't like cruelty, even though these guys were just messing around.

"I can get us going because I've been thinking about this game," Robby said. "Stephen is taken by helicopter and dropped naked into the desert one hundred miles north of Chihuahua. He's given a jackknife, a foil blanket, a compass, and a small canteen of water. And an Urban Remedy salad. That's it. He has to carry it all in a *Thanks, Obama!* tote bag. He will die of dehydration and fear."

Rebecca's mouth dropped open. Was she hearing this correctly?

"But he may not die, man," Dominic objected. "He's a very tough motherfucker."

"No, he's not," Robbie said. "He's a pussy at heart. They're all pussies at heart, they all have bone spurs, they're all fucking cowards."

"Well that's true," Ben agreed. "Okay. That's one corner. I have an idea." Ben was inspired. "He gets poisoned like Joffrey on *Game of Thrones.* It's a rare kind of poison, extracted from frogs in Costa Rica. Stephen Miller's nanny puts it on his food or something. He's poisoned by an illegal immigrant—that's ironic! He dies grovel-ing on the ground, gasping for air, foam coming out of his nose."

"That's a good one," Robbie approved. "That goes in one of the corners."

Rebecca had had enough. "Okay, that's it. You guys are insane. Can we stop this?"

"We still have two corners to go."

"No, we're done. I'm not going to listen to this anymore."

"Rebecca's right," Dawn said. "You guys are going too far."

Robbie was defensive. "We're just having some laughs. What are you getting all twisted about?"

"I'm not getting twisted," Rebecca said. "You're twisted. This is wrong. You don't talk about people this way, even a dick like Stephen Miller."

"Oh. Do you think we're hurting Stephen Miwwer's widdle feewings? Poor widdle Stephen. Fuck that. That guy's made of steel. He doesn't have feelings. He's the fucking Terminator. Just look at him."

"He has feelings. Everyone has feelings. This is too ugly. What you guys are doing is just ugly."

"Rebecca's right," Dominic said. "We're sorry, Rebecca. Let's move on." He paused for a moment, while the tension in the room faded. "But it's funny how satisfying that was. And how funny it was."

"It wasn't funny," Rebecca insisted.

"No, it was kind of funny. That guy has caused so much pain, and he has so much power. No one can touch him. It was funny to think of him getting justice, being made to feel a fraction of the pain he's caused."

"Well," Dawn agreed, "he's definitely one of those people who you think, it would be better if they had never been born."

Robbie, who had been quiet while the conversation took a saner turn, came roaring back to life. "He should have been aborted," he said.

This shocked the room into silence, and Robbie continued. "What if Stephen Miller's mother was one of those baby-killing fanatics the right claims we all are? What if she had said, *Oh, honey, I'm pregnant again. Let's get rid of little Stephen-to-be. Let's get a new car instead.* What if her husband had said, *What is wrong with you? Why do you keep getting pregnant?* And she said, *Honey, I just keep forgetting to take the pill. Why don't you wear a condom?* And he said, *I hate condoms, and you don't like them either.* And she said, *You're right. It's okay. I'll just get an abortion. La la la.*"

Rebecca had met women like that, in the Oakland clinic. Comfortable, well-coiffed women getting their fourth or fifth abortion. Abortion was their birth control. This made what Robby was saying even more horrible to her.

But Robbie wasn't finished. "Think of all the pain and hate this guy has caused, ever since he was a teenager and humiliated the janitors at Santa Monica High School. Man, even Jesus would say, *You know, I really don't like abortion, but this time, okay.*"

Rebecca stood up. "I'm going home."

"Oh honey, don't go," Dawn said. "Robby, you dick."

"No, it's okay. It's not Robby. It's okay, guys. I'm just drunk and stoned and tired. It's been a long week. I was about to leave anyway."

Dawn walked her to the door and Rebecca left. As she turned away, she heard Dawn close the door behind her and say, "You dicks."

~ * ~

Rebecca thought about that conversation all weekend long. Nathan worked at the winery and they chatted casually in the evening when he came home. From what she could tell, their crazy talk had slipped entirely from his mind. Rebecca didn't think they were bad guys. Who knew where that talk had come from?

It certainly wasn't typical of life in Napa. In Oakland she had felt suffocated in toxic rage, but Napa was different. Every store didn't have posters advertising safe spaces. People didn't wear t-shirts bearing outrageous slogans. The cars didn't have bumper stickers. You could walk downtown without seeing constant reminders people were hurting. It was just another little town where nothing happened, and the poor people lived in dilapidated apartments down by the river. Food and wine. Food and wine. In Napa it was easy to believe America was working just fine.

But Rebecca knew that was not true. She still could not believe a thing like "President Trump" was possible in America. It was like a poisoned bug had crawled into her brain and died there, contaminating the tissue around it, and the rot was slowly growing. In her brain. She had gone to the Hillary victory party her co-workers had organized; they knew it was going to be tight but not one of them seriously thought they would be doing anything but celebrating. Nicole actually broke down, crumbled into a ball, sobbing, cried, *It's like I'm being raped again!* They all wound up holding each other, hugging each other, telling each other, *We'll get through this.* Things got very ugly very fast at the clinic after the election—really, all around her. The Black Lives Matter rage was still bubbling. It was all too much. She had to get out.

Part of the problem, of course, was being on the front line of the abortion war, and she considered leaving Planned Parenthood and just starting over at something else. She rejected those thoughts; she wasn't going to let them chase her away from work she found so important and rewarding. She came out of UC Davis with a degree in Sociology; originally, she had majored in English but turned "practical" in her junior year. Hah! That was dumb. Sociologists weren't being hired either. She should have stuck with Chaucer and Saul Bellow. But she wound up finding a job as a Reproductive Health Specialist with Planned Parenthood in Oakland and began what was starting to look like a career. She wasn't going to quit.

Her co-workers in Napa were not brittle and scarred. If it wasn't for that little group of protesters camped outside this job would be exactly what she needed to get her head right. But they were there, nearly every day.

One afternoon she finished her lunch and decided to go outside. Two protesters, a man and a woman, both in their seventies or so, sat in lawn chairs eating sandwiches, their signs leaning against the hedge: *Abortion is murder. God Save the Children.*

"Hello," Rebecca said.

The man went on eating and did not reply. The woman looked up, considered her, and said hello.

"My name is Rebecca."

"Frances."

"I work here. I've been here for a couple months. I've been meaning to come out and ask you why you're here. We don't do abortions here."

"We've been told."

"So why are you here?"

"You give out abortion drugs, don't you? You give women those drugs so they can have abortions."

"Yes, we do. If they ask for them."

"That's why we're here."

"But we're basically just a health clinic for women who don't have insurance. We're just trying to help women stay healthy. We do breast exams, pap smears. Women who have urinary tract infections. We just help women who have problems and can't afford a regular doctor."

"Yes, that's what you say."

"Don't you want women to have those services?"

"I told you. You give abortion drugs. You give women contraceptives. You're Planned Parenthood. You're the face of Satan, as far as I'm concerned. You're murdering God's children. All that other stuff doesn't matter. Women can get that elsewhere."

Rebecca made a conscious effort to control her breathing. "Okay. Well, have a good day." She went back inside.

That didn't go so badly, she thought. Maybe the woman just didn't understand the full picture. The next day she came out again. There were three of them this time.

"Hello Frances."

"Hello."

"Just so you know, I'm a counselor, not a doctor. I screen the women who come here. Especially the teenagers. I try to make sure they know what they're doing. I give them information and help them make good decisions. You know, I talk all the time about abstinence. You're right, some of these girls shouldn't be having sex, and I talk to them about abstinence. I always tell them abstinence is the best way to stay healthy and not get pregnant. We don't just hand them birth control devices when they walk in the door."

"Hmm," Frances smirked. "This is just a candy store. No one goes into a candy store to be told they don't need candy. You go into a candy store, you get candy."

"Well, candy doesn't keep you healthy. We don't provide candy. We provide healthcare. We practically give it away. We're trying to keep poor women healthy."

The smirk disappeared and Frances stared hard at Rebecca. "These young girls who come here: they're looking for candy. You talk about healthcare, but you lead them into temptation. It's a sin to have sex and not be married. And it's an abomination to have an abortion. You lead these girls into sin. The most horrible sin there is. Murder. God is judging you."

Rebecca took a breath and disengaged. "Okay. I just wanted to make sure you know we talk about abstinence here. Have a nice day." And she went back inside.

It's not about information, she thought. Frances did not scream at her; she listened to what Rebecca said. That was an opening.

The next day she brought out a folding chair and her lunch.

"What are you doing?" Frances asked. It was just Frances and the man this time.

"I just thought I'd come out and have lunch with you guys. Is that okay? It's beautiful out here today."

Frances didn't say anything. She and the man looked at each other and kept eating.

They ate together in silence for a while. Then Rebecca said, "Frances, do you have health insurance?"

"That's none of your business."

"It's not, I'm sorry. I don't mean to pry. I was just thinking that you probably do have health insurance, Medicare, and it's sometimes hard for people who have health insurance to understand what people who don't have health insurance are going through."

"This is not about health insurance," Frances quietly insisted. "This is about abortion and premarital sex. You clothe what you are doing in all this talk about health care. You're killing babies. That's what you're doing. You're promoting free sex. God is judging you. We are here to serve God."

Rebecca looked down and continued eating in silence. Then she said to the man, "Oh, hey, I'm sorry. We haven't met. I'm Rebecca. I work here."

"Yes, I know you do. I'm Bill."

"Hi Bill. I guess you and Frances go to the same church?"

"We're married."

"Oh, that's nice." Rebecca mulled this over before continuing. "Do you guys have any children? If I may ask?"

Bill looked at her intently before answering. "Yes. We have six children."

"Six children? Wow, that's great." Rebecca smiled broadly. "That's a big family. There's only me and my little sister in our family."

"Yes, we had a very noisy house when they were little. Now most of them are married. We have nine grandchildren."

"Nine grandchildren? Wow, that's exceptional. My mom really wants me to have a baby. She really wants grandchildren, I can tell. She's not pressuring me or anything, I don't mean to say that. But whenever she's around a baby she just kind of goes to pieces, it's kind of amazing. She just loves babies. She's going to make the best grandma. You must be very happy."

Bill nodded and Frances smiled, pleased at this recognition. "We are very happy," she said. "We are very blessed by God. There's no joy like the joy children bring."

"Yes, I believe that," Rebecca said, nodding sincerely. Then she was silent, thinking. "Are any of your grandchildren girls?"

"Oh yes, two of them. The oldest and the youngest. With seven rowdy boys sandwiched between." Frances smiled, thinking of her little scamps, her grandsons. "The boys are always up to something, always getting into mischief, always pulling their toys out, all over the floor. Running around like little Indians. Annie, the oldest, is like a little mother. She's so mature. She's always carrying one of her little brothers around, or one of her little cousins. Always reading to them. So patient with them. And Mara, the youngest. She's the smartest little firecracker you'll ever meet. She knows all the dinosaurs. All of them! You show her a picture of one and she'll say, *That's a brontosaurus, grandma*. Or that's a traekiosaurus, or, I don't know, whatever they're called. I don't know their names. She knows all their names. *Traekiosauruses lived in Canada,* she'll say. *They were plant-eaters.* She's just so smart."

"Wow, that's great. Maybe she'll be a scientist someday." Rebecca was silent, thinking. There was someplace she wanted to go with this conversation, but she didn't know how to get there. "You must really love those girls."

"We do."

"So." She fumbled. "You want them to be happy and healthy when they grow up, don't you?"

The smile left Frances's face. "Of course we do."

"So, what if they get into trouble someday? You'll want them to be able to get help somewhere, won't you?"

"If they get into trouble we will help them. God will help them. Their parents will help them. They will not have to turn to strangers for help."

"But what if they're far away? What if they're all alone? You'll want someone to help them, won't you?"

"I know what you're suggesting." Anger washed across Frances's face, and the walls came back up. "You're suggesting that you're helping these girls, who come to this clinic. And you're suggesting we don't want to help them. That we're trying to hurt them."

"No, I didn't mean to suggest that at all."

"You did. You're suggesting we have no compassion for them, that we're their enemies. You listen to me, young lady. We love these girls, and these women, who come to this clinic. We pray for them. We pray for God's mercy on them. We pray God will open their hearts. You don't know what we do here. You come out and eat a sandwich with us, but you don't know what we do. You never see us, you're never with us. We stand here and we pray for these girls. We pray God will rescue them from their darkness. We pray God will open their minds and their hearts, that they will see the beautiful life inside them, that they will treasure that life. Life is precious, those little lives are precious. We pray these girls will understand, that the light will come into them and they will see."

Rebecca was stunned, listening to this. She felt foolish, thinking she could reach this woman. "Okay. I'm sorry. I didn't mean to offend you." She looked into Frances's eyes, which seemed to soften now as she saw the apology in Rebecca's face.

"Do you also," Rebecca said, stumbling, "do you also pray for yourself? That God will open your eyes, and your hearts?"

Frances did not reply. For a few moments the two women looked into each other. Then Rebecca folded up her chair and went back inside.

~ * ~

When she was nineteen, Rebecca had an abortion. She and Charlie were very careful, but one time they weren't. Charlie was her first real boyfriend; she met him at a frat house party. One rich golden morning they woke up together, having slept well; they turned to each other and embraced and kissed. His mouth was so sweet. It was a Saturday morning, no classes that day, nothing planned, a beautiful warm spring morning, and she was in bed with her boyfriend, who all her friends liked. They kissed and aroused each other, and she put him inside her. She knew she should take out her diaphragm and put some fresh spermicide in it; she knew she should make him put on a condom; often they did both. But on this beautiful spring morning she was naked and lazy with her boyfriend who loved her, and she thought, *It'll be okay.* But it wasn't.

When she knew she was pregnant, she didn't tell Charlie and

she didn't tell her mother. She told her best friend, but Rebecca already knew what she was going to do. Angela talked it out with her and understood and hugged her. Then she told Charlie.

"I'm so sorry, babe. It was my fault."

"No, it wasn't your fault. It just happened. We were careful. Just not careful enough."

Charlie told her if she wanted to keep the baby he would help her, but they both knew her mind was made up. Both their lives were on a golden track; a baby would plunge them into complication, frustration and uncertainty. It wasn't the right time to have a baby. It wasn't that hard a decision. He went with her to the clinic and was sweet and supportive. But six months later they broke up; they both wanted to date other people.

Rebecca was certain that one day she would get married and have children, but she never stopped looking backward and thinking about her abortion. She didn't dwell on it and she felt no lingering guilt, but it was a sad, important decision she never forgot. She should have been more careful. It shouldn't have happened. But it did.

She made a decision about her body, her life, and the life inside her. It never occurred to her, nineteen, a California girl, digging college, looking ahead, that it was anyone else's decision to make, or the country might somehow go back in time and try to put women back into submissive little boxes. That was unthinkable.

Because of her abortion, she brought focus, seriousness, and compassion to her work. She listened to every woman, asked the right questions, answered theirs, clinically and thoroughly. Each woman brought a galaxy of concerns, understandings and confusions into the clinic with her, whether it was about virginity or safe sex or having an abortion, and Rebecca was with them and helped them pick their way through. She felt needed and valuable.

Then Trump was elected, and #MeToo, and embers of resentment and injustice she had always felt got fanned into hot life. She just wanted to live in a fair, just world, with a level playing field, and clean air. A world that wasn't burning up. Where everybody wasn't shooting everybody. Why was that so difficult? They made her so mad sometimes, those Republicans.

Bill and Frances were Republicans, no doubt. Her stepfather was one. There were a lot of them, and they all seemed to love the bully in the White House. Was there no talking to them? None at all?

Rebecca went to work each day, juggling all this, trying to stay positive. She would look out the front door to see if Bill and Frances were there, and often they were. Sometimes she'd wave. But she didn't go out to join them.

~ * ~

One day it occurred to Rebecca that she hadn't seen Bill in several weeks. Frances was out front with two other women. She went out to talk to them.

"Hello, Frances."

Frances considered her and nodded. "Hello, Rebecca."

"I haven't seen Bill out here in quite a while. Is he okay?"

"Bill is fine. He's in the hospital. He had a stroke."

"Oh my god. But he's okay?"

"He's okay. He's in Acute Rehab. I'm going there this afternoon."

"What happened?"

"He worked too hard out in the yard, in the heat. I kept telling him to come in and he kept saying one more bush. He was pruning our bushes. I was holding the stepladder for him and he just dropped the clippers and fell off. It was very frightening."

"I'm so sorry. Is he going to be okay?"

"He's going to be okay. He can talk. He seems to have his memory and most of his faculties. He's having trouble walking but they're helping him."

"That must be terrible for you. I'm so sorry."

"Well, he's getting a lot of attention. He has his kids and his grandchildren with him all the time. He's not doing too bad. But it's a trial."

"Tell him I said hello. Tell him I'm thinking of him."

"I will." Frances smiled warmly. "Thank you, Rebecca."

The other protesters, two women, stood quietly by and listened while she and Frances talked. They seemed to appreciate Rebecca's interest. They smiled and nodded to her when she went inside.

A few weeks later, Bill was back on the sidewalk, in a wheelchair. He had a new sign: *Welcome Children to Life*. Seeing it Rebecca felt anger: was she someone who rejected children? She felt fear: it was an effective sign. But she also found herself thinking, *How do we do that? How do we welcome children to life? All children?*

"Hello, Bill," she said, as she went up to him. "You're back. You're looking good."

He nodded, smiled. His smile wasn't quite right. Frances stood beside him, with her hand on his shoulder.

"How are you feeling?"

"Not my...not myself. But okay. Can't...can't walk too well."

"But you're here. Looks like they're taking care of you."

He nodded.

"I'm glad you're okay. I prayed for you; you know."

Bill nodded. "Thank you."

"We have an umbrella inside if it gets too hot for you out here."

"Thank you."

"You're welcome. I like your sign."

Bill lifted it and waved it, a little feebly.

"I really like it," Rebecca murmured. "It makes me think. You know those kids down at the border? The ones who are being taken away from their parents? We should welcome them too, don't you think?"

Bill quietly nodded. "What's happening to those families is horrible," Frances said. "We pray for those families every day."

"That's good. I'd like to talk to you about that. About what else we can do to help them."

"We should talk about that," Frances agreed. "Something needs to be done."

Rebecca returned her attention to Bill. "Your grandchildren are taking care of you?"

"Oh yes."

"I'd like to see pictures of your grandchildren, if you think of it. Do you have any with you?"

"No," Frances said. "But it's kind of you to ask. I'll try to remember to bring some."

Rebecca was silent, considering Frances and Bill. They weren't going anywhere. They were going to be here every day. They were going to keep coming.

"All right. Have a good day, you two. I'll see you tomorrow."

"Bring your lunch," Frances said.

"I'll do that," Rebecca said, and she turned and went back into the clinic.

~ * ~ * ~

Brad Shurmantine (bradshurmantine.com) lives in Napa, Ca., where he writes, reads, tends three gardens (sand, water, vegetable), keeps bees, takes care of chickens and cats, and works on that husband thing. His fiction and personal essays have appeared in *Monday Night, Flint Hills Review,* and *Deep Wild*; his poetry in *Third Wednesday* and *Blue Lake Review.*

He backpacks in the Sierras and travels when he can, and has a serious passion for George Eliot.

In Other Words

Lisa Timpf

Tall and thin, Mike Brownley grinned at his best friend Aubrey as he held the basketball. A quick fake to the left got Aubrey leaning, and Mike drove past for the layup.

"Okay, you win this one," Aubrey said grudgingly. "Ready for a break?"

Out of breath, Mike could only nod as he dropped into one of the white plastic chairs set up courtside just for this purpose.

"What would you give to be at those talks?" Mike asked after a few moments.

Their fathers, part of the Special Forces unit of the Confederation of Nations, were currently assigned to support the negotiations with the Galavians. The black-furred humanoid aliens had cruised into Earth's solar system a month ago, and discussions had continued since.

"Wish I could have seen the pictures from their side," Aubrey said with a grin. Familiar with the process both as a result of his own research and information gleaned from his dad, he knew the first step in building a language database was to show images from each side's planet and have individuals from each planet say out loud their word for that image. Aubrey was burning with curiosity about the images of their planet and culture the Galavians would have provided.

"After the pictures, what comes next?" Mike asked. "I mean, I know you try to start with identifying each side's words for the same object, but then what?"

"They're using a special translation computer," Aubrey explained. "After the computer identifies common words for the same objects, members of each side read literature, news stories, and so on so the computer can also develop a sense of how words are organized into sentences, how ideas are expressed. When they figure they have enough information, the computer starts translating live conversation. They use an android linked to the computer for the face-to-face discussions; that makes it seem more personal."

"How well do you think it will work?" Mike's forehead

furrowed.

"The computer has been shown to be reasonably accurate for Earth languages, but you're talking about human thought patterns," Aubrey said. "We hadn't developed this technology yet when the Ptomians came five years ago, and everyone saw what happened then."

Both boys were silent for a space, Aubrey thinking of his mother, a fighter pilot, who'd been a casualty in the last push by the aliens.

Concerned by the serious look on his friend's face, Mike rose to his feet.

"Rematch?" Mike waved the ball in Aubrey's direction.

Before Aubrey could respond, a commanding bark from Max, Aubrey's yellow Labrador Retriever, brought both boys to attention. The dog, who had been lying patiently beside the backyard basketball court, was suddenly interested in something at the front of the house, and even the boys could now hear the hum of a hover car coming in for a landing in the driveway.

"That'll be my dad," Mike commented as he reached for his zip-up hoodie.

The two friends headed for the gate leading from the back yard.

Sure enough, there was the Brownleys' silver hover car, sitting in front of Mike's house. Dark-haired Rupert Brownley stuck an arm out of the driver's side window to wave, while Aubrey's dad Cole popped out of the passenger side. Just returning from work, both men still wore their military uniforms.

"Talks go well today?" asked Aubrey.

"Slow, but with the translation computer we're making progress," Cole said, absently running his hand through his crew-cut silver hair. "We were finished calibrating the languages a couple of days ago, so it's coming along." Cole's face showed the strain of the day's efforts. "The next two weeks will be critical," he added. "We can't afford the mistakes that set off the conflict with the Ptomians. We just don't have the firepower left, nor can we afford the damage, frankly."

Mike's usually cheerful face was somber. He only needed to look at the skyline, recognize the gaps where the landmarks he'd known all his life were missing or damaged, to know the truth of those words.

"See you tomorrow," he said to Aubrey with a nod as he hopped into the recently vacated passenger side of the sleek hover car.

~ * ~

The next day was a Saturday, but both Cole and Rupert had to work. There was no time to waste with the negotiations, and the heat from the media and the public was mounting. The sooner the two sides could come to agreement, the better.

When Rupert arrived to collect Cole, Mike clambered out of the hover car, lugging his paintball gear in a gym bag.

"Have fun, boys," Cole called out as he boarded the vehicle. Clad in her uniform, Aubrey's older sister, Jackie, had already climbed into the rear passenger side seat and was fiddling with her shoulder-length brown hair as she waited for liftoff. Working as a first-level runner at the talks, she too had to work this Saturday.

"We'll be missing our third for paintball today," Mike said with a shrug, gesturing toward Jackie, who was a crack shot. "May as well head over anyway and see who we can scare up."

Aubrey watched the hover car lift, turn, and swing out of sight. The whole, long summer stretched ahead of them, and with all the tensions from the talks, it was clear there wouldn't be a lot of family time in the near future. Cadets meetings had been suspended, too, with the leaders caught up in the negotiations. There'd be a lot of time to fill, Aubrey thought as he shouldered his gear bag.

He looked longingly at his family's Goosewing II gold hover car as he walked beside Mike down the driveway. He'd just gotten his license a few weeks ago but with the fuel rationing still in place, taking transit made a lot more sense. Besides, their fathers were trying to set an example by carpooling to conserve fuel, so he and Mike ought to follow suit. Parking was always a hassle in the downtown section anyway.

Aubrey and Mike walked the short distance to the tube stop, paid their fare, and boarded. Not unusual for a Saturday morning, the tube was fairly full and they reluctantly squeezed in beside a young man who looked around their own age and close to Aubrey's height, a good six inches shorter than Mike. The stranger was wearing a toque pulled low over his face, sunglasses—unusual for the

somewhat overcast day—and a surgical mask, customary for someone in the crowded city who had a slight cough, as a courtesy to
avoid infecting others.

Aubrey studied the stranger out of the corner of his eye, not
wanting to stare. Odd. Now that he looked more closely, Aubrey
noted the stranger didn't just have his face shielded , he was completely covered head to toe—a scarf closed the gap between the
surgical mask and his hoodie, and ill-fitting jeans covered his legs
down to high-top runners. He also wore black leather gloves.

The stranger shifted position, and Aubrey let out a gasp.
When the boy beside him moved, a gap opened up between the
gloves and the hoodie, showing an arm covered with dense black
fuzz. Aubrey elbowed Mike and jerked his head toward the stranger.
Noting the same thing, Mike's left eyebrow shot up.

The stranger was one of the Galavians!

When Mike and Aubrey stood to get off the bus, the stranger
rose too. Aubrey's heart beat faster. If they played this right, they
might actually get to meet a Galavian, face to face!

Once they stepped onto the sidewalk, the stranger seemed
uncertain which direction to go. Aubrey waited till the area around
the tube stop had cleared, then stuck out his hand.

"I'm Aubrey," he said as the stranger slowly extended his own
hand for a tentative greeting. "And we know who you are."

~ * ~

Half an hour later, Aubrey and Mike had company as they
walked through the entrance of the paintball gym. The Galavian
they'd met on the tube turned out to be Vrynx Vcznk, the son of
the lead negotiator, Zmyd. Vrynx had decided to take an excursion
from the compound where the Galavians were staying, hoping to
learn more about Earth culture. He was cautious enough to wear a
disguise, recognizing not all Earth residents were receptive to dealing with the aliens.

After a brief explanation sketched out mainly through gestures and a few words, Vrynx indicated his desire to join Mike and
Aubrey in their paintball game, noting all Galavians were encouraged to become expert marksmen and markswomen from an early
age. This encouragement, Aubrey and Mike gathered, had ramped
up after the Galavians had suffered severe damage to their planet

and population at the hands of a Ptomian invasion force.

Aubrey quickly handled the rental of the required gear for Vrynx, his mind racing as he and Mike assisted the Galavian in discretely suiting up.

Just as Aubrey and Mike made the final adjustments to Vrynx's gear, muscular Marcus Howerby, captain of the opposing team, strutted over.

"New player this week, I see," he said, sizing up Vrynx with a penetrating stare. "No matter. You'll still lose." He waved a hand dismissively as he turned to go.

"As I recall," Mike said with a sarcastic grin, "we won last week."

"Whatever," Marcus grunted. "We're ready whenever you are."

~ * ~

Two hours later, the boys walked out of the paintball facility, with Vrynx's street disguise firmly in place.

Aubrey's head was spinning. Not only had they won, they had thrashed Marcus and his two friends soundly, thanks to Vrynx, who had proven to be agile, quick-thinking, and deadly accurate. If all the Galavians could shoot like him, getting a treaty in place was all the more important.

"Weather is nice," Aubrey gestured to the sky. "We can walk back to the compound." He pointed to his feet. Vrynx had picked up many words in the English language, but he was far from fluent, so gestures and short phrases supported the communication process.

"Yes," Vrynx said simply. "I like that."

As they walked, signs of the Ptomian conflict were every-where—stately trees shattered, houses with roofs blown off, abandoned storefronts.

Vrynx gestured to one of the shattered, boarded-up houses. "Our planet, damage like this also."

Aubrey and Mike nodded.

Near one of the parks that had somehow emerged from the war unharmed, a gray squirrel ran up a tree. Vrynx stopped and stared.

"Small," he muttered.

"Small?" Mike questioned. "Squirrel. Normal size for us."

"Our planet, much larger." With his hands, Vrynx sketched

out an animal the size of a horse. "Fly from tree to tree. Sometimes, we ride."

Just then, Aubrey's phone buzzed. He pulled out the device, read the screen, and turned pale.

"What is it?" Mike asked.

"Message from Jackie," Aubrey said tersely. "There's trouble with the talks."

Vrynx looked directly at his two new friends. "I worry," he said. "Something wrong with words."

"Words?" Aubrey asked.

"Words not correct, sometimes," Vrynx said carefully. "I listen radio, TV, I learn some English. Machine make wrong words. May be problem."

Mike and Aubrey exchanged glances.

"Change of plan," Mike said. "We need to get to the negotiation chamber."

"I come, too," Vrynx sounded determined, and neither Mike nor Aubrey argued.

~ * ~

The three boys hurried as quickly as they could to the compound where the talks were being held. Outside the main gate, their progress was slowed as they worked their way past a crowd of protesters, who were holdings signs with messages like, "No Talks Are Good Talks," and "Remember the Ptomians".

"It's the Earth First Alliance," Aubrey explained to Vrynx. "I'm sorry. Some people don't think we should negotiate with your people."

"Our planet, same issue," Vrynx said calmly.

"Don't they get it?" Mike snarled. "It was because we couldn't come to terms with the Ptomians that we ended up in a war."

Aubrey's shoulders tensed as a loud, angry buzz arose from the crowd. He crouched in a ready position, determined to defend his new friend if it came to that, then noticed no-one was looking in their direction. Instead, they were looking up at the sky.

The stark, crisp lines of the Galavian space vessel, which had been orbiting so high up it was barely visible, were now distinct in the sky. Also distinct were a significant number of the Conferation's Cobra fighter jets, looking like gnats beside the alien ship.

"We need to hurry," Aubrey muttered.

Pushing through the crowd, they worked their way to the building's ornate entrance, where the double doors bore the crest of the Confederation of Nations. For the sons of Cole Johnson and Rupert Brownley, both cadets in their own right, entry to the general area where the talks were being held was difficult but not impossible. Once inside the building, Vrynx took off his surgical mask and glasses to reveal his identity, and he was also allowed in.

"This way," Aubrey took the lead as the trio sped toward the viewing area.

When they arrived, it didn't take long to size up the situation. As each negotiating team made their comments in turn, the four-foot-high translation android in the middle of the table uttered a string of sounds in the other group's language.

As the talks continued, the body language of each side made it clear that anger and frustration were rising.

It took only ten minutes of this before it seemed some kind of physical conflict was brewing. Vrynx stood up suddenly.

"Different words," he said with absolute certainty. "Computer say different words."

"We need to tell someone," Aubrey said.

Before Aubrey finished talking, Vrynx was sprinting to the lower door, and from there, racing out into the chamber. Aubrey and Mike, stumbling in their haste, were right behind him.

~ * ~

Whenever he thought back on the events that followed, Aubrey marveled that he'd had the nerve to proceed despite the icy blue-eyed glare his father initially fixed on him. He also realized how incredibly lucky they were the guards stationed around the room were disciplined enough to refrain from shooting when the three boys burst into the room unannounced.

While Vrynx talked urgently to his father, Aubrey and Mike told Cole, Rupert, and the other members of the Earth negotiation team about Vrynx's suspicions.

Fortunately, unshakably calm Mbana, nicknamed Mab, had been selected as the chairperson for the proceedings. The tall, solidly-built Afro-Caribbean had seen a lot in his sixty years—including a five-year stint on the lunar colony—and was prepared to give the boys the benefit of the doubt. Ever observant, he too had noted the increasing tension in the room and this, at least, would provide an explanation for why things were going so wrong, despite good intentions.

"I suggest we look into this matter," he said. "Let's declare a recess and get started again tomorrow."

To avoid any risk of further misunderstanding, Vrynx translated this message for the Galavians. At the same time, the translation android interpreted what Mab had just said.

The Galavians turned as one to stare at the android.

"My idea right," Vrynx said after a brief pause. "Computer said, 'We have no common ground'—not what you said at all."

Amid the hubbub that burst out in the chamber in two languages after that comment, Rupert and Cole exchanged glances.

"We need to get to the bottom of this," Rupert snapped. "I'll get my team started."

~ * ~

Too anxious to go home, Aubrey and Mike hung out in the chambers while Rupert and Cole sped off into the labyrinth-like building. After some heated discussion with his father, Vrynx drifted over to join them.

"He ask our ship to move back into space," Vrynx told Aubrey.

"If we can't trust the computer, what now?" Mike asked worriedly.

"We need to work the old-fashioned way," Aubrey commented thoughtfully. "We've been relying on a machine to translate for us, but we may be better off making sure we truly understand each other."

"Easy for you to say, you're good at languages," Mike snorted.

"Aubrey right," Vrynx said. "Start at beginning. Truly understand. Better."

"How did you pick up English, anyway?" Mike asked.

"Listen radio waves. My hobby," Vrynx smiled.

"Oh, like a ham radio operator?" Mike said.

"You call me pig?"

"No, ham radio operator means someone who works with radios as a hobby," Mike replied.

Vrynx's shoulders rose and fell in a sigh. "Many confusions," he said, raising his hand to his head.

~ * ~

It took Rupert's security team three hours to track down the details, but it soon became clear the garbled translation was no accident.

"Looks like the work of the Earth First Alliance," Rupert explained to Cole and the other Earth leaders. "They hacked into the program and set it up to make the translation increasingly insulting and divisive."

"Their motivation is clear, then," Mab commented.

"More to it than that," Rupert said. "We've suspected for some time the Alliance is actually linked to the Ptomians. They most of all would want to ensure the various other civilizations don't join forces."

"Why would anyone from Earth support the Ptomians, after what they did to us?" Mike's voice shook with anger.

"Everyone has their motivations," Cole explained. "Their families may have been threatened. They may have been promised things. We don't really know at this point."

"What we do know is the talks have to start from the beginning —without machines this time, so we can be certain," Rupert said. "It'll need more manpower, and be slower, but it's the only way."

"Well, boys, looks like the cadet force will get put to work," Cole told Mike and Aubrey. "We'll need to cooperate with our guests at all levels, and that includes getting to know as much as we can about their culture."

Mike and Aubrey exchanged grins with Vrynx.

"You know what this means," Mike said, once the two were on their own.

"Not much spare time," Aubrey groaned, pretending to be upset.

"No, it means we have a new hobby, when we can find a few minutes," Mike said, pausing for effect. "Riding lessons."

"Whatever for?" Aubrey rolled his eyes.

"For when we get to see those giant flying squirrels in person."

~ * ~ * ~

Lisa Timpf is a retired HR and communications professional who lives in Simcoe, Ontario. Her speculative fiction has appeared in *New Myths, From a Cat's View, Third Flatiron, Future Days,* and other venues.

You can find out more about Lisa's writing projects at http://lisatimpf.blogspot.com/.

Ten Pfennings Worth of Chocolate

Charles Robertson

Gisela rushed out of school, but she didn't accompany her sister straight home as she usually did. Instead, she ran the ten-pfennig coin her father had given her for her birthday through her fingers and headed for Hauptstrasse to browse the shop windows. So many things to buy. The stores were packed with beautiful dresses, shoes, and dolls, but she only had ten pfennigs. Not enough to come close to buying any of those things.

She peeked in window after window, but nothing she could afford interested her, until her eyes landed on a platter of chocolate, each stamped with a pretty rainbow pattern on top. Her mouth watered as she imagined the chunks on her tongue. She looked at the coin again and wondered how much she could get for it. Gisela touched the doorknob and stopped. The window had a bright yellow star hanging on it.

She looked down the street. All the stores on this block had stars. She glanced back at the direction she had come from. She had accidentally turned down Waldstrasse—the street of the Jews. Father had told her to never visit there alone. If given the chance, they would hurt her.

She inched backward. What could buying a little candy hurt? After all, it was her birthday.

She walked in. The Jew was busy sweeping the floor, not counting his money. His nose looked like anyone else's. He smiled at her. His teeth were not pointed as in all the posters she had seen.

The man stopped sweeping. "Good afternoon, *madchen*. What brings you here on such a gloomy day?"

Gisela's stomach tightened, as it always did when she was around strangers. Finally, she handed him the coin. "How much chocolate can I buy with this?"

She regretted what she had just done. The Jew only wanted her money. Now that he had it, she would be lucky if he gave her even one mouthful.

The man carved several chunks from the block in the window and dropped them into a paper bag, along with a receipt. He handed the sack to her. "Enjoy."

She looked inside. It contained more chocolate than she could have imagined. She smiled at the man. "It's my birthday, you know."

The man widened his eyes in an exaggerated facial expression. "It is? How old are you?"

"Ten."

He picked two more chunks and dropped them into the sack. "Well then, happy birthday."

She peeked at the extra two pieces. "What are these for?"

"Because it is your birthday."

A boy wandered in from the back room and set a box onto the counter. He looked over at her and gave her a half smile. He appeared about her age, but she had never seen him in school. Did Jews not go to the same school?

Gisela clutched her treasure. Just before stepping outside, she remembered her manners and turned back to the man. "Thank you."

She skipped on the way home, making sure to get off Waldstrasse before anyone she knew spotted her there. She popped one piece of candy, then another into her mouth. Mother would be angry she had eaten so many sweets before supper, but after all, it was her birthday.

Her house came up on the right, one of a number of identical homes with tiny courtyards, all scrunched together until they looked like one long building. The aroma of boiled cabbage met her nose at the door. She wandered inside, clutching the sack.

Father sat on the sofa, reading a newspaper by the light of the fire. He glanced up when she entered. "Hello, *Liebchen*. Happy birthday."

She ran to him and climbed into his lap. The fire warmed her almost as much as the pleasant feeling of being near him. The familiar smell of cigarettes and oils from the factory surrounded him. Gisela snuck another piece of chocolate into her mouth. Her parents were bound to disapprove, but surely would allow her to get away with it on her birthday.

Father's smile evaporated. He snatched the sack and stared inside. He pulled out the receipt. "Where did you get this?"

Her heart pattered. She knew her parents would not approve of her eating sweets before supper, but didn't think it would make her father this angry. "I bought it with the coin you gave me."

"Where?"

"At a store."

"What store?"

A store her father had told her to avoid. Gisela wanted to lie to avoid his anger. If her lie didn't fool him, however, he would be even more upset. She looked at the floor. "A store on Waldstrasse."

Father flung the sack into the fireplace.

Her eyes blurred. The coin she had carried around so proudly had been spent, and she had nothing to show for it. The worst pain, however, came from knowing she had disappointed her father. Sobs formed in the pit of her stomach and forced themselves out her throat. Huge sobs, so huge they prevented her from telling Father how sorry she was for disappointing him. She buried her head in his chest and let his shirt soak up the tears.

Father gently held her chin between his thumb and forefinger and lifted her head. "I am sorry for reacting so strongly. You must understand these people cheat and deceive. I want to keep you safe."

She sniffed back a tear. "The man at the store seemed nice. He even gave me extra chocolate when I told him it was my birthday."

"They all seem nice to your face. Please, Gisela, promise me you will never go into the neighborhood with the yellow stars on your own again."

She wiped the tears. "I promise."

"That's my *Liebchen.*" He set her gently onto the floor and rose from his chair. "Now let's go to the kitchen. Your mother has baked you a special surprise."

~ * ~

After supper, Mother buttoned Gisela's blouse and tugged at her skirt. She stepped back and looked her up and down, then gently nudged her toward the mirror in the hallway. "My, how mature you look in your new uniform."

Gisela stared in the mirror at her pressed white blouse and dark skirt. She frowned at the tie. It made her look too much like a boy.

Anna grabbed her hand. "Come, Gisela. We don't want to be late to your first *Heimatabend.* We're going to have so much fun tonight.

Gisela followed her sister along the darkening streets. A cold, damp wind blew through her skirt and around her legs. The warmth of the party headquarters lay ahead. She couldn't get there fast enough.

She passed the turnoff to Waldstrasse and glanced at the shop she had been in just today. A yellow light glowed in the upper floor windows. What were the boy and the man doing now?

Anna tugged her along. "Don't waste your time looking there. We have more important things to do."

The gigantic hall with the magnificent swastika banners sat at the head of Hauptstrasse. She'd passed it so many times, but had never been inside. Gisela paused at the steps. There were people inside she had never met. The same rumbling in her stomach she felt every time she was around strangers returned.

Anna put her hand on Gisela's back and gave her a gentle push. "There's nothing to be afraid of. Everyone is friendly and we'll have cake and cookies after the meeting."

Gisela stopped before entering to stare at the huge banners hanging on each side. They seemed to reach to the sky. She felt so small next to them. Inside, chairs surrounded a long table. Above the fireplace a portrait of the Fuhrer hung, like the one in her classroom, but this time looking thoughtfully into space. The swastika on his brown uniform displayed prominently. She felt as if he were watching her now.

A dozen or so other girls in identical uniforms stood around the room, a couple from her class at school and the rest from the higher grades. One tall girl, who looked old enough to be in high school, stood at the head of the table.

Anna nudged Gisela toward the older girl. "I want you to meet *Fraulein* Dienst. She runs the meetings."

The Fraulein smiled at Gisela, who looked down at the floor.

Anna squeezed her hand. "She's a little shy."

Fraulein Dienst patted Gisela gently on the shoulder. "There is no reason to be shy. We're all friends here. Have a seat."

Anna chose a chair near the center. Gisela sat next to her sister. A pudgy girl a year or so older sat on her other side.

The girl turned to Gisela. "My name is Marta. What's your name?"

"Gisela."

"This should be fun, once we get through Fraulein Dienst's boring lecture."

Fraulein Dienst stood at the head of the table. She cleared her throat. The room went silent. "Let's begin with our salute to the Fuhrer."

Everyone stood and faced the portrait. They lifted their right hands the way Gisela had seen her parents do so many times before at parades. They looked silly when they did it, but all the grown-ups took it seriously. "Heil Hitler!"

Always uncomfortable in crowds, Gisela remained still and silent. Anna prodded her in the arm.

"Heil Hitler!" This time Gisela mumbled the words and raised her hand slightly.

Fraulein Dienst walked up beside her. "Here, let me show you. Raise your arm to a forty-five degree angle. Lock your elbow. Remember, you are a proud German."

"Heil Hitler!" Gisela joined the rest of the crowd, raising her arm just as Fraulein Dienst had shown her. She didn't understand why they did it, but everyone left her alone after she joined in.

Anna looked over to her and smiled. "Good job."

Fraulein Dienst signaled for them to sit. "Before we move on, let me share with you a few words about the dangers of dealing with Jews."

Marta leaned toward Gisela. "See, what did I tell you?"

Fraulein Dienst paused and stared at the girl. "Marta!"

Marta rose. Her face grew pale. "Yes, Fraulein Dienst."

"Is interrupting a superior a good example of German community spirit?"

The girl stuttered. "N—no, Fraulein Dienst."

"You may sit back down. And do not interrupt again."

Fraulein Dienst stepped away from the table. "Now as I was saying, you must be careful when around the Jew. Don't ever turn your back on him. You never know what he is planning."

The girls slouched and stared with uninterested looks. They reminded her of how she felt in math class, waiting for it to be over.

As she listened, Gisela recalled the experience in the store today. The Jew there had been kind to her. He had even given her extra candy. He sounded nothing like Fraulein Dienst's description. She needed to say something. But Fraulein Dienst obviously didn't tolerate interruptions.

Gisela raised her hand. She never got in trouble in school when she did. Maybe it would be the same here.

Fraulein Dienst stopped talking. "Yes, Gisela."

Gisela paused, summoning the courage to speak. "The Jew I met today was nice to me. He even gave me extra candy when I went into his store."

"I'm glad you brought that up. This is an example, girls, of how the Jew deceives you. He pretends to be nice, but all this time he's plotting against you. Whenever around the Jew, you must be on your guard at all times. Even better, avoid them altogether."

Fraulein Dienst's lecture droned on. Even after it ended, her words continued to swirl around in Gisela's mind. The image of that smiling Jew stuck in her head. His kindness had seemed so real. Had he really been planning to trick her? Was she really that easy to fool?

She was still thinking about that when the meeting ended. Anna grabbed Gisela's hand and led her into the damp darkness and toward home. "How did you like your first *Heimatabend*?"

"It was fine." Gisela really didn't know how she felt about it.

"I know you're shy, but Fraulein Dienst is very good. In no time she'll have you fitting in."

They passed the turnoff to Waldstrasse. Gisela couldn't resist the urge to peek again. The lights in the shop were all out now. Were they asleep? What was the boy's bedroom like? Did he have a normal bed?

Anna tugged her past the alley. "Have you learned nothing? Don't waste your time thinking about those people."

~ * ~

The clouds parted overnight, giving way to bright, yellow sunshine. The moment school let out; Gisela walked home with her sister. On the way, she couldn't help but take another look down the forbidden street.

This afternoon, the doors to all the shops were open. People carried clothes, furniture, tools and every other kind of object she could think of from the stores. They were entering empty-handed and coming out with the loot. Why would the Jews give all their things away so easily?

Anna walked on a few steps, stopped, and retraced her path. "What's the matter?"

Gisela pointed down the street. "What's going on there?"

Anna clutched her hand again and tugged her toward home. "Who cares?"

They reached the house. The fire burned brightly in the fireplace, but Father's chair was empty. He usually got home from his shift at the factory before she did. The girls dropped their homework onto the dining room table.

At the sound of the door opening, Gisela dashed to the living room, with Anna following close behind. Sure enough, it was Father walking into the house. He carried a sewing machine under one arm and the other arm held a chair. A cloth bag was draped over his shoulder. He set the chair down, put the sewing machine on top of it and shook his arms out.

Mother walked into the room and glanced at the chair. "What's all this?"

Father smiled. "You always said you wanted a sewing machine; well we have one now. And this chair will make a nice addition to the kitchen."

She narrowed her eyes. "Where did this come from?"

"Waldstrasse. I managed to get there before all the good stuff was gone."

Gisela leaned in. "They just gave it to you?"

"They were Jews. They don't give anything away for free. But there's nobody there now. They don't need it anymore."

The man and the boy she had met yesterday didn't appear to be getting ready to leave. In fact, the man had been tidying up the shop when she had walked in. "Where did they go?"

"Who cares? All that matters is they're gone, and we won't have to deal with their treachery anymore."

"Are the children gone, too?"

"I'm sure they are." He reached into his pockets. "I have something for you girls."

In Father's hand were several necklaces. He put one around Gisela's neck then turned to Anna. "You said you like lockets. I found a nice one for you."

Anna opened the locket. A tiny photograph of a young man and women was inside, with the woman holding a baby. She picked the picture out and tossed it into the fire and hugged her father. "This is so beautiful. Thank you!"

He handed Gisela a small sack. "And I have something just

for you."

She looked inside. It contained chunks of chocolate. She recognized the stamp on top of each one. They were from the same shop she had visited yesterday. "I thought you said I was not supposed to have this."

"It's all right now. The Jews are gone. They can't control us with their merchandise anymore."

"But you said it was wrong to steal."

Father sat at his favorite chair in front of the fireplace. "We're not stealing. All we are doing is taking back what they have stolen from us through the years."

Gisela took one chunk out of the sack and examined it. The memory of the man and boy caught in her head. The chocolate did not smell as nice this time. She popped the piece into her mouth. It did not taste the same. She spat it out.

Anna glared at her. "If you don't want that, I'll eat it."

Gisela stared at the next piece. The motion to put it into her mouth was a simple one, but she still could not bring herself to do it. It was as if a plate of glass stood between the candy and her mouth and she could not press her hand through it. A thought clung to the back of her mind and would not let go. She had no explanation for the thought, but something told her enjoying it would be—wrong.

She dumped the chocolate into the fire and watched it burn.

~ * ~ * ~

As a teenager, **Chuck** spent many hours reading Clarke, Asimov, and Heinlein. He started his career as a science teacher, but ended up in the information systems field. He has been married for twenty-five years to a registered nurse but most of all a compassionate wife and mother. They live in the Missouri Ozarks and have two college-age children.

His short stories have appeared in *Stupefying Stories, 4 Star Stories, Devolution Z,* and *Page and Spine,* among other publications.

When not working, doing family things or writing, he likes to build military models or play with model trains. They never travel far because if you live in the Ozarks, you are already there.

THE ENEMIES

Thomas Cannon

Phillip Biggs hurried through the lobby of the hotel. Although his candidate polled slightly ahead of Joan McGaffee, the campaign needed a savior. His boss's skeletons were about to fall out of the closet like rolls of battered wrapping paper. By the time certain facts came out, his candidate had to be ahead by double digits.

Ashton Gold, the campaign guru, could get it done. He turned around every lost cause he took on. Mr. Gold was also Washington's best kept secret. So much so Phillip didn't know what Ashton looked like. All Phillip knew was one of his many idiosyncrasies were the white sneakers he always wore with his suits. That and he was at this hotel for a conference. This was enough information to make Phillip confident he would find the sneaker-footed genius. The tricky part would be to get him to work his magic for Senator Britton.

Phillip broke into a run/jog, thankful for the sneakers he wore so Ashton might notice him. Not that everyone in Washington didn't know his bald head save for the narrow band of gray and his twinkling blue eyes. Sure Ashton would see through the gesture, but Phillip hoped he would also acknowledge he was committed to do whatever it took to win.

The session had ended early, and Phillip was suddenly fighting a sea of suits. By the time he made it into the ballroom/meeting room, it was nearly empty. He immediately turned around and dove back into the crowd, holding his briefcase out in front of him, his shirt dampening under his jacket. While Gold was one of the good guys, a Democrat, he had made some interesting conservative comments since January 6th. If McGafee's campaign swayed him to their side, it would be all over.

The overnight polls already showed the public had not responded well to Britton's complaints of the press attacking her because she was a woman. Phillip had told her she couldn't cry sexism when her opponent was also a woman, but she had been too angry to listen.

He pushed his way through people, looking for white sneakers and feeling the people around him were intentionally slowing him down. Without Gold, the campaign was over and along with it, his career. While no one else could have sweet-talked Gold's secretary into revealing his itinerary for the day, McGaffee's young staff had been known to hack an email or calendar. They might have gotten to Gold. Phillip held the fear of this in the pit of his stomach as everyone around him had instantly worked his or her cell phones once they hit the hallway. Technology was the future of reaching the voters and he was the past. The ancient or at least obsolete history.

As people continued to meander towards the bathrooms and snack tables, Phillip realized his downward gaze was catching less and less feet. He sat on an empty chair off to the side and watched black-shiny shoed feet and nyloned feet in heels until he thought he would develop a fetish.

This is my last race, he thought to himself. He no longer felt the rush he used to get by out-campaigning everyone else. If fact, the more tricks he used, the more useful he had felt because it meant he had won the campaign for his candidate. Now he didn't think he had any more tricks up his sleeve.

Then, afraid someone would identify him leering at people's feet, he looked around to see who might be watching him. A surprisingly young man in a suit and white converses was doing just that.

"Hi, how ya doin'?" this athletic, early thirtyish guy said with a nod. "Right interesting election season, huh?"

"It absolutely is," Phillip responded as if these were the passwords to identify each other. He had heard Gold had a unique way of speaking.

"Something sure needs to be done. Everyone says they want to put a stop to politics as usual, but you still get the typical smear campaign from the other side."

Phillip leaned in toward this guy who was young enough to be his kid. It didn't seem right to him Ashton Gold could be so young, so successful, *and* have a big smile and dimples. On top of that he had a thick pile of hair. Still, Phillip knew how to get him. "We're compatriots here, right?"

"You're Bert to my Ernie."

Phillip raised an eyebrow. "What?"

Yes, we're compatriots. Small differences but otherwise simpatico. I'm Abbot to your Costello. Partners. You're Dean Martin and I'm Jerry Lewis."

This guy was clearly different. Which was a good sign. Phillip tried to be different as well. "Before the breakup, right, Dean?" He smiled at his own cleverness. "We simply have a hell of a time in this day and age, because we do not want to sink to our opponent's level while they Nixon every way possible to win."

"Yep, Bert. While they dole out the fear mongering, we keep a positive message. And actually stick to our principles."

Phillip leaned back and relaxed because it was clear this guy was still a true believer. A lunatic, but on the right side. "Ernie, I'm glad we see eye to eye. Of course, we may have to sink to their doom and gloom messages because it works. But if we can attack them enough on their 'end of America as we know it' ads, then our positive messages can be heard."

"Yeah," he replied, leaning toward Phillip. "Couldn't have said it better myself. But we also gotta git the people to ignore the attacks on our candidate just because she's a woman."

"Isn't that incredible?" Phillip knew he wasn't doing too well talking in an eccentric way, but things were going well. They were definitely kindred spirits. "You'd think they wouldn't go that far with their own candidate being a woman. But I suppose that chick is such a ditz they have to."

"And a whiner. Good God. 'The press is sexist. They have a double standard.' It's all a bunch of gobble-de-gook, double talk."

"Exactly." Phillip nodded his head in complete agreement. "Why can't she be like our candidate? I really respect how she doesn't whine; she just works harder to prove everyone wrong."

The young guy stretched out his legs. "Unfortunately, our side can't be heard over them sons-a-bitches with their dirty campaign. There's just too much bias against us."

Phillip put his hand out. It seemed like the time for a handshake. He got a nice firm one. "I'm so glad you're saying this. I thought you had gone over to the other side."

"What other side? Which I'm sorry for name-calling. I forgot you used to be one of them."

"What?" Phillip looked at the kid's white shoes. "I assure you, Mr. Gold. I was never a conservative."

"Mr. Gold?" The young man looked at Phillip's tennis shoes. "You're Mr. Gold."

"No. I'm not."

People had gone to their next session and the foyer was empty. Phillip looked over at his Ernie trying to figure out what was going on. Finally, he asked, "You wore the sneakers to grab Gold's attention as well, huh? I figured you McGafee guys would infiltrate the reception tonight and make your pitch."

"We will. So you're from the Britton campaign?"

Phillip didn't know what else to do so he said, "I'm Phillip Rhodes."

"Jake Bell." He stuck out his hand. "I guess our problem is our candidates are a little too similar." He pulled his hand away and drew it to his mouth in mock horror. "You're not going to repeat that, are you?"

Phillip shook his head. "No. I'd rather no one know about this little scene."

"If it's any consolation, there's been a bear attack in Colorado and your candidate's comments last night haven't gotten any airtime. She'll take a small hit in the polls and then it'll be forgotten."

Phillip noticed Jake's strange diction was gone. He had heard Gold had a strange, informal way of talking, but hadn't found exactly what that meant. This McGaffee guy had done his homework. "Well," he said and slouched down into his chair.

"Such is political life," Jake said, relaxing back as well.

They sat in the quiet hallway. Phillip thought back to how his dad bought a new black Cadillac every five years and how he refused to trade his old one in. Instead he put a for sale sign on it and drove it around until it sold. At night, the old car with the faded paint and worn tires sat next to the shiny new one. Phillip was the soon to be replaced car. He and Jake were the same model of Cadillac, but Jake was newer and better. Phillip just didn't know which was worse, being not as good or being the same.

What he did know was their candidates were also very similar. The winner would just make fewer mistakes.

Coming through one of the double doors of the conference room and shutting it quietly was a fortyish-looking guy with shaggy straight hair. He wore a suit and a pair of white Nikes. Jake jumped out of his chair and was to Gold before Gold got past the sign on a tripod that read Session II: The Plight of the American Family.

Jake introduced himself and revealed he worked for Joan McGafee's campaign. Then Phillip's new friend pointed over to him. "That there is Mr. Rhodes from the Britton campaign. Now I reckon he is over there to woo you, but let me tell you—"

Phillip stood up and walked out to the lobby, not bothering to hear the rest. Finding the nearest chair, he opened his briefcase and brought out his dress shoes and put them on. If he was going to fail, he wanted to go out looking professional.

A few moments after he got his sneakers into his briefcase, Ashton Gold came around the corner. It was instinct more than a plan, but Phillip pulled out his old non-smart phone.

"I reckon you all want to talk to me," Ashton said. "Your whipper-snapper of a colleague back there didn't have much success, but let's hear your pitch."

Phillip held up a finger and waved his phone that had been to his ear. "I would be pleased to have a few moments of your time. But right now I'm on the phone with my daughter. Family is very important to me."

~ * ~ * ~

In August of 2021, **Thomas Cannon** was selected as the inaugural Poet Laureate of Oshkosh, WI. He is the author of the book *The Tao of Apathy* (available on Amazon) and the lead contributor to *Cup of Comfort for Parents of Children With Autism*. He is also published in various journals such as *Midwestern Gothic* and *Corvus Review*.

INITIATION

Charles Kyffhausen

"Yet success, though incalculable, can be overwhelming; and failure, though undetectable, can be mortal," Jillian remembered from Cordwainer Smith's book on psychological warfare. She had studied engineering in college, but she had also learned in her history classes the enormous danger of malicious propaganda. Yellow journalism started the Spanish-American War by convincing Americans, without much actual proof, Spaniards had blown up American sailors on the USS Maine. Inflammatory propaganda had later pulled the United States into the First World War at the cost of 115,000 dead and countless more soldiers maimed for life.

The instant somebody tries to tell me why I should hate somebody I never met, Jillian thought, *I need to question his or her motives.* She had forced herself to read the propaganda chapter in Mein Kampf where she learned Hitler had unfortunately been the German who learned the most from Germany's failure to counteract the Triple Entente's propaganda. He had then used propaganda to perpetrate some of the worst atrocities in history, and her new employer had published unspeakably vile material that supported the Nazis' racist ideology. Now she would discover the truth and expose the Morgan Armory's dirty little secrets for the entire world to know.

Jillian was apprehensive because the three other college graduates whom her civil rights group had recruited had never reported back. They were, as far as anybody knew, working happily for the company, but they refused to discuss the vile leaflet Edward Morgan had published in 1938.

Jillian didn't need the job. She vowed to herself she wouldn't be silenced like the others, no matter what the Morgan Armory promised or paid her. "I'd like to work here," she told Jake Martin, one of the assistant Superintendents, during her interview. "Maybe I can ask you about this concern, though, because we're both African-Americans. This company was responsible for one of history's most appalling pieces of racist propaganda, and it has never explained it." She took out a German-language leaflet, and put it on the desk for emphasis.

"*Not for the Aryan Craftsman*," read the caption below the first picture, which showed half a dozen slack-jawed men who were working on a moving assembly line. One wore a Jewish yarmulke, while two others had Polish and Romany name tags for the benefit of readers who couldn't identify the three Caucasians as ethnic minorities. "The racial inferiority of the Slav and the Negro speak for themselves, and even the normally cunning Jew cannot be trusted to tighten the bolt he places in the assembly. None of these inferior races can be trusted with more than a small part of a very simple assembly task."

"Jewish Comedian Shows how to run a Factory" was the caption of the second picture, a frame from the movie Modern Times in which Charlie Chaplin fell into a conveyor belt. "The moving assembly line is beneath the dignity of the lowest-ranking member of the Master Race, and the Aryan must preserve his dignity with individual craftsmanship. The superior Aryan workman must place each screw or bolt himself, select the proper tool, and tighten the fastener to ensure the highest quality work."

"The current Superintendent's grandfather circulated millions of copies of this leaflet in Germany before and even during the war, but nothing about it makes sense," Jillian continued. "Edward Morgan never released it in English or published it in the United States. He sued Nazi sympathizers for copyright violation when they tried to circulate English translations on their own."

"You will understand after you join the Order of Vulcan," Jake assured her. "All I can tell you now is that Edward Morgan did right."

Jillian barely managed to conceal her elation. Nothing could possibly excuse *Not for the Aryan Craftsman*, and she would discover the secret during the initiation. She would then tell her civil rights group even if it got her fired. She had connections as well as top grades, she didn't need this job, and money would never buy her silence.

"There's also a rumor the current Superintendent is only the Steward of the Order," she said while she hoped her expression did not betray her real intentions. "I know none of this company's CEOs have ever bothered with the title of President, but there is a Grand Master. Stories say it has been the same person for more than eighty years, but that's impossible."

"Don't push me. You know the only way to discover a fraternity's secrets is to join," Jake replied with a wide grin.

Jillian was hesitant because of the three other graduates who had, at least as far as her civil rights group was concerned, essentially disappeared. This branch of the Morgan family, which was reputed to have descended from Mark Twain's Connecticut Yankee, did have a reputation for acting like ancient aristocrats with powers of high and low justice, including the power of life and death, over those to whom it took a dislike.

Edward Morgan's son William had earned the nom de guerre of Rat-Catcher in the Second World War for brilliant combat engineering that disabled a Landkreuzer Ratte; the biggest tank ever built. He retired from the Army as a lieutenant general to win the 1968 Presidential election, and ended the Vietnam War by ordering the bombing of Hanoi and Haiphong. "How do you feel about the people in Hanoi and Haiphong?" Jillian ventured to Jake.

"I didn't like it, and neither did President Morgan; remember he first tried to buy out the enemy leaders to end the conflict without further violence. He saw, however, what totalitarian governments do to their victims when his battalion liberated a concentration camp in 1945, and he expected the Communists to do something similar. As matters stand, the Republic of Vietnam, including the former North, is now as prosperous as Taiwan and South Korea, and it has the same level of human rights. I don't know exactly what the Khmer Rouge planned to do in Cambodia, but most people are glad they never got a chance to do it."

"I suppose that, when you look at matters that way, he did the right thing, but it's hard to accept it," Jillian admitted. There was also, she told herself, the matter of the current Superintendent's daughter. Diana Morgan had, after 9/11, gotten herself involved in some kind of secret government organization. She had then led an Afghan tribe to victory at Kafiristan, where Al Qaida had died to the last man. Evildoers who crossed the Morgan industrial family, Jillian realized, usually didn't even live to stand trial. What, she wondered, might happen to an ordinary person who crossed these people?

The three members of Jillian's civil rights group had not experienced foul play, but something had nonetheless silenced them. *They won't silence me*, she resolved even as she accepted the employment offer.

~ * ~

Jillian, along with thirty-five other new professional employees, began their initiation by putting on blacksmith's aprons. "The smith's apron is a proud part of our tradition," Jake Martin, who now wore the apron of a Master of the Order of Vulcan, explained. "Mark Twain's Connecticut Yankee and his brother Charles, our company's founder, were blacksmiths before they became one-man industrial revolutions. We will now pass through the Hall of Weapons to the Chamber of Ignorance, the first step of our journey to Truth."

The Hall of Weapons, the Morgan Armory's military museum, was lit dimly for the initiation, but this enhanced its majesty and solemnity. "I'd hate to have somebody point that at me," Jillian said of a sixteen-inch gun while the initiates walked the length of the gigantic artillery piece.

"This gun won the competition for the main armament of the Montana battleship class," Jake explained. "Edward Morgan was proud of this weapon, and he was very unhappy when the government cancelled those ships. The Navy's interest had shifted to aircraft carriers, so we built parts for those instead."

The group passed the gun to arrive at a heavy wooden door in the old factory's brick wall, and it required a special key to open it. "This is the Chamber of Ignorance," Jake continued while he ushered the initiates inside. "Take a look around you, and remember what you see."

The room contained a copy of Aldous Huxley's Brave New World, in which Henry Ford's My Life and Work was the Bible while the Sign of the T (Ford's Model T) had replaced the Christian cross. There were photos of Charlie Chaplin trying to keep up with an assembly line in Modern Times, and there was also a copy of *Not for the Aryan Craftsman*. *I'm glad that racist leaflet is in the Chamber of Ignorance where it belongs*, Jillian thought.

"This room contains the mistaken perceptions many people have of industry," the Assistant Superintendent continued. "Now you shall see Truth against the contrast of Ignorance." He gave the door ahead of him several ritual blows with a blacksmith's hammer, and it opened slightly.

"Who seeks entry into the Chamber of Truth?" Diana Morgan,

the Superintendent's daughter, and Shield-Bearer of the Order asked. She also wore the apron of a Master, as did the other Assistant Superintendent; Charlie Jones, who was the Plow-Bearer.

A half-mask that resembled the head of a resolute falcon, after her Welsh middle name Gavina, covered the left side of Diana's face. Jillian knew the other woman had required maxillofacial surgery after the Battle of Kafiristan, and was now undergoing reconstructive surgery to repair the rest of the damage. The story was; she had picked up a live grenade to throw it away from some hostages without knowing how much time was left on the fuse. These were not people one wanted to cross, Jillian realized, but she was determined to do exactly that.

"Those who pass through Ignorance to find Truth," Jake answered Diana's ritual question.

"Enter and learn the Truth," Charlie gave the ritual reply. The initiates walked into the room, and he closed the door behind them. Jillian knew the secret behind *Not for the Aryan Craftsman* was almost in her grasp, and there was nothing the Morgan Armory could do to stop her from revealing it.

The dimly lit room contained a table with mounds of iron ore and coal, a brazier, and a pail of water. A velvet cover concealed a book, and another drape hid a picture on an easel near the stone wall. Another brazier, which had already been lit, contained a red-hot sword blade. The widescreen television, however, seemed incongruous for a secret initiation.

Diana and Charlie took their places beneath the Shield and Plow that constituted the Morgan Armory's trademark and coat of arms. The motto underneath read Iustus et Prosperitas: Justice and Prosperity. "Why do you bear a shield, Diana Morgan?" Jake asked the ritual question.

"Vulcan forges the arms with which Minerva, the archetype of wisdom and righteous warfare, upholds Justice and defends Liberty."

"Why do you bear a plow, Charles Jones?" Jake continued.

"Vulcan forges the implements with which Ceres, the archetype for agriculture and plenty, fosters Prosperity so none might want for the necessities and comforts of life," Charlie gave the ritual response.

"Justice and Prosperity are the foundations of the Order of Vulcan, of which I am Steward," Superintendent Richard Morgan proclaimed. The master of the greatest manufacturing establishment the world had ever seen was in his mid-fifties, but the gray streaks in his blond hair only enhanced his dignity and bearing.

So that rumor is true, Jillian thought despite her amazement at the fact the firm's CEO was spending his own time on the ceremony. *He doesn't call himself the Grand Master.*

"What were the four ancient elements?" Richard began the ritual catechism.

"Earth, Fire, Air, and Water," the Shield and Plow Bearers replied.

"Here is Earth," Richard said while he pointed to the mounds of iron ore and coal on the table before them. "Earth is nothing by itself. How does it become our treasured servant?"

"Through the agencies of Fire and Air does Earth become steel," Diana replied while she lit the brazier on the table. Then she cued the widescreen television to display an operating blast furnace.

"By what instrumentality is steel strengthened?" Richard asked.

"By the agency of Water is steel strengthened," Charlie replied. He used a pair of tongs to pick up the red-hot sword blade, which he plunged into the pail of water. "This is the art and science of the Blacksmith."

"People once believed Nature's mightiest forces belonged to the gods," Richard continued. The television screen showed flashing lightning below a ghostly image of Jupiter, the king of the gods. "Then Man, armed with Knowledge, harnessed the lightning and made it his servant." The lightning played across the earth far below, only to be seized by Benjamin Franklin, Thomas Edison, and Nikola Tesla.

"Who now holds the power of the mythological gods?" Richard Morgan demanded.

"We, the engineers and artisans of Mankind, hold the power of the gods," Charlie and Diana replied.

"Whose hand wields the hammer?" Richard continued the ritual catechism.

"Our hand wields the hammer!" Charlie and Diana answered while the television showed one of the Morgan Armory's gigantic forging machines in action.

"Whose hand wields the lightning?" Richard demanded.

"Our hand wields the lightning!" the Shield and Plow Bearers replied while sparks flew from an electric machining tool.

"Who wields the power of the Sun itself?"

"We wield the power of the Sun itself!" Water glowed blue around the core of a nuclear reactor.

"For what purpose do we command the power of the mythological gods?"

"To uphold Justice and foster Prosperity, so all might live in peace and security, and none might want for the necessities and comforts of life"

How could people like these ever create something as vile as Not for the Aryan Craftsman? Jillian wondered while she felt the solemn majesty of the ritual that symbolically invested her and the other new employees with the powers of the ancient gods, along with the responsibilities that came with them. Maybe Edward Morgan had been a white supremacist, and his descendants were trying to make up for it. In any event, the truth was going to come out. Jillian would call her civil rights group that very night even if she had to get its leaders out of bed.

"I now open the induction of the Initiates into the Order of Vulcan," Richard Morgan proclaimed. "You may have heard we have had the same Grand Master for more than eighty years. I'm afraid he can't take an active part in the ceremony, but he is our Teacher." He drew aside the curtain over the easel to reveal a famous portrait and continued, "I give you Henry Ford, whom we adopted as honorary Grand Master of our Order. This," he continued while he removed the book's velvet cover to reveal My Life and Work, "is his Book."

"Don't say a word; I have been called 'Your Fordship' and 'Mustafa Mond' more times than I can remember," he told the gaping initiates. "We are not going to worship this book, or make the sign of the T as they did in Brave New World. It contains, however, the true heart and soul of American industrial supremacy. The Morgan Armory has never forgotten this book's principles, and you must pass an examination on its contents to rise from Novice to Apprentice of the Order. Then you must apply its principles to your everyday work to advance to Journeyman and then Master."

"Remember what you saw in the Chamber of Ignorance," he continued. "Charlie Chaplin's hopeless attempts to keep up with an assembly line were a parody of how a real factory is supposed to work. That was why, when my grandfather recognized Hitler for the monster he was, he bought copies of Modern Times, added German subtitles, and circulated them lavishly in Germany. Hitler laughed his head off at the sight of Chaplin falling into the conveyor belt."

If Edward Morgan thought Hitler was a monster, why would he have reinforced Hitler's racist beliefs? Jillian wondered to herself.

"You also saw a very offensive leaflet outside, didn't you?" Richard continued. "The best place to hide a secret is in plain view, which is why *Not for the Aryan Craftsman* ridicules a Jewish worker for placing a bolt but not tightening it. If the worker who placed the fastener also had to tighten it, he would have spent more time picking up and putting down the wrench than on assembly. My grandfather's success in getting Hitler's 'Aryan craftsmen' to do exactly that destroyed more of Germany's production capability than the Army Air Force and Royal Air Force put together."

Jillian's jaw dropped with sudden realization while that last sentence thundered in her brain. Now she understood why the three other members of her civil rights group had never reported back, and why she also would not report back. *Yet success, though incalculable, can be overwhelming; and failure, though undetectable, can be mortal*, she remembered Cordwainer Smith's words. Edward Morgan's propaganda had deceived Hitler, the grand master of propaganda himself, and it had hurt the Nazi war effort far more badly than anything she had seen in the Hall of Weapons.

"Here are two of the men who posed for that picture," Richard continued.

"I'm Chaim Levy, the 'Jew who couldn't be trusted to do more than place the bolt,'" one retiree said. "The superior Aryan workman must place each screw or bolt himself, select the proper tool, and tighten the fastener to ensure the highest quality work" he recited from the leaflet while he acted out those motions, only to be unable to avoid laughing halfway through the process. "Can you see how much wasted motion is built into this job?"

"We do this as an exercise in the Morgan Trade School," Diana elaborated, "and the wasted motion comes to roughly forty-eight seconds out of every minute. My great-grandfather therefore destroyed eighty percent of Hitler's industrial capacity before the war even began, and he didn't notice because the factories, their equipment, and the workers were as yet untouched by a single Allied bomb."

"I'm John Kowalski, the 'Polack who couldn't be trained to do more than tighten the bolt,'" the other said. "When people ask how much the Morgan Armory had to pay us to pose for such a degrading picture, we just smile at them like the cat that ate the canary."

"The company didn't pay us," Levy elaborated. "We volunteered to choke the Berlin paperhanger with his own racist poison, and we enjoyed every minute of it. I went so far as to study pictures from the Nazis' The Eternal Jew, and I imitated the most degrading ones as best I could. This is why," he explained while he held up a picture of a gigantic tank with a German cross on its side.

"That's a Tiger," Kowalski said, "and it was made by Aryan craftsmen in the good old-fashioned Aryan manner: very slowly and meticulously, and one at a time. That was why there were never very many of them, and that was good for our side. There was, however, a German translation of My Life and Work, and Hitler had read it—"

Jillian could no longer contain himself. "If you hadn't used the Nazis' own racist ideology to convince them the moving assembly line was only for 'inferior races,' our troops would have been up to their necks in mass-produced Tiger tanks, V-2 missiles, and jet fighters. That's why Edward Morgan never allowed that leaflet to appear in English, wasn't it? It was for nobody but the enemy to read."

"That's exactly right," Charlie Jones affirmed with a broad smile. "Plenty of German industrialists and military men wanted to implement Henry Ford's methods. Once Der Fuhrer made up his mind such methods were 'Not for the Aryan Craftsman,' however, they knew enough to keep their mouths shut. President Truman said in public Not for the Aryan Craftsman was the most disgusting, sickening, and vile piece of racist propaganda he had ever seen. He also gave Edward Morgan, in secret, the nation's highest civilian decoration for winning the Second World War."

"My grandfather paid the price of derision and public condemnation to exercise the power of high justice, to the extent of life and death, over Nazism," Richard Morgan added. "He may as well have shoved that pistol into Hitler's mouth and pulled the trigger himself."

"Then Edward Morgan was one of the greatest heroes who

ever lived, and this 'Order of Vulcan' is an employee training program disguised as a fraternity," Jillian said with a wide grin. "Why, though, didn't he explain his actions after the war rather than living with the opprobrium?"

"Remember that *My Life and Work* is the foundation of the Morgan Production System, but it's only the foundation. My great-grandfather began to improve on its content, and my grandfather, my father, and I have continued that process. Let's just say our operations are now considerably more efficient than Toyota's. If somebody is going to sell the best manufactured products on earth while starting hourly workers at thirty-five dollars an hour, that somebody is going to be us."

"It is how you keep the secrets that have made this company the most successful manufacturing firm in the world for almost a century," Jillian said. *And I will keep our secrets as well*, she pledged to herself as she became part of an adventure from which she would not retire for another fifty years.

~ * ~

"So, Jillian, what are you going to tell your civil rights group?" Diana Morgan asked while she took the other woman aside in the Hall of Weapons.

"You knew?" Jillian asked, her heart pounding with terror. Would the Morgans fire her before a career, with which she had fallen in love, had even begun? She was on Diana's left side, and the falcon mask told her nothing of the other woman's expression. She suspected she would not want to see what was under that mask until the other woman's reconstructive surgery was complete. These were not, she remembered, people one wanted to cross, and that was exactly what she had done.

"My father and I both knew. That's why we had our head-hunters practically drag you in for an interview."

"What?" Jillian stammered while her head spun.

"We didn't like what your group was doing, of course, but we gained the absolute loyalty of everybody it sent once he or she learned the truth. You'll be the last because the only people left in your group are now those whose grades are too low to interest us," Diana said while she turned to show Jillian a crooked smile on the uninjured side of her face. Jillian thought again of the cat that ate the canary.

"We knew you were willing to do the right thing," she continued, "regardless of what it cost you, up to and including a job whose starting salary exceeds those offered by our competitors by thirty-five percent. That means, if you ever see anything wrong with our production processes or quality controls, you'll speak up about it. We reward our people for doing that instead of punishing them for bringing bad news. Now, if you would be good enough to carry this for me." Diana handed Jillian the Shield of Minerva.

Jillian stammered while she did so. Diana had just said she and her father had chosen her personally, and now the Morgan Armory's heiress wanted her to carry a heavy shield the way a servant might. "Think back to medieval times and customs," Diana hinted.

Jillian did, and she realized the truth yet again. Almost every lord had a man-at-arms whose official job was to carry the lord's shield until he needed to use it in battle, and that meant the lord had to be able to trust this man with his life. The shield-bearer was therefore also often a trusted friend and confidante who could tell the lord what he needed to hear whether he liked it or not. Diana would also need a loyal shield-bearer when she succeeded her father in a couple of decades, and she had chosen Jillian to be that friend.

~ * ~

"I'm quite well," Jillian insisted when her civil rights group called her the next day. "I know I told you I didn't need this job, but now I want it. No, the company is not intimidating, bribing, or threatening me. I'd want this job even if I was as wealthy as Richard Morgan must be."

"You know I can't tell you what goes on in an initiation," she replied to the next inquiry. "It was just a silly little ritual anyway; you know, the usual mumbo-jumbo. I really can't talk about *Not for the Aryan Craftsman* either. All you need to know is that Edward Morgan did right."

~ * ~ * ~

Charles Kyffhausen is the SF/Fantasy pen name of the author of stories published in *Fear and Trembling*, *Strange*, *Weird and Wonderful*, *The Lorelei Signal*, and others.

Time for Murder

John Taloni

I have died more times than I can count. One endlessly repeated day, the same actions in the same sequence, each ending with a unique death. Each death has imprinted itself in my memory with searing clarity.

Today's executioner approaches, grim faced and unspeaking. He lifts his hand to show some form of energy weapon. I raise my arms just as I did the first time. I see a flash of light illuminate the nearby trees before the beam strikes my head.

And then, limbo. I float in an awareness that is not quite consciousness.

As usual, I come to in the subway. My left hand holds my phone, open to a book app and a paragraph I've read countless times.

From there I walk to work, each step the same as the first day. I log in to my workstation, just as I did then. The repetition numbs my brain, but I cannot change. I have tried to tune out, but my consciousness remains alert, experiencing an endless searing eternal present.

The rest of the day proceeds exactly as before. Work ends and I make my way to a local park, to wait out the worst of the rush hour jam. I sit on the same bench.

Then, and only then, is the one item that changes. A new executioner appears. This one carries a projectile weapon. It seems to be a pistol, similar to ones I have seen many times on TV and film, but with a shorter barrel flared at the end.

Tonight's killer is a talker. He levels the pistol at me. "Don't move," he says. "You have to die. Not for anything you've done, but for what you will do. We have to prevent it." I have heard similar speeches over and over.

He presses the trigger. I raise my arms...

I come back to consciousness on the train. The sting of my previous death reverberates through my body. My hand grips the phone, locked into the day's activities, but my mind wanders. If I cannot change the actions my body takes, then I can try to free my mind.

I pay special attention to the sky as I walk to work. Cumulo-nimbus clouds cluster together, implying rain for a tomorrow that never comes. At lunch I focus on the taste of the food, though I have eaten it more thousands of times than I can count.

At the end of the day it is the same, with the one change. Each killer is different, each method used to kill me unique in at least one small way.

Yet each one ends with the same result. The killer fires, shoots, swings an ax, thrusts with a sword, stabs with a knife. Each night the moment comes. I raise my arms, uselessly, and the killing stroke lands. Some deaths cause agony that lasts for minutes. Others finish me off in seconds. All end in a fugue state before I come to on the train.

After a string of a dozen quiet deaths, I get a talker.

"The timeline keeps resetting," he says. I come out of my haze to look him over. Average height. Odd-looking jumpsuit made of a shimmering material. Energy weapon in his right hand.

"We don't know how you're doing it," he continues. "No matter what we do to the timeline, history doesn't change. You murder tens of millions." I look at him—indeed, I have to. His eyes blur with tears.

"The history books say you're still an innocent at this point. That is not important. You do not remain so. You've got to be stopped. I have to stop you. Even if you are not yet guilty of your crimes. I'm sorry."

He raises the weapon and points it at my head. He hesitates, the gun wavering.

I raise my arms...

He fires. The shot goes past my head, setting a tree behind me ablaze.

And I...*I am past the moment.*

The time loop has ended. I am able to move of my own volition, no longer bound to past events.

For a split second, one that feels like an eternity, I remain motionless. Then the realization dawns and I strike.

I hit my would-be killer with frustration born from a century of days, each of which ended with my death. But not today. I would not die this time. Not ever again.

I leap forward and strike a flurry of blows to his face. With a desperate reach I grab his forearm and twist. He steps back and tries to yank his arm out, but my grip would not be broken. I step in and stomp his foot, making him double over. With a wrenching heave I tear the weapon from his hand, breaking two of his fingers and one of mine in the process. He gurgles in pain and I punch him in the solar plexus, forcing the breath from his body.

He looks up at me with agony-filled eyes, a dawning horror in them. My attempted assassin wouldn't feel the pain for long. I place the grip of the weapon in my right hand and find the trigger. Aim down the front of the barrel and fire. A bolt of light flashes, illuminating the darkness of the park. He moves no more.

I stick the weapon in my belt. With a swift decision I rip the jumpsuit from his body. It tears to shreds, exposing wiring and a material that was not cloth. I take his boots as well.

I run from the park, looking for the nearest dark alley. I couldn't go home. I would have to hide.

The suit and the weapon are a treasure. I would examine them, find a way to reverse engineer the technology and figure out a way to protect myself. After dying so many times at last I could live. Live, and take my revenge for so many deaths.

They want a monster? I'll show them a monster.

~ * ~ * ~

John Taloni has been reading SFF for five decades. He finally decided to put finger to keyboard to express the "what if" stories swirling in his head.

LABELS

Bob Rich

Dear Mom,

I know you love me, so this will hurt you terribly. I am sorry. Hurting you is the last thing I want to do. Still, I need to kill myself. I can't see any alternative.

I am fat and ugly. No other kid wants to be my friend, and many think the funniest thing in the world is to humiliate me. And I'll never have a boyfriend, not with my looks.

OK, I am good at studying, but so what? When I graduate from school, I'm sure to get into college, so we can build up a huge debt, then nobody will ever bother to employ me.

If I lived somewhere else in the universe and was offered a ticket to visit another planet, Earth would be my last choice. Oh, the place is OK, but the monsters inhabiting it are something else. I can't stand all this hate and fighting and selfishness.

We love Greta Thunberg. She is right, but so what? Demonstrate all we like, but the moneybags won't listen. Going to hell with billions is so important to them! So, my generation can expect a life of horror and misery. I am only getting off the sinking ship a little early.

~ * ~

Shelly leaned back. Tears might damage the keyboard. She opened the second drawer of her desk and found a carefully hidden Hershey bar—the best antidepressant in all the world.

Someone laughed behind her. She spun her chair around—who could that be, at 4 a.m., in her bedroom?

A boy about her age stood there, a friendly smile on his face. He wore blue jeans and a yellow t-shirt. "You're not ugly," he said. "Fat, yes, thanks to that thing in your hand, but if you lost fifty pounds, you'd look beautiful."

"Who are you, and what the hell are you doing in here?"

"My name is Jakablatioini, but Jake will do. And what I'm doing here should be obvious: saving your life."

She felt her face flame. Here she was in her summer pajamas, fat tits half out of the top, all the bulges she usually hid under loose clothes visible. "Go away!" she shouted.

"Shh! You'll wake your mother."

Shelly crossed her arms over her chest and once more couldn't help crying.

"You can change everything," Jake said. "Start with what you eat, and do some exercise. Tomorrow is Saturday, right? You'll need a sleep-in, then we can go for a walk."

"What the hell for? If I got skinny, I'd still be a black girl who got born because some bastard raped my mother. She never even saw his face."

"You're not black but brown. I got a friend, now he IS black, like coal."

"If they could get away with it, half the people in this town would call me a nigger anyway. In elementary school, the favorite thing thrown at me was 'Shitface monkey' because I'm brown. Oh, go away!"

"Look, I've got to save your life, or I don't live either."

"Huh?"

Jake bowed, grinning. "I'm your great-great-great-great grandson from the future."

Bloody nonsense. "Who're you kidding?"

"Okay, let me explain."

The door opened, and Mom came in half asleep, with a dressing gown over her nightgown. "What are you doing awake this late? And who are you shouting at?"

"Only you can see or hear me. I'm here as a projection," Jake said.

If he really came from the future, not that he could have, there were no bets on technology.

Shelly saw Mom look at the screen and lifted a hand to control-tab to something else to hide her letter, but too late. A strong hand grabbed her wrist.

"Oh no. Oh darling, no! I couldn't live with myself if you died! You're all I've got!"

Then Shelly was standing, held in a comforting hug, and both of them were bawling their eyes out. Past Mom's shoulder, she saw Jake was crying, too.

"Promise me you won't harm yourself. We'll get you to see a psychologist."

"They cost money. You work hard enough washing ancient bums for a pittance."

"There is a lot more to my job than washing bums. The oldies call me Sunshine. Anyway, money is a tool. No point having it if we're dead."

"No psychologist. They can't take away my problems, only spout some nonsense about changing my attitude or something." She pulled away from Mom and looked her in the eyes. "But okay, I promise not to kill myself."

"Right, see you tomorrow," Jake said then disappeared.

Shelly woke at 11 a.m. Naturally, Mom was at work. She hoped Jake wouldn't turn up while she was showering and dressing, but thank God, he only appeared when she got to the kitchen. "Hi Shelly," he said. "Start eating healthy: have the same breakfast as your mom."

"Who are you to tell me what to do?"

"Temper, temper. Do you want to show up those stupid school bullies?"

"How do you know all this?"

"You could even ask; how can I speak your ancient version of English and wear clothes from your time. Look, please have a healthy breakfast, none of that maple syrup and stuff, and I'll explain, okay?"

Shelly shrugged. It was easier to comply than to battle. "Go ahead. Tell me." She got out a couple of eggs and heated the frying pan.

"Every time someone makes a choice, the universe splits in two. If a rat under your house has to choose between turning right and turning left, you get two universes, one for each."

"Bullshit." Shelly buttered two slices of bread and put the jug on. "Hey, you want something to eat, too?"

"You forget. I'm not really here, only a projection. Anyway, most of those universes are very similar, but some choices make huge differences. If you kill yourself, my universe doesn't exist. And out of her mind with grief, your mom will go for a drive in one universe, and crash the car and die. In another, she'll survive the crash, but as a quadriplegic. And in others, she comes home okay, but…you get the idea?"

"You're trying to put a guilt trip on me." She made instant coffee and sat down to eat.

Jake's white teeth flashed in a grin in bright contrast to his face, which was slightly lighter brown than hers. "The records show you're highly intelligent. Shame to snuff out all that potential. Of course, I'm putting a guilt trip on you. I want to live, don't I?"

Shelly used a sip of coffee to wash down the egg taste. "But isn't coming back to influence the past logically impossible?"

"Bullshit back to you. There are infinitely many futures. It's making sure one happens."

"And that's an infinite cycle. You're born because you came back. But you can't come back unless you were born." She rinsed the dishes.

"Leave the theory to the physicists. Look, do you know how your smartphone works? Just trust the experts. I'm here, so my theory is right. C'mon, walk time."

~ * ~

Sunday morning, Shelly managed to get up before Mom and prepared breakfast for both of them. Jake sat at the table, silently approving.

Walking in, Mom said, "That's a surprise! Not your usual?"

"No. I'm gonna get rid of my fat."

"Wonderful! What brought this on?"

"I…met this cute boy called Jake who reckons I'd look beautiful if I lost fifty pounds."

Jake laughed.

"So, I'm going for a walk before studying for tomorrow's math test."

"Darling, you're beautiful inside with all your passionate care for every living thing. But listen, only Friday night you were desperate. Next time you feel like that, remember, the sun always shines, even when something blocks its light."

In a half-hour, Jake and Shelly strode along under sunlight that could have benefited from a few clouds to block it. She had a thought. "Hey Jake, so humanity will survive?"

"In some futures. Obviously, in the one I come from. But other futures have nothing but primitive life for millions of years."

Shelly shivered, never mind the heat. "Climate change?"

"Yes, that's devastating and will get worse, but the main idiocy is poisoning everything. You're killing all the insects and other small creatures, and—"

"ME?"

"Keep your shirt on. The people of your time. If insects die out, everything dies out. They're at the base of all the food chains, and pollinate plants, and so on."

Taking her shirt off was a horrendous thought. Shelly sped up to burn off more bulge material. "I know that. But can you tell me what people of my time need to do to survive?"

"I don't know. I could find out, but the krionter only teaches me what I ask for."

"The what?"

"It's a sort of a machine."

Then hell intruded: Gillian sped past on her bike, shouting, "If it's brown, flush it down!"

Tony and Harry rode behind her, screaming with laughter. Tony slowed enough to shout, "Nah, the big lump would block it up!"

This of course spoiled Shelly's mood. She walked silently beside Jake until she noticed a nasty pain in her thighs. She said, "I've got a chafe between my legs. We better go home." By the time she entered the front door, her thighs were on fire and she could hardly walk.

Monday morning, thighs lathered with cream from Mom, she hobbled off the bus. Avoiding eye contact with the usual torturers, she still couldn't close her ears to little oft-repeated gems like "Wish they built the corridors wider so Ms. Blimp could fit, hahaha!"

First period was the math test. Shelly finished in half the time, then got out a sheet of paper and a soft pencil and sketched Mr. Barlos. He did have a nice face with gray eyes, a sharp nose, and a firm, square jaw.

He must have noticed her repeatedly looking at him then down, and walked over. He smiled at seeing the drawing. "Give me the test," he murmured.

At the end of the period, he called Shelly to stay behind. As the last kid left, he said, "I've scored your test. One hundred percent as usual. Congrats."

"Thank you, sir. Math is fun."

He laughed. "To you and me. To most of humanity, it's torture. Look, have you heard of the Math Olympiad?"

"Vaguely."

"The first round is online here with me supervising, but if you do well enough, it's an all-expenses paid trip to MIT in Boston. If you enter, I'll coach you after school."

"Oh…sir, you really think I have a chance?"

"Probably not to win the first time, but it can be practice for next year."

Extra study fills empty time, right? "Only sir, I do babysitting Monday, Tuesday and Wednesday evenings. And won't your family miss you?"

His eyes glistened, and the corners of his mouth turned down. "No family anymore. My ex has moved to New York, and I only see my kids on Skype except for twice a year. But okay, we can spend an hour on preparation after school, Thursdays and Fridays."

Great. Lost in her thoughts, Shelly forgot to steel herself for the usual as she walked out.

"Did you sit on his lap?" Kathy screeched. "He'll now be two-dimensional!"

"Hey Shel, how is the baby?" Tony poked toward her stomach.

"That has to be an immaculate conception," Cade said with a mock adoring look. "I mean, who'd want to?"

Somehow, she got through them and hid in the restroom.

At lunchtime, she visited Mrs. Corter in her home economics classroom. "Ma'am, I've decided to lose weight. Can you please help me design a diet?"

"Excellent, Shelly. First, change the language. You're not losing anything You're reducing weight and gaining health. You know the nutritional facts. Avoid fad diets, eliminate sugar and as much processed foods and takeaways as you can, and just eat less of everything. One trick is to use a smaller plate. It still looks heaps, but the quantity is reduced."

"Sure, by Pi-r-squared."

The teacher looked puzzled. "A square pie?"

Shelly hid her inner grin. "The mathematical concept of Pi,

ma'am, not food wrapped in pastry."

After the hell of school, it was the usual heaven of caring for Ellie and Tim. With Jake smilingly watching, she entertained them, fed them, bathed them, put them to bed and got out *The Lorax*. Ellie could recite it word for word.

As she kissed Tim's little face, he said, "Oh Shelly, loveya." Ellie hugged her. "See you tomorrow after school," she said, very proud of being a schoolgirl.

Then Shelly studied for three hours until Mrs. Dorian got home from work and paid her. On the short walk home, as she was passing the 24-hour supermarket, Jake challenged her. "You're not doing your usual, are you?"

"Stop nagging!" But she walked right past, at the tortoise pace imposed by burning thighs and too much fat, without putting money in the vending machine. In fact, at home she extracted all her hidden antidepressants, stripped them of wrapping and popped them into the compost bin under some other muck. Emptying that was her job anyway.

On Thursday, Mr. Barlos drove her home after their study session. Mom was in the process of opening the front door, surrounded by cloth bags full of shopping. The teacher looked at her. "Hello Sunshine!"

She turned. "Oh. Alex, right? You visit your mother nearly every day. Didn't realize you were the teacher coaching Shelly. Come on in."

Mom produced three cups of coffee and a plate of cookies. "No cookies!" Jake said.

Shelly surprised herself by pushing the plate closer to Mr. Barlos and keeping her paws off them. Last week, she'd have tried to grab them all. All three of her companions—two humans and one projection—gave her surprised smiles.

"Ms. Gorton, you have one bright daughter," Mr. Barlos said.

"Please, Lynette."

"Or Sunshine?"

"Sometimes. But we do have hard times, too. Shelly, does Mr. Barlos know about the bullying?"

The teacher's face went hard. "Shelly, you know the school rules. Bullying must be reported. Tell me."

Shelly managed not to cry. "Sir, I went to elementary school with these kids. They started on me then, and I told my teacher, which made things worse. I got hit, and spat on, and my things stolen and wrecked. If I just suck it up, at least it's only words. I can survive that."

"Report to me in detail."

Friday morning, there was an announcement. "Gillian Treloar, Antonio Florino, Harold McTave, Katherine Harter, Cade McWilliams, and Michelle Hirsch, you're required at the Principal's office." Off they went. When they returned, Shelly caught a barrage of toxic glances, but surely, they couldn't do worse than the usual shit?

During breaks, she got the invisibility treatment, which was much better. After everyone else left, she had the joy of learning with Mr. Barlos, working on matrix algebra, which was new to her. Again, he drove her home and this time had dinner with them.

During the weekend, she immersed herself in math, did her share of housework, and during their walks, asked Jake about his life.

"Oh, where do I start? There are only five million people, so by your measures, everyone is a billionaire, only we don't have money. You want something, you order it from Gaia. If you compare an abacus with your computer, that's the step up from your technology to Gaia. She is everywhere and organizes everything."

"How do you spend your time?"

"Lots of ways. I enjoy growing beautiful plants, using something like you now call genetic engineering to make amazing variations. We don't eat animals, and many kinds have developed speech, and they're also people. And I play music, and hang out with my friends."

"Do you go to school?"

"No. That's what the krionter is for. You put on this helmet and go to sleep, and wake with all the knowledge you specified. Skills are something else. They need practice."

"Wish you could take me to your time!"

"Sorry, Granny, ain't gonna happen."

Monday at school, things were peaceful enough, and Shelly enjoyed her evening job, with Jake watching. Ten past ten, she was walking from one streetlight to the next when something slammed into her back. Then Tony was in front of her, with a baseball bat raised high.

Then nothing.

~ * ~

Beep…beep…beep…

She lay in an unfamiliar bed. Pain gnawed everywhere, but distant, like looking through a veil.

Someone was holding her left hand. Shelly opened her eyes, to see Mom leaning toward her, a tear hanging on the lashes of both her eyes. Those eyes were swollen and bloodshot. "Thank God, you're back," she whispered.

"Back from what?"

"Do you remember anything?"

"Uh…Jake and I were walking on Sunday, and he told me a little about his life."

Mom smiled. "I'll have to meet this Jake. But what about Monday night?"

Shelly tried, but there was nothing.

"John Carlisle was driving home and saw this bunch of people putting the boot into someone on the ground. When the headlights shone on them, they ran away. He saved your life, but, oh, you had a depressed skull fracture, and four knife wounds, and three ribs broken, three other fractures, and internal bruising…." Then Mom was crying. "You had emergency surgery and stayed in a coma until now."

"What day is it?"

"Friday afternoon, love."

"Shouldn't you be at work? And what about Ellie and Tim?"

"Mr. Cartwright is being very generous. Both Susie Dorian and I are on paid leave, although we don't have that in our contracts."

Shelly heard footsteps, and Mom let her hand go. "Wonderful, she is conscious!" Mr. Barlos said.

Shelly managed to turn her head left and saw Mom and the teacher hug. She approved.

Still holding onto Mr. Barlos, Mom said, "Alex kept me alive. He's been here almost every moment when not working."

"Welcome back, Shelly," he said, smiling. "The police will want to talk with you. Can you identify your attackers?"

"She has no recall after Sunday night," Mom said.

A middle-aged lady's face came into Shelly's limited range of vision. "Honey, I'll take your vitals and I've called the neurosurgeon. She wants to talk with you."

A Chinese lady soon arrived. "Good afternoon, everyone. Hello, Shelly, I'm Dr. Kwong, and spent three hours Tuesday on fixing your skull. I'm afraid we had to shave your hair off, but that'll grow back. Now, I need to test for any psychological effects of the brain trauma."

Actually, that was interesting. It started with her name, birthday and address, then general-knowledge questions, then about recent events.

She correctly answered everything, up until going to bed on Sunday. After that, nothing. "Doctor, I want to check if my math is affected," she said. "Mr. Barlos, can we do some matrix algebra?"

"Good idea," Dr. Kwong said.

Mr. Barlos came into Shelly's view. In a few minutes, they determined she could still solve the problem they'd worked on a week ago, which was a great relief.

"Unfortunately," the doctor said, "You won't be any use as a witness for the police."

Shelly thought about those six hateful, hating kids. She didn't want them to go to jail—what good would that do? "I have an idea. Mom, please organize a visit from Ellie and Tim, and take a video of them seeing me like this And Mr. Barlos, show it in class. Mom, you can talk on it too, telling the world how the attack on me made you feel. Maybe, just maybe, we can get them to realize I'm not merely a lump of lard but a person with feelings like them?"

Jake appeared beside Mom. "Love you!" he shouted, making Shelly smile inside.

~ * ~

Saturday morning, two nurses washed her. She hated them seeing her fat belly and fat bum and… She reminded herself, dozens of people had seen her during the past four days, but she still squirmed inside. Then they propped her in a sitting position, much better than lying flat. She took stock of herself during this. Both lower legs were in plaster. A frame encased her right upper arm. One of the nurses explained it was to apply tension so the broken arm would set straight. *What kind of a person would do that to someone!*

Bandages covered much of her. A tube carried yellow fluid into her abdomen, another dripped clear into the back of her right hand, and two tubes removed body waste. She asked for the hand one to be moved so she could type and draw, and at least they attached it further up her arm.

As soon as the nurses left, Mom and Mr. Barlos entered. She'd brought Shelly's laptop, phone, drawing pad, and pencils. He handed her a CD. "These are study materials from all your teachers. All of them are rooting for you to get better."

"Oh. Thank you, sir. I—"

"At school, I'll still be 'sir' and Mr. Barlos, but in private, please call me Alex."

A pink cloud of pleasure filled Shelly, never mind the background pain, the shock of being assaulted like this, being tied to a bed. It'd be so wonderful to have a father!

"Alex, can we please do some math now?"

"No, darling," Mom said. "Susie and the kids are coming, to do our video."

"Great, although…I hate to distress the littlies. But something else. How can we pay for all these medical expenses?"

Alex answered, "The state has a medical insurance program for victims of crime. It won't cost you anything."

Shelly thought of what Mrs. Corter had said about losing weight. "I am not a victim. I am a survivor!" As Shelly expected, Jake appeared on Mom's other side, and cheered.

The door opened, and Mrs. Dorian led Ellie and Tim in. They looked at her, and both started crying.

Shelly said, "Darlings, I'm still alive."

"Mom told us not to touch you 'cause you hurt everywhere," Tim said with a sniff, "but I wanna kiss you better!"

Mr. Barlos—no, Alex—stepped to the foot of the bed, and Shelly felt the bed moving down. Mrs. Dorian lifted the little boy, whose blue eyes seemed too large for his face, then she felt the butterfly touch of his kiss on her cheek.

"Thank you, I'm better already!"

"You're my best friend in all the world! Why would anybody do this to you?" Ellie asked, sparks flying out of her eyes, hands forming fists, face like a little tiger's.

While thinking about her answer, Shelly thought their golden hair and pale skin would emphasize the lesson. "I don't know. I can't even imagine wanting to hurt somebody. You know I don't even kill insects. But suppose you could talk to these people who attacked me. What'd you say?"

"Shelly is wonderful! My teacher told me I'm the best in my class, because Shelly taught me to read and count and write. And she is the best friend, ever, and if I could find you and had a gun I'd shoot you!"

"No, Ellie darling," Shelly said. "That'd make you the same as them. I've read lots of things a man called Gandhi said. One is: an eye for an eye leaves the whole world blind. Do you understand that?"

"Uh...no."

"They hurt me. That's a bad thing. If I hurt them back, that's two bad things. It goes round and round forever: they hurt me and I hurt them so they hurt me so I hurt them, on and on."

Mrs. Dorian asked, "What would you do, then?"

"I...I'd like to rescue them from their sick way of thinking." She couldn't help crying. "Ellie, ever since I was your age, every day they tortured me. Isn't it horrible to be like that? To be so full of hate that all you want to do is to hurt someone? I feel sorry for them, always have."

"Shelly's mother is a nurse at The Haven nursing home where my mother lives," Alex said. All the old people call Ms. Gorton 'Sunshine,' because she makes them feel good. She's their favorite nurse, and all her colleagues enjoy working with her. Since the attack on Shelly, I've spent many hours in her company, watching over an unconscious girl, and I can see why she is so popular. Ms. Gorton, please tell us what this horrible event has done to you."

Mom passed her phone to Alex. Shelly had forgotten everything was on video.

"I have no family. Shelly is it. For the past fifteen years, I've lived for her, and she's been worth it. She is the gentlest, kindest, most decent person I know, and the smartest, too, and I feel honored to be her mother." Tears cascaded down her cheeks, but she kept a level tone of voice. "I didn't know she's been bullied for years. She never told me, but I saw her sliding into depression. Then she put on weight. We now know it's because sweet things helped her to fight the pain. The other night, I caught her writing a suicide note to me."

Mom stopped—had to stop. Mrs. Dorian pulled her close, and it was beautiful to see blonde and black hair mingle, brown cheek against white.

Mom again looked at Alex, well, at the camera. "If you-all simply treated her like another kid, she'd be a great friend to you too, like she is to every person and even animals. You know, before she got terribly depressed, she only had to hold out her hand to a wild bird, and it'd come to her?"

There was a knock on the door, and a young man entered. "Oh, sorry. I'm the physical therapist, here to give Miss Gorton her first session."

"Mom, it's okay for you to return to work.," Shelly said. "I'll study, and draw, and play chess and Sudoku on my computer."

She got a kiss from Mom, Mrs. Dorian and the two little kids, then they left.

The physical therapist's name tag stated he was Steve Billings. He moved her covers off from over her, and Shelly wanted to pull them back. She didn't want a nice guy to see Ms. Blimp, but he seemed not to notice. After a few minutes of instruction, she could swivel in the bed, lower her legs to the floor and pull them back, then he taught her to stand with a frame, and sit again. "That'll do for the first time. But your plaster has gotten loose. I'll report it."

Maybe she was losing...reducing weight?

Her lovely people returned on Sunday, but Shelly nodded off after an hour. When she awoke, she enjoyed seeing the vase holding a bunch of roses, hand-drawn cards from Ellie and Tim, and Jake sitting by her bedside. "Don't you have anything else to do?" she asked, but with a smile.

"Currently, getting you well is my most important project."

"Can you play chess?"

"Give me an hour and I'll learn. But don't you need a set?"

One of us can use my phone, the other the computer."

Jake disappeared. Shelly worked on her biology homework, then slept again. When she woke, they did play chess, only Jake was unbeatable. "That's the instruction from the krionter," he explained. Still, it was fun.

Never mind how smashed up her body was, Shelly was happy.

~ * ~

Shelly's phone tinged Monday morning: an email on her school email address. The sender was Michelle Hirsch. "Oh bloody leave me alone!" she shouted, then felt stupid, and lucky she had a private room. Was the abuse starting again? She didn't want to read the message. Couldn't they leave her alone even after a murder attempt? "Jake?" she called.

He stood by her bedside, smiling.

"Please read this message. If it's abuse, I don't want to know what it says."

"Fair enough." He leaned over, then said, "Wow! You've got to read it."

Thank heavens for Jake, and how he was always there when she needed him. Reassured, she read the message.

Hi Shelly,

> I am taking a risk, but I want to visit you to apologize and make friends.

Michelle,

> She thought, *Well, she never hit me even in elementary school. It's not like Gillian or Tony wanting to come.* So, she replied:

Michelle,

> I am delighted. Mr. Barlos will visit me after school to coach me for a math contest. Ask to come with him.

Shelly

That would also be protection, in case Michelle meant to cause trouble after all. Shelly still slept long periods—maybe because of the analgesic still dripping into her right arm? In between, she tried to study, but worry over Michelle got in the way.

Again, two nurses washed her, and again, she wished they couldn't see her body, then they replaced her leg plasters.

And, soon after what was lunchtime to people who were able to eat, a young man in jeans and a short-sleeved shirt entered. And great, his skin was the same color brown as hers.

"Hi Shelly, I'm Dr. Jim Holroyd, a psychologist working for Victims' Services."

She'd imagined psychologists as white-bearded old men, or wise old ladies with spectacles and wrinkles, not someone she wouldn't mind for a friend. To get a rise out of him, she answered, "Dr. Holroyd, you look too young to have a doctorate."

He laughed. "Good, healthy living. I've been told you've suffered bullying at school for ten of your fifteen years. Tell me about it."

Once she started, it kept pouring out. Dr. Holroyd quietly sat there, and Shelly felt safe. She told him all of it—except for Jake. She didn't want anyone to think her crazy.

When she finished, he gently asked, "How do you feel now?"

"Like...I stopped carrying a mountain. But...they still hate me for no reason, and if they're jailed, their lives will still be wrecked, and if they aren't, they'll still torture me."

"I'll be working with them, too, and their families. You're safe now."

She didn't think he'd make any difference with Gillian and Tony. The others, maybe.

"Shelly, I'll return Wednesday, same time. Now you've started on the path to inner strength, you'll get there."

Shelly again needed a sleep, then, after Dr. Holroyd's visit, had more energy, and worked on her history essay.

Later, Mom returned with a lady in police uniform, who gave her a friendly smile. "Shelly, I'm Detective Christine Jardin. I know you have post-concussion amnesia but need a statement from you regarding the bullying at school, because that little gang are our chief suspects."

"Oh, ma'am, I wish I could get out of that!"

She looked surprised. "You can report it. We'll keep you safe."

"No, ma'am, it's not myself I am worried about." How to put it? "Um...if they go to jail, they'll only come out worse criminals. Can something be done by the court to lead them out of hate instead?"

"My dear, the law does what it does. I'm a servant of the law, and we're all required to obey it. Never mind the outcome, your duty is to answer my questions honestly, to the best of your ability. Now, Ms. Gorton, I need your permission to record this interview."

~ * ~

Alex and Michelle walked in the door. He was smiling. Shrunk in on herself, she seemed even shorter than her little-girl height. She was looking down, and as usual, her brown hair masked much of her face.

Shelly thought, *She looks terrified,* so said, "Michelle, thank you for coming."

"Uh…you don't know, but I've always been a coward. Right back to being little kids, the safest thing was always to do what Gillian told me. You know we live next door to each other. She used to beat me up even before we started school, and if I told on her, it was worse. So, all these years, I had to join in their games against you. Sorry!"

"I was watching those six," Alex said. "Michelle was crying when I played the video."

Michelle shook her head. "Yeah, but later, during the break, Gillian said, excuse me sir, 'So what, shitface monkey mother crying over shitface monkey daughter,' and I had to pretend to laugh with them."

"Michelle, listen," Alex said. "Now you'll probably go to jail. One way out is to tell everything to the police."

She shivered. "Oh, sir, they'll kill me!"

"They'll be in jail, and chances are, the judge will let you off with a rap on the knuckles."

"Mr. Barlos, Shelly, you got no idea. Gil's father…if I stand up in court and send them to jail, he'll stop at nothing. Look, his house is full of guns. He has them as decorations on the walls of his living room. All legal, but scary as hell. And Shelly, that's where the bullying comes from. I've often heard him say, excuse me, sir, shitface monkeys should be got rid of, shouldn't have the right to live near people."

"So, to him I'm not even human?"

"That's it."

Shelly felt the tears come. "What a bastard! Oh, excuse me, Mr. Barlos. But you know what, I feel sorry for Gillian. She is the horrible way she is because that's normal to her, from home. It's, I don't know, a rotten father spreading his rot into his child."

~ * ~

Tuesday morning, Shelly's phone rang. It was Mom, sounding

terribly upset. "Darling, remember that psychologist you told me about yesterday evening?"

"Dr. Jim Holroyd? I really like him."

"Somebody called Craig Treloar murdered him!"

Oh no. That nice young man! "That's Gillian's father."

"Detective Jardin was talking with me at work. She needed me to sign the transcript of your interview. Her phone rang, and I heard her side of the conversation before she rushed off. That's how I know."

After the call, Shelly cried. A young man, perhaps with a young family…he may have endured all sorts of hardship to study so he could help people…snuffed out by an ignorant, toxic monster. For a moment, she felt like Ellie: if Mr. Treloar were in front of her, and she had a gun, she'd shoot him. Except, she knew she wouldn't. *Stupid, misguided, destructive*, she thought, *he may be a cockroach, but I can't even kill real cockroaches.*

She hadn't prayed for years, thanks to the bullying—God had permitted it, hadn't He? Now, she tried to pray for Mr. Treloar and the five kids. Michelle, she thought, needed support, but not prayer.

Only, no words came to her. Aloud she said, "If I could, I'd forgive you all. I can't, I just can't, but I do wish you'd climb out of your horrid pit and become humans. You look down on me and Mom and Dr. Holroyd because of skin color, but you're the ones who have thrown away God's grace."

She fully expected Jake to appear, and here he was. "Well done," he said. Then they sat in companionable silence until a nurse came in to replace Shelly's near-empty food and analgesic bags.

"Do you think you can draw me?" Jake asked after the nurse left.

In a half-hour, she had an excellent likeness of his smiling face, lighter than hers but still brown, with wavy dark hair.

He took a small object from his pocket and pointed it at the drawing. "Thanks, I'll treasure this." Then he was gone.

Shelly started on integral calculus, and soon got lost in Alex's tricky problems.

He arrived shortly after 3:30 p.m. and inspected her work. They were still at it when Mom arrived, wearing her uniform. Shelly glowed inside seeing them smile at each other. She decided, the many hours they'd spent together in her ward was the silver lining on her cloud.

To spoil their mood, Mom carried a copy of the local newspaper. The headline was "Murder!" above Dr. Holroyd's photo. The report stated, Mrs. Hirsch (Michelle's mom), saw him drive up and enter the Treloar house. She heard Mr. Treloar shouting obscenities, then multiple gunshots, so she called the police. When they arrived, Mr. Treloar shot at them through a window, but police managed entry, and he suffered multiple gunshot wounds. He was in the hospital under guard.

The paper reported that Dr. Holroyd had two children, aged four and eighteen months.

Shelly couldn't help crying. Mom joined her. Alex hugged Mom and stroked Shelly's hand.

"Alex, Mom, I wonder if I can get into a wheelchair and visit him, Shelly said. "After being shot and arrested, he may be open to seeing the world differently?"

"Not a chance," Alex answered. "There'll be armed officers guarding him, keeping out everyone except authorized medical personnel."

"Mom, please ask Detective Jardin. At the worst, the answer is no."

Mom explained the situation on the phone, listened, then thanked the detective. "The Captain himself is here, and Detective Jardin said he is coming to speak to us!"

Soon there was a knock on the door, and a fit-looking middle-aged man in a suit entered. "Good afternoon, I am Captain Gray." The name suited him: he had wiry gray hair, and gray eyes. He looked at Shelly. "Young lady, I've heard remarkable things about you. And, I've also got good news. We've searched the homes of all six of the bullies. Antonio Florino's baseball bat has traces of blood despite having been washed. We're sending a sample for DNA analysis, and I'll take the opportunity now to request a sample from you. He is singing like a canary. Of course, it's not his fault. Each of the six blames the others."

"Sir, I'm convinced Michelle Hirsch didn't take part in the assault on me, although she was there because she was scared of Gillian Treloar."

"I understand you have no recall of the event. What makes you say so?"

"Sir," Alex said. "Michelle came with me from school yesterday to apologize to Shelly, and I agree with Shelly's assessment. Oh, I'm their math and science teacher, Alex Barlos."

"She is still an accessory to attempted murder. But Shelly, why do you want to talk to this criminal?"

"Sir, he suffers from a very common illness, that of hate. Maybe if he comes to see me as a person, not an animal because my skin is brown, he may change. And if he does, Gillian will, too, and the others may follow her."

"Well, it can't do any harm. During the arrest, he was shot in both arms and one knee, so he is in no position to do worse than swear at you."

Mom pushed the bell. While waiting, Shelly thought about putting her body on public view. "Er, Captain, Mr. Barlos, when I am transferring, can you please wait outside? And I'd like myself covered with a sheet or something while in the chair."

When two nurses helped Shelly to transfer to the wheelchair, Mom said, "Hey, you've lost heaps of weight!"

"Reduced, Mom." It was to be expected, with no food, but only some yellow muck dripping into her intestine.

Alex pushed the chair, Mom a pole with the liquid bags on it, Jake walking on Shelly's other side. Soon, they were outside a door with two armed policemen guarding it.

Shelly swallowed. It no longer seemed such a good idea.

"You can do it," Jake said as a guard opened the door.

Mr. Treloar sat in an armchair, plastered left leg on a footstool. Both bandaged arms were in slings. A third policeman sat on a chair near the door.

When they entered, he didn't look anything out of the ordinary, just a man with short-cropped blond hair, but then he saw Shelly and Mom. His face transformed into something horrible. "Fuck'n shitface monkeys!" he roared. "Get outa here!"

"Treloar, shut up," Captain Gray ordered. "Now listen. You're in here for murder. You—"

"Nah! Pest extermination!"

"Mr. Treloar," Shelly said, hating the tremble in her voice, "what makes you think I am not human, just like you are?"

"Uppity little bitch, aren't you?"

"Sir, I study biology. A sixteenth of an inch under the skin, we're the same."

"Get outa here and stop stinking up the room!"

"Mr. Treloar, do you consider yourself to be superior to colored people?" Mr. Barlos asked.

"They are not people. But yeah."

"This girl is fifteen years old. I challenge you to outdo her in any mental activity. She runs rings around students three years ahead of her in every school subject. I'm helping her to prepare for a very high-level math competition, in which she could win a lot of money."

"So?"

"So, who is superior, who inferior?"

The man tried to stand, but his movement pushed the footstool away, and he landed on his bum, the leg still up. His roar of rage filled the room.

Captain Gray and the policeman grabbed him under the arms and hoisted him back onto the chair, even as the door opened, and the two guards rushed in, guns in hand.

Shelly started breathing again. "Sir, I am not superior to you. But also, the same the other way. You're not superior to me. I happen to have been blessed by God with good intelligence, and so what. But—"

"Oh, shut up!"

Shelly found her hands forming fists, and she could feel her pulse in her temples. "Why? Are you afraid to hear me out?"

"Afraid? AFRAID? I'm not afraid of anything."

"No? Only of people who are slightly different from you. Look, suppose I am an animal. A bird just flew past the window. That's an animal. Do you want to exterminate birds?"

"They don't pretend to be people."

"Why is it a problem that I pretend to be a person?"

"Because you don't know your place, daring to argue with me!"

"Why is it my place to not argue with you?"

"Huh?" The man glared at her but couldn't come up an answer.

"You see, sir, this is your fear. I'm challenging the position of privilege you imagine yourself to be in. How are you worse off if I am as good as you?"

"Shelly," Captain Gray said. "he is a lost cause. Not enough brains to follow a logical argument."

She shook her head. "Captain, I don't think Mr. Treloar is

stupid, just prejudiced. And I think he follows my reasoning all right. Mr. Treloar, Mr. Barlos has white skin. He is a teacher, with knowledge and authority you don't have. Nevertheless, he is no threat to you. You're a mechanic. You have knowledge and authority he doesn't, but you're no threat to him. Would it be any different if his skin was brown or black or purple?"

"Look, why are you here, pestering me?"

"Hate is an illness. I want to help you get cured. That poor young man you killed because his skin was brown had a lot of training, a lot of wisdom. He wanted to help you improve your life. Instead, now you'll spend, I don't know, maybe twenty years in jail. And because you've spewed your hate during all of Gillian's life, she's going to jail, too. Is that what you wanted for your daughter?"

Silence filled the room. A tear rolled down Mr. Treloar's face.

"I don't hate Gillian, or you. I'll pray for you both, and the others, too. Now, I'll leave you, and I hope you think about things." As Alex turned her wheelchair, she couldn't help the thought, *It does feel good to take you down a peg or three, you bastard!*

~ * ~

The weeks passed. Mom changed her shifts so she could look after Ellie and Tim while Mrs. Dorian worked at the nursing home. As Shelly's stomach healed from the knife wound, she gradually started eating, and the various tubes were removed. Now the major challenge was to regain her strength. Eventually, she went home, and returned to school, where kids vied to be her friends.

Looking in the mirror, having other people see her body, was no longer painful, and as she said to Jake, she was determined to stay slim for the rest of her life.

"Yeah, slim and beautiful. If you weren't my granny and I wasn't a projection, I'd ask you for a date."

"So, will you keep visiting me, now that my life has improved?"

"That's up to you. Remember when you said, a visit from the future is bullshit?"

"Yeah."

"You were right. It is bullshit. I don't exist. You invented me as a way out of your deep hole. You always had it in you to slim down, and be brilliant in math, and thrive."

Now what the crap! "You mean, I've gone schizophrenic,

hallucinating?"

Jake laughed. "Haven't you had enough of labels? It worked, didn't it?"

~ * ~ * ~

Bob Rich is an Australian storyteller, with 19 published books in a variety of genres including both fiction and nonfiction. Five of his books, and over 40 short stories, have won awards. He has retired 5 times so far, from 5 different occupations, but is still going strong as a Professional Grandfather. Any human born since 1993 qualifies as his grandchild; anyone born after 1987 as his child. Everything he does, including his writing, is working toward a survivable future for them, and one worth surviving in. This means environmental and humanitarian activism: an attempt to change a worldwide culture of greed, hate and fear into one of compassion and cooperation. He carries on much of this work at his popular blog: Bobbing Around, https://bobrich18.wordpress.com.

He has been writing since 1980, with a byline column in "Earth Garden" magazine and several other periodicals. His first book, "The Earth Garden Building Book: Design and build your own house," was published in 1986, and went through 4 editions, the last going out of print in 2018. He has had four other self-help books published, the latest being "From Depression to Contentment: A self-therapy guide." A biography, "Aniko: The stranger who loved me" has won 4 awards. Two of his three novels are science fiction, with "Ascending Spiral" having gone through 4 print runs.

SECOND WIND

Tammy Higgins

I blinked fast after the vision came, swallowing the burning, bitter, bile nugget in my throat. I faltered stumbling into a parked copper colored PT Cruiser, regained my balance then stood frozen looking at the dark low hanging clouds.

I couldn't have stopped it anyway, I thought. The strength of *this* vision had floored me with its intensity. Instead of the storefronts looming before me at the bottom of the hill and gas guzzlers lined up in single file on my right, I'd been suddenly assaulted by a brilliant, blinding, bright flash of light.

I saw warriors with M-16s hurt and mangled. The devastation of homes and villages ripped apart and smoldering from bombs. And, to my disbelief, heard the earth thudding explosions and shattering glass of windows. The wailing of mothers crumbling to their knees in the streets and the frightened confused cries of children with their innocence and desire to play, lost forever, blurred my vision.

I walked dazed, loping down the black topped and concrete hill to the townhouse exhaling hard a white plume of air. It began to snow, landing in big wet splats coating my long dark hair and navy-blue wool coat.

I passed a *Bring Jimmy Back* sign shoved into the ground as I rounded the corner. 'Jimmy' was a nationally known cardboard artist named James Grashow from Connecticut who creates art from cardboard. The guy was a genius who could make small and delicate pieces to huge installations to fit a room. Our local arts center was trying to bring him back in residence at the gallery. Another vision came and went as I chucked up the five steps in front of the townhouse. A vision again this time of cold, tired and lonesome men out on patrol and screams of pain and deep voices, deep moans and deep sobs.

"Hey peace freaks," someone shouted. I snapped back to reality as eggs were flung from a passing red Mitsubishi, full of local teen-age boys, landing, CRACK, broken, on the sidewalk and on the steps in front of me. I heard gasps of surprise and annoyance among the gathered crowd. The car jetted off with the sounds of the *Beastie Boys* song 'You gotta fight, for your right, to Party!' blasting from the car sound system. This is what our troops fight for too, I guess. The freedom of speech.

I stood outside the double doors with the others who had come today. I glanced around surprised at the number of people gathering at noon on a Saturday. Must be about seventy or so I guessed.

"Hello everyone. Does anyone here have something they'd like to share? Some good news maybe?" I asked, scanning the faces with my best hostess smile. I stood waiting in the winter chill as the snow began to fall faster. I lit the hurricane lamp I held in my left hand, gazed at the flame and began to relax as my breath slowed and deepened. I turned to my right handing the lamp to a red bearded man standing next to me. The lamp went from him to another, each alighting their wick eventually coming back to my possession with a gentle touch on my forearm from a lanky teenage boy towering over me.

I don't want to be an advocate but well, here I am. It's what I and some others have become. But that's not it either. More like patriotic and human I suppose without all the bells and whistles. A voice pulled me out of my thoughts.

"Well, yes I do have something to say," a woman said. I took in a stern matronly looking woman in a forest green hooded parka, who was standing to the left up in front. "First off, I'd like to say…I hope they bring Jimmy back," she said. Everyone laughed. Echoes of *yeah* and *Kickstarter* rippled through the crowd mixed with whistles and claps. She held up a hand then once again turned serious.

"I think the whole thing is wrong," she said. The herd gasped and sputtered. "But I respect our troops for doing what they do," she said to lukewarm scattered applause. "I also believe, everyone's here to show their support, hopes and prayers." She paused to cough and clear her throat. "I read somewhere, one person can make a difference and if enough like-minded gather together they can, through their collective energy, send out healing positive emotions and thoughts to where it's needed. So, I'd like to thank all of you for coming today. God bless you." She waved her arm in a casual sweeping gesture that included everyone, as she looked around at the gathered crowd. More applause. She lifted the homemade sign she carried higher in the air. *Bring them home.*

"Ahem." This was a blonde, pony-tailed woman in her mid-forties, wearing a green and yellow checkered flannel shirt and dark hued goose down vest standing in the back. We all turned towards her.

"Hi. I just wanted to say, my son Ryan is on his second tour. He's a supply clerk near the front line and when he gets the time to *write*." Her voice cracked, and she paused a moment to gather herself before continuing. "He says he's fine, a little homesick and he and his unit are doing well and are busy helping the displaced refugees start over and giving the kids toys and candy and...I miss him so much," she said. A single tear rolled down her cheek. Hands reached out to give her pats and squeezes.

"Well, hi everyone. My name is Gordy and I'm a veteran of two wars. I'm a widower now and have no children but I'm a proud American patriot full of the Ole' red, white and blue, for my country and our troops," he said. He was an older silver haired thin but average man. He clutched a flag tightly in his gloved right hand while his crippled left hand, hung by his side. The applause erupted once again with cheers and mumbled thank yous. I mumbled my thanks to him and turned to the next voice.

"Every bud-dee! Hey! My mommy's in the army and she's a captain and she's..." he said. I peered over to the side, taking in a little boy in a wool cap and a camouflage jacket with U.S. Army sewn on the front left pocket. All of five years, I supposed. He noticed the attention from the big people was now all on him and became shy again. "She's a nurse and I...I don't know when she'll be back," he said toeing the ground with his hiker boots. "And my name is Caleb," he whispered. He held a toy tank in his camouflage gloved hands and fell silent once again as he looked away. I knew without looking, some of us swallowed hard, trying to choke back sobs and not break down in front of our little trooper. A few hands reached out to tousle his hair or squeeze his shoulder for a few beats. I swallowed hard and downed an hors d' oeuvre of emotional sawdust.

"You people make me *sick*," a deep voice said from the back. We all turned to see who it was. He slammed his wooden handmade sign reading *Seek truth* down on the steps. He had a military style black crew cut, unkempt whiskers, in his mid-forties, about 5'8", with a beer gut, wearing a navy pea coat and faded jeans. His eyes burned red, either from allergies, a cold, drinking or a combination of the three.

"You're a bunch of pansy cowardly ostriches," he shouted. "You come here spouting peace in this little here social gathering. You're patriots?" He looked hard at a few of us, giving us the once over, then sneered and barked. "You're in denial, you *ass*holes! You come here Saturdays with your KOOM-BY-A Gandhi bullshit but you aren't getting to the root of the problem." He glared again. "None of the damn one of ya," he spat. "As Thomas Jefferson said, 'Question *Everything*! Don't believe all you hear or are told. Find the truth. Seek justice'."

Ahh, a nut job. Great, I thought, *just what we need*. A woman in front started to speak but he unplugged her before she'd even pushed play.

"Shut it miss. Not your turn," Peacoat said. He paused to pull a pack of Pall Malls from his jacket pocket and lit one. He looked around at us again. "I want to ask you something." Think about this for a second," he said exhaling. He bent his head from side to side to loosen the kinks then inhaled his cigarette again, exhaled then spoke. "What if...and I'm talking fifty-fifty here. What if, our government did instigate nine-eleven?" A few groans went up. He silenced them by raising his voice as he continued. "No, that can't be." His reflected shock, but only in mocking. "There ain't no conspiracy going on, you all whine. Well, what if they DID? Standing here as a peace pacifist is all nice and safe, but you wouldn't be here if someone hadn't fought for your freedom, to be daisies and girl scouts. I know this because I'm an ex-marine who flew in combat missions, for your Nancy asses. You can thank me later."

Now people murmured asshole and jarhead. Too *much* combat buddy, someone whispered. Pea coat ignored them.

"What if they did start this war? What if it was an inside job? You my friends, are not doing any justice to those innocently killed, maybe by our own government's bloody hands, by remaining neutral," he said, in a calmer, steadier, yet pleading tone. He looked at a few of us, then at the ground then up at the snowy sky and lit another cigarette.

"Folks, do you really *trust* our government? Thing is, there's a thin line between believing *in* something and in dumb shit, we've been told existed. Everyone is always at odds whether there is a

God or not. Whether the Easter Bunny, Santa Claus and the Tooth Fairy exist cause it's what we've been told. The government's different. We get the right to vote. We hire these sons-of-bitches to look after us and our country. We trust them." He let that sink in. "But what if you just can't? What if there's a possible truth…that we've been lied to and people have died for the wrong reasons? Reasons other than what we were told," he said. He pulled gloves out of his pockets, slipped them on, then moved to pick up the sign he'd thrown, standing it up at his side, fingertips steadying it.

"Think! Think on these bank bail outs, these oil and gas wars we keep having. Think on those poor New Hampshire folks, The Browns, getting arrested for not paying their taxes when boss man's been stealing ours? Something isn't right here, my fellow Americans. All I'm saying, is check er' out for ourselves. Investigate. Then do what's rare these days. Do the *right* thing." He pounded his hand into his fist for emphasis. The wind blew rattling the stop sign across the street as snow fell harder.

"That's *bullshit*! You shut your mouth." A long-haired blond man, wearing a blaze orange hunting jacket, probably in his early thirties moved fast, lunging at pea coat in the back but was blocked.

"The nine-eleven conspiracy theory is bs We were attacked by friggin' terrorists. Freaking sand jockey towel heads," he yelled spraying spittle. They faced each other, nose to nose, eyes hard and glaring fists clenched at orange blazed side.

"You sure about that, Elmer Fudd? Better check that video footage of the Twin Towers again and rethink your position. Oh, right. Our government wouldn't do something like that. We're only losing jobs left and right, being taxed to death, spending our money and buying us debt and spying on us. Wake up dude. Get enlightened," said Pea Coat, as he tapped the side of his head with an index finger.

"You son of a…." Blaze orange drew his arm back to swing.

Eeeeeeeeeeeppppp! I jumped, startled by the fire stations fire whistle shrieking loudly at that instant.

"Police! Stop what you're doing and step back. *Now!*" a voice said through a bullhorn. Two local cops in uniform pushed their way through the crowd pulling blaze orange and dragging pea coat away from each other and away out of sight.

Cars squashed their way through the snow as they drove by.

Confusion and mixed feelings took over. Some people glanced at each other nervously and then looked quickly away. Others shoved hands deep into their pockets while others stared at the ground or off into space. I stood, playing with my car keys, watching the falling snow begin to cover my shoes.

I thought of my own family. My oldest brother Luke had been killed by a roadside bomb three years ago, leaving behind a family of four. My baby sister Maria who had just turned twenty-one in June had been blinded instantly from the powerful explosions and flying debris that rocked the infirmary where she worked. She was discharged after a brief hospital stay then committed suicide shortly after returning to the states. My heart felt heavy and ached within for the past my siblings and I had shared and the future memories now stolen.

The lanterns flame wavered and flickered in a sudden gust of wind as I stood lost in my thoughts. The song 'Winds of Change' by the Scorpions came to mind. I wondered if these candlelight vigils did any good. Sometimes while I was out and about here in town, I could see the same question in people's eyes and faces. I overheard it in conversations in the next aisle over, at the pharmacy. Or while waiting in line at the grocery store.

But they kept coming back here each week to gather peacefully with their beacons of light and I guess it was a good thing to at least be doing something. Maybe it was for the soldiers and perhaps even the enemy's protection and safety and done out of simple love and goodwill. Maybe it was out of sadness by some for all the tears, loneliness, thirst and hunger pangs both sides suffered from. Perhaps just realistic and weary acceptance of all the hurting, pain, killing and dying of so many brothers and sisters in the name of God and illusionary beliefs we inflict on each other. This overwhelms me deeply and I feel helpless suddenly. I think on what pea coat said. Am I scared of it being true and should I unite with others to do something or is he just a nut job?

But I rise back to the surface trying to make peace with my inner demons. I'm touched by the power and goodness of a handful of people who in this fast-paced electronic age want to connect with other birds of a feather, for a few nano seconds of an hour and pause time, to become one. Here and there. Everywhere. For whatever the reasons wars are started...to just bring it to an end. I wonder deep inside, if there will ever be total peace, in this thing we're born into, called life.

I blow out the flame in the lantern as the moment is over. We begin to disperse and scatter waving our good-byes and as we drift away the sun suddenly breaks through the dark clouds and falling snow.

"Jimmy's coming back. They're raised the ten thousand dollars they needed to bring him back to the Arts Center and get involved with the 'Children's' Giant Puppet Parade' next Spring," a group of women talking on the sidewalk across the street said. Cheers went up.

My name is Indie and you can even call me Liberty, but my name doesn't really matter because now I understand and this is my vision. That sometimes, all we're left with, when there's nothing else we can do while we wait, when there are no right answers blowing in the wind, is to keep putting one foot in front of the other and *light that candle*. There is hope here and a second wind.

~ * ~ * ~

Tammy Higgins has been published in *Amulet, Atlantic Pacific Press, Conceit, Iconoclast, The International Library of Poetry, Noble House, Out in the Mountains, Ultimate Writer, Samhain Secrets of Irish Horse Anthologies* and won a contest sponsored by *The Oak* magazine among others.

Tammy is 54 has MS and was born in Northern NY in the Adirondacks. She is currently living in southern New Hampshire.

STANDING FOR THE FLAG

B. Craig Grafton

The old hippie sat in his seat at the stadium waiting for the game to begin. He wore a tie dye T-shirt of many colors, camouflage shorts, no socks and sandals. His long grey hair, what was left of it, was tied back in a ponytail and he wore a red bandana around his head.

Down the aisle came an attractive young female reporter, Paula Periodista, on her first assignment. All excited was she, her hair and makeup perfect, her clothes the latest fashion.

Behind her came veteran middle-aged cameraman Glenn. His hair tousled, shirttail out, belly over his belt buckle. He was nondescript, a generic looking type of guy.

"We'll start interviewing people as soon as the anthem is over," Paula said to Glenn. They were there to find out what people had to say about African-American athletes who don't stand for the national anthem.

A young Hispanic boy in a charro suit sang the national anthem and sang it beautifully.

The old hippie never rose. He remained rooted to his seat.

Paula spotted him. *What a colorful looking character. He should make for an interesting interview.*

The anthem ended to the cheers of the crowd and Paula approached the old hippie.

"Sir, would you mind being interviewed?" she asked, sticking her microphone in his face.

"I'd be honored," he answered politely.

Paula signaled for Glenn to start filming.

"Your name sir?"

"Mr. Unaverage American Citizen" he responded in all seriousness.

Mr. Unaverage American Citizen, she repeated to herself. *This is great. What a hoot this will be. My boss will be impressed with this interview.* Her enthusiasm was bubbling over.

"Mr. Unaverage Citizen sir why did you not stand when the anthem was being sung? Were you joining with the African-American ballplayers in calling attention to racial injustice and inequality in this country?"

"No, I'm not joining with them."

"Then what sir?"

"I'm calling attention to all this flag waving, national anthem singing nonsense that goes on at a ball game. That's what I'm calling attention to. There's no reason for it."

Well that's different, Paula thought, *a new angle. Maybe I'm onto something here. I should keep this going. See where it leads.*

So she asked, "Just what do you mean by that sir?"

"I mean that I'm protesting against all this flag hoopla whoop tee do that's been going on forever. I've been against it ever since grade school and been against the military industrial complex that exploits it all my entire life. That's what I mean by that," he said defiantly.

"Really? All your life?" Paula asked without thinking, forgetting to stay focused on the black athlete issue.

The old hippie's eyes lit up. His loquacious button had just been pushed. "Yes really. All my entire life. I started back in grade school, at the height of the cold war itself, when I refused to stand and repeat that mantra they call the pledge of allegiance. Saying a pledge of allegiance that's something you'd expect in the Soviet Union, Red China, North Korea. We shouldn't be doing that in America. We shouldn't be indoctrinating the minds of innocent school children with stuff like that. Kids should go to school to learn not to be politically brainwashed or be taught how to be politically correct as they're teaching them today. That was what was wrong with this country then and that's what's wrong with this country now, too much political bull." The old hippie was proud of his oration. He held his head up high, chin firmly jutting out as he spoke.

"They want everybody to stand and show respect for the flag. Stand and sing patriotic songs, at a ballpark of all places. For God's sake you're at a sporting event, a ballgame, not a political rally. If you want to go to a political rally, go to the Fourth of July parade, a veteran's day parade, a Labor Day parade. Don't force patriotism on a captive audience at a ballpark."

You know this guy's got a point, Paula reflected. *I'm onto something here. I need to milk it now for all it's worth.*

"Are you suggesting, then sir, that they do away with singing the national anthem?"

"You bet I am. All that singing the national anthem nonsense started during World War II. I looked that up on the internet. It was meant as a morale booster during the war. Now after nine-eleven they've started singing God Bless America at baseball games for the same reason. It's all part of the military industrial complex's plan to control America. If you have to sing at a ball game, then sing the team's fight song. They all got one. Sing it instead of the anthem. A ball game is supposed to be a place to have fun, not a place to sing about your damn country."

This guy really does have a point, Paula repeated to herself. *I never thought of it that way before. I never knew how the tradition of singing the anthem came about. This is fascinating. I learned something here today. This funny looking old guy is actually making sense. Who'd have thunk it.*

But she knew she had to stay focused and tie this into the ball player issue somehow because that's what her boss had instructed her to do. So, she redirected the conversation.

"That's all interesting and informative sir but what about the players' protests recently? Aren't their protests really just like yours?"

The old hippie couldn't help but smile. "Like mine? You have got to be kidding me young lady? Am I going around taking selfies with fans, getting on tv, tweeting on the internet? These big tough guy football wusses don't know how to protest. They ever take over the dean's office, shut down a university, stand across the commons and look down the rifle barrels of the National Guard. Hell, we stopped a war, brought down a president. What have all their selfies accomplished? Nothing I tell you but their own self-gratification." The old hippie paused and looked off into space reflecting into his own world of the past. "We put our lives on the line back then. These guys don't even put their money where their mouths are; and they all make millions."

Just then another old man walked up holding a couple of beers. "Excuse me Miss, may I get through to my brother please," he said to Paula while nodding toward the old hippie.

Paula and Glenn made way and let him by.

He started to hand his brother a beer but stopped.

"Hold onto it for me will ya Brother. I gotta go take a leak." The old hippie rose from his chair, excused himself, and left.

"I hope he wasn't bothering you, Miss," the brother said to

Paula. "He gets kind of wound up sometimes, imagines he's somebody else and runs off at the mouth. I'm my brother's keeper so to speak, so if he said anything offensive, I apologize for him."

"No, he was fine," she answered. But now this threw a different light on things. Paula now questioned the old hippie's veracity so she asked, as politely as she could, "Is he okay, uh, well you know, mentally that is?"

"No, not really. My brother's never been quite right since he got back from Vietnam. Took some shrapnel and a lot of drugs over there. Been in and out of the VA hospital ever since. They let me bring him to the ball game today. Thought it might do him some good. So, if he misbehaved in any way please let me know so I can tell his doctor. My brother pretends he's somebody else sometimes. Runs his mouth. Lives in his own made up world."

Paula's news story was rapidly disintegrating.

"Was he a college protester back in the day? He led us to believe he was," Paula asked hoping against hope her interview didn't totally implode.

"No, he was drafted and sent to Vietnam back then."

Just then the old hippie returned and stared at Paula nonplussed. His mind could not connect the dots. "You're gonna introduce me to your friends here Brother."

"That's okay we're just leaving." Paula tugged Glenn's sleeve and drug him away and down the aisle.

"Sorry Glenn," Paula said. "It's my fault. I just thought he would make for an interesting interview about singing the anthem."

"He did make for an interesting interview."

"Yah but we can't use it now."

"Who says we can't. Look kid, I've been doing this for years. We just edit it the way we want it and go with it. Do it all the time."

And they did. And her boss told her, "Job well done."

~ * ~ * ~

B. Craig Grafton's latest book *Willard Wigleaf: West Texas Attorney* is a legal fiction humorous western thriller about the diversity of and social issues of the American West in the 1880s. His next book, released in September 2021, is *Jill Driver: Trail Boss*. It is the story of a female trail drive boss and her crew of many ethnicities on a trail drive from Texas to Missouri. Both are available on Amazon.

SUSPICIOUS WORDS

Duane L. Herrmann

"Do you think anyone will notice?" Terrance grinned as he asked his wife who had come outside their house to see what he was setting up in the front yard.

"How can they NOT notice?" Sharon exclaimed, astonished. "They're Christmas lights—in April!"

"No." Terrance emphatically replied. "They are *not* 'Christmas Lights.' Colored class and electricity have no religious beliefs. They are religiously neutral. These are *Electrical Decorations*."

"Well, all the neighbors will think they're Christmas lights."

"Let them," Terrance replied. "Or they can ask. They decorate for their holy days, I want to decorate for our holy days, or at least *these* holy days."

"They won't understand…"

"I've told them decorations will be coming, I just didn't say when." Terrance smiled in satisfaction. He was demonstrating some seasonal diversity to his block.

"I understand that, but…" muttering to herself, shaking her head, Sharon went inside the house.

Terrance continued setting up his decorations. He had worked on them over the winter and was ready this year. He was excited. At Christmas time this block looked like one huge neon sign. The decorations went up Thanksgiving weekend and stayed up, and on, until after the new year. All except for his house. This upset several neighbors; they felt his dark house kept their street from winning the city's annual Christmas decoration contest. Terrance had noted that on some prize-winning streets not every house was decorated, but some people don't want facts to confuse their minds. He sighed as he got out and set up the letters. He'd cut them out of plywood, painted them bright, cheerful colors and attached electrical decorations around the edges. Each letter was two feet tall. He was proud of them. They had taken a lot of work—and a lot of space in the garage! Now he could get them out, set them up, and see what they would really look like when they were in position.

When he had them assembled on the front lawn, each one

anchored in place, and all in the right order, he stepped back to the street to survey the results: perfect!

Here were words that proclaimed the diversity of his city. There were more than just Christians, Jews and Muslims in this town. There were also Buddhists, Hindus and Wiccans. Here was proof of even more than that. It was time for the religious diversity to come out of the shadows. If Christians could proclaim their faith spectacularly every year, why not anyone else, everyone else? Terrance would be part of that.

His house would not be as decorated as most others were at Christmas, but it would stand out, especially now. The weather was warming, more people were taking walks outside in the evenings, they would see. The letters would be impossible to miss! It was the most joyous holy festival of the year. He wanted to share his joy in these days, just as they shared their joy for Christmas.

The holy days would begin in just a few minutes when the sun set. He was ready to turn the lights on. Terrance had connected the cords so he could flip one switch in the house and all the lights would go on outside at the same time. One part of this project had been to install a new, quadruple, weatherproof outlet outside, connected to a switch inside. It made turning the lights on and off much easier.

Terrance watched the sun set behind the trees and when it was gone, the new day, the first of the twelve holy days, had begun. The Most Great Festival had started! He flipped the switch. The house came to life! Amidst the small utilitarian lights of the other houses, his blazed forth!

He left the lights on that evening until they went to bed, then turned them off. Most of the neighbors left their "Christmas Lights" on all night, which made sleeping difficult. He didn't want his decorations to do that. He wanted to share his joy, he didn't want to annoy.

He planned to have the lights on only during the evenings of this twelve-day festival. There was no point having them on past the holy days. These days commemorated, and celebrated, the declaration by Bahá'u'lláh of His mission in the Garden of Riḍván. The Persian government had found Him innocent of all but His beliefs, so He was not executed. Indeed, His family was part of the aristocracy, royal blood flowed in His veins. It would take a greater crime than heresy to find a reason to execute Him. Instead, He had been stripped of His wealth and properties, and exiled from His home country forever. His family was impoverished, and they were all, technically, prisoners, even the children. That had been ten years before the first exile, the one out of Persia. He was being exiled further from the Persian border because His followers would walk for days to Baghdad to see Him. Many would bring letters for Him from others. His answers guided their lives. Now that trek would be longer and more dangerous. It was hoped the further exile would stop them altogether. It didn't.

It was the announcement of His mission of fulfilling past religious prophecies and bringing a new revelation to mankind that was celebrated in these twelve days. Those twelve days He and some companions had spent in the garden. Visitors came there instead of crowding the house while the packing was going on. Roses had been blooming then in that garden, but it was not yet the season for Roses to bloom where Terrance lived. They would come in summer. The lights would make up for their absence.

Terrance did not notice various neighbors peeking through their windows, most just shook their heads. They knew the Harrisons were "different," but *this* different?

Some had accepted the Harrison's invitations to participate in the small devotional gatherings they held once a month. At first it had seemed odd to go to someone's house to pray, but the Harrisons were welcoming hosts and people could pray as they wished. There was no agenda, hidden or overt. It was a time to come together and simply pray. There was no harm in that. The world certainly needed prayers. And, with no sermons, no doctrine, the gatherings were refreshing and comforting. The Harrisons had shared their own prayers, and many found them beautiful and com-forting. They had grown closer through praying together.

"Harrisons must have something going on," Sam said to his wife as he looked across the street at the Harrison's house. "Must be some special occasion. I don't know what. They do have differ-ent holy days. Maybe that's the reason."

"Come to bed," Barbara urged. "They can do what they want. They're not bothering anyone. They're nice people. Sharon did say some special time was coming up. I'll ask her tomorrow."

For nine evenings the lights came on and neighbors began to get used to them. On the ninth night, well after the lights were out and everyone was soundly asleep, a dark van pulled up in front of the Harrisons' house. Several figures got out and walked about the yard inspecting the decorations. After several minutes they left.

"We got them Islams," the leader of the group said under his breath as he got back into the van and began to shut the door. "Now get us out of here," he ordered the driver who had already started the engine.

But what if they're not? The driver wondered to himself as he drove away. They were friends at work, but now was not feeling good about this turn in the relationship. How to get out of it and not make an enemy of the other man? He drove away pondering his options. Did he have any?

The next morning Terrance was leaving for work when he glanced at the decorations and noticed a power cord down from the roof slightly swaying. As he approached the cord, he could see it had been cut. He also noticed words had been spray painted on the front of his house: "GO HOME ISLAMS!!!"

"Well," Terrance said to no one in particular. "Considering my Native American ancestry—I AM home. This is MY continent! Everyone else is an invader! They're the ones who should go home! And, I'm not Muslim. I never have been. Why would they think that? They are so ignorant. My parents and grandparents were Episcopalians before they left the church."

As he walked closer, Terrance noticed all the cords connecting the lights, had been cut. The electrical decorations had been destroyed. He would have to replace them all. New ones would be on sale in the fall, just before Christmas. He could get more, that was no problem. That would be easier than cleaning the paint from the bricks on the front of his house. He'd never cleaned paint off brick before. It didn't look like it would be an easy job. The spray paint on the letters could be painted over.

And, he would need to notify the police. It was obvious he would be late to work today. This was a hate crime and that couldn't wait.

"Barbara, come look!" Sam called as he looked out the window across the street at Terrance surveying the damage. "Someone thinks the Harrisons are Muslims and attacked their house."

"NO!" Barbara exclaimed. "They're Bahá'ís, not Muslims. Bahá'ís get enough of that in Iran, not here!"

"At least the letters are intact," Sam observed. "The spray paint doesn't look nice, but the letters can be repainted easier than the bricks of the house can be cleaned. I'm going over to help. The police will have to look at it first, though."

"I'll call others on the block," Barbara replied. "Everyone should want to help. No one has ever destroyed anyone's Christmas decorations here. The Harrisons have the same right to their decorations too! It couldn't have been someone who lives on this block, we all know each other and like each other. We're all *friends*! This is awful! It doesn't matter what time of year it is. These are their holy days! This is outrageous!"

In the clear, beautiful, late April morning, the letters, though defaced, continued to proclaim:

"JOYOUS RIḌVÁN."

~ * ~ * ~

Duane L. Herrmann, a reluctant carbon-based life-form, was surprised to find himself in 1951 on a farm in Kansas. He's still trying to make sense of it but has grown fond of grass waving in the wind over the prairie, trees, and the enchantment of moonlight. He aspires to be a hermit, but would miss his children, grandchildren and a few friends.

His work has been published in many real places and online, even some of both in languages he can't read (English is difficult enough! Spellling????).

He is known to carry baby kittens in his mouth, pet snakes, and converse with owls, but is careful not to anger them! All this, despite a traumatic, abusive childhood embellished with dyslexia, ADHD (both unknown at the time), cyclothymia, and now, PTSD.

He's still learning to breathe and perform human at the same time.

THE GREEN LINE

Sarah Edmonds

Stones clattered softly in Akram's pockets as he made his way out of the bustling heart of Ramallah. It was for a morbid sort of sport he and many of the other children lined up in the streets to throw stones at the Israeli patrols and convoys that occasionally drove through the town. Akram hoped he wouldn't need them as he ran through the streets towards school. His tattered grey backpack weighed him down as he crossed the community square, dodging the bumpers of impatient drivers. His final assessment was coming up—the exam that would decide whether or not he could continue into secondary school—and Akram had prepared by shoving every book he owned into his bag for review.

Making it safely across the street, Akram paused at the foot of a massive painted statue of Nelson Mandela. The likeness looked out across the square as if he were waiting as Akram waited. For years, Akram and his best friend Khadem had met at the statue's feet to walk to school together—their parents always warning them it wasn't safe to cross the Green Line alone. However, Khadem had stopped coming to school two weeks ago, his father keeping him hidden away at home ever since his mother disappeared.

Still, Akram waited every morning at the foot of the statue just in case.

When it became clear Akram would be late if he waited any longer, he turned his back on the statue and jogged past the sprawling array of housing complexes and businesses. The closer he got to the Green Line the more he saw familiar faces. An elderly woman his mother sometimes brought to the market shouted after him as he ran past—something about running like the devil was after him. Akram spun on his heel and waved, nearly tripping over a chair at an outdoor café. A rumble of laughter surrounded him as Akram caught his balance on the shoulder of a stranger, a large man with an even larger beard.

"Sorry, Uncle," Akram apologized.

"You'll be late." The man waved him on, turning back to his companions seated at the café.

Akram thanked him and continued on his way. Each morning he passed the same group of men at the same time smoking cigars and drinking tea at the same table of the café. They had never spoken before, simply nodding as he—and Khadem, when he had attended school—passed, but there was still a kinship. The people of Ramallah looked out for each other.

Akram and his parents had no relatives left in Ramallah, the rest of their family having evacuated back in the 1980s, before he was born. His father had wanted to leave with them but his mother refused. Palestine was her birthplace. Ramallah was her home. She would abandon neither.

~ * ~

As the border wall came into view, the people vanished. Graffiti covered the tall cement dividers that marked the Green Line between Palestine-ruled Ramallah and the Israeli settlement of Psagot. The artwork showed quotes from the Qur'an and murals of missing people, interrupted only by a gap in the wall where the guard station stood. A few cars were lined up, their occupants standing outside of the vehicles to be searched. Akram's school—a foreign-funded private school his parents could barely afford—stood just beyond the Green Line.

Instead of heading directly to the guard post, Akram turned left and made his way to the base of the wall itself. He knelt down and slid his backpack from his shoulders. Pulling the Kaffiyeh out of his bag—the checkered material of which had been waving from a half-zipped pocket like a flag as he walked—Akram set the headscarf on the ground and piled the stones from his pockets on top of it so it wouldn't blow away. Several other mounds of stones and scarves were lined up against the base of the wall. Akram counted them—seven. It seemed none of his friends had run into any convoys on their way to school. He was relieved.

Oftentimes the soldiers came to Ramallah to steal people without warning or explanation from their homes. People like Khadem's mother. Gone, in the blink of an eye. Akram wished he could do something more to stop them. Something more than barely putting a dent in their SUVs with their tinted windows and mounted rifles.

If he did well on the final assessment, he would be able to leave Ramallah. To leave and learn the ways of men who took power to get what they want and then he could find a way to do something more. Until then he was helpless; so, he threw stones with his friends, cursed the soldiers under his breath, and tried to make the most of that small rebellion.

"Late today?" Sahar called. She was a petite border guard with a long black rifle cradled in her arms. Several of the waiting drivers grumbled but none argued when Sahar let Akram cut in front of them.

"Thank you, Ma'am," Akram replied as he dropped his backpack at her feet.

Sahar was one of the kinder guards he had met over the years. She didn't jab him with her rifle as she patted him down and she always set his things on the ground gently rather than tossing them aside as she searched his bag. Akram still remained stiffly formal with her, though. She would be gone soon, anyway. The guards always rotated stations as a precaution against forming personal relationships with the people of the city. After all, kindness could get you killed.

"Clear." Sahar nodded to her fellow guard, stepping aside so Akram could gather his books from the ground.

Compared to Ramallah, the land across the Green Line was barren. Akram passed few civilian buildings—all abandoned except for the homeless who dared to occupy them—and several military outposts. Clumps of tents guarded by barbed wire and armed soldiers were interrupted by cement bunkers, shoulder high hills along the horizon, charred with ash from the all-too common burning tire thrown against them. Rifle barrels followed Akram's every step as he moved towards the heart of Psagot.

Psagot was one of the more vulnerable Israeli settlements surrounding Ramallah. The settlement itself was the main reason why Ramallah could not expand to accommodate new businesses or residents and why the city was cut off by miles and miles of cement walls. Psagot was made up of hundreds of buildings and encampments, gathered close together and surrounded by armed forces. It was as if the buildings themselves were huddled in perpetual fear.

Akram's school sat just within the first few rows of inhabited civilian buildings—a fact for which he was grateful. He didn't have to suffer the mistrustful glares of the residents for long.

The school itself was a tall building, an abandoned office complex that had been converted so the first two stories could function as classrooms for students from grades one through twelve. It was one of the few non-vocational schools that even offered grades eleven and twelve. Parents paid to have their children attend up through their tenth year. After that, students had to qualify for the secondary classes through their final assessment.

The secondary classes were taught by foreign teachers preparing students to escape to foreign countries for university. The demand was so high students from all over Palestine competed to get in. Akram's parents had paid for him to get a tutor in hopes he would be able to stay in his current school for secondary classes. They were willing to send him to vocational school, if need be, but foreign teachers looked better on foreign applications.

Akram had always been like his mother; he loved Ramallah. He loved the constant stream of music that carried through the city streets at night. He loved the warm smell of tea and tobacco that hung around every market, restaurant, and park. He loved the way street art was constantly springing up from nothing on the sides of buildings and the border wall. He loved his community, his family.

He didn't want to leave but it was because of his love that he one day would.

By the time Akram passed through the school's metal detectors, the halls were already empty.

"Bell just rang," the lone security guard explained as he handed Akram his bag back. "You can tell them I held you up, if you think it'll help."

"Thank you, sir." Akram nodded over his shoulder as he jogged down the hall towards his class. He wasn't sure which would be better, admitting he was late or letting his teacher think he had tried to bring a weapon to school.

Resigning himself to admit his tardiness, Akram paused outside of his classroom door. He took a deep breath, prepared himself for the inevitable lecture, and stepped inside.

Mr. Bukhari, a tall and haughty man whose appearance was far more intimidating than his reputation, turned away from the board as Akram pulled the door shut behind him. "Akram Marzouki."

"I'm sorry I'm late, sir. I—"

Akram glanced over to the rest of his classmates and froze.

Khadem was sitting at his desk for the first time in weeks.

"You pass over the border, don't you?" Mr. Bukhari asked.

"Yes, sir," Akram answered mechanically. Khadem kept his eyes downcast.

"Holdups have been getting worse there. Be sure to leave earlier tomorrow." Mr. Bukhari turned back to the board. "Take your seat. I'll let it slide this once."

"Thank you, sir." Akram rushed to take the empty seat beside Khadem as Mr. Bukhari picked up his lesson. Leaning over towards Khadem as he pulled out his book, Akram whispered, "You're back."

"No shit." Khadem raised his eyes to the board but the corner of his mouth twitched up to a smile.

"Are you okay?" Akram pressed.

Khadem opened his mouth to reply but Mr. Bukhari cleared his throat loudly from the front of the room. His stern gaze lingered on Akram and Khadem pointedly for a moment before turning back to his lesson.

Try as he might, Akram found it nearly impossible to keep track of Mr. Bukhari's lesson. His attention kept slipping and he would catch himself watching Khadem instead.

He wasn't the only one.

His classmates turned around in their seats to glance back at his friend's face. He couldn't blame them. Khadem was almost unrecognizable from the lively prankster they had all known. His skin was sallow and there were dark circles under his eyes. His thick brown hair was disheveled and much longer than Akram remembered. Khadem sat stiffly in his chair as if following Mr. Bukhari's lecture attentively but the open notebook in front of him remained blank. He didn't even have a pencil.

By the time the bell rang, Akram's own notebook was filled with half-finished equations and a series of unhelpful question marks where he had caught a problem's solution but not its process. He cursed his own inattentiveness as he shoved the useless notebook into his already crammed bag. The last thing he needed was a missed lecture right before the assessment.

As he and the other students rose, the usual classroom banter was replaced by a tense hush. Akram could feel the students' eyes on him and Khadem as they made their way towards the hall. Khadem trailed Akram slowly as if to prove to everyone he really was there.

The two boys had just reached the door to the hall when Mr. Bukhari called out, "Khadem Odeh. A moment, please."

Khadem rolled his eyes and waved Akram on his way. Akram followed the throng of students out into the hallway. Mr. Bukhari shut the door after them.

Once free of the room however, a prickling sense of unease held Akram back from heading to his next class. He leaned up against the wall beside the classroom door and waited, watching the students jostle past each other in an attempt to beat the bell.

A minute passed and then another. As the hallway began to empty Akram could hear the low droning of Mr. Bukhari's voice coming from the classroom behind him. However, the thick wooden door and complaints from the students of Mr. Bukhari's next class, waiting to get in, made it impossible to make out any clear words.

Akram jumped slightly when the bell for the next period rang. All of his hopes for a productive day of exam prep were slipping away.

At last, however, the classroom door reopened. Mr. Bukhari held it wide for Khadem to exit, raising an eyebrow at Akram but saying nothing.

"What was that about?" Akram whispered as he followed Khadem down the hall.

"Beats me." Khadem shrugged. Akram noticed a pencil tucked behind his ear. "I don't think I can sit through another class."

"We'll be in trouble for tardiness, too." Akram shuddered at the thought. Their literature teacher was a rigid disciplinarian.

"Nah," Khadem smirked, "I mean I'm getting out of this place. You in?"

Akram hesitated. It wasn't like he and Khadem had never skipped school before. There were plenty of times when they were small where they had snuck through the fire escape—the door on the east side had a faulty alarm that was the worst kept secret of the whole school—but that had been years ago. If they were caught when they were young, they could get away with nothing but a cuffed ear. Ever since they turned twelve, Akram and Khadem were old enough to serve jail time—especially if someone in Psagot claimed they were participating in "suspicious activity."

"You don't have to come," Khadem continued when Akram failed to answer. His tone wasn't judgmental or taunting. "I don't stand a shot at that assessment, but you? You might actually make it out of this place."

Khadem's words made Akram grimace, even though they were spoken with only a hint of bitterness. Meeting his friend's eyes, Akram shook his head. "Let's go."

~ * ~

Once they had managed to slip off the school grounds, Akram followed Khadem away from the building with growing apprehension. They were not heading towards the inhabited areas of Psagot where, if they were lucky, the pair could pass as two of the many unemployed teens who had failed their final assessments and didn't have a father whose cousin could offer them a job.

No. Khadem was leading them back through the first rows of residential buildings. Back towards the Green Line. They took a circuitous route, far from any of the guard stations. There were fewer military outposts but that didn't make Akram any less nervous.

Determined not to show his fear while his friend seemed so calm, Akram tried to distract himself with conversation. "So, how are you? Really?"

Khadem stopped and, for a second, Akram thought it was to answer. However, Khadem remained silent as he scanned the mostly barren landscape. His gaze landed on what looked like a small hill nearly a hundred feet away. Upon further inspection, Akram realized it was a half-buried bunker.

Before Akram could repeat his question, Khadem sprinted off towards the bunker, shouting, "Last one there buys knafeh for a week!"

"Khadem!" Akram's voice cracked as he stood, frozen, watching Khadem run full speed towards a gunman's shelter. Khadem had always taken risks but not with his life. That level of recklessness was no better than a death wish.

Akram trembled as Khadem climbed on top of the bunker and raised both hands in triumph. Only then did Akram begin to follow, his steps hesitant and faltering. He kept his eyes focused on Khadem, his heart nearly stopping when his friend sat and slid down around the far side of the bunker.

As soon as Khadem dropped down out of sight, Akram broke out running. With every step he expected the sound of shouting, of screaming, of gunfire to break out from inside the bunker.

There was only silence.

"Khadem!" Akram called out as loud as he could manage, out of breath from the sudden exertion and panic.

"It's okay." Khadem's head popped up over the opposite side of the bunker as Akram skidded to a stop. His grin faded as he saw the shock on Akram's face. "It's abandoned. I noticed it on the way to school this morning."

Akram glared at him, too out of breath to shout any of the curses running through his head. Circling the bunker, Akram settled for punching Khadem twice on the arm, hard, instead.

Khadem let the punches go unreturned—it was as close to an apology as Akram expected to get—and ducked back inside the bunker. "You have to see what's here."

Akram scanned the horizon nervously. No one else was around; the nearest hill—the nearest bunker—was merely a speck in the distance. Letting curiosity get the better of him, Akram crouched down and followed Khadem inside.

It took several seconds for Akram's eyes to adjust to the shadowy interior. When they did, it took him another second to realize that part of what he had taken for darkness or black paint was actually scorch marks scarring the walls and ceiling of the structure. A partially melted tire sat in the center of the small space. The smell of gasoline still lingered in the dust.

"Come on." Khadem waved Akram over to a back wall of the bunker. The side of his face lit up as he clicked on a flashlight and wedged it against the wall.

Akram shuffled over to his friend and sat, relieved the ceiling was just tall enough for them to sit fully upright. As he looked down at the object Khadem had pulled out to show him, however, Akram was disappointed. "It's just a box?"

"Just a box, he says!" Khadem threw his hands up in exaggerated disbelief. With a smug smile, Khadem gestured to the box. "Open it then."

Khadem's smirk gave Akram pause but he was already embarrassed at his earlier show of panic; so, he squared his shoulders and lifted the blackened metal box into his lap. It was surprisingly light for its size. About the same dimensions of a shoebox, Akram had expected it to be full and weighty. Instead, when he pried open the lid, the paint flaking off onto his hand, he found it half empty.

Sitting at the top of the box's contents was a vacuum-sealed bag, a remnant from the soldiers' manat krav, that, even when he tore it open, Akram couldn't discern what kind of food it was trying to be. He handed the open bag to Khadem who took a small bite of the odd rectangular ration and immediately spat it out.

Underneath the manat krav was a pack of cigarettes. The red and white box was labeled in English—probably an American brand—and, surprisingly, it was almost full. As Akram set the pack to the side, Khadem rummaged through his own bag and pulled out a shiny blue lighter.

"Where'd you get that?" Akram paused in his search as Khadem lit one of the cigarettes and inhaled deeply. The one time Khadem had been caught filching tobacco from his father's pipe his mother had banned all smoking in the house. Akram's parents had followed suit as a precaution.

Khadem grinned, blowing smoke out of the corners of his mouth in place of an answer.

Akram held his breath as the smoke swirled around his head, letting the subject drop.

Next, Akram pulled out a handful of rubber bullets and let them fall back into the metal container; they bounced with a startlingly loud sound.

"See?" Khadem reached into the box impatiently. He balanced one of the bullets on the palm of his hand and flicked it back at Akram. "Cool, huh?"

"There's something else in here." Pushing past the pile of rubber ammunition left in the box, Akram pulled out a round metal object about the size of an orange. He leaned closer to the flashlight against the wall, turning the object over in his hand before he recognized what it was.

A grenade.

"It's probably a dud." Khadem spared no more than a glance at the potential explosive, more preoccupied by flicking bullets at the wall and dodging the ricochets. "If it worked it would've gone off in the fire."

Akram rolled the grenade over in his hand gingerly. He had no idea if Khadem's assumption was right—it made sense, in a way —but the weight of the explosive was real. The cool glinting metal against his skin was real. The idea of death behind it was real.

Akram set the grenade back in the box and pulled a cigarette from the discarded pack. Khadem raised an eyebrow as he lit it for him. Akram inhaled and immediately started coughing.

Shoving the box with the grenade aside, Akram and Khadem sat back against the wall and smoked by the light of the flashlight. The bunker walls seemed to deaden all outside noise—not that there was much in the no-man's land between the Green Line and the settlement—and the only things that intruded on their silence were the occasional thud of a rubber bullet flicked against the wall and Akram's coughing every time he tried to take a drag on the cigarette.

"They found her; you know."

Khadem was staring at the ceiling, knees drawn up to his chest. The cigarette hanging from his fingers had burned so low it must have been hot on his skin.

"Beaten in a back alley," Khadem continued. His voice was flat. "Broken teeth, broken nails, broken bones. Half her hair was missing. They said it was probably pulled out when they grabbed her. When they raped her."

"They let you see?" Akram asked without thinking. He instantly regretted speaking but he was too surprised to stay silent. Usually when people went missing, they were never found.

Khadem turned his head sideways to look at him but otherwise remained as still as stone. "She was the right age. They could tell that much. But her face was too broken. Unrecognizable, they said. So, they had all the families come."

Akram didn't bother asking how many people had shown up to try and identify the body. Anyone missing a woman around the same age as Khadem's mother would have been brought in to see if they could recognize the corpse. To see if they recognized a friend or a wife or a sister or a daughter or a mother underneath all of the swelling and bruising.

"My dad couldn't bring himself to go so I went." Khadem inhaled sharply, in pain, and flicked the last bit of cigarette away. It bounced off the wall and landed in a pile of bullets. "They said nothing was conclusive. Everyone thought it was who they were looking for. But it was her."

"You're sure." Akram offered Khadem his still-lit cigarette.

He took it, breathing the smoke in and blowing it out in a single large cloud. He nodded. "It was her."

"At least you know," Akram remarked after a beat of silence. He didn't know what the right thing to say was but what he did say certainly didn't feel right.

"At least I know," Khadem echoed, grinding out what was left of the cigarette in the dirt. Shifting abruptly to his knees, he began picking up the rubber bullets and shoving them in his bag. "We should get going if we want to meet up with everyone else."

"You're taking those?"

"Catch." Khadem plucked the grenade out of the box and tossed it at Akram. Akram caught the potentially deadly explosive, his heart nearly jumping out of his chest. Khadem grinned, adding, "If we go through at the same time as the rest they probably won't check."

Akram clutched the grenade in both hands. He knew he should leave the grenade—dud or not—in the box where they found it. But he also knew if he didn't take it, Khadem would. The idea of leaving the explosive with his friend scared Akram even more than the beating the guards would give him if they found it.

He would drop it. On their way back, Akram decided, he would find a chance to drop it without Khadem noticing. If that didn't work, then at least Khadem was right; most of the time when the primary grade students crossed the Green Line together the guards would only do superficial checks. Their duty was to protect Psagot, after all, not Ramallah.

"Come on," Khadem urged, picking up the flashlight. "If you're not going to take it then I will."

Akram looked up as Khadem held out his hand for the grenade. The light from the flashlight bounced up off the floor and walls and cast unnatural shadows across Khadem's face. His eyes looked hollow. The shadows looked like bruises. Khadem had always resembled his mother.

Akram put the grenade in his pocket and pushed past Khadem, emerging into the light.

~ * ~

By the time Akram and Khadem had packed up the items from the bunker and reached the guard station the rest of the students were already waiting to be ushered through. Akram had failed to find a chance to drop the grenade. The weight of it bumped against his leg as they walked. He felt nauseous.

Along with the usual chatting from the crowd of commuters, rhythmic shouts echoed up over the opposite side of the wall. Akram recognized the chant of the local activist group as a small crowd of people—mostly university age students—came into view on the Ramallah side of the guard station.

"From the river to the sea, Palestine will be free!"

"Perfect." Khadem grinned as he and Akram pushed their way into the center of the small group of commuter students.

Akram furrowed his eyebrows, confused. The protestors were little more than a hassle. A publicity stunt. Then again, throwing stones at armored cars never helped anyone either.

As the group swelled forward between the two guards on duty —Sahar and a stern looking man—Akram became hyperaware of the weight of the grenade in his pocket. A cold sweat broke out across his skin. He hoped the protestors would distract the guards enough for them to break through unnoticed.

Keeping his head down, Akram let out a breath of relief as he and several of the other students passed by Sahar with little more than a quick check of their backpacks. The half of the group Khadem was with, however, was not so lucky.

One by one, the stern looking man pulled the students aside and patted them down, rooting thoroughly through each of their bags. Akram watched anxiously as he and the other students collected the piles of rocks they had left under the graffiti along the wall, many of them running to join the protestors, shouting insults and curses rather than fancy slogans. Akram followed more reluctantly, making sure to put the rocks in the pocket not occupied by the grenade.

"From the river to the sea, Palestine will be free!" The protestors continued.

Akram stood at the front of the protest line, bodies pressing against his back and shouts droning in his ears as he wrung his Kaffiyeh in his hands anxiously. He felt like he was about to be sick when he saw Khadem pulled out of line to be searched.

The way Khadem held himself as the guard searched through his bag—shoulders slouched back, looking down his nose at the hunched over man—put Akram somewhat at ease. Maybe Khadem had managed to hide the rubber bullets or discard them without Akram noticing. After all, Khadem looked completely disinterested, his expression unchanging as the guard turned towards him to search his person.

However, even from where Akram was standing several meters off, he could see Khadem's expression change when the stern guard jerked upward on the boy's tucked shirt and a jumble of rubber bullets fell out and bounced up off the ground. Khadem lunged away but the guard grabbed the neck of his shirt and threw him on the ground.

Chaos erupted the moment Khadem's head bounced against the road.

Akram tried to run forward, shouting at the guard to stop, but he was tripped up by the crowd of protestors surging behind him. He caught himself, the hard ground tearing up the skin of his hands, and shoved his way through the crowd as chanting turned to shouts of horror.

Sahar had her rifle out, shouting warnings as she shoved back against the line of protestors.

The commuter students were pelting her stones.

Khadem was on the ground.

Akram fought his way through to the front of the line to where most of his fellow students stood screaming. The stern guard stood over Khadem, his rifle raised towards the sky as if he would slam the butt of it down on the boy's head.

As if he already had.

Khadem wasn't moving.

Akram screamed at the guard to stop even though the man was doing nothing more than staring down at the limp boy at his feet. Akram felt hands on his shoulders and he struggled against them. Sahar had pulled out her radio and was calling for backup.

It was hardly a minute before a massive tan and grey SUV pulled up to the checkpoint from the Psagot side of the Green Line. At least ten soldiers piled out of it, guns aimed indiscriminately at anyone standing on the Ramallah side of the border. Another two stood in close conference with the stern guard, their backs to the crowd, attempting to block Khadem from view. He still hadn't moved. There was blood on his face.

All around him the protestors continued to shout. Students turned their stones on the newly arrived soldiers. They rattled off riot shields and the SUV like thunder. Akram felt the weight of stones in his own pockets and reached down to grab them.

Gunfire sounded, shot at the sky. The guard was poking at Khadem's arm with the toe of his shoe. Shouting continued.

Akram pulled his hand out of his pocket and stared blankly down at the shining metal grenade balanced on the palm of his hand.

It was probably a dud anyway. That's what Khadem had said when he tossed it at him inside the abandoned bunker. What harm could it have done? What harm?

What harm could Khadem have done?

Through the raging shouts and chaos, the shock of what had happened finally came crashing down on Akram. Khadem wasn't moving. He wouldn't move. The guard had seen bullets and maybe Khadem had made some harsh comment or maybe he hadn't and the guard had hit him. Too hard or at an odd angle, the guard had hit Khadem in the face with the butt of his gun and Khadem had stopped moving.

So Akram moved. With a sudden jerk and a half-choked scream Akram pulled the pin out of the grenade and threw it. The grenade rolled, unnoticed amongst the stones, between the feet of the soldiers and underneath the SUV. He had at most six seconds to shout—they learned that during drills in school—to warn the soldiers, the protestors, and his friends about the armed explosive.

But the instant that grenade fell away from his hand he felt stuck. Unmoving.

It was probably a dud anyway.

Four seconds.

Akram watched as the other students continued to throw stones. He watched as the protesters shouted at the soldiers and pulled out their phones, taking pictures of the wall of riflemen blocking Khadem from view. Akram watched as the soldiers shook their weapons in their faces, no longer aiming at the sky. He stared down the barrel of a gun.

Two.

Akram said nothing.

One.

He said nothing.

~ * ~ * ~

Sarah Edmonds is a queer author and filmmaker from southeastern Pennsylvania who specializes in fantasy, horror, and queer fiction. Her films have won recognition at multiple national and international festivals and her poetry has been featured in *Backchannels Literary Journal* and she has upcoming work in *Ethel Zine.*

Currently, she works as a technical writer for an immigration-advocacy law firm and serves as Co-Chair for the Communications Committee of the APHA's International Health Section.

THE HISTORY SONGS

Russell Hemmell

City, explosion, debris, corpses…rivers of blood?

Heloim scribbled the last word with a shaking hand and abandoned her quill. Writing poetry in Ancient Age's dactylic hexameters had looked difficult before; but now she had the impression her brain was going to burst.

She pushed aside the dusty tome and rested her head on the desk.

Interpreting the bizarre alphabet had taken longer than she imagined, and she wasn't even sure she was making any progress. After several days spent on a single page, those cryptic verses still refused to give up their meaning, no matter how many hours she dedicated to them. She had gone to the extent of copying it down and taking it with her at school to keep working in her spare time, with no appreciable results.

Heloim stood up, observing the empty library, remembering the first time she had ventured inside: she had found it huge and somber, populated with volumes nobody read, young people like her in particular. The building itself, the Itemenaki Palace, didn't appear on any of the city maps, and from the exterior it had the same appearance of a faceless military compound, which belied the impressive *richesse* of the internal structure of superposed vaults and the exquisite, old decorations.

And the subtle tang of incense pervading the high-vaulted ceilings…why perfume a place almost everyone seems to ignore the very existence of? Apart from the dreadful Inquisition, of course. After a few weeks, however, she found that scent eerily appealing, almost inebriating.

And one fateful day what had begun with reading rare poetry in a secluded place had turned into something different.

"I suggest you take a break."

Heloim turned into the voice's direction. The Master Librarian had materialized out of nowhere, silent like a shadow.

"I'm not going anywhere." She rubbed her eyes. "I'm stuck, Sima Qian."

"You're not," the monk replied, looking at her notes. "Everything you've written is correct."

"But I don't make any sense of it."

"Patience, young mistress. Languages require time."

"I speak five if we include the local dialect. Why is this one taking so long?"

A faint smile appeared on Sima Qian's mouth. No matter if there were no wrinkles or sign of age on that eerily handsome face, she sensed the librarian was far older than he appeared.

"Because it was conceived by a mind structured differently from yours. Your brain is human. This is a non-human product."

Heloim bit her lips. "You told me these volumes tell the history of a thousand-year war, or so you called it once. The one my people won against the non-humans and denied ever happened. But, if there were no survivors from the loser side...who did write these lines?"

"This is not the right question." The monk's eyes, as clear as water crystals, shone up in a glint. "What is the reason for that denial?" He took her hand and put it delicately on the tome. "That's what you should ask yourself."

~ * ~

"What are you thinking about?" Marthel came nearer, kissing her cheek.

Marthel. Her supposed boyfriend, except she had never committed to anything.

He had been the only one persistent enough to stay after she had consistently refused all the other boys' attempts at romance. She warned him she had no interest in taking it to the next level, but he decided to stick around anyway.

"Only that I need to study more," she said, throwing a quick glimpse at her desk. Heloim was always careful not to leave her notes around, but one moment of distraction could spell doom. She was positive nobody would have appreciated her extra-curriculum activities, let alone Marthel.

"Is this why you spend almost all your evenings in...what's that, a library?" he asked. Then noticing her expression, "I didn't spy on you. Your brother told me."

She stared at the boy in surprise. "What does he care?"

"Fritz believes you're still in love with your former classmate

—the one who joined the Inquisition—and you go to that place because…because you still see each other in secret."

Heloim snorted. Fritz knew her friend Treuwan too well for thinking he would've broken the celibacy rule for the Inquisitors in training—or any other rule, for that matter. But he wondered what she was doing so often in the Itemenaki Palace, and what better way than putting Marthel on her case?

"You should not go there, Heloim."

"It's not illegal. Or at least I'm not aware of any law preventing me, or anybody else, to visit."

"It's discouraged. If nobody teaches us to read old books except to access official repositories, there must be a reason."

Heloim put her hands on her hips and lifted her chin. "And this looks good to you. Somebody else decided in all their wisdom what's appropriate for you to know and what to ignore and you're happy with that."

"Listen, dear," Marthel said, taking her hand. "We enjoy a good life, and if we got where we are, at the pinnacle of humankind progress, it is because we've all worked together toward a collective goal. If this means focusing on what's important and leave behind the rest, it seems to me a pretty good deal, yes."

Heloim observed him, aware he was watching her reactions, and made an effort to keep her face expressionless. Had she not been like him one year before, before Treuwan had found out about books that were never supposed to be written and a forgotten apocalypse that was the foundation of humans' stolen prosperity? History told by the vanquished, the ones who had lost not only their lives but their right to have ever lived.

"That's my brother talking. What a role model you've chosen." She withdrew her hand and brushed her short blonde locks. She had to take heat from her teachers when she cut her luscious hair, but she had never repented. Toeing the official line was one thing, but at times she needed to give vent to her frustration. "Don't stress out. I go to the Itemenaki Palace to read forbidden poetry."

It was only half a lie. Hadn't Sima Qian told her the Annals were composed as epic poetry?

"Why is it forbidden?"

"Because it's beautiful, and we didn't write it. The non-humans did. Dangerous enough to restrict access, isn't it?"

~ * ~

From that day onward, Heloim stopped visiting the Palace to give her brother and Marthel the impression she had sobered up but redoubled her efforts to learn the language itself. She memorized all Sima Qian's grammar notes and learned by heart an entire dictionary of words.

Instead of trying to understand somebody else's writing, she forced herself to think in that way and composed her first, faltering pieces. Her internal discourse began occurring in the coveted language and, even though she was unsure about how correct her understanding was, slowly but steadily, she surprised herself by having spontaneous thoughts. Images made words and sounds. Her sentences became better, more fluid, their unfamiliar words quivering with weird sonority.

Until one night, she had a dream. Her uniform, of a fifteen-year-old Officer-in-Training, was covered in blood. She saw herself stomping into an arena of devastation, with a pervasive stench of death and mauled bodies on the terrain. Heloim woke up, screaming in panic.

She rushed to her desk and took out the text she had copied. It was the one that had eluded her for so long, and she translated it as she read it out loud, her mind opening up like a carnivorous flower.

I walked among the ruins of a fallen city,
I stumbled on the debris of a damned land.
Nothing stood still in the day when the sun bled in front of our astonished eyes.
Corpses—the corpses were everywhere.
At times they weren't dead bodies but what remained of them
—a stump, a lock of hair, a shred of broken wings
—a reminder of something once alive and breathing.
Rivers of blood.
I couldn't recognize any of my siblings,
not because they were safe,
but because they were long gone before that carnage.
I was, then as today, the last one of my Clan,
survived to bear witness and gather warm embers for already-destroyed urns.
Kneeling on the collapsed tower's scorched ground,
I said—nevermore—
knowing, as I know now, there will be a never-ending return, again and again,

because nothing will prevent it from happening.
We are the last and the first, of a past genocide and a coming apocalypse.
Free creatures once, vanquished today—forsaken, forgotten, and forever in
rebellion.

Heloim put down the text, grabbing her hands to keep them from trembling.

She breathed with difficulty as if the air had become too rich. She didn't try to get back to sleep. She kept staring at the stars looming beyond the glass ceiling of her room and, at the first lights of dawn, she went out straight to Bysanthium, the capital city where the Inquisition was based.

~ * ~

"You look well, Treuwan," Heloim said, glancing at her old friend.

It had taken her an entire day to get an audience. Inquisitors in training were not supposed to receive visitors from the outside world, but an exception had been made in her case. Perks of belonging to one of the most influential families of Founders, she sneered. At times, it came in handy.

She studied the surroundings. The place was exactly what she had expected it to be: dark, silent, and controlled. But the complex itself was architectonically well built, with beautiful halls. It would have reminded her of the Itemenaki Palace, except for the fact there were no books in there.

"I've heard the Inquisitor apprenticeship is the harshest of all. Not even us military trainees suffer as much as you," she continued, in a light tone. "I've decided to do as Fritz suggested: I dropped Art & Belle Lettres and joined him in the Vedrekruis Elite Corps. It seemed a reasonable thing to do, right? You've done the same. Big Sis Kerstin is Chief Inquisitor. The rumors say she's even more than that."

"Why are you here, Heloim?" he asked, offering her a cup of herbal tea.

They were sitting in the South Hall, where a few other students were busy debating theology. Heloim looked at them, all dressed in the same way, hair cut short in a sign of contrition, no ornament on their hands, and got back to him.

"We are the last and the first, of a past genocide and a coming apocalypse. Free creatures once, vanquished today, forsaken, forgotten, and forever in rebellion," she recited in a low voice, speaking those words as if it were a dangerous incantation.

Treuwan's eyes narrowed. He put his forefinger in front of his lips and gestured for her to follow him outside. They went out to the park that encircled the complex and ventured along the river stream for a mile, stepping across the woods. When they reached a clearing, he pointed at the cone shadow an old oak projected on the terrain. They sat down.

"This is the only spot where our activities are untracked, I suppose."

"You've learned the language."

"How do you know it was not Sima Qian to read it out for me?"

Treuwan tilted his head. "Because he wouldn't have phrased it the way you did."

"Why not?"

"Elleniki is not a human language, Heloim, no matter if we can learn to use it up to a point. We need to change and adapt it to our mental structures, so each person will read those words differently. In time, they modify the way you experience reality, reshaping your perception, rewiring your brain. That's the reason its knowledge has been forbidden. If you become too close to your enemies, you might start appreciating them."

"So why did your sister make you learn Elleniki in the first place?"

"Because I was deemed to become an Inquisitor since day one. We're the ones who need to intimately know the non-humans so we can devise the most efficient ways of destroying them."

Heloim looked at him. "She made a mistake with you, though. You're a sleeper."

"When you love somebody, you become selectively blind. Her love for me is her weakness."

Treuwan's polite smile made her cringe. She remembered only too well the torments her friend had gone through before bending his neck to his sister's will.

"You're the one who retrieved those tomes I'm reading now and put them into Sima Qian's custody. Who did speak the words I've just recited? You must know."

Treuwan sighed. "It was the last Chief of the Faen Clan.

Karelhein. They murdered him in one of the last acts of that conflict, exterminating all his people and then burying the truth together with the records of the entire war." His lithe fingers traced a circle in the air. "It was you, Heloim, who noticed there were seven hundred years oddly missing in our historical records, when we were in the Itemenaki Palace. Without you, I'd never discovered the truth."

She thought it over. "Sima Qian told me there were no survivors. Where did these volumes come from?"

"Karelhein belonged to an oral culture. His people have never recorded anything the way we do. All that existed has been passed down generation by generation, over a thousand years, and far back in the past," he said. "But Sima Qian's ancestors, who belonged to a different species of the non-human Clade, were aware only too well of the terrible power of history and told the story for those who couldn't talk about it anymore."

Heloim shuddered. Sima Qian's features came to her mind, pale and beautiful like an Old-Earth fresco. It had always haunted her the fact he looked so similar to them, to her—the same shade of blond in his hair, the same aquamarine eyes almost transparent in their sheen, the same long and delicate hands.... They all looked the same, her people and Sima Qian, when they did not even belong to the same species. What had happened when their two worlds collided in that war nobody among humans knew about?

She grabbed her own arms, as to protect herself from an invisible wind, stretching the light fabric of her uniform.

Maybe the others did not, but she did. She knew. She could feel the cold steel of the sabre over her skin. Tasting their blood in her mouth. "What good is a truth everybody ignores?" She murmured, almost talking to herself.

He touched her shoulder. "You only need one person to remember for those million dead to exist."

~ * ~

"Where are you, Heloim?"

"Just here."

"No, you're not. You're always with your head in the clouds, as if you lived in another world. What's wrong with you?"

It was not the first time Marthel and her quarreled because of her lack of enthusiasm, but things had been going from bad to worse since she had started living in the military academy, giving her a good excuse to avoid his company.

"I'm sick and tired of seeing you wasting away like a ghost." His eyes flared up in sudden anger. "This must stop."

"It's none of your business."

Who were you, Karelhein? she asked herself for the nth time, once back in her room. After the meeting with Treuwan, Heloim had visited the Itemenaki Palace only once, to collect the tomes from Sima Qian and inform him she was not coming back. The monk asked no questions, because none were necessary: their conversation had taken place in Elleniki.

She had come back to her day-to-day life—studying, eating, surviving her training.

Trying to ignore, and, if not, to forget, ghastly visions of rivers of green-tainted blood and cities in ruin popping into her head in the most unexpected moments of the day. But at night, in the silence of the dormitory, she found it increasingly difficult to sleep. She had the wrenching feeling in her stomach that she was betraying an old friend, living as if nothing had ever happened. A friend separated from her by centuries, more, by aeons of time, by species, culture, biology, even. A friend she had never seen but in her dreams—or nightmares—and whose black hair and dark green wings reminded her of a frightening demon of the officialdom's legends. But still a friend.

The night after she came back to her house, tiptoeing in silence to her old room. But when she opened the cupboard where she had hidden the volumes, she found nothing.

Marthel.

She returned to the dormitory and curled up on the floor, waiting for the inevitable.

The morning after, they came for her.

~ * ~

The prisoners' features were hidden in the semi-obscurity of the dungeons, but their screams were loud and clear. When her eyes got used to the shadows, Heloim distinguished the silhouette of a boy and what looked like an interrogator standing by a massive hoop of iron, with a hinge in its middle. The victim was forced to crouch on one side of the hoop while the other side was pressed over his naked back.

A tall, fully cloaked Inquisitor was questioning him with methodical, patient accuracy, and at every profession of innocence, he tightened the hinge a bit more, making the prisoner howl.

Heloim averted her eyes, looking at the marble pavement. A sticky red liquid was pouring out of the tortured boy's toenails.

"Where did you find those books? Did anybody give them to you?"

The voice of the Inquisitor assigned to her jerked her back from her reverie. Heloim herself was not strapped to any gruesome device, only seated on a wooden chair, but the environment was scary enough.

They had been holding her for about one week, in the same Inquisition complex where she had visited Treuwan but in a different wing, the jailhouse. She could hear, at night, the inmates' desperate cries and, at odd times during the day, screams of agony.

That afternoon, unhappy with her lack of cooperation, her interrogator had taken her to the wheelhouse, where enhanced questioning took place. It was the first time Heloim could actually glimpse at the man, cloaked in black and masked like all the others, monotone voice devoid of accent. He could have been a hologram, for the level of empathy he radiated.

"On which occasion did you read them for the first time?"

A high-pitched, prolonged yelling came from the left corner of the vaulted hall, followed by a hysteric cry. In spite of herself, Heloim cringed. A young girl, just about her age or a couple of years more, was having her breast torn apart by a metal claw. Tied to the wall, she could not move, only wriggle in agony while the torturer cut her tender flesh into shreds.

But that was not an interrogation: Heloim knew enough of the Inquisition procedures to know hot pincers and the rack were reserved for heretics, as punishment for their crimes. Their tongues were the first body parts to go, for they had sinned against the truth. That girl was going to die on the wheel in a public execution, in the middle of Bysanthium, among thousands of cheering fanatics.

"This language is not taught anywhere in our city. How can you understand what's written in these pages?"

In the beginning, Heloim had eaten and drunk nothing, afraid she was of being drugged and mindscanned. That procedure terrified her even more than the physical tortures. But after 24 hours, thirst had started to torment her, and she had to relent. Over the days, however, things had progressively worsened; albeit the interrogation routine had remained the same, with the identical questions voiced over and over again.

Heloim's whole world had started melting away in nightmarish, hallucinatory visions. She could perceive reality slipping away from her grasp, while fear slithered like a giant worm in her brain, making her thoughts the same substance as her darkest dreams.

In the evening, when the sunset rays from her cell's small oval window burnt her pupils like a flame, she could finally glimpse Karelhein, emerging from the shadows of a blood-stained past. He glared at her with the clear eyes of Sima Qian, eyes too old for an ageless face and which had seen too much. No matter how hard she tried, Heloim could not shut down visions of his non-human siblings' martyrized bodies. Their blood was not crimson red, but livid green, flowing over the city alleys in rivers, dripping on her face and mingling up with her tears.

I won't betray you, she cried in silence. *I will never forget about you. One day, I will tell your story and oblige everybody to listen and atone.*

At dawn of the ninth day, she was lying on the floor, agonizing from the lack of fluids, in a bottomless sorrow. The door opened, and somebody stepped inside. The shadow caressed her forehead, pouring drops of water over her dry lips and giving orders to carry her outside.

Heloim lost consciousness.

When she came back to her senses, she was no longer in the jailhouse. The light was coming in from the glass-paneled window of a luxurious hall. Heloim found herself resting on an ivory-carved triclinium, covered with a silky blanket. The shadow was standing beside her, and now she could see those features in the orange glow of the sunset: Kerstin Auren, Treuwan's all-powerful sister.

"I have read some of your writings, young Jennings. Beautifully worded, accurate, sharp. You're gifted with logic, and your discourse terse and persuasive. But with power comes responsibility."

Heloim raised her eyes, staring at the woman in front of her, at her long black robe, at the flawless line of her chin. She had known Chief Inquisitor Auren since she was a child and was astonished to see the woman had not changed over the years. The beauty of an ice queen with the subtle charm of a praying mantis, and just as dangerous.

The Chief Inquisitor's lithe hand rose in the air, her forefinger like a sword pointing to the sky. "There's a time in your life when you have to decide what you're going to be. It's the moment you choose your battles, and you learn when to harden up, when to concede, and when to bleed. This is what happens when you become an adult."

"Do you think I'm going to tell you what I've kept from your colleagues, Madame?" she asked, keeping the fear out of her voice. "Are you going to torture me, like the others I had to watch and hear in the dungeons? Is it going to be me, the next one burnt at the stake on Mount Taigetos?"

The woman bent to pour water in two goblets and took one herself, drinking it in slow sips. It was well known Chief Inquisitor Auren never drank anything stronger than water or herbal teas and, while one of the wealthiest, her austerity was legendary.

"You're one of us, a Founder. Nobody is going to touch one golden lock of your precious hair. Things don't work in this way."

Heloim stood up, ignoring vertigo and forcing her legs to remain steady. "Then let me go."

"After we're done here, I will. Yes. But I'll share something with you first." Kerstin Auren smiled, but her smile was like the sneer of an infernal god, hungry for human flesh. Heloim shivered. "Your brother is going to be arrested, young Jennings."

Heloim laughed. "I don't believe it."

"Soon. He's going to take your place in that cell, even though we won't interrogate him. There's no need."

"How bizarre. I thought you people cherished fanaticism and blind devotion."

The Inquisitor walked toward the glass window, which allowed for a unique view of Bysanthium. Old spires and marble columns made the city an architectural jewel, nested and secluded like a portal to another world, lost in time. "You're bright but naive. There's nothing blind about Fritz. He has a precise agenda, and beliefs I do share. But your brother is not a politician, and he hasn't realized yet that war is fought, but not won on the battlefield."

Heloim drank the water, fighting her pulsing head and a migraine that didn't want to go away. "I'm sure you appreciate him anyway."

"I do. Still, no matter what I may think in private, he must be condemned for sedition," she said, looking at the skyline behind the glass. "He's too vocal for what we need right now."

"So, this is the deal?" Heloim said, studying the woman's demeanor. "You're going to free him afterwards if I tell you where I found those volumes?"

Kerstin laughed, a dry laugh that sounded like a feral snarl and made Heloim shudder.

"I'm not offering you any deal. I know exactly where that garbage came from and who gave it to you. If it were not for my little brother, we wouldn't even be talking here; the offender would've already been taken care of, and those books gone forever." Her teacup took its place back on the table. "Treuwan has eventually learned his lesson. And, so will you. I deem your brief stay in our jailhouse proved to you how determined we are in our pursuit of the truth and in the preservation of our people's immortal souls." She turned her back to the window, her eyes now shining in contempt. "No, what I want from you, girl, it's for you to chase the foolish ones who believe these stories are true. Hearing reason from the crystalline voice of one who was seduced by them in the first place will be far more persuasive. I'm well aware there are many among our own kind, God only knows why, who still bask in fantasies."

"They are not fantasies."

The Inquisitor came nearer, her black robe covering every inch of her body leaving only her pale face in view. Her gloved hand opened, showing tiny white flowers on her palm. "That's all they are: sheer fantasies. Anything that comes to existence must linger long enough to trickle into something solid, concrete—like facts—to turn into reality. Otherwise, it's just a ghost. A chimaera. A non-entity."

"People have died—"

"No, somebody said they died—long ago, in a time you're not able to conceive. It is as good as a fairy tale," Kerstin Auren snapped, "and this is the choice upon you, Heloim Hyeemal Jennings. Being part of the narrative our people are telling, part of our history and mission, or joining the vanquished in their hell, which is not eternal suffering but oblivion. It's your call, and yours alone. Compared to that, the fate of your brother is meaningless." A soft smile appeared on the Inquisitor's delicate features. "Fritz's precious to me, now more than ever. I'll free him at the right moment, whatever you do."

THREE YEARS LATER

The old dungeons of Telluria, located in the city's outer circle, were a far cry from the gloomy perfection of the Inquisition complex. They looked ramshackle, decaying, almost crumbling under the sheer weight of age and inmate overpopulation. Telluria was reserved to the lowest classes and the non-humans. The official excuse for their arrests was terrorism. The non-humans had recently attacked and destroyed cities in the colonial belt. They constituted a mortal threat, and they needed to be dealt with. Of course, all those now languishing in the hell of Telluria were born in the colonies themselves, for non-humans had never inhabited the sacred land of the ancestors. Or so the officialdom pretended.

Heloim knew better.

"They're here, Vaandrig Jennings. The three non-humans you inquired about. We've rounded them up in the latest operation," the guard said to Heloim, standing to attention when she passed under the iron gates of the dungeons. "They'll be deported tomorrow to the mining fields, where they'll remain until their deaths."

Heloim caressed her long hair, trapped into a neat braid in the Vedrekruis military fashion. Three years had passed since her forced stay in Bysanthium's jailhouse, but she had not forgotten the Chief Inquisitor's words. Heloim, a fresh graduate from the Vedrekruis military academy, was already a commended junior officer in the Vedrekruis Elite Corps, with an impeccable record of ruthlessness and efficiency.

Her first assignment?

Rounding up and arresting all the non-humans from the City's territories, where they had lived for centuries, well disguised among humans.

Heloim gave the guard a brief nod and turned to Treuwan. "In this case, we'll have to interrogate them straight away."

"I don't understand."

"You have no need to."

Vedrekruis Vaandrig Jennings gestured for the man to open the door and she walked in, followed in silence by Inquisitor-in-training Treuwan Auren. The prisoners, two women and one young man, were on the floor in chains, one of them wounded but attentive, the other two unconscious. Their wings had been clipped with a ring at the left extremity near the upper bone spear, the only vulnerable point of a species who was built as a war machine without the hunger for power. How well the Vedrekruis who had arrested them knew their prey. Old genocide lessons kept delivering against modern enemies, Heloim sneered inwardly.

A pair of green eyes with split irises stared at her. Neither fear nor hostility in them, she realized. Only cold contempt.

"Leave us," she ordered.

The guard flinched. "We're not authorized to let you alone with them, Ma'am. Chains or not, they remain dangerous beasts. Predators, you, see. It's for your own safety—"

"I authorize you, right now." Heloim raised her chin, challenging him with her eyes. Young or not, she remained a Vedrekruis officer. And a Founder. "Just to make things clear: we can do whatever we want to these animals, even killing them, if they don't cooperate." She smiled, but her hand went for the sword at her waist, grasping the silvery hilt. "Nobody can stay over or record details of our sessions, soldier. It's classified."

"I know what the Vedrekruis Commander-in-Chief said, but these three are not terrorists." The man looked at her, puzzled. "We have examined them already. They don't know anything."

"It's our job to decide."

The guard hesitated. Then he shook his head and obeyed. The door closed behind him with a loud thud. She proceeded to deactivate the surveillance system, while Treuwan went to help the unconscious prisoners.

Heloim then came over to the woman who had observed the whole scene in silence. "Talk to me. I want to know everything you've heard from your kind. The genocide, the apocalypse, what came after that—no matter how outlandish you think it may sound."

"What are you talking about?"

Heloim released the grip on her sword and knelt near the woman. "Karelhein, and the Millennium War he fought and lost."

The woman's eyes widened in surprise. "How do you—"

"It doesn't matter," Treuwan said, in his usual, gentle tone.

Heloim could read disbelief more than lack of trust in the

woman's expression. That was probably the first time in her life she heard a human uttering that name, or anybody at all. Heloim didn't need to ask to know.

"It has remained buried for too long," Heloim added. "We're going to write history today. Of a war nobody knows when started, and that has never ended but only become more insidious. And we will write it from your side."

"Why?"

"When civilizations clash, one may devour the other, but the price is always higher than people imagine, let alone what they are willing to pay." Treuwan's voice was sweet, almost suave, but his eyes were cold as stone. "Humans need this truth as much as you do. For the common good of both of us."

"*Djet Isfet Maa-Kehru*", the young man, now awake, said in a low voice, staring into Heloim's eyes.

"Forever in rebellion," Heloim repeated.

She searched in the chest pocket of her uniform and took out a biomagnetic pulse generator, unlocking their wing-clipping devices without removing the ring itself. They were going to need the pretense until they were ready to escape. At the moment they'd decide.

"I will start with Karelheim Clan," the boy said, smiling at her for the first time. "He was born not far away from here."

The three encircled Heloim, answering her questions and narrating their ancestors' stories in eerie-sounding verses, which Treuwan wrote down in his elegant calligraphy. His hand danced on the ivory sheet, and tiny Elleniki letters in golden and red shimmered like flames, alive under his quill.

~ * ~ * ~

Russell Hemmell is a French-Italian transplant in Scotland, passionate about astrophysics, history, and Japanese manga. Winner of Canopus Award of Interstellar Fiction.

Recent stories in *Aurealis, Cast of Wonders, Flame Tree Press, The Grievous Angel*, and others. SFWA, HWA, and Codexian.

Find them online at their blog earthianhivemind.net and on Twitter @SPBianchini."

THE KILLERS

Carlton Herzog

I was a sniper assigned to the 82nd Airborne in Fallujah. My job was to shoot and kill the enemy without warning. On my last day, I had an Al Qaeda in my sights, when I felt a gun barrel pressed into my head. I turned to face my executioner. In that moment, my life stopped. All I could think about was the muzzle and his finger on the trigger. Then his head exploded from my sergeant's shotgun at close range. Chunks of bloody skull and brain flew into my mouth and nose. I'll never forget the burning bitter taste of copper mingled with gunpowder along with the chalky bits of teeth.

After my tour ended, I returned to the states. The thing that got my attention was the epidemic of gun violence. I could see that as the norm in strife torn countries, but not in democracy's shining city on the hill. It seemed the height of absurdity that the conservatives were hell bent on regulating a woman's uterus but not lethal weapons of war like the AR-15. As a conservative myself, I vowed to do something about it.

I fell in with a band of like-minded veterans. To protest the epidemic of mass shootings, we intended to assassinate NRA members gathering at a gun rally. Easier said than done. For after we had sequestered ourselves in an abandoned bunker, we began to squabble among ourselves about the rightness of the project. Distilled to their essence, the two overarching questions that paralyzed our call to action were: How do you claim the moral high ground when everyone is standing in the mud? Do you make your claim based on the gross facts of life or the minutiae of theory?

Our leader was Ruby, an Afghanistan veteran. She had a voice so husky it could pull a dogsled. She had nothing but vitriol and fury for "gunnies". Understandable because her daughter had been gun downed along with six other children during a mass shooting. As she checked the cyanide cannisters for leaks, Ruby demonized the gun lobby.

"The scary thing about gun lobbyists is that they can vote, and they can breed. Their whole Second Amendment argument is bullshit. The Framers never meant that every Tom, Dick, and slack-jawed yokel should have the right to carry weapons of war like the AR-15. They were talking about the collective rights of the states to maintain National Guards. Those who wrap themselves in the Second Amendment to justify gun ownership are nothing more than cowards. They are little people with small dicks and even smaller brains that want to be bigger."

Finn, whose son had been injured in a school shooting, began having misgivings about the moral arc of the project.

"I get that you're burned up about the mass shootings. But locking down an NRA convention and gassing over one thousand attendees is not the way to go. Gun violence isn't happening in a vacuum. We live in a warrior nation, the culture of which glorifies violence in its movies, sporting events, television, and video games. We pride ourselves on having the most lethal weapons of any nation on the planet. The Pentagon takes pride in the destructive capacity of our nuclear arsenal. It expects us to do unspeakable things to others in the name of patriotism. Frankly, I see myself as having been the lapdog of whores with chests full of metal too afraid to do the killing themselves."

Ruby conceded the points. "I agree man is a loaded gun pointed at the head of the planet and at himself. And leaders in general all have clay feet. But that doesn't matter because the angels of our better natures are dead. All that's left is devils. And my inner devil tells me the only thing those inbred, gun-toting cowboys will understand is a taste of their own medicine. When the bullets are flying in their direction, then we'll see how truly committed they are to keeping those guns. Because in the end, the only way to deal with evil is to kill it, and the only way to kill it is to be meaner than evil."

Tyrus, another war veteran, drilled deeper into the psychology of gun owners taking a more scientific view of the matter.

"The gun issue is all about neuro politics. I think we can all accept the premise most gun owners and lobbyists are conservatives. Recent studies at Harvard and MIT show liberals and conservatives use different cognitive processes when thinking about risk. When confronted with risk, liberals show greater activity in the left insula, which is the area associated with social awareness and responsibility. They are more reluctant to harm living creatures or act unfairly. By contrast, conservatives, when given the same scenario, will show greater activity in the amygdala, which is home to the fight and flight response. They tend to be obsessed with managing anxiety. They do that by imposing a sanitary cordon around themselves that denies the validity of change, compromise, and complex facts. Atheists, agnostics, gays, evolution, migrants, people of color, pro-abortionists, transgenders are anathema to them for no other reason than they represent the advancing tide of change. Thus, it should come as no surprise they refuse to acknowledge the shameful aspects of a gun-crazy society, and by association, their own dark nature."

Ruby belly-laughed, "Thus real science proves gunnies are retrograde genetic misfires, for what is evolution if not the forward march of change."

Omar, an African-American who had done two tours in Iraq had this to say:

"That's one way of looking at. Another is that conservatives are monsters. When it comes to a mass shooting or anything else that requires empathy, they will duck the issue or wrap themselves in empty soundbites. Less a matter of impaired cognition and more one of shameless indifference. That sort of nonsense is straight out of the Dictator's Playbook written by the three abominations: Putin, Assad, and Kim Jung Un."

Nelson, who was on the fence about the mission, refused to lend it his imprimatur.

"I can't sanction the mass slaughter of people even if it is to further a greater good. It's murder, irrespective of how much you demonize them."

"The problem is you are confusing murder with positive social engineering," Ruby retorted. "Human society is based on the notion some lives are worth more than others. We abort unwanted babies. We pretermit the sick and elderly and call it assisted suicide. We execute criminals so we can be safe in our homes. We send our young to kill and if need be, die to protect our way of life. Our lawmakers constantly make value judgments that categorize some lives as expendable."

Omar, who knew something of military history, expanded on her point.

"Five hundred thousand Americans died in the war to free the slaves. We nuked Japan, not once but twice. You can still see the victims' shadows scorched into the walls and pavement. We carpet-bombed North Vietnam. One hundred thousand Iraqis died to be free of Saddam. Many were women and children. Was all that murder? We have a chance to make a difference here. Like John Brown at Harper's Ferry. Or the Israeli raid on Entebbe to free the hostages. And what is this nation if not hostage to the gun lobby? Those motherfuckers need to die."

In objecting to Omar, Nelson drew a distinction between national and personal responsibility.

"I can't deny your historical truth. But I alone decide whether I want to go along with this cock-eyed scheme."

"Would you agree terrorist groups like Al Qaeda, the Taliban, ISIS, and Boko Haram, need to be eradicated if they don't change their ways?" Omar asked.

Nelson called him on his point. "Apples and oranges. There's a big difference between killing terrorist groups with finality and doing the same to all gunowners across the conterminous U.S. Believe it or not, most gun owners favor background checks and bans on assault rifles. So, like it or not, you are contemplating terrorism—the unlawful use of intimidation and violence against civilians for political gain."

"First, gun owners don't claim to be civilians," Ruby said. "They consider themselves to be militia men. So, let them own their bullshit. Second, groups on the terror watchlist are composed of psychopaths who have zero regard for human life. Unlike us, they think nothing of raping and killing women and children. Should we just sit around and pray they see the light. The gun lobbyist who ignores or downplays school shootings is like the German who went along with the Nazi death camps. He may not have turned on the gas, but the Nuremberg trials showed he knew about Hitler's mass extermination program. He was just as culpable as those who rounded up the prisoners, stuck them on crowded cattle cars, and marched them to the gas chamber. Gun lobbyists and their political allies know full well they are enabling mass shootings. They need to be held accountable the way Adolph Eichmann, Ernst Goebbels, and Hermann Goering were. And that's not going to happen from any turkey necked conservative senator."

Finn offered a pointed rebuttal. "I'm not shooting anybody. I'm a Christian. I get my marching orders from God. not a bunch of zealots with a messiah complex. Besides, murder is not in our Lord's playbook."

Ruby laughed. "Are you kidding me? If you believe the Old Testament, the Devil killed only ten people while God slaughtered two point three million. God was more than willing to eradicate all of humanity with the Flood, the righteous and the wicked alike, including children. He allowed his own son to be tortured and killed. In Revelations, He promises to exterminate all life on earth with fire, the way he did Sodom and Gomorrah. Let's not forget, the lethal rampages of His genocidal bagmen Joshua and Moses. In city after city, their conversion method consisted of killing everyone who didn't kneel before their God. They killed all the married men and women, raped the unmarried ones, sold the children into slavery, and butchered all the domesticated animals. Slaughter is baked into Christian DNA, marinated in bullshit, and seasoned with over-weening self-righteousness."

Omar echoed her sentiment. "What puzzles me is how any-one can speak highly of Jesus. Neither he nor the church spoke out against slavery in ancient Rome, or during its heyday here and in the Congo. If you ask me, Christian morality is nothing more than a con for the greedy and the power hungry, and Jesus is their front man. The only thing most Christians move in their lifetime is their bowels and the dirt it takes to bury them. They're snake oil salesmen with stretch limos, private jets, and armies of braindead followers. If Christianity is your gold standard for human morality, you're sunk."

Until this moment, Zachariah had done nothing more than listen. He decided it was time to set the record straight.

"You all make valid points. But you do it from a very narrow perspective and a flawed methodology. Calling someone stupid or evil doesn't make you smart or good. Ask yourselves if name calling and violence are the only viable solutions to our problems, and if so, then where does that leave us? If we can't find common ground with the gun lobby and conservative America, then how can we expect to find it with our global adversaries, three of whom have nuclear arsenals? Taken in the aggregate, the current stock of opera-tional nukes if launched have the combined capacity to eradicate all life on earth a thousand times over.

"Where precisely is humanity supposed to go in that eventu-ality? We still haven't gotten back to the moon, so where would humanity find a safe harbor to start again? Mars? We haven't figured out how to sustain a colony of ten there, let alone billions. Even if we could then how, pray tell, would we get them all there? And the whole let's move to an exo-planet is nothing more than pie-in-the sky. Like it or not boys and girls, Star Wars, Star Trek, and The Expanse are pie-in-the sky futures built on wishful thinking.

"What everyone seems to forget is: humanity is a thin slice of life smeared across a grubby ball of mud and rock hurtling through the lifeless void. All this infighting within the species is like a bunch of idiots adrift in a lifeboat squabbling over which flag they should fly. To make matters worse, the survivors in that lifeboat have decided poking holes in the lifeboat makes perfect sense. If lifeboat earth is the only game in town, then killing it with pollution is a new level of stupid. Clearly humanity's collective face should be next to the word idiot in the Great Galactic Dictionary.

"This all reminds me of *Gulliver's Travels* where the Lilliputian Big-Enders and Little Enders squabble over where to break an egg. Literary satire played out for real in our sporting events where opposing sides demonize one another for honoring or not honoring a particular musical arrangement or colored cloth. My God, isn't it obvious such energy would be better spent on preserving the environment or developing better astronautical propulsion systems? It would be comical if it were not so pathetic.

"Now you mean to improve on that stupidity by escalating from name calling to murder. And you mean to do it as if your actions will take place in vacuum. If you go kill those people, do you honestly think there will not be reprisals? Did it ever occur to you that you will be justifying the very position you are hoping to undermine? All you will be doing is inducing people to buy more guns for protection, to shoot first and ask questions later, and hate one another more than they already do.

"The sad truth you are illustrating is that human cognitive architecture is too impoverished to solve its own problems. That's a fancy way of saying we don't learn from our mistakes, and more importantly, we don't learn that we don't learn. We need to accept moments like this and learn from them. This is a time when we either come together or fall apart."

"Calm down," Ruby said. "In an ideal world, we could all sit down, respect each other's essential dignity, use due process, and find common ground. But Zack, your view of humanity is far too charitable. Essential dignity and due process are the weasel words of a permissive and promiscuous society. To my mind, human dignity is not a given. It must be earned. Our actions define us, not our beliefs. It's not about what you believe but how you believe.

"Each day we must dedicate ourselves to transcending our bestial heritage. When I look at our primate ancestors, dignity is the farthest word from my mind. Genetically, our closest cousin is the murderous, sometimes cannibalistic, chimpanzee. That we are not a consistently reasoning animal, that our heads contain dark animal impulses, and that our brains are imperfect instruments should come as no surprise. The shadow of our checkered evolutionary past often falls over our so-called civilized lives. For despite our trousers and phones, we remain beasts of the dark woods and caves. The hair and elongated canines may have shrunk, the screeches and ululations may have given over to language, and ballistic fecal matter may be a thing of the past, but we remain intimately tied by our very chromosomes to those voiceless souls we cage and medically exploit. We claim we are better than they are because of our larger brains even as we slice them open to see what makes them tick. If I had my way, I wouldn't stop at the gun owners. I would kill all the factory farmers and do it in the cruel manner they use on the defenseless animals.

"The same kind of thinking that allows the torture and murder of animals who already have short fucked up miserable lives is the same bullshit that can condone and facilitate mass shootings of innocents. Kant said as much."

At that moment, Zed entered the bunker with Jake and Amber.

Omar pressed them on their reconnaissance of the convention center.

"What's the layout?"

"In addition to the main entrance and rear exit, there are eight emergency side exits. We can access the ventilation system from the roof. The night before we'll install the cyanide cannisters and remote release valves. Then we wait. Once the place fills up, we shoot whatever security and stragglers are outside, then chain the doors shut.

"Listen to yourselves" Finn said. "You sound like the Nazis who poured poison through the shower heads at Auschwitz."

Ruby laughed. "Don't be so dramatic. The Nazis killed based on nothing more than ethnic affiliation. We're doing it based on the pragmatic consideration of protecting people, especially children, from gun violence. Get off your high horse."

"I'm not going to help you," Nelson said. "It's wrong to murder innocent people regardless of their politics. Besides that, did anyone here stop to think the proliferation of guns among the civilian population contributes to national security. It's a powerful disincentive for any would be conquerors."

"Right," Ruby said. "That just makes the nuclear option more appealing. We've heard enough from you. Now sit down and shut up before I put a bullet in your head."

"What are you doing Ruby?" Omar asked in exasperation.

"Making sure our friend here doesn't have a come-to-Jesus moment and run to the police," Ruby said. "We'll need to hog-tie him until this is over."

Now it was Nelson's turn to laugh. "No, you'll kill me long before that. Just as you don't want me throwing a wrench in the works, you don't want me naming names after it's over. I'm a dead man Omar. You might be able to rationalize the poisoning as an act of social necessity but killing me in cold blood is nothing more than murder. You were a Marine, Omar. You did two tours right? Is strapping somebody to a chair and shooting them part of the Marine Corps honor code?"

Omar and Ruby exchanged glances.

"We all need to take a breath here. Because this thing is spinning out of control before it starts," Zack said.

"No it's not," Ruby said. "Nelson here is a traitor who has chosen them over us. He always was a pussy. Your basic limp-wristed latte sipping liberal. As for the marines, they shoot those who go AWOL in time of war, and that is exactly what Nelson is trying to do. I did not come this far to turn back now."

"I will not be a party to murder," Zack protested. "Of Nelson or the convention goers. This was a bad idea from the start, but I was afraid to admit it because there seemed to be no other solutions in the offing."

Omar pointed his Glock at Zack. "You too? Fine. You can join Nelson at the bottom of the river."

Amber, Finn, Jake, and Zed had stayed quiet throughout the heated exchanges.

"I have no intention of being a fugitive or going to a federal lockdown. If these two clowns don't want to play ball, then we have no other choice than to ice them" Amber finally said. "Zed?"

"Maybe there's another way," Zed said. Suppose we use sleeping gas, put them all to sleep, steal their guns and wallets. Set their cars ablaze. That way killing is off the table, and we have hurt them financially while making them look stupid."

"Where are we supposed to get sleeping gas in a day?" Ruby demanded. "No. We stick to the plan. It's now or never."

Finn pointed his gun at Ruby's head. "No, it's not. Untie those two. We're walking out of here. Nobody is going to the cops I give my word. I didn't say you shouldn't kill those gunnies. Only that I didn't want their blood on my hands. So, just let us go."

"Can you vouch for these two?" Omar asked.

"If they go to the cops, then I'll shoot them myself."

By now Amber and Zed had untied the three dissenters. As they moved toward the bunker door, Ruby grabbed an AR-15 and shot the three of them where they stood.

Ruby smirked and swung the barrel around onto Amber and Zed. "Questions, comments?"

Nobody said a word. They stared down at the three bodies gushing blood on the iron floor. A few shivers, some chattering teeth, a blinking eye, and then all three were still.

"Let's clean up this mess," Ruby ordered. "There's plastic wrap and mops in the storage area. After that, we need to reconfigure the plan for fewer people. In the end, you will also see the rightness of the thing. Cause whenever it comes down to us or them, the only ones left standing will be us."

Epilogue

The reader is no doubt curious how I reproduced the foregoing exchanges with such high fidelity yet seemed absent from the exchange. I am embarrassed to admit I had accidentally discharged my weapon. Two bullets fired and ricocheted off the bunker's iron walls. One grazed my head and knocked me unconscious, the other stuck in my shoulder.

Omar and Ruby, in addition to their other skills, both had ancillary medical training. They removed the bullet, patched me up, and put me on a lovely fentanyl drip. I came to a few days after the go date of the mission. No one was present in the bunker.

The first thing I did was playback the digital feed we had set up as a historical record of our glorious mission. Hence the precise dialogue and minimal descriptive language of the players.

The news crawl indicated the gassing had been successful. We got "them". The perpetrators, dressed in clown suits and masks, claimed victory on the Web. They mocked the NRA, conservative political leaders, and gunowners in general.

In retrospect, I'm not sure what we won. This was a hair on fire moment for the country, and all we did was add fuel to the flames. The gun lobby is stronger than ever. The news media remained nothing more than echo chambers divided along information lines.

I have decided to sit tight and wait. The bunker has enough supplies to sustain one person for two years. I figure sooner or later my compatriots will return. Until then, I'll pray for us all.

~ * ~ * ~

Carlton Herzog is a USAF Veteran with a B.A. and J.D. from Rutgers University. He writes in all genres. He is also a sculptor and digital artist.

Some of his writing can be found on Facebook and on Amazon at: www.amazon.com/author/carltonherzog.

Us Versus Them: An Aged Fable

Christopher Welch

The Aged Books recall that prior to the Great Slaughter, neither Us nor Them had expected that *Another* would appear at midday; thus, each side fulfilled the ancient rituals and preparations for Battle Day unaware of what was to come.

Every ten years, on the tenth day after the tenth full moon in the decade's final year, the drafted citizens re-constituted the soldieries of Us and Them. Duty-bound by nature, blood-thirsty by nurture, and invigorated by the centuries-old ceremonies and invocations, thousands of Us and thousands of Them paraded out of the kingdoms and into the neutral plains of tall grass and prairie flowers bordered by the knolls and foothills beneath the great mountains. The legions of Us and Them were armed with keen spears, swords, and battleaxes. Dozens of snapping banners waved above the marching armies' heads and the monumental god-idols—stone-carved and bronze-smelted—placed atop horse-drawn wagons driven by acolytes from the ecclesiastical classes reminded both returning veterans and new conscripts to pray for a decisive war zone victory over the incessant enemy.

The frontline engagement, always led by the King of Us and the Queen of Them, began at mid-day and ended at sunset, no matter how many noble champions or greenhorn gladiators remained standing in the moonlit field amidst the trampled flowers, the demolished gods, and the teeming piles of ruined corpses, both human and equine.

"Leave Them bodies for the worms," Us said, staggering off the plain.

"Leave Us bodies for the crows," Them said, limping back home.

The Aged Books note Battle Day had always been observed in such manner. No one, neither in the realm of Us nor in the realm of Them, recalled the exact reason *how* Battle Day became so important once upon a time, but everyone was taught *why* it was so important. Indeed, it was the first lesson for all elementary-aged children in both realms.

"Us is not like Them," Us said.

"Them is not like Us," Them said.

"Them have different hair," Us said.

"Us have different eyes," Them said.

"Them have chiseled gods," Us said.

"Us have the molded gods," Them said.

Outside of Battle Day, rarely did one of Us see one of Them or one of Them see one of Us. Occasionally, on off-years, one of Us would follow a river too far upstream into Them lands; Us would be found days later floating homeward face-down, throat slit. Occasionally, on off-years, one of Them would get lost in the wilderness and cross into Us territory; Them would be found hanged from a tree and left dangling for weeks as a warning for any other encroaching Them to retreat.

The eldest of the Aged Books tells the fable retold by parents to children in each realm; and like all myths, the purpose was to educate the young and to frighten away conceptions of improper behavior. The fable states, once long ago, one youthful Us and one youthful Them sparked a romantic relationship which required secluded meetings in the foothills; each one knew the love was forbidden, and the risk was great.

Soon, rumors were hatched, and those rumors took nimble flight within each youth's social sphere. One day, the youths were away from their mansions a long while, and both immediate and extended family members frantically searched for the minors, desperate to outrun the escalating accusations within the communities of the upper class; the gossip and innuendo could flourish into reputations of dishonor, corruption, and abasement among all of the youths' kindred. Us and Them, together? *Never.* The families, often seen in royal functions at the courts of the King or the Queen, could barely withstand the insinuations; neither family would survive the scandalous truth unless it was extinguished properly.

The well-armed families finally discovered the couple, who were enjoying a book of poetry, under a tree on a grassy knoll. The youths' fathers, conjoined in disgust yet unable to speak a single word, either to each other or to the youths, struck quickly. The fathers pierced the youths' hearts with war-sharpened spears—heirlooms from previous Battle Days. Shortly thereafter, each father paraded a punctured child through the kingdoms' streets, and up to the respective royal mansions, to celebratory applause from the echelons, the plebeians, and the ecclesiasticals alike. The citizens appreciated that the punishment was proper and just, and this teachable moment would serve as a proper warning to other youths. Honor had been restored to the families, and each were shielded from any new, ignominious gossip.

Was this fable based on a truth? Was it based on a lie? No one really cared enough to discover whether it was real or not, for the tale served a greater purpose: it enforced the long-established norms of both Us and Them, and that was all any proper youth needed to know.

And so, Battle Day had arrived once more.

On the plains, the armies approached one another on foot. Leading the frontline from the northeast was the King of Us and leading the frontline from the southwest was the Queen of Them. The columns stopped ten paces apart; only prairie grass and field flowers separated the combatants, the banners, and the idol wagons. The King raised an axe, and the Queen raised a sword, each ready to shout the sacred war-cry to commence Battle Day—when *Another* appeared on the closest foothill.

Weapons lowered, the King and Queen stared in unstated but shared shock. The perplexed acolytes stopped prayers to the idols in mid-chant. Whispered apprehension filled the armies' ranks on both sides.

"This person is not one of Us," the King said. "The hair is wrong."

"This person is not one of Them," the Queen said. "The eyes are wrong."

Another had no weapon and was clad differently than either Us or Them. *Another* descended the hill with sure-footed strides and walked into the field between the frontlines. *Another* stood between the King and Queen, and spoke.

"I am I, and I come from land beyond the great mountains."

"Impossible," the King said. "The peaks are too jagged to climb. Us cannot do it."

"Untrue," the Queen said. "The paths are too narrow to hike. Them cannot do it."

"But I can, and I did, and now I am here," I said. "And since many things are possible, I have come today to advocate for peace between Us and Them, and I call for an end to Battle Day."

"Peace with Them?"

"Peace with Us?"

"Yes," said I. "There is no need for conflict or bloodshed. Is Us and Them really so different, after all? Do Us and Them have hair? Do Us and Them have eyes? Do Us and Them bleed red on Battle Day?"

"Them have different hair," the Queen said.

"Us have different eyes," the King said.

"Do these peculiarities truly matter?" asked I. "These are meaningless differences and details of no consequence. Us and Them speak alike, and think alike, and—most certainly—fight wars alike. So, why not have peace alike? There can be communication. There can be prosperity. There can be philosophy. There can be shared knowledge and educational exploration. There can be no limit to what *We* can do."

"What is *We*," the King asked.

"What is *We*," the Queen asked.

"Us and Them and I, together, become *We*," said I. "With sisters and brothers from the other side of the great mountains, We, together, can work towards peace and end the carnage of Battle Day."

"Work with Us?"

"Work with Them?"

"Yes," I answered.

"Brothers and sisters not like Us? There is more of I?"

"More of I? I is different than Them."

"I is not like Us."

"And I wants to be We with Us?"

"And I wants to be We with Them?"

"Enough! I will be no more!"

"Death to I!"

With a quick thrust, the Queen of Them ran the sword through I's body. Striking at the same moment, and with an equally fast blow, the King of Us smashed the axe into I's skull. I did not have time to scream as the weapons rapidly struck again and again. The King and Queen hacked and slashed at I until I's blood coursed through the tall grass and field flowers. The blood flow stopped, finally, when it met the boots of the frontline soldiers.

The King and Queen rage-screamed as the weapons clanged

above the butchered corpse of I—the war-cry resonated through the ranks. Shocked from wide-spread apprehension, the armies launched into full Battle Day assault.

The Aged Books call that day the Great Slaughter. The fierceness and savagery between Us and Them was more vicious and brutal than any previous Battle Day chronicled before it. It is written the sun descended faster than ever before on that fateful day, as if nature itself was horrified by the ferocity of the conflict and the innumerable heaps of corpses left in its wake. When the moon was finally noticed by the wearied fighters, the havoc halted. Neither Us nor Them had suffered so many casualties in the centuries-old, ritualized conflict. The exhausted survivors, wounded and traumatized, retreated in silence. For the first time ever, both sides ignored the traditional welcoming of worms and crows to the carrion field.

The last and youngest volume of the Aged Books recounts three curious events following the Great Slaughter. Breaking with tradition by ignoring the rule of decades, a dozen of Us and a dozen of Them—unaccompanied by royalty or idols—returned the plain of the Great Slaughter on the first anniversary of the massive battle. Us and Them gazed at each other over the flowerless field, which was still swampy with blood from the fallen. Neither Us nor Them drew their weapons, and each departed in silence after several quiet moments.

On the second anniversary, the veterans returned to the plain, and discovered the grass was growing again. This time, neither Us nor Them carried weapons, but once more both sides walked away in silence.

On the third anniversary, Us and Them returned to the field yet again, and both sides were pleased to see a few flowers had finally spouted. Us and Them stood closer to each other than the two years before.

"Could there be a *We*?" Them asked.

"Can there be a *We*?" Us asked.

The youngest of the Aged Books ends here.

~ * ~

The Moral of the Story:

I alone cannot end violence, but working together,
We *might* be able to do so.

~ * ~ * ~

Christopher Welch is originally from Akron, Ohio but currently lives in south-central Wisconsin. He was a reporter for 16 years, and for the last 12 years, he's been an English instructor at Madison College. His creative and non-fiction works have appeared in various small press and professional publications. His short stories have appeared in the anthologies *The Anthology from Hell, Blood Lite, Blood Lite II: Overbite, Catopolis*, and *Dark Wisdom: The Best Dark Fiction.*

Welch previously served on the juries in the Long Fiction and Poetry categories for the Horror Writer's Association's annual Bram Stoker Awards™.

Are We a Thing?

Bennie Rosa

Tracey wanted to know.

"The long answer is yes," Fyler said.

Tracey looked warily at Fyler. "You mean we are?" she asked. They held hands loosely as they walked through the milling crowds of Times Square. If there was a short answer, he wasn't about to tell her, at least not then.

There was never a doubt Fyler Stinson loved Tracey Astonish, and vice versa, and they both knew it even though Tracey was insecure about it at times. It was just that Fyler was always too busy pissing people off. He spent most of his free time pumping iron to protect himself. Too many years of getting his ass kicked as a kid learning his craft. There's a lot to learn when you want to be the best disturber you can be, like right now, wearing a MAGA cap and a Black Lives Matter t-shirt at the same time.

This was Times Square in September. The heat suffocates in September and it takes its sweet time doing it. It is the most persistent of months, filled with summer's lame duck heat and endless whys. For instance, why end summer and begin fall if there's no difference?

~ * ~

EatMe was a giant walk-in vending machine on Broadway, the newest incarnation of the old Automat. Fyler and Tracey were hungry and, for them, it seemed the best place to eat. Why? Because, it was totally self-contained. And here's another answer to why; they were from Brooklyn, that's why.

Before they began their meal, Fyler tipped his hat back and rolled up the sleeve of his t-shirt. He said 'watch this'. She was and wasn't surprised by his new tattoo. It was a cartoon inside a heart, of George Floyd with his knee on Donald Trump's neck. The title was 'I Love You Donald'. When he flexed it, the knee bounced up and down.

They began to eat. Tracey noticed a police officer eating next to them. He glared at her after he noticed the tattoo, stood up, wiped his mouth, threw the napkin on his half-eaten sandwich and stopped next to Fyler on his way out.

"I'd be careful if I were you," he said.

"Which you're not, so…"

The cop left and Tracey gave him the look. Fyler flexed for Tracey one more time, before giving her that lovable smirk she'd seen so many times before. She smirked back.

~ * ~

The Black Lives Matter Shop was right next door to the MAGA Shop in the New American Strip Mall on 43rd St. Business was brisk at both. It was time to go back to Brooklyn, but as Fyler stopped in front of the MAGA Shop Tracey had one of her premonitions.

She played with her watch as the MAGA Shop swallowed her man. She couldn't make herself look in the window. Yelling and scuffling could be heard inside. Fyler came stumbling out, t-shirt ripped, bruises on his face. He was laughing and smirking his way toward Tracey. Tears were starting in her eyes.

"Quit crying."

She did, sort of.

"Let's go home Fy."

Not yet." He pointed to the Black Lives Matter Shop and went in.

The first thing that came out was the MAGA hat spinning into the gutter, then Fyler, then an angry clerk at the entrance telling him to keep his hatred to himself because he was bad for business. Fyler sat on the curb. Tracey tried to help him up but he was too heavy.

That's when the same police officer who gave Fyler the warning in EatMe came along and lifted him up and rested him against a streetlamp. At first, the cop didn't say a word. Tracey thanked him for helping.

The cop waited.

"I told you to be careful son," the veteran cop said.

Fyler stood on his own. "No you didn't. You said if you were me, you'd be careful."

Some people never learn was all over the cop's face as he walked into another day of doubt.

Fyler and Tracey held each other as they walked down the

steps to the subway home. Turns out there was no short answer after all.

~ * ~ * ~

Bennie lives in the high desert of Central New Mexico where he writes short stories, flash fiction, novels, and drama. His writing has recently appeared in the *Charleston Anvil* and the *IHRAF Journal* as well as *Dream Pop Journal, New World Writing, The Writers Club, Barrio Beat* and others.

THE LIMIT OF THE SKY

Holly Schofield

Morgan Howard stretched out her arms, letting the rising thermal take her higher. Hundreds of feet below, treetops drifted past. The treetops became rocky shoreline, then whitecaps marring the waters of the strait. She admired the palette below; November on the western shores of San Juan Island came in shades of pearl, blue, and soft gray.

She banked toward shore then initiated a steep dive, grinning as she imagined wind rushing through her feathers. The tallest fir swung close, a lone veteran with a broken, dying spar. The eagle nest, a sharp bundle of sticks perched on the top-most branch, drew near. She tensed for the landing.

The loud ring of her cell phone jackhammered through her skull. She lowered her arms then closed the eagle-riding software with a twitch of an eyelid. The intracortical connection and the visual linkage ended with only a small mental jolt. That figured. The day she was dumping the project was the day the eagle "mind meld" was finally getting bearable.

Her phone, set to maximum volume and the most irritating ringtone she could find, continued to ring stridently, almost hard enough to rattle the row of empty eagle cages on the far wall of the laboratory. She removed her unauthorized prototype—a modified pink swim cap studded with tiny magnetic field generating "coils"—and diverted the eagle's visual feed from the swim cap over to the holographic display monitor on the lab's countertop. Willy, the eagle she'd been melding with, gazed over his territory of forests, ocean, and cliffs.

The phone continued to ring. Morgan raked her fingers over her stubbled scalp where the electrodes had left tingles. It was probably yet another call from Major Andrew Anissette, the military liaison to the university; if she answered, she might say things she'd regret. And if it was the dean, trying once more to convince her not to torpedo her career, well, there weren't any arguments left for him to give.

She worked quickly, shoving the swim cap into her purse then boxing up the official Brain-To-Brain Interface (BTBI) equipment in the cardboard boxes supplied by the military. In four hours, she could be out of Seattle traffic and at her father's old cabin—now hers —on Vashon Island for her well-deserved vacation. She taped the box shut and hefted it onto the dolly. The satisfaction she got from rehabilitating Willy and the other dozen eagles from their wartime trauma and brain surgeries was at an end. It was unlikely anyone would use the equipment again. Very few people had her cross-disciplinary qualifications in wildlife biology and neuro-science and, certainly, no one understood the neuro-chips or the eagles like she did.

Movement on the display caught her eye and the view changed to green and brown blurs: Willy was bobbing his head as he cleaned his talons. She reached a hand towards the screen as if she could give Willy a pat on his feathered white head twenty miles up the Oregon coast then let her hand fall. In a perfect world, she would be able to completely extract the eagles' God-awful neural chips and throw them in the ocean, but attempted surgery by army veterinarians had killed several eagles already, and she wasn't about to risk such a procedure on Willy. No, the best plan was just to walk away from the whole project.

And part of that damage control involved sneaking her prototype out of the lab. All the materials were her own and it actually might be deemed her intellectual property in court; but she'd rather not have to trust the military to play fair. She shoved the swim cap into her large purse below a scarf and a pair of gloves. Her dedicated hands-on training with the unit went far beyond any cognitive neuroscience advancements the military had ever made. Maybe it, or a subsequent generation of equipment, could eventually even cure the Major, that uptight prick.

The phone had started clanging again. She'd have to answer it if only to appease her aching head.

The call display showed a picture of a young girl. For a minute, she couldn't place the face. Then she recognized the Major's daughter: a failing university student with whom Morgan had reluctantly suffered through "Take Your Daughter to Work Day" at the Major's behest.

With a sigh, Morgan put her phone on speaker and laid it on the counter. The military in general, and the Major specifically, seemed to bring her nothing but trouble. "Charlotte?"

"Oh, Morgan, you've got to help!" Fear hung from every word.

Morgan's stomach clenched. "Where are you? Switch to holo!" She flicked on a monitor beside the one with Willy's feed and began to pull up a GPS mapping tool.

A thumb loomed on the phone screen, then Charlotte's head and shoulders appeared, framed against a U-shaped settee. Ocean waves rolled behind her and, in the far distance, a green shoreline stretched.

Morgan hardly recognized the tear-ravaged teen. The spark of intelligence she had tried to set afire that day last month in the lab had disappeared. Yellow stains, probably vomit, defaced the front of the girl's shirt. Tattoos spread across her temples down to her cheeks. Most alarmingly of all, a beige shower cap clung to her head.

"Morgan, please!" Charlotte's eyes jerked like a spooked horse. "I need...aw, screw it!" Her head twitched and she touched a silver control pad on her wrist. Instantly, a beatific yet lopsided smile spread across her face. The transformation was incredible. "Hey, Morgan. I'm jacked and I can't get up." She giggled and the image slewed as the girl abruptly slid off the vinyl seat and onto the metal floor of what had to be a boat.

Morgan fumble-dialed the Major on the seldom-used landline. "It's urgent." She drew a long breath before explaining. What she thought of him, and what he thought of her, was irrelevant now. The girl needed help.

Morgan's departure would have to wait.

~ * ~

The Major had been nearby, at a project-closeout meeting in the dean's office. He strode through the lab door and barked, "Report, Dr. Howard." His usual clipped sentences were no sharper than usual. Had it been her own daughter in trouble, Morgan knew she would have been rather more upset.

She pointed to the blinking green dot on the map. "There's her phone signal. Puget Sound. A couple of dozen miles up the coast from here." She'd propped up her cell phone on the dark blue counter, so the tiny 3D image of Charlotte appeared lost on a plastic sea.

"Details?"

That was all he could say? The man was impossible. "The only detail is that she's jacked. Which you would know if you'd talked to her today. Why'd she phone me and not you, anyway?"

"Blocked her calls. Tough love. Jacked?"

"Slang for wireheading, Major." The latest unwise teenage thrill required only a couple of household sponges for the anode and cathode, along with a simple fabricatable chip and a good template. Basic medial forebrain bundle stimulation—easy enough to jolt the pleasure centers of the brain. A very crude version of the pink cap that lay in Morgan's purse.

The Major gave a single nod, studying the tilted image of Charlotte's legs splayed out below the seats, short skirt hitched high. They could both predict the eventual outcome of repeated stimulation. Numerous lab studies had shown if a rat or a monkey could push a button to self-stimulate the pleasure center of their brains at the expense of eating or sleeping, they would. There was no reason to think a human wouldn't make the same choices.

For a moment, the Major stood ramrod straight, staring at the counter. Morgan looked at him, really *looked* at him for the first time since he'd entered into the lab. His uniform jacket was unbuttoned, his hair out of place, and there were bags under his eyes. Maybe he wasn't as insensitive as she'd thought: he looked like he'd been awake all night, maybe searching for Charlotte on campus or something.

The teen must have heard Morgan's voice over her phone. She opened her eyes. "I'm on Broan's boat. Broan's boat. Broan's boat." She giggled until tears ran. "Shhh, here comes Broan." The holo image blurred, the bared legs shifted off-screen, then a gray sky with a few tattered white clouds came into view. Charlotte must have sat up and laid the phone on the decking.

A thin man with a brush-cut leered up out of the holo field, or rather, Morgan realized, he was leering *down* at Charlotte, towards her phone.

"Girl, we're gonna have some fun once you come down from that jack-shit. Party time." His jean-clad leg appeared, blurred, and Charlotte grunted in pain as his foot struck her just out of camera view. Several more kicks then, "Is that thing on holo? Shit!"

The image distorted: sky, waves, water, then blackness.

Morgan kept tapping keys, futilely, but the GPS signal was also gone.

The phone connection had been completely broken.

~ * ~

"You don't *know* that Charlotte went overboard. Maybe just her phone did," Morgan said for the second time in five minutes, staring at the map, Charlotte's cell phone now a steady red dot tagged as Last Known Location.

Andrew, on hold with the Coast Guard, grunted a second time. How do you comfort a guy like that? Not with a hug. She tried logic again. "She'll be okay. There must be other people on the boat."

"No, Dr. Howard, doesn't appear to be. Coast Guard says it's registered to a pimp, John Broan. Boat's a fast one, Formula Four Hundred." He rubbed his face. "Coast Guard says they think they can intercept it in half an hour, based on the coordinates and some guesswork."

"The boat sure was going fast." Morgan's eye caught motion on the other screen as her favorite eagle turned his head, and therefore the camera view, to admire his incoming mate, Elsa. On a side panel, the bird's endorphin reading jumped. "Andrew," she said, realizing it was the first time she had ever used the Major's first name. "Willy. Willy can help us find her."

"Who? Oh, W-One. Yes, of course." Andrew's regular visits to the lab these past months and old-school insistence on face-to-face meetings had made him familiar with the eagles' names and their progression through the rehab procedures.

The box with the BTBI equipment, which one was it? She scrabbled through the stack on the dolly. "If there was ever a time to use this equipment..." Morgan plucked out a standard military headset. The intended purpose of the eagles' cognitive implants as a weapon would never sit well with her but, as a tracking device they were better than a drone, able to soar for hours at a time and adjust to changing weather and circumstances instantly. Never mind their attacking capabilities.

Willy chose that moment to launch himself from the nest and soar high above Puget Sound, his view covering several square miles.

Morgan tweaked the joystick and zoomed in on the speeding boat. "They're heading north of Whidbey Island, near the Canadian border." International boundaries didn't really matter: the winding waterways in both countries offered Broan numerous hiding spots.

As the view enlarged, Andrew's daughter became visible, sprawled near the stern. Her white legs were apparent even from Willy's six hundred feet above the waves. "She's there! Thank Goodness!"

The view twisted away as Willy headed east to the shoreline. Fir snags and arbutus crowns came into view. The boat became a tiny dot as Willy caught an updraft and rode higher.

Morgan fit the gray metal headset over her scalp and plugged it in to the computer. "I'll activate Willy's chip link". The primitive chip in the eagle's head simply sent impulses into the somato-sensory cortex, similar to a radio receiver. A mild jolt to the neurons on the right cheek and Willy would turn right, a similar tickle on the left and he'd turn again. But only if he wanted to, much to the frustration of army commanders. It wasn't all that effective, hence the much more painful but inconsistently performing Warbird software that resided somewhere in the military servers at Fort Lewis.

Once the dean had signed the joint agreement with the military, Morgan had been requested to stop working on real-time transfer of sensorimotor information—research that could potentially rebuild nerve pathways in animals, maybe eventually even help humans with motor neuron diseases, At that point, she'd changed her focus to the eagles' rehabilitation. Then, last month, Andrew had been ordered to reinstate the Warbird software research for one last hurrah.

Morgan swore under her breath as she tapped the touchscreen. It would be wonderful to go back to those earlier times, back when the project was forging a different path, uncovering new understanding of the brain.

Back when her job had been without moral conflict.

Back when the sky had been the limit.

While Andrew phoned in the new location to the Coast Guard, Morgan flicked her way through various cortical ensemble templates. Guiding Willy with the chip link alone was as cumbersome as steering a bus by remote control. Useful for guiding a rat in a maze but difficult in the three dimensions that made up Willy's world. She stabbed at the screen. Clumsily, with many over-compensating actions and corrections, she managed to angle the obliging Willy northward. He must not have had a particular location in mind and was just out for a spin around his territory.

The boat emerged back into view, its wake two diverging white lines. Morgan zoomed in on the boat deck. Charlotte, shaven head now bare of the shower cap, hung onto the railing, leaning into the wind, her mouth a rictus of fear. Broan had one hand on the boat's wheel and the other waving a shotgun in the air. His lips moved. The silence made it even more unnerving.

After five minutes, Willy curved east again. Morgan increased the prickling sensation on his left cheek until he arced his head and raised a claw, trying to scratch his face. Eagles didn't normally fly in straight lines and the unnaturalness must have begun to grate on him. She could feel it too—like fingernail scrapes deep within her mind.

Willy headed deep inland, most likely for a treetop where he could brush the imagined wasp off his face.

"The link's not strong enough to override his instincts. It's not working." Morgan sat back and rubbed her hands over her upper arms.

To her surprise, Andrew's eyes were shiny. He stumbled over to the lab sink and washed his face. His voice was flat as he mopped his face with a paper towel. "We need to activate Warbird mode."

"No, Andrew. Just…no."

"Just to follow the boat, not to attack, damn it."

"The software doesn't *work*. That's why your offensive, immoral project failed. All it does it cause pain to Willy."

"Charlotte's only seventeen, Morgan." In the six months he'd supervised the eagle project, he had never called her anything but "Dr. Howard."

Morgan wrenched her eyes away. "It doesn't work," she said again, shaking her head. She walked over to her purse, each footstep weighing a hundred pounds. "But I have something that does."

She'd never tried the swim cap in conjunction with the Warbird software. The thought disgusted her. She continued shaking her head even as she took off the standard headset, opened the Warbird software link and gestured for Andrew to enter his high-level passwords.

The innocuous pink swim cap settled heavily on her head, out of all proportion to its weight.

She spread her arms wide and blinked the interface on.

~ * ~

A tilted arena of green tree crowns, brilliant blue water beyond. Morgan soared, lost in the sheer glory of being airborne.

The scent of the fir trees rising from below was almost tangible.

Andrew coughed, somewhere far away. Morgan exhaled long and slow and used the visuals for a meditation focal point before sending Willy a direct thought: *lower*. He dropped instantly, then, at her next instruction, angled out into the strait. If the earlier apparatus was comparable to steering a bus in a rainstorm, the sophisticated performance of her own apparatus was like a driving a sports car on a dry and sunny racetrack.

Among the whitecaps, the blemish of the speedboat was easy to pick out.

Broan loomed larger, his wild eyes catching the light. He swigged from a half-filled liquor bottle and propped it next to the shotgun by the wheel. Charlotte huddled in a corner, head down. Soon, the boat would enter a narrow maze of channels and disappear from view.

A murmur on Morgan's right. Andrew, his voice rough, was on his phone, feeding the Coast Guard revised GPS coordinates, his other hand half-raised in a fist.

Then his voice blared in her ear. "The Coast Guard! Won't get there in time! Got to stop the boat now!" He slammed his fist on the counter.

Morgan clenched her jaw so hard pain radiated right to her ears. She had to save the girl, even at the expense of Willy. She focused on single, discrete thoughts: *Attack. Claw. Fight.*

Willy swept in a tight circle, then he cried, a high-pitched wail of confusion and distress. She tried again. *Defend the girl.* And again. *Save her. Please, Willy, please.*

For long moments, she repeated the phrases, using every mind calming technique she knew.

Finally, she lifted the swim cap. Voice raw, she shouted at Andrew. "It's no use! Even with my enhanced connection, Willy simply won't react to direct neuro-commands!" The abuses the eagle had endured by those military combat operators, those *jerks*, must have dampened his response receptors irreparably. "He doesn't *feel* pleasure anymore. There is no way you can reward him for attacking."

Andrew's eyes glinted, yellowish in the harsh lab lighting. "Carrots, Dr. Howard, are one way. Sticks are another. Pain avoidance. Poke Willy a bit with your mind. Minor phantom pain, momentary twinges, is all it is. Willy will instinctually avoid that even if it doesn't hurt him much. Let the Warbird software help. Have him dive at the boat, slash at Broan's hands."

She stared at Andrew. He was right. There *was* no other course of action. But he had misunderstood her explanation. Willy couldn't feel pleasure but he *could* feel real pain to the same degree as any animal—the two hemispheres of the amygdala were not related. She could tell him how much poking at Willy's mind would hurt Willy and herself—tell this man who had sent men off to their deaths in Iraq and was now at risk of losing his only daughter—and add to his misery.

Or she could keep the knowledge to herself.

She settled the cap to her scalp, ignoring the tears running down her face, lifting her impossibly heavy arms.

~ * ~

Attack, Willy. Do it! Now! Like dominos falling, electrical signals passed through her neural connections at lightning speed. Pain shot through her temple like a live wire, transmitting Willy's agony directly to the most primitive areas of her brain. She felt herself almost fall and groped for the countertop.

Fighting for control, she managed to lock some of the pain away. *Fight! Slash!*

Eons later, she couldn't take it anymore. Willy was shuddering now, his mind a black hollow of pain. Sharing the agony, she steered him to the shoreline several hundred feet away, where he circled and cried.

She threw the swim cap on the counter and clawed at her sweaty forehead as if she could gouge out the last few minutes. Her lab coat felt constricting and she wrenched it off.

She'd rest for a minute. Just for a minute.

"Keep trying, Doctor. Failure. Not an option." Andrew had taken off his uniform jacket and loosened his tie. Large sweat patches darkened his shirt.

"The pain is too unfocused! It's only making Willy panic."

"Need a higher signal-to-noise ratio, that's all."

"That's the *reason* the Warbird project failed in the first place," Morgan snapped, then berated herself for her loss of control. She took a Buddha-breath, deep from her belly, her momentary rage dissipating as she achieved partial zazen state again. Andrew's PTSD could perhaps be alleviated if he learned this ancient yogic methodology, she thought absently.

She paused, swim cap in hand. *Huh*. Maybe *that* was why there had been inconsistent results with the Warbird software in all the military testing. Perhaps *rage* was the answer. She just wasn't angry enough to get through to Willy.

But she knew someone who was.

She turned to the dolly and dug through one of the packed boxes. "Here." She thrust a spare headset—a standard military one—at Andrew. "Put it on. Channel your anger to Willy. He'll sense it."

"Doubt it, Doctor. No experience. No training."

True. And, although he had amazing self-control, without her years of meditation practice, he wouldn't have her degree of focus.

She'd have to connect in tandem with him.

~ * ~

"Failure is not an option, remember, *Major*?" She pushed him into her chair and placed the headset on him hastily. No time for an MRI. She found a splitter in the boxes and pulled up compatibility software. Another Buddha-breath, then she raised her arms.

The instant she blinked the twinned set on, Andrew gave a loud gasp. Morgan's view immediately clouded with Andrew's overlapping and uncontrolled inputs. Interference, manifesting as a sudden murky gray fear, clogged her view. Willy lurched and went into a dead fall, like stooping on a rabbit. Morgan fought the panic, most of it this time from Andrew, and Willy leveled out, then rose.

"Oh, my Lord, that's magnificent!" Andrew's voice was hoarse. His panic lessened, the neural handshake steadied, and Morgan's vision cleared a bit. She ached all over from the strain of Andrew's aura, like she'd caught a bad flu. Was this how he felt all the time? How did he live with such fear and guilt and sorrow? She squeezed her eyes shut for a moment.

By the time the boat reappeared below them, Andrew's presence had receded to an aching brown mist blurring the scene. Morgan directed the visuals onto Broan's face.

"Picture the creep as if he was a male rivaling for Willy's mate's attention, as if some guy was hitting on your wife," Morgan said through gritted teeth, as she refined the close-up image. She knew eagles were more faithful than humans, but she also needed to enrage Andrew more. She was vaguely aware of Andrew leaning forward in his chair. The haze intensified, making Broan's sneer indistinct and her arms heavy as lead.

Morgan ignored her thudding head and issued commands rapid-fire. *Slow. Stop.* Obedient despite the agonizing throbbing in his skull, Willy propped out his wings and halted, allowing the boat to pass underneath.

Broan raised his shotgun and fired at the bird, seemingly just for sport. Willy flailed and panicked, flapping madly. Charlotte dove for the gun and the two humans wrestled for control.

A bird, another bald eagle, zipped past. *Elsa!* Morgan yelled and Willy cried out to his partner, high and wild. Broan wrestled the gun from Charlotte and fired again. Elsa plummeted downwards, into the water behind the boat. Her body rose for a moment on a swell, then disappeared into the white foam.

Andrew seethed inside Morgan's mind and red-hot flames momentarily filled her view. Time to act, before Andrew's burgeoning rage eclipsed her sight entirely. She put Willy into a steep dive, wings folded. Pain seared through her mind like saltwater on an open wound. She pulled Willy up just short of the wheelhouse, claws outstretched towards Broan, beak open. Charlotte grabbed the gun barrel but Broan thrust her aside. A shout. A shot. A feint, then another, then a confusion of wings, feathers, and claws, and red-black blood.

Enough.

Morgan tightened her mind, pulling Willy away.

Nothing happened.

She pulled away again, almost blind, pain blistering through her skull. Again nothing. Andrew's anger, intense flames now white-hot, overwhelmed every command she gave. All Willy had left were his primary instincts. After Elsa's death, base survival had been subsumed by the instinct to kill.

More blood, black tufts of hair, some kind of fluid. A shot of the decking and a blurred close-up of some rivets.

Then, nothing.

Andrew stood so violently his chair crashed backwards. He tore off the headset, gave a hoarse inhuman cry, shoulders shaking.

Morgan stood in stunned silence, not bothering to disconnect the now-lifeless equipment. She lowered her aching arms.

It was a long twenty minutes before the Coast Guard phoned. Charlotte had taken the wheel and had been on her way back to the harbor when they'd reached her. The officer who took over as pilot was kind enough to aim his phone at Charlotte, sending the image back to Andrew's phone. The teen had wrapped Willy's lifeless body in her jacket and was sitting on the bench, just rocking back and forth, back and forth.

~ * ~

"Here, let me help." Andrew said, closing the lab door behind him and taking the heavy box from Morgan's arms. "Charlotte sends a hello. First round of therapy's done."

Morgan let go of the box warily. Three weeks at her seaside cabin had gifted her with rainy days full of rest and introspection. She followed Andrew's glance around the lab. The sun shone feebly through the blinds, striping the cages and dusty scattered boxes. A lone eagle, a juvenile male, perched sullenly in the only occupied cage, his magnificent chest plumage a glory of brilliant white and chestnut brown.

"All packed up?" Andrew placed the box in the stack on the dolly, then put his hands at his back, a kind of parade rest, and frowned at her.

Morgan reached for the next box. She and Andrew were now comrades-in-arms, she thought wryly, with their own little secret about the unauthorized use of government equipment, the scientific leap ahead her swim cap was capable of, and Andrew's later wiping of his software access. "I'm glad Charlotte is all right." Sitting on the porch at the old cabin, she'd realized everyone had their burdens to carry, Andrew included.

"Updates for you, Doctor. You'll have seen Broan's sentencing, life in prison. You might not have seen his attempts to elicit public sympathy. Online uproar. Media circus."

"I've glanced at newscasts. Some kind of petition and various lobbies?" She had spent her vacation mostly offline: meditating, hiking, and eagle watching. Headaches and gut aches still remained; sort of like PTSD, she figured—something else she now shared with Andrew.

"Seems Broan's eyesight was ruined by what the press are

calling a 'rabid' eagle and social media are calling a terrible bout of misfortune. Signed on to be a guinea pig. Someday, may get an experimental optoelectronic prosthesis that will translate the visual signals via intracortical—"

"—microstimulation," Morgan finished. "A spin-off of the technology he was dealing. The very technology we are helping to advance." Something in her chest eased even farther than it had these past few weeks. But she still had to get her own life in order. She lifted the box of electronics—there was still a lot of equipment to dismantle.

Andrew touched her arm, halting her. "Best news last, Doctor. The military responded to the media outcry about eagle welfare in urban areas. Amazingly fast, if slightly off kilter in goals. The remaining Warbird eagles will all be quietly rehabbed and released. The Warbird program shut down forever. Funding increase will facilitate that. That is, if you're willing to stay on?"

Morgan set the box back onto the counter. "Help rehab the Warbirds? Wonderful! I'd like that." It would be a satisfying project to complete and after that, she could take stock of her ambitions.

She opened a box lid and unpacked a bundle of electrode connectors, setting them next to the row of cages. Timmo, the juvenile male eagle, rustled his feathers and glared at her as if he knew which cages had belonged to Willy and Elsa. Morgan wiped her eyes on her sleeve. Her grief would linger for a while. And Andrew still had bags under his eyes. It seemed some burdens were harder to lay down than others.

Andrew still stood at the window, his eyes on the brilliant clear sky. She put down her next handful and joined him, squinting into the infinite blue.

She'd been thinking about a refinement to the pink swim cap for a week or so, one that heightened the wearer's pleasure feed and allowed it to be communicated more strongly. It might help Timmo, the juvenile male in the cage, rehabilitate faster if she could bounce his joy of flying back to him, ramping up his pleasure like an infinite series of mirrored reflections. Further, if more people could feel the exhilaration an eagle experiences in flight, their mental wounds might heal in some small way, too.

Meanwhile, the swim cap was the best sensory apparatus they had. She turned and dug it out of her purse. Thin, pink, and lightweight, it dangled from her hand as she offered it to Andrew. "Timmo is really keen for a flight. Want to go along for the ride?"

~ * ~ * ~

Holly Schofield travels through time at the rate of one second per second, oscillating between the alternate realities of city and country life. Her speculative fiction has appeared in many publications including *Analog*, *Lightspeed*, and *Escape Pod*, is used in university curricula, and has been translated into multiple languages. She hopes to save the world through science fiction and homegrown heritage tomatoes.

Find her at: hollyschofield.wordpress.com.

PHOTO SYMPATHY

Ray Daley

Monday

The morning was my Harvest Time. Time to go through all the online papers, time to see what news the world was feeding on.

FAMINE IN SUDAN

I clicked on that. The bot did its scrobbling. It was more like an arcane procedure than a few lines of Python script, but it always did its thing, shooting the results back to the main server. In the bad old days of manual inputs, it used to take me several hours to manually check all the news sites. The scrobbler bot did it in a little under three minutes these days. By which time I'd got a cup of coffee on the go and was working on the day's new output.

Then I got the usual daily call from the Boss. "Hey, Mays. Your stats are in, nice work on the over-nights!"

"Thanks, Boss. Any requests today, or should I just start working on the regular stuff?"

"Can you prepare a few post-tsunami shots? The normal fare, buildings wrecked, boats beached, cars floating on a river that used to be a road. That kind of thing."

I nodded. I knew what he wanted. "Any bodies? Or is it just a Stage One?"

"Not yet, Mays, Stage One will do me fine. Can you have them ready before five, your time?"

"Sure, Boss. I'll put the standards on hold. I can pull archived stuff if the need arises. You need me to check in later?"

"That's okay, Mays. I wouldn't want the great artist thinking he was at my beck and call. Work your magic, like I know you can. Toodles!"

I spent three hours roughing out a series of pictures for the tsunami job. People always seem to like the little boats, so I worked extra hard on those. I made sure the cars were local, nothing fancy or too expensive. It didn't get the heartstrings going, seeing people with a nicer car than you, even if they were losing it to a natural disaster. I was just about to shoot the pictures off to the Boss when I had a brainstorm.

The tiniest of inserts on one of the debris shots, a child's doll, washed up in the foreground, right where the eye would be naturally drawn. Yes, it was perfect. That was a really nice touch! Then I sent them in.

"Recorder on. *Pull archived shots of avalanches, mine cave-ins and rockfalls. Return all images over twelve years old. Commence search.*" And that left me free to fill a few freelance jobs to pad out the rest of the day. A couple of abandoned dogs, a premature baby born two months early, more images of that haemorrhagic fever outbreak. Then I punched out for the day.

Tuesday

FAMINE CONTINUES!
TSUNAMI HITS ISLAND CHAIN!
3 TRAPPED AFTER CAVE-IN.
MISSING DOG FOUND!

The bot commenced scrobbling as I ate my cheese on toast, quietly burning the roof of my mouth as I read. It was getting more hits this morning, firing them back to the server.

Then I heard the daily alarm, "Hey, Mays. Nice work on the tsunami stuff, it's being picked up by all the global outlets. Is three percent all right or should I haggle for four?"

"Four if you can, Boss, half a percent in it for you if you can?"

"The Dailys loved the dog shots and the baby. You do great baby, Mays! If you can work up some underwear shots of that Minister, I'd be super grateful?"

"I thought you'd already contracted that job out to the independents, Boss?"

"That asshole let me down, Mays! He's in bloody rehab!"

"I bid you eight percent on that one, right?"

I could hear the clicking of his keyboard through the speakers. "That's right, Mays. He bid five. Would you take six and a half on that? I'll pay seven if you rush it before the end of today?"

"Seven and a quarter, and I'll get it to you before noon. Deal?"

"Hell, yes. You pulled my arse out of the fire on that one, Mays. I'll let you cherry-pick our jobs for the rest of the week. One second. *'System. Set over-ride code, let current feed be priority one. Confirm?'* Hang on Mays, okay?"

I could hear his machine clicking over time, then the muted female voice saying "Confirmed."

"Right, Mays. You'll get all the feeds first, until next Monday. Are you working this weekend?"

"I haven't decided that yet, Boss. You'll be the second to know."

"Second? Who else are you working for, apart from me I mean?"

"Me, you idiot!"

I could hear him slapping his forehead, trying not to groan, and failing miserably. "If you finish that Minister job, can you see about doing a more hardcore haemorrhagic fever shot for me?"

"No promises. I want scale plus two if I send it in though?"

"That's fine, Mays. I can cover that with my offsets. Get on the case. Toodles!"

I set a search bot looking for pictures of the Government Minister. He was an under-secretary of something or other. Not that it mattered to me. I never voted. It returned a dozen good images of him from all angles, enough for me to mock-up what the Boss wanted. I could have easily 'shopped him onto a cross-dressing nude from any of the porn forums but I always do everything manually myself. I had a decent body match in my tools file. Then I had a thought. "Call Boss."

He picked up right away. "Hey, Mays. Problems?"

"No, Boss, just a question. This Minister job. You want I should maybe do it sans panties? Erect, perhaps? Or would that be too much?"

He laughed. "I like your mind, Mays. They can blur out a cock shot, that'll get the news-hounds baying for his blood too."

"The full eight percent for that then, Boss."

"No arguments from me, Mays. Make it hard. Toodles!"

And I was straight back on the case. Nose to the grindstone. Minister without panties, and soon to be without portfolio too. It took a few sweeps through my tools file to find a good enough erection, one that wasn't too long or thick. I didn't want to make him look good, after all. Another twenty minutes spent working on the background, some extra kinky lingerie just casually draped about the room. Perfect. Right at eye level too.

"Recorder on. *Pull archived shots of haemorrhagic fever. Return all images over fifteen years old. Commence search.*" That left me time to go make myself some food, and take a much-needed bathroom break too.

I wolfed down my ramen, along with a cup of lukewarm fresh green tea. I decided to make an afternoon of the fever images. I managed to get eight completed before the end of day deadline.

Wednesday

3 DEAD AS FEVER STRIKES!
MINISTER DISGRACED IN NUDES SHOCKER!
BABY ABANDONED!

Another morning, deep into scrobbling. It was getting major league hits, right out of the park in some cases. All I had was a minor indie lead for a job that just read '*Wheelchair*'.

"Recorder on. *Feedback on wheelchair job. Request further details, more info is required before I can go forward. Thanks.* Send that to them with a rush on it. File stats A and stats B from Monday and Tuesday. Run the numbers on productivity to percentage points and money made, before and after deductions. And send a message to that software guy. *Query on new tools files, when should I expect to receive them? Payment is being held for now.* Send that as a rush too."

Then came the alarm, almost as if on cue. "Morning, Mays. Good work on that Minister job. They offered another three percent and I took it, I assume that was okay?"

"Fine, Boss. Take two percent for yourself. Everything else seems to be scoring too?"

"Confirmed, Mays. I've got an offer of credits on the fever submission. There's no exact word on how many outlets want the pictures yet but I've heard offers on everything. Was the baby yours as well?"

"Yes, Boss. I'm not taking any subs today though."

"But I had three twelve percenters lined up for you, Mays?

All sure things too?"

"Sorry, Boss. I'm having a rare day off. Gonna go and see my kid."

"You get the restraining band off then?"

"Not yet. So yes, still from twenty feet."

"That sucks, Mays. A man should be able to see his kids. Be able to hug 'em too. Not have to be twenty feet away. How much longer you gonna be wearing that band?"

"Another month, unless the appeal goes through. Speaking of which, didn't you mention you knew a Judge? When we discussed the para-legal job back in June?"

I could see him scratching his head, which meant he was about to give me an excuse. "Wilson. Yeah, about him?" *Here it came.* "He got disbarred. So no-go on that avenue. I could ask around, see who else is in the contacts book?"

"Screw it. I can wait another month. I've already waited two years. If you get any emergencies, leave them with the scrobbler bot, okay, Boss?"

"Sure, Mays. Toodles!" I could tell it was killing him, not to be leaving any work with me.

I left the various bots searching, collating data and waiting on incoming calls. I spent the rest of the morning watching my boy from a park bench. At least he waved at me this time. I guess he still remembered me today. He was with the Nanny. Hitler in high heels, as I called her in my head.

As much as I'd tried in the past, she'd never talk to me, the ex was really tough on enforcing that rule. The poor kid's had no end of nannies who cared too much and lost the job through speaking to me. I made sure he went home chock-full of sugar. Something to keep that hell-witch busy. I miss being able to talk to him though. Just one more month.

I didn't even bother logging in when I went back to the flat. I just sat on the bed quietly broadcasting hate at my ex until it got dark.

Thursday

I guess I slept on top of the bed last night then? I didn't bother logging in until I'd inhaled my first cup of tea. That was four slices of bacon into a proper breakfast. I've decided to go easier on myself, I have to be there for the kid when the restraining order expires.

The screen was flashing seven different kinds of alert messages at me when I finally decided to sit down and sign in. "Display messages in order of importance. Outstanding jobs?"

Nothing came up. That was a good start then, it meant the Boss hadn't weakened and sent me stuff anyway. "Display message feedback?"

"Hey, Mays, it's Joey. Sorry about the delay on those folders. I totally understand you holding my payment. They should be with you in twelve hours. It's a big chunk of data and I'm passing it over as fast as my servers can manage. Check it out once you've got the whole thing. Pay me when you're entirely happy. Any issues, flash message me and we'll deal with it immediately. I like my clients to be both happy *and* satisfied. Once again, massive apologies for the delay. Peace, out!"

Sweet. He was a decent guy most of the time, sometimes he could get a little flaky around things like deadlines. He didn't always have his shit together. It was good to see him on top of this one though. The message bot was showing all data received. I'd check that later. There were no new jobs, a few payment confirmations from completed stuff though. Mostly automated daemons, few places rarely involved people with payments these days.

The scrobbler had got everything I wanted, even a couple of extra things from the inference routine. I like that code, it sees what I'm doing and asks itself what else might be useful in similar fields. That gets me a lot of side work.

I still hadn't got anything back on the wheelchair job yet. I set a crawler bot running, just to make sure they weren't farming the work out to anyone else. I'd been stung by people like that in the past, they send you a vague outline and expect results but then pass the job on if you dare to ask for more information. I was taking a massive chance working with them, but it wasn't a big payday if I lost out.

Then it was that time. *Ting-ting! Ting-ting!*

"Morning, Boss. I haven't seen the headlines yet; I'm running a little behind. How's the news?"

He didn't look his usual enthusiastic self. "No takers on the fever stuff, Mays. I'm not sure what's going on but it's like everyone suddenly turned their back on your work. I've got one job but it's to be filed anonymously, they'll never pay out otherwise. You wanna take it?"

I nodded. "Sure. If there's nothing else, Boss?"

He shook his head and signed off. Things must have been bad, he didn't even say Toodles.

I scanned the job info. *Dead news filer.*

Ouch. That was a bit close to home. Then I saw the name. I didn't know him as such, but I did recognize the filer code. I should, I'd only taken on one of his jobs a few days back. He was the guy who'd flaked out on the Boss over the Minister story. Either someone had hit back at him hard, or they'd missed the fact he hadn't done the job. I had filed it under his credit, but I had got the money.

It took well over an hour with the scrobbler set on its widest search terms before I even found one remotely usable image of him. Lass Tass. Probably his byline name, I never found another ID on him.

Three hours scanning the scrobbled image, rendering different angles and dimensional projections. I eventually made two decent profiles and a torso shot.

Then the message daemon went haywire. *"Don't file! Don't file! The hits are out! Lass Tass."* A message from a dead man? Interesting. Sent in the last ten minutes too, according to the header info.

Then another, "They know it's you. Bug out! Find a safe haven. Use q codes. Q-33." Q-33 was the Boss. Shit. It was bad if *he* was telling me to get the hell out of Dodge!

I looked around the place. I grabbed the cash I kept stashed in the wall, and the burner phone too. I couldn't take anything else, but I left the renderer running, I had a feeling this might be its last job.

Friday

"Incoming news file, Q-86."

"Thanks, scrobbler bot. ID on that account please, Admin?"

"ID confirmed, Boss, Mays Philays. Forward payment?"

"Hold, for now, Admin. Open filed story?"

"Opening as requested. Audio on?"

"Go ahead."

"The body of an independent news filer was found at his London flat in the early hours of Friday morning. The man confirmed to be news filer Mays Philays appears to have been shot several times. Examination of local CCTV footage has yielded no clues as yet. In other news, the Government are said to be standing by the Under Secretary for Education. It appears pictures recently released by the gossip tabloids may have been manufactured in an attempt to influence public opinion against the current Cabinet."

"Audio off. Forward all payments to the alternate account. Account holder, James Philays, current age, nine years old. When the outstanding payments are sent, delete all files pertaining to Q-86. Purge today's logs, too. I'd like to wake up alive tomorrow, and not on the front page if I can help it."

"Processing as ordered. Okay, Boss."

~ * ~ * ~

Ray Daley was born in Coventry and still lives there. He served 6 years in the RAF as a clerk & spent most of his time in a Hobbit hole in High Wycombe. He is a published poet and has been writing stories since he was 10. His current dream is to eventually finish the Hitch Hikers fanfic novel he's been writing since 1986.

Tweet him @RayDaleyWriter

THE LONG AND THE SHORT OF IT

DJ Tyrer

The ripe fruit hung heavy on the branches of the trees in Mytherim Wood, the scent of it sweet upon the summer air. Flies droned lazily between the trees as they waited for the fruit to soften and spoil, offer nourishment for their offspring. In the dappled shade, it was nigh paradisical.

"Give me a hand," Adegar said.

"Gladly." Orvan picked up the Halfling in his beefy hands and lifted him up towards the branches where Adegar grabbed several fruits before being deposited back onto the ground.

To the memories of all, it had ever been thus. The strapping Woodfolk and the stout Halflings lived side-by-side in a forest that offered them all they required with but little effort. Life was good.

Had been good.

"There is less fruit this year," Arpan told Orvan when they met later that day in the shade of an age-bowed fruit tree.

"You said that last year," Orvan replied even as their friend Toldan nodded.

"Well, it's true," Arpan grumbled. "Last year, there was less fruit than usual. This year, there is less still…"

He gestured at the branches above them. "Oh, yes, there may be fruit here, but there is little in the Grove of Pesos and none at all on the east bank of the Lire."

"It's because the rains came late," Toldan opined.

"Still, there's plenty," Orvan said before taking a bite of one.

"Not at the rate those little sack-bellies gobble it up," Arpan told him.

"Share and share alike. We help them pick the fruit and they cook lovely pies—just as we hunt and share the meat we cook."

Toldan sneered. "For every pie they share with us, they scoff down three or four. Oh, you know it's true—they're always eating!"

"Aye," Arpan said. "They're half our size and don't labor as we do, yet they eat so much more."

"So?" Orvan shook his head in bemusement. "What does it matter? That's how it ever has been."

Another snort escaped Toldan's nostrils. "What does it matter? Have you not been listening? We have maybe half the fruit we usually have—and, our wheat has been sparse, and fewer deer have been seen—yet the Halflings continue to stuff themselves as much as ever."

Arpan nodded. "They are eating most of our food—our *limited* food—and contribute nothing but a few pies."

"They're good pies," Orvan said.

"Not *that* good, no." Arpan shook his head.

"It isn't fair," Toldan said.

Orvan scratched his head for a while, then said, "I guess you're right, friends, but what are we to do about it?"

"Give them less," Arpan said, firmly.

"But, that doesn't seem fair, either."

"Look," Arpan explained, "they're too short to reach the fruit without us. We do the work—whether picking it or lifting them so they can reach it. We're the ones who hunt and bring in fresh meat. As we do the work, we should get the most to keep our energy up."

"We're not saying they can't have *any* fruit," Toldan added, "only that we should get the most and they, perhaps, could be put to work in some productive way to help out."

"That does make sense," Orvan admitted.

"Of course it does," Arpan told him. "And, if you'll back us, I'm certain the others can be convinced."

Reluctantly, Orvan gave a nod.

"Good," Arpan said. "We'll call a moot."

~ * ~

"Give me a hand," Adegar said, the next day.

Orvan shook his head. "No."

"No?" The Halfling looked up at him in wide-eyed confusion.

"No," the tall man said with a note of finality.

"Are you hurt?"

"It's nothing like that. You see, we held a moot last night and it was decided that no longer shall Woodfolk help Halflings to fruit. There isn't enough to go around and we have to think of ourselves. Only those who do the work deserve the benefits."

"But," the Halfling's lip quivered and he stamped his foot in indignation, "the trees are ours. We share them. We've always shared them ever since the Woodfolk came to these woods."

"Times change, my friend, and they are no longer 'ours' together, but the Woodfolk's alone." Orvan shrugged. "I'm sorry."

He looked away, shifting uncomfortably.

Adegar shook his head. "This won't stand."

Orvan almost laughed, but managed not to.

"That's the way it is…"

~ * ~

"The little runts have started using ladders," Arpan told the gathered Woodfolk.

Jeers and angry shouts answered him.

"They're stealing *our* fruit," Toldan cried.

Orvan held up his hands in placation.

"Brothers, please…. Don't get agitated. Our anger was that the Halflings were taking advantage of us, using our height. If they can reach the fruit through their own effort, well…" He spread his hands. "…I'm not sure we have a complaint."

"But, it's *our* fruit," Arpan said.

"Is it? Doesn't it just grow upon the trees with no effort on our part? It dangles there for any who can take it."

"Don't go soft on us, Orvan," called someone from the crowd.

"Look," Toldan said, "given our height, we stand closer to the fruit. Therefore, it is ours. It stands to reason, my friend."

Orvan sighed. It had to be wrong, but he couldn't argue against Toldan's reasoning.

"Let the Halflings have the roots and berries and we'll have the fruit," his friend continued.

Arpan nodded. "Right."

"What about the deer?" Orvan asked. "They run upon the ground."

Arpan laughed. "Have you ever seen a Halfling hunt?"

"And, the wheat?"

"They can have the stalks to chew and we'll take the ears—it grows tall."

Orvan could see there was no swaying them, so shrugged and stayed silent as Arpan called upon the assembled men to defend their food supplies.

"Break their ladders," Arpan shouted.

"Break their ladders," came back the answering cry.

Orvan sighed.

~ * ~

The bonfire blazed merrily and the gathered men laughed and sang as they shared baked fruits sweetened with honey.

Had the fire not been fueled with the smashed remains of the Halflings' ladders, Orvan might have enjoyed the evening. Instead, he remained silent, and the mouthfuls of fruit tasted like ash on his tongue.

Never had he known anything like it—the rage, the cathartic release after. It was as if his kinsfolk were in the grip of madness.

~ * ~

"You can't do that," Orvan exclaimed as he came upon Adegar throwing sticks up at the ripe fruit, trying to knock it free from the branch.

"They're our trees," the Halfling huffed, throwing another stick and finally scoring a fat fruit.

"You know how the others will react if they see you."

"Snap my twigs and build another bonfire?" Adegar snorted. "The wood is full of twigs, my friend."

There was a sneer to his last two words that made Orvan glance away, embarrassed.

"Just don't let the others catch you…" he said as he hurried away, an unpleasant feeling of guilt churning his guts.

~ * ~

The sweet scent of ripe summer fruit had been replaced by the heavy smell of smoke that tickled the back of his throat unpleasantly and made him cough.

Orvan wasn't certain what had set if off—someone had seen Halflings throwing sticks up at the fruit, rumors claimed they had made themselves bows and taken to shooting at the deer and had, if not taken some, spooked them—but, the results were clear: A band of men had decided to burn down the homes of several Halflings, that of Adegar amongst them. The fires had spread and taken a number of trees with them.

Shaking his head, Orvan considered that such rash behavior

could see them deprived of all their fruit if they weren't careful.

"They deserve it," Toldan said.

In a sense, perhaps they did—he had warned Adegar, after all —and yet, Orvan couldn't shake the feeling they had done something terrible.

"With any luck," Arpan said, "the little maggots will take the hint and go away, leave us in peace?"

"Leave us in peace?" Orvan murmured to himself. He didn't recall the Halflings doing anything to threaten them. Quite the opposite…

But, he didn't dare raise his voice in protest…

~ * ~

Orvan found he missed the taste of Halfling-baked pie. His wife's was passable, but nothing like it. More than that, most of all, he missed Adegar.

The Halflings had retreated across the Lire, leaving the western half of the woods, and its fruit, to the Woodfolk.

The arrangement seemed to suit Arpan, Toldan, and the others, but Orvan could see no real advantage in it. Fruit had become scarce, and winter was coming and the woods seemed dark and foreboding. The world he had known ever since he was a child seemed to be gone forever.

~ * ~

"There's no fruit," Arpan snarled when summer finally came round again.

"The trees look sick," Toldan said.

"The rains were even later this year," Orvan pointed out.

"No." Arpan shook his head. "It's those damn Halflings— the little rats have done something to the trees. It's their revenge because we wouldn't let them steal our fruit."

"I'm sure it's not," Orvan said.

"Arpad's right," Toldan said. "It makes sense."

"You know," Arpan said, "they're probably growing fruit over the river. We should go get it."

"But, if they are, then it's their fruit."

Arpan laughed. "Oh, Orvan, you fool, you just don't understand."

"No, I don't."

"We're the ones who deserve it all, not them; it's as simple as that!"

Orvan just shook his head, confused.

"Come, let's gather the others and go to war."

Toldan nodded at Arpan's words and they set off, leaving Orvan to his confusion.

~ * ~

The battle didn't last long before Arpan and the few survivors came limping home.

"The runts ambushed us!" Arpan ranted as Orvan tried, futilely, to calm him. "They shot us up with arrows and broke men's skulls with sling-stones."

Fists clenched in anger, he cried, "They cheated!"

Orvan snorted. "You deluded yourself. You didn't think they could fight, but they could."

"But, we're better than them!"

"Listen to yourself, man. You didn't think about the possibility. You didn't think about *anything*."

"Oh, shut up. Look, they'll come for us, now, finish the job. We have to be ready to fight—unless you want your wife to be murdered by one of those maggots. They'd probably eat her—stuffed with fruit!" He paused to suck in a pained breath.

"Here," he thrust a knife into Orvan's hand, "get ready."

Orvan looked down at the blade clasped in his fingers, then up at Arpan. There was madness in the man's eyes.

"We have to kill every last one of them," Arpan cried, "before they kill us. Got it?"

"Got it." Orvan plunged the blade into the man's chest.

Arpan sank to his knees.

"It ends, now," Orvan told him as the man's eyes dimmed; "*if* the last of us are to survive…"

The man collapsed and died and Orvan let out a sound that was somewhere between a sigh and a wail.

Then, he turned and began to walk away.

He would talk to the Halflings.

"Pray I can resolve this," he called back to the wounded men he left behind.

~ * ~

The Halflings had appointed Adegar their spokesman, but any hope that raised in Orvan's heart was soon dashed.

"We cannot go back to how things were," the Halfling told him. "Too much evil has been done to just be undone."

Adegar shook his head. "I know you, personally, did us no harm. You even sought to warn me of the danger. But, you did nothing to stop them. You remained with them, no matter how reluctantly. You remained one of them…"

"I'm sorry," Orvan said.

"Sorrow is of no value to us. You and your kind must go, leave the wood and start anew elsewhere."

Orvan sighed, then said, "With the trees dying, it may be the best course, after all."

Adegar gave a bitter laugh. "You never understood, did you? The trees *were* ours. We planted them and nurtured them. The lateness of the rains was a problem, but the trees would have recovered —they always do. Without us, though, the trees die…

"Things are bad, but we can restore their health."

He stared hard at Orvan. "Not that it will benefit you. I'm sorry."

Shaking his head, Orvan turned and, sadly, walked away. They had lost everything. And, worst of all, it had all been for a false premise.

The fruit had never been theirs for the Halflings to steal.

But, there was no time for him to dwell upon their foolishness: They needed to find themselves a new home.

A home, he knew, that would never be as bountiful nor as peaceful as the one they had thrown away.

~ * ~ * ~

DJ Tyrer dwells upon the northern shore of the Thames Estuary, close to the world's longest pleasure pier, in Southend-on-Sea. They studied history at the University of Wales at Aberystwyth, worked in education, and have a particular fascination with language, spending any free time working on conlangs. DJ is the person behind *Atlantean Publishing*, which has been going for more than two decades, and has been widely published in anthologies and magazines around the world, such as *Crunchy With Ketchup* and *Misunderstood* (both Wolfsinger), *Winter's Grasp* (Fantasia Divinity), *Tales of the Black Arts* (Hazardous Press), and *Pagan* (Zimbell House), and issues of *Fantasia Divinity, Broadswords and Blasters*, and *BFS Horizons*, and in addition, has a novella available in paperback and on the Kindle, *The Yellow House* (Dunhams Manor).

DJ Tyrer's website is djtyrer.blogspot.co.uk and you can visit Atlantean Publishing at atlanteanpublishing.wordpress.com.

THE OTHER SIDE OF THE CAGE

Radar DeBoard

Zeepholt saw them for most of his formative years. He had to. The only way he could get to his school out by the shoreline was by walking right by the Luminantis' enclosure. They would always be pressed up against the wiring as he passed by, looks of sorrow shown in their yellow eyes. Zeepholt learned later it was nothing more than a show. A trick the Luminantis pulled to lure unsuspecting fools to the fence, where they would then grab hold of the rube and tear them apart.

In his early years, before he knew any better, Zeepholt took pity on the freaks. He couldn't understand why there were so many of them kept in what looked like a prison. They seemed so harmless to him, and Zeepholt had convinced himself the Luminantis would never harm anyone. It wasn't until instructor Maltorph told him the truth his view of the Luminantis took the correct heading. That formative experience didn't happen till just after Zeepholt's seventh molt. After such an event, it was clear Maltorph decided it was time for his students to learn the truth.

"Has anyone ever seen the creatures trapped in the apparatus several clicks from the shoreline?" Maltorph began with his rough yet wavery voice.

"Zeepholt has!" a classmate shouted with a sneer, "He has to walk by them every day because his family is poor!"

Maltorph reacted to the student's comment by scuttling across the room at a surprising speed and snapping a claw right next to the instigator's face. It was simply a warning to tell the bully to stop, and it served its purpose well.

"Does anyone know what they are called?" Maltorph asked as a follow up to his initial inquiry. When none of the students replied he calmly informed the class, "They are a race of creatures called the Luminantis." Maltorph had then added in a lower tone, "They are incredibly dangerous."

The overwhelming curiosity of Zeepholt's young mind had forced him to ask, "Why?"

"Why!" Maltorph suddenly yelled as he slammed his left claw

against the wall. A passion he rarely displayed to his students spilled out as he explained, "Long ago, the Luminantis invaded our world. They stormed across the dry surface, wrecking all in their wake. Thankfully, they didn't begin their rampage at the coastline, otherwise we would have been exterminated. Their key error gave us time to prepare for them."

Instructor Maltorph paused for a long moment, which left the class in complete silence. A lone student decided to brave the situation and asked, "What happened?"

"We killed them!" Maltorph screamed.

The look of pure anger that filled his instructor's face in that moment stuck with Zeepholt through the years. It was a face of pure hatred. An emotional response Zeepholt could tell was directed solely at the Luminantis.

"We killed them," Maltorph repeated before justifying his words, "For what they did to our people. The atrocities they committed against us. We did what we had to do to beat them." The instructor shook his head in disgust, "After we pushed them back, broken their numbers and driven those monsters to the breaking point...we...backed off." Maltorph slammed his claw against the wall once more while he tried to hold back his distain. "Our leaders," he growled, "In their wisdom...decided to negotiate for peace. After all we had been through...all the atrocities the Luminantis committed...we were just supposed to let it all go."

In every moment since that day, Zeepholt had learned to bite his tongue in any situation, but he did no such thing at that point in time. "Is that what we did?" he asked, "Did we make peace with them?"

"Yes," Maltorph hissed before scuttling across the room at a surprising speed towards Zeepholt. Once he reached the student's desk, Maltorph bent down and poured a gaze of pure hatred into Zeepholt's eyes. "We made peace with them," he replied in a low whisper.

Zeepholt felt his instructor's breath brush against his visage, each exhale left him more uncomfortable than the last. He wanted to break his gaze from Maltorph, but he was afraid of what would happen if he did so. Zeepholt had been completely aware of the rooms' silence in those tense moments. He could feel all eyes were focused on the unintentional standoff Zeepholt had created between him and his instructor. Finally, Maltorph silently rose up and scuttled back from the desk a bit.

"Can anyone tell me what happened after we signed a peace treaty with the Luminantis?" Maltorph asked even though he knew no one would be able to answer him. He gave it a few moments before informing the class. "They continued to inhabit our land." Maltorph grimaced before continuing, "This was not part of the treaty mind you. The Luminantis had made a ridiculous accusation that we had destroyed all of their space vessels, so…they insisted they were stuck here. They would have to wait for others from their world to come and pick them up."

A student in the back of the room who clearly had not read the atmosphere of the situation correctly joked, "Well they haven't left yet!"

"That's right!" Maltorph screamed in the direction of the student to silence them. There was a long pause before Maltorph continued. "They haven't left yet. There are thousands of those enclosures across our world because the Luminantis refused to leave. We put up with their behavior for years. Their strange customs and inability to follow our rules were tolerated for a time. Eventually, they started to take all the jobs available on the land. Then all the homes. They started to create their own neighborhoods, all while laughing in the face of our laws and hospitality." Maltorph paused for effect before positing, "So ask yourself this …if someone lies to your face, breaks your rules, and takes what is yours…should you simply allow it to happen again? Or should you seek retribution."

That question clung in the back of Zeepholt's mind for weeks after that lecture. Though it was particularly lingering as he journeyed home from school that day. He was focused more on it than on his surroundings, which had been the reason why some antagonistic students had been able to follow without him noticing. Zeepholt hadn't even known they were there till the rocks started flying at him. The bullies outnumbered Zeepholt four to one, so their attacks easily pushed him to flee across the dry land. It wasn't until he was nearly in front of the enclosure he passed every day that one of the rocks caused some true damage.

An errant stone managed to smack into the left side of Zeepholt's visage, which tripped him to the ground in front of the enclosure. The fall had given the bullies plenty of time to catch up to him, but instead of delivering more physical punishment to Zeepholt, they started to verbally abuse him. They openly mocked his poverty, adding horrible remarks about his parents for good measure. Zeepholt brought his gaze up to the enclosure as he struggled to get up, and noticed the large group of Luminantis starring at him. Eventually, the bullies grew tired of abusing Zeepholt and they left, leaving him alone in the dirt. Yet, all the while, Zeepholt never looked away from the Luminantis.

A sensation of annoyance built inside of him while the bullies had been verbally assaulting him, but, the negative emotion hadn't been directed at his tormentors. That sense of gradually building anger was placed on the Luminantis who just stood there and watched with the same sad look they always wore on their faces. Zeepholt had wanted them to look away, to not stare at his humiliation, but they didn't move. This inaction, for some reason, seemed to affirm everything Maltorph had talked about, and continued to add fuel to the fire that burned inside of Zeepholt. It took a few tries for Zeepholt to stand, but when he finally managed it, he had a burning fury towards the group of Luminantis that drove him towards the fence of their enclosure.

Zeepholt screamed at the gathered mass on the other side of the fence. He threw obscenities at them while his temper raged on. The more he yelled, the more his body began to shake from the force he was putting behind his words. Zeepholt scanned the Luminantis during his rant, and the more he stared at them, the more he found their features disgusting. The pain the bullies had caused him thusly became associated with the enclosed group of aliens. Eventually, Zeepholt's rage subsided, and he stopped his screaming. The group of Luminantis just continued to stare at him with the same looks of sadness stretched across their twisted faces. Zeepholt scoffed at the mass of beings, insulting their intelligence, for they clearly had not understood what he had been screaming at them.

All the combined factors of that day started a notion inside of Zeepholt. The small idea the Luminantis were just disgusting creatures who tried to seize control of Zeepholt's world and failed. A growing feeling the beings behind the fenced in area were not worthy of equal treatment compared to Zeepholt's people. Afterall, the Luminantis were the ones who tried to hurt them. What right did they have to be sad for failing so miserably? Zeepholt found each time he trekked by the enclosure, the sight of the Luminantis filled him with slightly more disgust than the last.

This distaste festered and grew as time passed while Zeepholt continued to be taught by instructor Maltorph. Zeepholt found the instructor's views and arguments made a lot of sense to him the more they were espoused. He began to idolize Maltorph for his service to their people, and the wisdom the instructor was giving to him. It took a while for him to realize it, but eventually, Zeepholt learned he wasn't the only one who thought the way he did about the Luminantis. Most of his peers shared the same view, and Zeepholt realized he actually had something in common with the others.

Zeepholt took advantage of the distrust for the Luminantis and developed a rapport with several of his classmates. He found if he badmouthed those inside the enclosure it created a positive reaction in his peers. This spurred him to amplifying the ferocity of what he said about the Luminantis, adding a bit more legitimacy to the sense of disgust he felt for them. One day, the feelings of pity Zeepholt had once had for the Luminantis were gone, completely replaced by rage.

After Zeepholt's twentieth molt had come and went, he was finally deemed a fully grown member of the world. As such, he had to choose a profession to immediately began work in and Zeepholt did not hesitate to become a guard at one of the Luminantis' enclosures. He feared what would happen if the Luminantis were to escape, and above all, Zeepholt wanted to make sure that didn't occur. So who better to undertake such an important task than himself? He was a true servant of his people, and he would do whatever was necessary to keep the disgusting creatures trapped in their cages.

Zeepholt took to his new position with vigor, doing everything he could to keep the Luminantis in line. The Luminantis, in his opinion, were given far too much freedom based on the crimes they had committed. Of course, though his vigor was admired by upper management, most of the other guards found Zeepholt a bit too eager to dole out punishment. The rules of the enclosure were clear, the Luminantis were to be fed twice a day and allowed to roam around the inside of the enclosure. Yet, Zeepholt wanted nothing more than to take away the Luminantis' ability to move as they pleased.

In his mind, Zeepholt felt the Luminantis were playing a very long con on them. His people had played right into their clutches, and as soon as they had their chance, the aliens would slaughter everyone he held dear. This rationale drove everything Zeepholt did, giving him more than enough energy to carry out his duties. It took some time, but he eventually gained the respect of many of his peers while intimidating the rest into silence with his ferocity. He regularly beat any of the prisoners he deemed too rowdy, and took out his personal problems on any alien that dared to even look at him.

The moment Zeepholt elevated himself to a high enough position in the encampment, he began to implement changes. They were small adjustments at first, like cutting back the portions given to the prisoners for all their meals. Zeepholt hid this punishment under the guise of a necessary cutback to allocate funds elsewhere. A statement that wasn't a complete lie, but did hide a more sinister purpose. Zeepholt used the unethically acquired funds to build a small holding cell into the very ground of the enclosure. The cell was placed in the direct middle of the prison, so the Luminantis would have to walk over it as they moved about. Any prisoner Zeepholt felt was acting up would be thrown inside, left for days in a chamber a grown Luminantis could barely fit in.

As Zeepholt continued his rise in power, the injustices he doled out grew in cruelty. The young child who once took pity on a sad group of beings stuck behind a fence was long gone and had been replaced with a truly malicious individual. Zeepholt eventually became director over all Luminantis enclosures on the planet, and quickly implemented his preferred methods of housing the prisoners. Each passing day, Zeepholt took more and more away from the beaten aliens, who were on the brink of having nothing left to take.

When he first started his campaign, many employees quit. Yet, some stayed, and over time they added more likeminded individuals to help guard the enclosures. Eventually, it grew to the point where any new guard could easily be indoctrinated through peer pressure and the threat of losing their job. In only a few years, Zeepholt had developed a cult of personality that obeyed his every command. He had created a place where he was the absolute authority, and with the outside world seeming to forget about the remaining Luminantis, Zeepholt could do what he wanted to them.

"It's them or us!" he would shout as his rally cry.

A simple phrase that worked those under Zeepholt's command into a frenzy. His guards morphed from individuals simply doing their jobs, to beings only focused on conducting new and terrible ways to hurt the Luminantis. All the while, Zeepholt believed he was doing the right thing for his people. He honestly thought he was protecting his world from a menace that would stop at nothing to escape and destroy them. To his credit, Zeepholt was certainly right about one thing, the Luminantis would stop at nothing to escape. Even if that meant hundreds of them sacrificing themselves so a few could reach a point to contact other Luminantis who were searching for them.

Though it seemed like it took several generations in the life of Zeepholt's people, it only took a few Luminantis' years for others to arrive, their ships touching down on the surface of the planet to Zeepholt's horror. There were millions of them traversing across the land towards the encampments where Zeepholt waited with an army of his own, which he had amassed via those working for him. Yet, when the Luminantis arrived, it became abundantly clear to all they were not there to fight a war. They had received a distress message and had come to take their own back where they belonged.

This answer did not agree with Zeepholt and he ordered his men to attack. It was while staring down the Luminantis who greatly outnumbered them, a group who were devoid of any weapons or malice in their yellow eyes, that the guards finally realized they had made a mistake. They ignored their leader's order and opened the enclosure, setting the imprisoned Luminantis free. Of course, before the Luminantis left, the guards allowed them to enact their revenge. So the imprisoned gathered around a screaming Zeepholt and slowly tore him apart piece by piece. After Zeepholt's execution, the Luminantis left the planet, happy to be departing from the savages who had attacked and imprisoned them, simply because they had dared to make an emergency landing on Zeepholt's planet.

~ * ~ * ~

Radar is a horror movie and novel enthusiast who resides in Wichita, Kansas. When he's not living in his own nightmares, he's writing horrifying tales to help others find theirs. He's had stories published by *Gypsum Sound Tales*, Eerie Lake Publications, Macabre Ladies Publishing, Black Hare Press, Black Ink Fiction, and Little Demon Publishing. He is also a regular contributor to *HorrorTree* and Siren's Call Publications.

HUMANITY

Joanna Michal Hoyt

The old man sat bolt upright, biting his lips and waiting for his trial to begin. He had always hated speaking publicly as a civilian; he didn't know what to do with his eyes and hands; and now the stakes were terribly high.

He didn't expect to save his own life. He had fought with the resistance at the end, had held his own for a long time against greater numbers and better weapons, and he'd pay for that. But if he could command any respect or sympathy, if he could intercede for his friend and co-defendant, the doctor, who had never fought…

Above the bench where his judges would sit were carved the words posted in every public building in every world of the diaspora, the final words of the Great Pledge they all repeated daily: "TO PRESERVE AGAINST ALL MENACE FROM WITHOUT, ALL DISSENSION FROM WITHIN, OUR COMMON AND PRECIOUS HUMANITY." That was what he and the doctor and all of the Pure had been trying to do.

His advocate, a harsh young man appointed by the court, had dismissed this argument. "Stop posturing. Let them see you're old, frightened, *human*. For humanity's sake don't quote your omnipestilent Commander." The old man hoped his judges would prove more understanding.

The judges filed in. Thick-skinned, small-eyed, squat men and women shaped by generations of Ipiu's harsh atmosphere and fierce insects. None of them were beautiful like his people, who had been shaped by Arraj's kinder climate before the earthquakes and eruptions forced them to take refuge on Ipiu two generations back.

He joined in the reciting of the Pledge. Like his judges he spoke in the clipped Unic of the Interworld Consortium. He might have solaced himself with the rolling cadences of Arraji, but he needed to remind his judges they were all humans—united against the common enemy.

An evidentiary declaimed the list of accusations.

Breach of the Code of Humanity—well, the Code was always interpreted by the party in power.

Land seizure—how could they claim that? The Ipiu had acceded to the Arraji's request for a new homeland as the earthquakes devastated Arraj, and the Arraji had never tried to take anything beyond Andek, the barren and *esur*-infested continent allotted to them.

"Murder; gross inhumanity; cruelty to noncombatants, to children..."

The old man rose. He knew what to do with eyes and hands and voice.

"You must not slander us so! My people have never killed or mistreated children or other noncombatants. Only your soldiers—and a few medics, I suppose—invaded our adopted homeland. None of your children came there. If they had come we would not have harmed them. We never attacked your medics...some may have been accidental casualties of our self-defense..."

Judges, advocates, evidentiaries, reporters, all stared at him in apparent bewilderment. Perhaps they were mistaken, not lying. What had they heard?

"We have never neglected our duty toward children and unfortunates. I chaired the Arraji Children's Aid Board before you destroyed their headquarters and confiscated their funds. I contributed more than my share to the Interworld Relief collections; you have paralyzed or destroyed our databanks, but if the lines of communication ever open again to the Interworld Consortium their records will bear me out." He took a deep breath, remembered his priorities. "But I am only an ordinary man, doing as all the Pure did. As, no doubt, Your Honors do. My co-defendant is a more striking case. He has devoted himself to medical research for the good of humanity. He has always been a noncombatant. He has a wife and a small son who are now deprived of his assistance, presence and comfort. Is this not cruelty to children?"

"Are you mad?" the old man's advocate hissed.

"No. Are they?"

An evidentiary rose to speak.

"With the Court's permission, we will begin by itemizing the evidence against the defendant who has just interrupted the Court's proceedings."

"Objection," the advocate said.

"No objection," the old man said.

The evidentiary held up a small black-bound book.

"Do you recognize this?"

"Yes."

"What is it?"

"My personal duty log from my time as a sanitary coordinator."

"You entered this information yourself? You can vouch for its correctness?"

"Yes."

"I will now show the Court an entry from this book. You may inform us if it has been changed in any way."

The old man nodded. The blank wall at the end of the court lit up, showed an enlarged image of a notebook page covered with his cramped Arraji next to a typed Unic translation.

"Ejeget, 6/17. Standard sanitary operation. Pestilentiaries thermoconverted: 137 mature male, 245 mature female, 44 juvenile male, 56 juvenile female. Energy profit: 46 amplissae."

"Is this entry correct?"

"It is." So many days, so many sites, how could he remember? But it was plausible, and there was nothing there that could be used against him.

"You still deny killing children?"

"Of course I do!"

"Would you tell the Court what you did in the process of this 'sanitary operation'?"

"My unit and I were sent to Ejeget by my superiors. Upon arrival we found the *esurin* verified and isolated in a warehouse at the edge of the town. That location was too close to human habitations for thermoconversion—exudates might have compromised air quality. My men removed the *esurin* to a quarry which was abandoned, stripped of useful material, and well downwind from the town."

"Go on."

"The *esurin* were marched into the quarry. One rank of my sanitaries stood at the lip of the quarry, prepared to shoot any who offered interference. The rest set up the thermoconversion booth, moved the *esurin* through in groups of ten, and interred solid byproducts. Then the booth and battery were removed and we set out for the next town on our list. We encountered no children."

He paused, thinking.

"No, I had forgotten. There was a young girl, the daughter

of a woman who after the daughter's birth had been seduced by an *esur* in our collection group. That girl ran after us, shouting. Two of my sanitaries returned her to her mother. She struggled violently, so her wrists may have been bruised, but there was no cruelty."

"No cruelty, either, to the children who died in your thermo-conversion unit?"

"I tell you, there were no children! To thermoconvert humans would be a clear violation of the Code of Humanity. We would never —I would never—have condoned such a thing."

"Then how would you describe the—juveniles—you killed?"

"They were not children! Not humans! All of them were *esurin*. This was manifestly obvious in most cases. A few were more...well-disguised...those who had interbred with humans, to our shame and to the danger of humanity—but the selection specialists were highly trained and conscientious. All those collected for disposal were *esurin*."

"You have used the Arraji word *esurin* several times. Can you not find an appropriate word in Unic?"

The old man frowned. Linguistics had never been his strong point.

"*Esurin* is one of the true names of the Destroyers, the Children of the Lie. They are not human, though they may appear so to the uninformed. There is no exact translation in your language. Your translators have rendered it as 'pestilentiary', which is close, but..." He turned toward the doctor, who was better at such things.

The doctor caught his glance, rose, and explained.

"'Pestilentiary' is often employed as a figurative term of abuse. Even in the literal sense your pestilentiary is most usually a victim of circumstances, someone who is infected through no fault of his own and who infects others unwillingly. '*Esur*' is always used literally. An *esur* is by nature diseased, and he deliberately spreads disease to humans. His goal is the destruction of humanity."

"This is how you define all non-Arraji?"

The old man shook his head. "No! You Ipi are humans like us."

"And on what grounds do you claim this is not true of the Verekei?" The evidentiary gave the *esurin* their false name.

The answer was too obvious to speak. The old man felt his knees buckle.

"Adjournment requested. My client is unfit." His advocate's

voice was flat.

"Adjournment granted."

In the hallway the doctor came up beside the old man and looked at him with concern before his guards hurried him away. The concern, the old man knew, was not about their impending sentence or the success of the Lie but about his unsteady gait and ragged breathing.

Finally alone, the old man tried to pull his thoughts together. How could he make them see? He could remember pieces of the speeches of the Commander of the Pure, but he could not recall the words, the tones, that had woven the pieces together into a clear and damning whole.

There was history. The *esurin*, who were resettled on Andek along with the Arraji, claimed asylum on the grounds that their population on Verek was being decimated by a fatal and highly infectious respiratory disease caused by an organism native to the planet. They complied with quarantine procedures before entering Andek. But they had lived four generations on Verek before the disease was identified. If it had been genuine and planet-specific, it should have struck the first settlers. At first some of the Arraji had suspected the disease was a fabrication, a way of claiming sympathy from Interworld Relief and acquiring land on a planet more centrally located than Verek. (Some of the *esurin* had the gall to draw parallels with the exodus of the Arraji, but that was a different matter; the earthquakes and eruptions that rendered Arraj uninhabitable were verifiable; those who said they resulted from Arraji fuel-extraction operations were politically motivated liars…) When the first generation of refugee *esurin* lived and died in apparent good health on Andek these suspicions seemed to be confirmed. Afterward, when the gut-wasting sickness struck the Arraji and some of the *esurin* also pretended to be stricken, the Commander recognized the truth of the situation. The *esurin* were creators of diseases, which gave them excuses to move into closer proximity to humankind and weapons with which to destroy them.

There was anatomy. The *esurin* might claim their large eyes with bloated pupils and shrunken whites, their translucent skin under which the veins showed blue, resulted from living underground to avoid the sickness on Verek's surface, but after the Commander's artists' work was publicized, who could fail to see these were clear marks of the alien nature of the *esurin*?

There were the loathsome crimes of the *esurin* that the Commander's investigative units had uncovered. Not content to wait for their sickness to destroy true humanity on Andek, the *esurin* had stolen human children and killed them. The *esurin* had denied the crimes and alleged a lack of evidence, but the investigators were Arraji of clean descent and good reputations who would not have lied.

The old man repeated the arguments until they were fixed in his mind. He would explain in the morning...

~ * ~

In his dream he was out of prison at last. He walked in sunlight on a high ridge, looking down onto a forest. The breeze sent shivers of silver and shadow through the leaves. Why had he never stopped to see how beautiful the world was?

He couldn't stop. The men with the guns hurried him along, hurried the others along in the line behind him. He went down into the shade of the trees, to the edge of the old quarry. Something down there was throbbing loudly. He didn't want to know what it was.

A harsh voice told him to keep going down. The stairs were steep, he wasn't sure of his balance, but he had to go down or they'd shoot him, he'd fall into the people below him, they'd fall. He went down. Saw the thermoconverter. Kept going. What else could he do?

The thermoconverter's door opened. The charging chamber was empty. He was in front. If he didn't walk in they would drag him as if he was an animal or a *thing*, not a human. He went in, set his back to the wall, turned to see who was with him. Just before the terrible light and the pain began he recognized the doctor.

~ * ~

He woke, sweating and shaking. He dressed with unsteady hands, returned to the courtroom. Entry after entry was read out of his book. The evidentiaries refused to call the *esurin* by their proper name or to admit their inhumanity. When he tried to explain they interrupted him. His advocate did not intervene. At the lunch recess the old man called his advocate for a conference.

The advocate stared at him, looking belligerent even for an Ipi. The old man stared back.

"Why do you not object when the evidentiaries refuse to allow me to explain the basic premise of…"

"You have already done yourself enough harm. Your so-called explanations would make things worse if that were still possible. Your chances…"

"I understand I will almost certainly be executed. I am merely attempting to clear my people and my cause of the slanders which have been advanced against us. And also, if it is possible, to save the life of my co-defendant—an obvious noncombatant—my friend—the doctor." He did not say, "Who is young enough to be my grandson, dear enough to me to be the son I never had."

"I am not here to salvage your delusions. I'm charged with saving your life, if that is possible. You haven't made that any easier." The advocate half-smiled. "Or maybe you have. Let me change your plea. Let me argue that you're mentally unfit. It may even be true."

"No! I do not want to live because of a lie. For myself I want justice or nothing. For the doctor…"

"Justice!" The advocate rose as he spoke. The old man half expected a blow. His guards had hit him before. He didn't cringe.

The advocate dropped back into his seat. "Don't ask for what you deserve."

"May I ask for a chance to speak?"

"Not at the evidentiary stage. They've almost finished questioning you anyhow. They'll be starting on your—*friend*—this afternoon. But defendants may make a final statement before sentencing. If you want the slightest chance of living you'll let me make it for you."

"No."

They watched one another in silence until a guard came to take them back to the courtroom.

~ * ~

When his turn came the doctor explained that he had researched possible cures for the gutwasting plague, which had spread among the Arraji to such an extent the eradication of the *esurin* alone did not guarantee control. To that end he had requisitioned juvenile *esurin* for experimentation, since the worst devastation of the plague had occurred among Arraji children. The doctor's account was carefully brought down to a level which his hearers could understand.

His advocate interrupted his explanation of the similarities and differences between *esurin* and humans to remind the court the children (as the advocate called them) whom he requisitioned would surely otherwise have been thermoconverted.

"That may be," the evidentiary said. "As some of his victims did not die, we have summoned one of them to appear in court during tomorrow's session." The advocate's hands clenched. The court adjourned.

The old man looked for the doctor as he was led away, but the guards kept them separate. He walked grimly upright to his cell. He slept and he dreamed:

He was in the field headquarters of the Southeastern Sanitary Campaign along with the doctor. This was at the beginning of the end; there were rumors of an Ipi invasion along the northeastern seacoast, but these had not been confirmed, and the old man had not yet begun training his sanitaries as soldiers. The coordinators discussed the rumors, still only half afraid. The old man, listening, envied them, pitied them, and then forgot them. There, across the room, looking out the window, was the doctor. He didn't know he was marked for death. The old man didn't plan to tell him. He only wanted to sit beside his friend once more, to talk about music, mountains, mathematics, all the lovely things that endured. He started across the room.

One of his colleagues asked where he was going. He turned to answer, but the words froze on his lips. Her voice was his colleague's voice, her uniform and her hair were right, but her veins showed blue under her skin, her eyes bulged obscenely—*esur!*

He recoiled, trying to see who else had seen, who might help him. All through the room eyes turned toward him, horrible, distorted eyes. She had infected them all with something far worse than the gutwaste. She had turned them into *esurin*. He had to warn the doctor, to get him away before he also was destroyed.

If he took another step he would be able to see himself reflected in the window. If he spoke the doctor would turn toward him. He didn't want to see the doctor's face, or his own.

~ * ~

He woke up cold and rigid. He sat up on his cot and tried

unsuccessfully to put together some words in the doctor's defense.

He dragged himself into court for the testimony of the juvenile *esur*. The ushers treated the juvenile with the gentleness due a human child, stood close enough to it to be contaminated. It took its place between the old man and the judges, facing the judges. It looked, from behind, very human, very young. The old man swallowed hard and silently recited the Revelation of the Commander of the Pure which he and his sanitaries had repeated daily along with the Great Pledge:

The esurin *are Children of the Lie. They practice to deceive. Their aim is the destruction of all human life. The torch that was kindled on the Mother-Earth, the spark that gave light to the worlds, they would extinguish. We must not fear them. We must not believe them. We must not pity them. When they are destroyed the wasting diseases will leave us. Fear, cruelty and shame will leave us. We shall be fully human again. We shall have peace. But until we are free of them there will be no peace. Therefore let us devote our time, our resources, our courage and our strength to the work of Purification. Let us never falter in our resolve to preserve against this worst of menaces our common and precious humanity.*

The old man remembered the first time he had heard those words, listening to the transmitter beside his brother, who had turned gray-haired and silent after his child died of the gutwaste, and his cousin, who had been gray-faced and voluble since the *esurin's* excessive-resource-consumption complaints to the Interworld Consortium closed the mine where he worked. He remembered the hope in those words. His cousin nodding. His brother's head lifting.

The young *esur* spoke in halting Unic. "I saw that doctor when I was in the…the bad place. They had away taken my mother and my father. I was alone with strangers except my cousin. I asked where were my parents and they didn't answer." He stopped, his lips quivering. "My…my aunt says they're dead. A bad way dead." He gulped and resumed in a higher voice. "They took us to a hospital, but before I had only to go to hospitals when I was sick, and I wasn't then sick, only scared. They made us line up. My cousin went into the room front of me. I heard him yell. Then they took me in. That doctor was there, in a suit that covered him all over. He weighed me and measured and asked my age, and then gave me a shot. It hurt much, but I did not yell. Then they sent me into a room with beds and no windows. My cousin was there and I sat with him and I told him shots were not to be afraid for and he told me my favorite story about the astronauts. We went to sleep."

He paused, looked down, continued, "I woke up because my cousin was screaming. When I touched him he was too hot. There were other ones screaming too, or crying, and one shaking so all her bed rattled. So I knew they were sick. My mother said always to watch for sickness and tell her and she'd call a doctor. I couldn't tell her, but I'd seen the doctor. So I banged on the door and I yelled and I said now there are sick people here and you need to help and he didn't come, and so I thought maybe it was night and he was gone home, but I looked and found a camera in the ceiling and I stood right under it and said the same thing and then I thought he would come and I went back to my cousin and I said someone would help, and he said no, and I thought he was crazy from the fever, so I told him about the astronauts while I waited for the doctor to come, but he did not come."

The old man sat with his head in his hands, remembering his nephew tossing with fever, screaming, then growing silent. Remembering his brother, smiling at the boy, telling him he would feel better soon; weeping, singing a lullaby; stone-faced, staring at the boy's body.

The young *esur*'s story went on. The housekeepers shoving trays of food in, slamming the door, not listening to the boy's—the *esur*'s—pleas. The orderlies coming in their protective suits, taking temperatures, drawing blood, giving nothing. Telling the boy, when he kept asking why, that they were the control group. The fevers, the screaming, the vomiting, the stench. Many deaths, including the cousin's. Then, finally, the three children who had not sickened and died being taken away for more tests under the doctor's supervision. Kept in another room for a week, monitored daily, having blood drawn, screaming at night from dreams not sickness…

"Are you all right? Can you hear me?" the advocate asked quietly. The old man realized his head was down between his knees. He couldn't straighten up. He couldn't answer.

"You're ill. I'll call the guard to take you back to your cell."

The old man rose, lurched, grasped at the guard's arm. The guard recoiled. The old man fell. Someone lifted him, bundled him into a wheelchair, rolled him away. He kept his eyes down, not wanting to see the disgust on the guard's face again, not wanting to look

at the doctor and feel a similar spasm of disgust crossing his own
face.

~ * ~

That night he dreamed. He ordered a file of *esurin* into the
thermoconversion chamber; one looked back at him with his
brother's haunted face. He ordered an example be made of an *esur*
who had attempted to interfere with a collection, and found himself
staring at the doctor's mangled body. He didn't notice at first when
his victims stopped changing, remained clearly marked as Verekei.
When he did notice his sick horror did not abate.

~ * ~

He called his advocate in.

"Have you decided to let me make your final statement for
you?'

"No…that doesn't matter. I needed to tell you…" The old
man groped for adequate words.

"You've already told me your *friend* deserves to live. I'm not
defending him. His advocate is doing what little can be done."

"No, not that. I had to tell you…I know now…I did not
know before, but I know now, that the…Verekei…were human."
He had said it. He had broken the First Law of the Pure. The voices
in his memory screamed at him: *Traitor! Corrupter! Hater of true humankind!* Newer voices, too sure for screaming, called him worse and
truer names.

"So you've decided it's safer to admit that after all? And you
think this…revelation…will impress the judges? It's too late."

"No! It isn't calculation, I…I did not know and now I do.
Too late to save them."

"You never knew?"

"No! We were told…we were all told…" So they had been.
Even before the Commander's rise to power. He remembered the
taunts when he failed a test, the scoldings when he was cross with
his younger brother. *Don't be such a verek!*

"What do you want now?"

"To confess. To apologize."

"This is not your time to speak in court."

"Must I go back and listen while I cannot speak?"

"No. Your part of the evidence is concluded. Let me know if you change your mind about your statement."

The old man nodded. The advocate left.

~ * ~

The next day was bad. The old man swung between cold horror at what he had done and furtive self-pity for his ignorance. First his statement sounded groveling, then cold, then merely stupid. The night was worse.

Back in court the next day, he listened while the doctor's advocate spoke unhopefully of the duty of victorious nations to be merciful. He stood when his time came to speak.

"I can say nothing in my own defense. My actions were indefensible. I have told this court what I believed, that the...Verekei were not human, that our campaign against them was waged on behalf of humanity. I know now I was horribly wrong. I did not know then, but that does not excuse what I did to my...fellow humans. Nothing can do that. I am guilty of murder, indeed, and of defamation as well. I apologize to those Verekei who survived." He swallowed. "I submit myself to judgment. Whatever sentence I receive, it can be no worse than what my actions have deserved. But I ask you to have mercy on my co-defendant, who shared my ignorance, and whose actions, however misguided, sprang from his love for humanity."

He looked at the judges, who stared coldly at him. He looked at the doctor, who did not seem to see his friend at all.

The sentence was death by thermoconversion. Publicly broadcast. In three days.

His advocate walked into his cell unannounced.

"It's over, then. Unless you wish to make an appeal."

"I do not. You are not sorry."

"Should I be?"

"Not for me."

"For humanity?"

"You loathe me. Why did you agree to defend me?"

"You never saw, did you? You stood there explaining the self-evident inhumanity of the Verekei, and you never saw what I was."

"You?"

"My paternal grandfather was Verek. He came to Iberra for

a scientific conference and met my Ipi grandmother, stayed there to raise his children, left his son there to marry another Ipi, went back to Andek himself as an old man. I have my mother's features. I was in law school on Iberra when we got word my grandfather was dead. Accused by your Commander of atrocities he never committed and sentenced to death in a sham trial, with no advocate. Then you were taken. No one wanted to defend you. I couldn't bear to have it said that you were killed unjustly like my grandfather."

The advocate left abruptly. The old man looked after him, shook his head, activated the viewscreen in his cell; anything to take his mind from memory and regret...

His own image was all over the newsfeeds, together with images of the doctor and the Verek child. Some of the images were photos. Some were 'artistic renderings' which caricatured the slenderness of the Arraji, made him and the doctor look more like insects than men, and gave them expressions that were anything but human.

Ipi commentators and decision-makers, speaking in solemn and elevated tones, discussed the ramifications of the case:

The trial had set a clear precedent for sentencing others complicit in Purification. Mass executions would be more energy-efficient, since so much power was required to activate the thermo-conversion unit.

The serum which the doctor had developed showed some promise against the gutwaste. It would be given to the surviving Verekei and, preventively, to the Ipiu presently on Andek, and to other Ipi if they chose to settle there to relieve the overcrowding which had begun to trouble Iberra. It would not be given to the Arraji. Why should they be allowed to profit from torturing children?

The ideology of Purification had spread throughout Arraji society, tainting even those who had not taken an active part in the sanitary campaign. Clearly that ideology posed a fundamental threat to humanity. In view of that threat, might it not be necessary for humanity's sake to eliminate the threat prophylactically?

The old man deactivated the viewscreen and stared into the dark. When he could find words he sent a message to his lawyer: *Have your people decided that we all are esurin? Have you been infected by the madness that possessed us? Where will it end? Can none of us help ourselves?* The lawyer did not answer.

He tried to write to the doctor, could not; he didn't know

whether he was writing to his friend or to a true *esur*.

A fragment of memory came back to him. The doctor, very early in the sanitary campaign, midway through his struggle against the gutwaste, sitting exhausted at the old man's kitchen table, talking, not meeting his friend's eyes. "Humanity. Did you know that in the source-language, on Old Earth, the word meant two things? They used it for the species, as we do, but it had another definition. It also meant kindness."

"They used the species-name for kindness? On Old Earth, where they killed each other over pigmentation and metaphysics?"

The doctor stared at his friend, stalked out the door. He did not turn when the old man called to him. The next day when they met the doctor apologized, saying he had been distraught after the death of three more patients.

The old man sat up straight on his prison cot, pulled out the paper tablet they had given him, wrote a halting message to the doctor recalling that night. He gave it to the guard to deliver. It was returned, unopened, by the same guard, who said that after hearing the old man's pre-sentencing statement the doctor had refused to receive messages. Since then he had not spoken.

~ * ~

The last morning came. The old man greeted it with relief. The only thing he had left to hope was that Ipiu would be a dead planet before its links to the Interworld Consortium were restored, before the plague he had helped to spread could reach beyond Ipiu. He walked out quietly between his guards.

The doctor walked ahead of him, half carried, and half dragged by guards. They reached a flight of stairs. The doctor's feet dragged, caught, and he lurched forward. The guard on his left let go of him. The other guard swung round and took the doctor's weight before his head could hit the stairs.

The old man saw the brief convulsion of pity on the guard's face and the hard look that came down over it. He stared, remembering:

He and the doctor sat in the park on a sunny spring morning two months after his nephew died despite the doctor's efforts to save him, two weeks after the first speech of the Commander of the Pure. They did not discuss death or politics. The doctor talked about a new fugue he had heard, whistled a piece of the theme. The old man nodded, listened, smiled; started when the shouting began.

A Verek man ran past them. A crowd of Arraji pursued him, shouting. Someone threw a stone. Then another. The Verek raised his arms to shield his head, stumbled, fell. The crowd fell on him.

The old man sat staring, cursing himself for a coward and an *esur* because he did not run to the lone man's aid, cursing himself for a traitor for pitying one of the *esurin* who had caused his nephew's agonizing death. The doctor rose abruptly and set off toward a quieter part of the park. The old man went after him, telling himself *It's all right, what could I have done, it didn't matter anyway, he isn't one of us.* He swallowed the Commander's next speech like medicine to cool the fever of self-accusation. In time he taught himself to believe. But he had chosen. He had known.

"Can I speak to my advocate?"

"Too late."

"Not a legal appeal. Just…Can I speak at the end?"

"You'll have a few minutes while the thermoconverter warms up."

They were outside, in a hard-floored courtyard. One thermoconverter, humming as it began the activation sequence. Two condemned men, four guards, seven judges, one cameraman, and another man. The old man's advocate.

"Your grandfather died alone?"

"Surrounded by men who hated him."

"I am sorry." The old man tried to meet his advocate's eyes, turned away, looked into the camera. "I have something to say. I…In court I said one thing that was true: that the Verekei were human, and that I and mine had murdered them. I said something, also, that was false. That I was deceived. That I had been an innocent pestilentiary. When I saw your people were beginning to see mine as *esurin*, to prepare to destroy us before we destroyed humanity, I thought you were innocent pestilentiaries as well. That you could not help yourselves. But this was false." He swallowed hard.

"I knew the Verekei were human. And then there were the shortages, and the plague, and the communications breakdowns, and I was afraid. My nephew died of plague, and I grieved. I did not know how to save the people I loved, and I was ashamed—I reproached myself with the name I thought was most shameful—I called myself a Verek. Then I heard the Commander blaming all our griefs and shames on the Verekei, and I wanted it to be true. I told myself the Verekei were not human. I did things that made me unworthy to lay claim to humanity. It…It is a word that meant kindness, once." He glanced at the doctor's blank face. "I chose to kill, to lie. I did not have to. Many of my people did not choose what I chose. It is not a plague, a fault in our race. It is not a plague in yours. It is a choice you make. You must not make it. Please do not do what I have done. Do not make yourselves into what I have become. We are all human, after all…the kindness, the cruelty, the cowardice, the courage…it is for all of us to choose, it is all human …Please choose better…"

The words were still wrong. He looked at his advocate, who appeared almost as blank as the doctor.

"Time's up. Machine's ready." The guard turned him away from the advocate and the camera, pushed him—not too hard— toward the open door of the thermoconversion chamber. The old man turned back toward the doctor hanging limply between his guards.

"Come on, my friend," the old man said. And, to the guards, "Let me take him." He forced himself not to recoil from the doctor as the guard had recoiled from him. He pulled the doctor's arm over his shoulders, leaned into the doctor's weight, moved forward with him. Eight careful steps. One last look back.

Just before the door closed, just before the terrible light and the pain began, the old man saw his advocate's face streaked with tears.

~ * ~ * ~

Joanna Michal Hoyt lives on a Catholic Worker farm in rural New York where she spends her days tending goats, gardens, and guests and her evenings reading and writing odd stories. She has loved ones on opposite sides of America's deepening divides. Her short speculative fiction appears in various publications including *Mysterion*, *After Dinner Conversation*, and *On Spec*. Her novel *Cracked Reflections*, about polarization, fear, and solidarity during the textile strikes of 1912, will be published by Propertius Press in fall 2021.

Read more at https://joannamichalhoyt.com/

ACCEPTANCE

Steven T. Lente

He walked into the hotel lobby wearing his covid mask with the letters "BLM" on the front; I knew it meant *Black Lives Matter*. On my mask was the thin, blue line flag representing the police, of which I was. We eyed each other, evaluated our options, subtly nodded our recognition, then went to our respective and opposite corners, which was probably in my favor since he had about 100 pounds on me and was about a foot taller: not fat, built.

My wife was with me, and I learned later the people with him were his family: wife, two high-school age children, another older daughter, and a son-in-law. We were in Vegas, and twenty-six of us were heading out to the Colorado River for a three-day, two-night Grand Canyon raft trip, and the lobby was the pickup and drop-off point used by the rafting company. It appeared the BLM guy and I decided it was not worth spoiling the next few days on our first encounter; however, it turns out we had more in common than not, which would be confirmed when the rattlesnake crawled into camp.

The next couple of hours was right out of the movie *Planes, Trains, and Automobiles,* only without the trains. We gathered onto a large commercial bus which took us to the airport in Boulder City. There we transferred to multiple nine-passenger single-engine planes. Before we boarded, the airport staff weighed both our bodies and our duffle bags and computed the total weight per plane. We were then divided into three groups and our weights balanced between three aircraft. The BLM guy and his family, plus a couple of other travelers, filled one of the planes.

We flew over Lake Mead, past Hoover Dam, and well above the Grand Canyon. We followed the rim of the canyon for about fifty minutes with the onboard sound system providing a narrative about the dam's construction, the formation of the canyon, and other pieces of trivia. When we landed in the middle of nowhere, the dirt runway instantly made me think of drug lords, guns, and kilos of cocaine. Parked at the end of the runway was a rusty school bus, which took us to another landing strip with a helicopter waiting and already running up its engine. The young man at the chopper pad again weighed us and our bags, divided us into smaller five-person groups, and precisely placed us on the helicopter to ensure it was balanced in flight.

The chopper flight was about nine minutes, and it took six flights to deliver all of us and our bags. The landing spot was a very small clearing at the river where two large rafts waited for us; each raft would hold half of our group, and the BLM man and his family took one and my wife and I loaded onto the other. In short, between buses, planes, helicopters, and now rafts, Mr. BLM and I had no chance, nor reason, to talk.

Because we were now outside, we no longer needed our covid masks, although we were all given new buffs stamped with the company logo. Our guides, two per raft, introduced themselves and we pushed off on the first leg of our ninety-mile trek back to Lake Mead. We made about twenty miles that first day before beaching at a sandy spot downriver. Our guides showed us how to set up our tents and cots, warned us to be aware of the potential hazards of the environment, including heat and snakes, and went on to set up the kitchen and, further away in the willows, the outdoor bathroom in a shower stall type of tent. The lead guide, Sam, told us he would sound a horn to call us to dinner. BLM guy and I finally connected before the first horn blast.

"I saw your mask in the lobby. You a cop?" he asked.

"Yep!" I replied.

"Where?"

"Atlanta."

"No way. I'm from Norcross," BLM guy responded and put out his hand to shake. "I'm Dennis."

"Steve; pleased we could finally talk." I took his hand.

"That was quite a ride getting here. I haven't been on a chopper since Nam," Dennis said.

"Me too. Small world." Aside from us both being from Atlanta metro, we now found our first real connection: the Army, I was an MP, and Dennis was a chopper mechanic. After Nam, in 1971, we both had Stateside tours in Forts Rucker and Hood, then on to Europe, where he landed in Germany and I in Italy. So, instead of defending democracy against the yellow hordes, we were defending her against the Red tide. Now, standing next to the Colorado River, we agreed to act out the Army commercials of the 1980's where on a beachhead at 6:00 AM one private says, "Good Morning First Sergeant" who then responds back, "Good Morning Trooper." So, I became "Trooper" and Dennis was "First Sergeant" for the rest of the trip. The dinner horn sounded, and we put our talk on hold.

The next day was the longest, almost fifty miles of river before we would again set up camp. Some of the rapids were serious but not really life threatening. Rapids are rated from Class I, small riffles with no obstructions, basically smooth water, to Class VI rapids, which are treacherous; in those waters someone who falls overboard will be difficult to rescue. Ours were probably Class III; none the less, it was a long and tiring day.

After setting up camp and before the dinner horn sounded, Dennis and I reconnected. He was now an electrical engineer with one of the local high-tech firms. His two younger children were college bound, and his son-in-law was a recently separated Air Force captain just back from Afghanistan and now flying with UPS commercial. My son had also made a career in the Air Force and was now retired. More common threads.

Then the conversation turned to race, or at least racial issues. Dennis opened with this question: "So, during the *Black Lives Matter* protests in downtown Atlanta, were you and I on opposite sides?"

"Yes. I was on the riot lines every day."

"They weren't riots," Dennis said.

"Nope, but we were prepared for the worst. What would you have had us do?" I responded.

Dennis continued: "Do you believe that Black lives matter?"

"Yes, I do. And I'm not even going to that other end that says Blues Lives Matter, too! I can separate the issues; I'm not just a pretty face you know."

"Now that you know me," Dennis asked, "would you arrest me?

"If you broke the law, yes. And would you hate me for doing it?"

"I don't know. It's such a hard question."

"Well, let's just hope we don't have to face that situation," I said. "Besides, if you didn't come peacefully, I don't think I could take you by myself. You're a big guy."

"Certainly, I'm not going to resist; I know what happens to Blacks who do!" Dennis added.

"I meant that as a funny, but I guess it's not really a laughing matter. My apologies."

We shook hands and started to bid goodnight, but then we heard someone yell for help.

Dennis and I ran towards the toilet closet where the cry came from. Sam, the lead guide, was limping down the path grabbing at his left calf. "Snake bit me. Keep the others away from the bathroom. Don't know where the snake went."

I supported Sam as he limped back to the main camp. Dennis secured the scene; he and a couple of the others did not find the snake, and we still don't know if it was already in the tent or crawled in just as Sam was dropping his pants, but it's irrelevant now.

Most snake bites are not fatal assuming you can keep the patient calm, medical care is relatively close, and the bite is not near the neck or head. The old formula of cutting into the bite area and sucking out the venom is only when all other methods fail or are not available, in other words, really the last resort. We had options, however: one of the guides had a satellite phone and started the air evacuation wheels in motion.

The chopper would be about forty-five minutes out, and we would have to clear the beach for the landing; Dennis took that lead. In the meantime, I had Sam resting in one of the folding chairs with some block ice from the food coolers wrapped around his calf. I kept the leg lower than the rest of his body to slow down the circulation of the venom and to keep it as far from his vital organs as possible. Dennis and the guides also had to calm down some of the other rafters as they were now concerned for their own safety as well. Two of them wanted to get on the medivac chopper and go home. Dennis convinced them we could post people in shifts to watch for other snakes, and if needed, would beat the bushes around the toilet area before anyone else went into the tent. Since our sleeping areas were raised on cots anyway, this seemed to soothe fears. We were, after all, leaving in a few hours on our last leg to the pickup on Lake Mead.

When the chopper was five minutes out, Dennis had everyone use their flashlights to outline the landing zone. The chopper would come in "hot," meaning the crew would not shut down the engine, but that was not new to us as the helicopters we rode into the canyon two days ago did the same thing. Dennis, however, reminded everyone to stay low around the rotating blades or just stay back and keep the LZ lit up. I stayed with Sam.

The medivac carried an EMT and when the chopper landed, she quickly checked out my first aid measures and Sam's vital signs; all were OK. She shook my hand and I transferred full caretaking over to her. We helped Sam into the chopper and the EMT strapped him into a stretcher; Dennis cleared the area for takeoff, and the chopper lifted away.

Few slept the rest of the night, either for worry of Sam's health or their own concerns. Dawn seemed to come quicker than usual, and the remaining three guides rallied us around breakfast. Dennis and I greeted each other: "Good morning first sergeant," I said. "Good morning trooper," he replied. "We did good last night," Dennis added. "Yes, we did."

The rest of the trip was back to the business of getting off the river. About ten miles further down we met the new guide that took us and our bags to a waiting bus, which, in turn, would take us back to the Vegas hotel lobby starting point. It was a quiet ride, each of us lost in our own thoughts.

At the hotel, a representative of the rafting company met us with the good news that Sam was well and total recovery was predicted. We shook hands all around, and Dennis and I got pats on the back. He and I never finished our *Black Lives Matter* conversation, and almost to prove that point, Dennis dug out his BLM mask and put it on. Following his lead, I took out my thin blue line mask and strapped it around my mouth and nose.

Dennis came over and said: "You take care out there trooper."

As we shook hands a final time, I responded: "You be safe as well, first sergeant."

Dennis and I gathered our bags, turned away from each other, and I knew we would go back to our own private worlds. Deeply, I knew we might again face each other in Atlanta on opposite sides of the protest lines, and being soldiers, I knew we would both do our duty to protect democracy.

~ * ~ * ~

Steve is a 20-year retired US Air Force veteran, where for over thirteen years he was in security and law enforcement. After retirement, Steve returned to Colorado where he joined the management team and security workforce at the Ute Mountain Casino, near Cortez CO. In 2000, Steve relocated to Colorado Springs CO, to start another career with an international contract security company serving a world-wide high-tech firm headquartered in Silicon Valley. Steve has since retired again, and he and his wife, Brenda, travel regularly, both with and without an RV. Steve is an ASIS International board-certified protection professional (CPP) Lifetime, Ret. Steve's education includes an MA in Organizational Management, a BA in Business Management, and AA's in Criminal Justice and Instructor Technologies.

More Great Anthologies from WolfSinger Publications

Crunchy with Chocolate – edited by Carol Hightshoe

It has been said that one should never meddle in the affairs of dragons—for you are crunchy and taste good with chocolate.

Come enter the dragon's lair and roll the dice. Within these pages you will still meet some of the biggest, baddest predators ever—but if you are *lucky,* you will also discover some that have a *sweeter* side.

Meet a dragon with a soft spot for hard luck cases and another who is a hopeless romantic.

Enjoy a musical battle between a dragon and the specter of one of the greatest guitarists to ever play.

Meet a dragon in trouble with other magical creatures because he enjoys hanging out with human children.

Join a mother and daughter and their teams of dragons on a dangerous cross-country race.

Reconnect with an imaginary friend – who is not so imaginary and escape the isolation of the pandemic.

And more…

Crunchy with Ketchup – edited by Carol Hightshoe

It has been said that one should never meddle in the affairs of dragons—for you are crunchy and taste good with ketchup.

Come enter the dragon's lair. Take your chances with other would-be heroes and heroines who decide to face off against one of the biggest, baddest predators ever.

Witness a dragon civil war.
Hear the true story of the Battle of New Orleans.
Find out what it's like in the belly of a dragon.
Discover why cats can spell disaster when stealing a dragon's egg.

Meet a group of dragon riders who protect us from nuclear devastation.

Follow legends of modern dragons, only to find something very unexpected.

And more…

Cat Tails: War Zone – edited by Rebecca McFarland Kyle and Dana Bell

Cats have been our companions since long before they graced the temples of Ancient Egypt. In addition to being members of our families, they have also stood with us through difficult times. From keeping pests and vermin away from our food stores to providing a comforting paw when we have been wounded; cats have been our sidekicks and friends in many different battles.

Cat Tails—War Zone contains twenty-five stories from Ancient Egypt to the far-flung future, about some amazing cats who have served as compatriots during war times. But beware, for they can also be tricksters sent to teach lessons.

The real heroes are the volunteers of SHADOW CATS, an Austin, Texas-based rescue that has saved the lives of 9,000-plus cats since 1997. Trappers, veterinarians, nurses, and adoption social workers volunteer to trap, neuter and return ferals, provide care for ill, injured and behaviorally-challenged cats, find perfect adoptive parents, educate on proper feline care, and advocate for real change in communities.

Proceeds from this book will continue their efforts.

Unintended Consequences – edited by Carol Hightshoe

For every action there is an equal and opposite reaction –
Newton's Third Law of Motion.

While Newton was talking about motion when he developed the above law, it can also be said that for every action or decision there is a consequence: sometimes good, sometimes bad.

Many times consequences can be foreseen and planned for. But there are times they are never seen. It is these unforeseen or Unintended Consequences that can have the biggest impact on individual lives.

An android working to pass as human.

A woman who loses her pre-destined 'soul mate' on world where they were marked at birth.

A Queen who uses magic to make her subjects more cooperative and helpful to each other.

A wife who authorizes a radical treatment for dementia to be performed on her husband.

And 16 more who will learn about the unintended consequences that will affect their lives.

Just Desserts – edited by Rebecca McFarland Kyle and J.A. Campbell

Whether you like your revenge with the molten fire of a fine old Scotch or the cool sweetness of a tasty meringue, the nineteen tales within these covers should offer something to assuage you.

Narcissistic co-workers, thieves of affection, and bad neighbors are given their due in ways imaginative and sublime.

Love 'em, Shoot 'em – edited by Dana Bell

One should never be afraid to love or shoot the one they care about. A famed markswoman once said that. Or so it's claimed.

Imagine a town with a dog sheriff from another planet.
A zombie attack clean-up woman.
An attractive alien who likes to play love goddess.
A magical concert with dead musicians that gets out of hand.
Or those of the old west who meet aliens.
Those from the far future hunted for not volunteering to die.
A woman who learns a lesson with a twist during war time.
And more…

Come along with our writers and travel the diverse trails of their tales, of loving and sometimes shooting, in these pages of Love 'em, Shoot 'em.

Extinct – edited by Dana Bell

What if those ancient creatures so beloved in fiction, myth, and science had not disappeared? What if they were real? What might have been developed to handle them, and how might man have felt about the thundering giants in yesterday's, today's, or tomorrow's worlds.

Imagine a sanctuary established for dinosaurs that displaces humans.

What if Raptors were used on a distance planet as scouts for the new colony?

Could Dodo birds have left a record about what happened to them? Dragons helping settlers? Inconceivable!

A conqueror learns a hard lesson from a goddess and two children create their own 'monster'.

Lovely, unique, tales of lumbering giants of old, ancient rulers of the skies, and many others once thought to be myth or legend appear here in Extinct?

Tales From the Fluffy Bunny – edited by Carol Hightshoe

Welcome to the Fluffy Bunny

We welcome everyone—especially those with a story to tell. Adventurers, mercenaries, guardsmen, merchants, noble and peasant. Whoever. If you have a tale to share, then come in and have a seat. First drink and a hot meal are on the house.

What's a tale without an audience to appreciate it? So, even if you don't have a tale to share, come in, pull up a seat and enjoy these 17 tales of how a warrior or their weapon earned their name.

Visit us at www.wolfsingerpubs.com for more information